THEY HAD FOUND
VIKTOR'S HIDING PLACE

About 15 miles away, turning slowly on the spokes of its twisted cross, was a gigantic swastika in a virtually identical orbital path with the Zon. It looked monstrous and overwhelming—and completely unreal.

"Christ, where did that come from?" Hunter gasped.

Looking through long-range binoculars, he saw that it appeared to be constructed of hundreds of heavy metal sections welded into place like the plates on a battleship. There was a large observation deck on the space station that looked very much like the bridge of a World War II-era ship, complete with a gaggle of antennas, receivers, and what could only be space periscopes.

"Do you think they know we're out here?" Ben asked.

"Probably," JT replied. "But what can they do? It ain't like they can come out after us or shoot at us or anything."

Suddenly Hunter felt his psyche start vibrating.

A hatchway at the end of one twisted arm opened, and small objects began drifting out of it. They looked like Messerschmitt Me-163 Komets, a type of German wonder-weapon rocket plane used by the Third Reich at the tail end of World War II. There were six of the stubby rocket-powered fighter planes, each carrying some kind of large muzzle-heavy weapon under its wings.

And now they were heading straight for Hunter and the Zon!

WINGMAN
BY MACK MALONEY

DEATH ORBIT

Mack Maloney

Pinnacle Books
Kensington Publishing Corp.

http://www.pinnaclebooks.com

PINNACLE BOOKS are published by

Kensington Publishing Corp.
850 Third Avenue
New York, NY 10022

Pinnacle and the P logo Reg. U.S. Pat. & TM Off.

First Printing: January, 1997

Printed in the United States of America
10 9 8 7 6 5 4 3 2 1

PART 1

One

It was a calm night in the Himalayas.

Where usually the winds blew at 50 knots or more and snow fell almost continuously, this night there was no gale, no frozen precipitation, no sign of the elements at all.

At the top of the mountain called Ch'aya, known as one of the coldest, windiest, most inhospitable places on earth, an eerie silence had settled around the small Be'hei temple and its row of guesthouses nearby. It was close to midnight and the stars above were twinkling madly. The monks within the temple grounds were awakened by the lack of wind; they were so unused to the silence, it actually roused them from their slumber.

Concern quickly gripped the Be'hei monastery. Candles were lit, prayer bells began tolling. The monks had read about this sort of thing. It was a phenomenon that had been written down in their ancient texts by hands that had passed on centuries before. No wind. No blowing snow. The sky seemed as if on fire. Be warned, the ancients had written. You are not being spared from the never-ending tempest that makes Ch'aya the holy place it is.

Rather you are in the eye of the eternal storm.

In one guesthouse, however, no candles had been lit. This was the small hut at the far end of the temple grounds, the dwelling closest to the edge. Inside slept a beautiful girl. Blond, supple, and youngish in face and form, she was named Chloe. She was naked, her enchanting body covered with a single layer of lamb-skin. She did not realize that a frightening calm had come over Ch'aya Mountain. She was too busy having a dream.

Out beyond the orbit of Pluto, in a region of space millions of miles from the sun, there is a place known as the Oort Cloud. It is here, scientists discovered years ago, that comets reside—massive chunks of ice and space dust, some weighing trillions of tons. Most are caught in a gravitational netherworld, slaved to travel long, looping flight paths, just out of reach of the pull of the sun. They are orphans, second-class citizens of the solar system that if not for a quirk of fate might have formed into planets 15 billion years ago. Instead, they are eternal transients.

But the universe could be a funny place as well as a mysterious one. Sometimes it would rely on the Oort Cloud to provide a cosmic joke. One of the comets would stray just enough toward the sun to get caught in its gravitational pull and thus begin a long, perilous journey inward. In Chloe's dream, she could see exactly that kind of thing happening. A massive comet many times larger than what would be considered normal had been captured by the sun's attraction and was slowly but surely heading into the solar system. But in her dream, Chloe could see a gigantic hand actually pushing the comet, steering it, controlling its move-ments as it began to tumble at a velocity rising to 100 miles per second. And behind the gigantic hand came a screech that echoed across the cosmos. It was a rather frightening sound—and an indistinguishable one as well. Was it a man's voice or a woman's? It was hard to tell. But in Chloe's dream, the voice belonged to what she perceived to be the Supreme Being.

God was laughing.

This hand had flicked the gigantic comet not just toward the sun, but right at the planet Earth. It must have happened centuries earlier, for the trip from the Oort Cloud to the inner solar system was a long one, even at a speed of 360,000 miles an hour.

That was the cruel thing about cosmic jokes.

It could take eons before the punchline was delivered.

When Chloe woke up in tears some time later, two monks were standing over her bed.

Though bound to a life of celibacy and denial of earthly pleasures, the pair of holy men could not help but look down at her lovely naked body and begin thinking thoughts they shouldn't.

She stirred and was surprised that her eyes and cheeks were so wet. The men startled her for a moment—she caught them looking and quickly pulled the lambskin back around her. But she knew them and knew they would not harm her and that the only reason they were here was because they were concerned for her.

"What is it? What's wrong?" she asked, wiping away the tears.

"We heard you weeping," one monk said, gathering his saffron robes around him. "And . . ."

"And?"

"And things are wrong . . . outside."

"What disturbed you?" the second monk asked. "Why were you crying in your sleep?"

Chloe thought a moment—then it came flooding back to her. The huge comet. The gigantic hand. The frightening laugh.

She told them everything and began crying again,

and the monks did, too. They really didn't have to hear very much. They knew what she had dreamed, knew what it meant. They sat down on her bed and hugged her. All concern of modesty forgotten, she allowed the lambskin to slip away and hugged them back.

"The stars have begun to fall," one of the monks whispered. "Just as it was written. Now it is only a matter of time . . ."

They sat there, the three of them, and cried until morning.

By that time, the wind outside had picked up again and the blowing snow had returned.

TWO

Saint Ann's Island, the Caribbean

The man they called Pooch was having a strange dream, too.

He was floating on his back atop the calm, clear waters off Saint Ann's Cove, barely flicking his hands and feet, yet moving quite quickly. He was surrounded by girls, at least six of them. They were all beautiful, all young, all topless. They had their hands all over him. On his chest. Running through his hair, down his pants. They were rubbing him, caressing him, stroking him. It was heavenly.

This was a very odd dream for Pooch to have for several reasons. First, he could not swim. Though he had lived more than two-thirds of his life on this beautiful Caribbean island, he hated the water, hated the thought of getting near it, for fear he would somehow stumble in and get caught in the undertow and suddenly be in over his head. To be skimming along the surface of the water was a very alien thing for him to be doing, awake or asleep.

Dreaming about six young, topless girls lusting over him was also very odd for him. Pooch was 71 years old, bearded, grizzled, with a serious case of roly-poly. Thoughts as graphic as these hadn't venture into his dirty old mind in nearly two decades. At least, not for this long, anyway.

The third reason this was all very strange was that Pooch was hopelessly drunk, lying in the gutter of Saint Ann's only paved street, his bulbous winestained nose pointing directly up at a sky that was gradually darkening and beginning to twinkle with stars. This was a normal state of affairs for him. Rum was indeed a demon, and it had had Pooch by the ass for as long as he could remember.

Dulled brain cells and all, though, when Pooch woke up, he remembered his dream in its entirety, right down to the little nipples on one of the girls and the giant bazzooms on another. A smile found its way across his crooked yellow teeth. With a rare spring in his shorts, he lifted himself out of the gutter and began the long stagger home.

Pooch lived on a small riverlet called the Dink which ran out from Smugglers' Cove, which in turn flowed into Saint Ann's Bay. His house was a two-story affair, much more ornate than one would have thought for a man of Pooch's demeanor. But the Poochman had a profession, and it was a profitable one by this day's standards. Originally from the hills of West Virginia, Pooch had been a pharmacist's mate in the old U.S. Navy. These twin experiences had ingrained two life lessons in him. From his upbringing, he knew how to make and bottle whiskey. From his service days, he knew how to make drugs. Pooch was Saint Ann's moonshiner and druggist, a beach-conch Dr. Feelgood.

He'd been dropping off a delivery of whiskey to the local saloon when the rum had gotten him again. That was twelve hours ago, and now at last he was going home to sleep it off. He trudged out onto the beach and then across the Dink; the water was only about a foot deep here and the stream was narrow, as the tide

was just about to turn. Reaching the high stairs to his
back door, he took each one with a grunt or a groan,
counting them off as he did every time he was in this
condition, knowing that once he made it to the twen-
ties, he was close to the top.

He finally reached the last step and now had only to
contend with the locked door and the balky key that
always gave him trouble, stinking drunk or not.

But this night Pooch had a surprise waiting for him.
His back door was open. Not just unlocked, but wide,
wide open.

He saw it and it gave him a start. Stinko though he
was, he damn sure remembered locking the door behind
him when he'd left that morning because he'd almost
dropped his case of precious hootch in the process of
getting the key to work.

Why was it open?

He got his answer as soon as he tripped through the
entranceway. Two men were waiting inside, sitting on
his couch and looking as relaxed and calm as if they
lived there. He stared at them for a long while, trying
to make some sense of their faces, reflected in only the
bare light of some candles and a single weak 25-watt
bulb. Did he knows these guys? He really thought not.

They were Asians, or at least, people from the Pacific
Rim. They were both about the same height, same
weight, and same frame, and both were wearing the
same nondescript sand-colored combat fatigues fa-
vored by mercenaries around the world. These uniforms were virtually free of insignia or levels of rank,
but each had a thin red braid running across the collar
and down the thin lapels.

Even Pooch's sodden brain knew what this meant—
and suddenly he thought he was going to lose control
of his bladder.

"Can . . . can I help you?" he managed to stutter. It

was not all that unusual that he would come home to find customers waiting for him; they were just never inside his house before.

"You are the man who makes drugs?" one asked, his accent thick, his English barely decipherable. "Speed? Coke? XTC?"

"I am," Pooch replied, settling down a bit at the thought that these guys might just be here to do some business. "All three of those and more."

"And whiskey, too?" the other asked.

"Again, yes," Pooch slurred, finally coming into the room and closing the door behind him. Outside, the sea suddenly sounded very loud.

"What quantities do you have of these things?" the first man asked. "You have much whiskey? Much drugs?"

Pooch couldn't get his eyes off those red braids. Why would these guys come all the way here to find him?

"I have large quantities of whatever you need, I'm sure," he stuttered in reply. "And discounted prices, at that."

The two men looked at each other and smiled, but not in amusement.

"May we see your stores?" the number one guy asked. "We would like an idea how much we will have to transport."

Pooch nearly fell over. "You want it all?" he asked, both terrified at the thought and salivating at what a payday it might bring if he sold them everything he had hidden in his cellar.

"Oh, yes," the second man replied. "All of it—and more."

Less than a minute later, they were climbing down into the vast storage chamber beneath Pooch's beach house.

One wall was covered with cases of bottled whiskey, 2,700 fifths in all. Another wall was similarly hidden by kegs of "Greed," a lethal combination of 150-proof rum and 99-proof whiskey which reminded some people of both mead and grog, hence the name. On the wall furthest from the ladder, three clear plastic vats were hanging. These held about 500 pounds each of Pooch's own recipe for "Scratch," a volatile mixture of cocaine, metaamphetamine, and XTC. In the fourth corner stood two huge wooden barrels, each containing 200 pounds of pure China white heroin, just set out to dry.

Pooch stood back and cast an admiring eye on this treasure trove of mind alterants, all of it produced by his own hand, most of it nonfatal if used wisely.

The two visitors seemed unimpressed by Pooch's stash, though. With a sniff, they noted that the China White wasn't really that white and the mixture of coke, speed, and XTC was a rather amateurish combination. The whiskey smelled bad, and the Greed, well, they didn't so much as take a whiff of it.

"But it is guaranteed to do the job," Pooch insisted, hurt that the pair was downgrading what was his life's work these days. "Or your money back . . ."

The two Asian men laughed slightly at this, though not because they were amused.

"Additionally," one said, "this isn't nearly enough for our purposes."

Pooch thought his ears needed cleaning. Before them were close to a ton of drugs and hundreds of gallons of liquor.

"Jeezus, how much do you guys want?" he asked them.

They laughed again and then led Pooch out the lower hatch door from the storage area. From here they stepped out onto the beach just below Pooch's home. It was now nighttime and the horizon was studded with stars.

"Take a look," one of the men ordered Pooch. "Out there."

Pooch was becoming very frightened now but felt it wise to go along with these two.

He squinted his inebriated eyes to the far horizon, and sure enough he could see first one, then two, then three, then a half dozen ships' lights blinking through the early evening haze. Even with his poor eyesight he could see the vessels were massive. The dark silhouettes of huge guns were also quite apparent.

Now a chill ran down Pooch's spine and up again. The Asian men. Their red braided collars. Their brash behavior. And now the huge warships anchored off-shore. All these things combined to make his worst fear come true. Just as he'd suspected, the two men were from the hated much-feared Asian Mercenary Cult.

He turned back to the men to see one was now brandishing a razor blade.

"Your puny collection is far too small for us," the man said with a sinister grin. "But we will take it anyway."

Pooch could hardly speak at this point. "Take it, yes," he stuttered. "For free. As a gift. From me . . ."

"You're very kind, old man," the razor-toting stranger said. "But not kind enough . . ."

In the flick of his wrist, the men slashed a hole in Pooch's neck just an inch above the jugular. Pooch bellowed, but his cry was cut short when the man savagely cut him again across his right cheek and then again above the left eye.

The wounds were ghastly and very bloody—and that was the point. The men knocked Pooch to his feet and kicked him twice in the stomach. Then one pulled out a small walkie-talkie and was soon speaking to someone aboard the nearest battleship. The brief conversation ordered those aboard to come ashore to raid Pooch's underground vault for drugs and liquor.

This done, the men picked up Pooch and carried him kicking and screaming to the small motor launch they'd hidden beneath the reeds near his beach house. Fighting the growing waves, they quickly puttered to a point about 200 yards offshore. The launches from the lead battleship passed them now, on their way in to steal Pooch's supply. There were sneers and laughter as these men saw what their colleagues had done to Pooch—and realized what they were about to do.

At about 300 yards out, they slashed the writhing Pooch again, tearing long gashes in his arms, legs, and chest. None of these wounds would prove instantly fatal—that was the whole point. Pooch was screaming— he hated being on the water as much as he hated getting sliced—but his cries were drowned out by the sound of the small navy of motorboats moving in from the battleships toward shore.

Finally the two men grew tired of cutting Pooch; now it was time to go for the kill. Taking handfuls of the old man's blood, they leaned over and wrung it into the water. Then they waited. Not a minute passed before they saw the telltale fins of a fast-approaching school of hammerhead sharks.

At this point, they picked poor Pooch up by his hands and feet and sent him screaming into the water.

"Drugs kill, old man," one yelled at him, as the sharks began taking chunks from his body.

"And drinking is bad for your health," laughed the other as Pooch, what was left of him, was carried below the surface. Seconds later, only an oily slick of blood and a few pieces of ragged clothing remained.

Their entertainment over, the two men restarted their launch's engine and headed back to the closest battleship.

They still had much work to do tonight.

Three

One hundred and forty three miles high, passing directly over the island of Saint Ann's at 17,500 mph, Hawk Hunter was strapped into a zero-G holding harness, sound asleep.

He was dreaming, too. Of solid food. Of his F-16XL fighter. Of the fiery launch that had put him in orbit. Of the girl named Chloe. Of his girlfriend, Dominique.

He'd been in orbit for three days now. He and five others had blasted off from Cape Canaveral in the heavily refurbished Russian-designed Zon space shuttle exactly 71 hours before. And even in slumber, Hunter knew he would never be the same again.

In all his years of flying—and he was widely regarded as the best fighter pilot ever—nothing had matched that 22-minute ascent through the cloud layer above Florida, across the Atlantic, and eventually into orbit. The Zon, a crude cookie-cutter copy of the old American space shuttle, bucked and bronked the whole way up. At one point it was shaking so badly, Hunter and the others had clasped hands, so sure were they that the Zon was about to break apart in the upper reaches of the atmosphere and kill them all.

But somehow the spacecraft had held together and attained the magical speed of 17,500 mph, or roughly

7 miles a second, the velocity needed to break out of the earth's gravity. And it had deposited them here, shaken, into orbit, safe and in one piece.

In surviving this, the most hair-raising experience of his life, Hawk Hunter had had an epiphany. Flying jets faster, higher, and better than anyone had been only a warm-up, a precursor to this, the ultimate high-flight. *This* was what he'd been working for all along; *this* had been his goal. Not so much the act of flying, which was, in exact terms, simply a way of fooling gravity. What Hunter had wanted all these years was to be *free* of gravity. To break those surly bonds completely—not just in his kick-ass fighter at Mach 2 or 3, but in a monstrous spacecraft: huge liquid-fuel tank, solid-rocket boosters, awesome shuttle engines, all combined for more thrust than what he'd summomed up in his many years of driving jets. Flying airplanes was just the first step to flying in space. He was convinced of that now—just as he was certain the Wright Brothers had been convinced of it way back when.

But this was not just a free ride in space.

There was a mission up here for them to fulfill. And a desperate one at that. The supercriminal, world-feared terrorist Viktor II was up here somewhere, too. This was his space shuttle they were flying, captured in a spectacular battle on the South China Sea island of Lolita, where Hunter, through many machinations and twists, had forced it to land.

He'd been chasing Viktor II for many months now, ever since the superterrorist had ignited separate wars in the Pacific, Southeast Asia, and the Mediterranean. An embodiment of everything evil in the world, Hunter was determined to catch the devilish-looking war criminal and put an end to his reign of terror once and for all. Hunter had even gone so far as to vow to kill Viktor II

with his bare hands if he had to. It was a promise he
was still intending to keep.

The catastrophic world war which had put the earth
into its present chaotic position was now five years past.
From the ashes, a new kind of pursuit of freedom had
arisen. Not the old, cobbled-together, illusory freedom
that politicians had bandied about in the years leading
up to World War III—no, this was real freedom, real
liberty, politician free. And it was not just for those who
were fortunate enough to be born into the prosperous
areas of the planet. This was worldwide freedom, individual driven, based on the concept that all men were
created equal and therefore should be treated that
way—might they sink or swim, do good or bad.

This new concept was at the heart of the determination of Hunter and his allies of the United American
Armed Forces. It had taken them four long years to
rid the U.S. continent of those who had imposed an
unequal peace at the cessation of hostilities of the last
great war. Gone now for the most part were the left-
wing terrorists, the far-right white supremacist armies,
the Nazis, the Mid-Aks, the organized crime families,
the air pirates, the greedy opportunists, the agents of
disinformation and discord—all of them taken on and
defeated by the United Americans, all of them now on
the outside looking in.

In the last year or so, the United Americans had
found themselves fighting offshore, first on some of
the very same Pacific islands where their great-grand-
fathers had fought during World War II, and then in
the haunted jungles of Vietnam, where their grandfa-
thers and fathers had also spilled blood.

Now they were in outer space, doing the same thing.

More than any other, it was Hawk Hunter who had
led the forces of freedom in these campaigns, and it
was he who was at the helm of this new expeditionary

force. As with much of his life, times of great joy were frequently spliced into times of great peril. He loved flying in space—yet he was here to find and eliminate the world's most dangerous criminal. He loved the freedom from gravity, the total unshackling of earth, yet he'd left behind two very personal entanglements. One was named Chloe. The other was named Dominique.

It was perhaps not so ironic anymore that his relationship with Dominique had started in the cold, dark aftermath of World War III. He'd met her during his long, lonely march back across Europe once the fighting had ceased, staying with her in an abandoned farmhouse before moving on, eventually getting back to the States and having her walk back into his life again soon afterward. Beautiful, blond, erotic, and widely lusted after, they had been together ever since, unmarried and with no children, but bonded by real love and the passion of the times.

Dominique was now at their farm on Cape Cod, the place called Skyfire, waiting, he supposed, as she always did, for him to finally return home for good. That had been Hunter's dream, too: that all of the fighting and wars and intrigue would finally be over with and he could simply go home and be with the woman he loved.

At least, that had been his dream before he'd met Chloe. This had happened barely a few months ago, while he was making his way through the Swiss Alps in search of a key tracking station being used by Viktor II and the orbiting Zon spacecraft. That Chloe was naked when he first set eyes on her, bathing in the frigid waters of an alpine lake near Saint Moritz, only increased the magnitude of the lightning bolt that struck him that day. The way she was, what she believed—it filled him up inside so much, he'd been tempted just to quit the whole hero business and settle down with her right then and there.

But duty called and she became entangled and he wound up rescuing her from the clutches of Viktor's minions and together they had tracked down the last possible landing site for the Zon, thus forcing the climactic battle which gave the United Americans a working space shuttle, but not the prize they were after, Viktor II himself.

Now, for the first time in his life, Hunter was torn between two women, both beautiful, both smart, both patient. Both willing to be with him for the rest of their lives. And neither one knew about the other. Yet.

No wonder he liked it so much in space.

Hawk woke up to find the still-sleeping form of Elvis Q floating by him.

One of the original United Americans, Elvis Q had just escaped several years of captivity by Viktor's allies, a time during which he'd been brainwashed *and* taught how to fly the Zon spacecraft. Now that he was back in the fold, he was probably the most rabid Viktor-hater among them all, if that was possible.

Also on board and floating nearby were Jim Cook of the elite JAWS special ops unit, and Frank Geraci of the famous NJ104 combat engineers. Both were close allies of Hunter. The only ones awake up on the flight deck at the moment were JT Toomey and Ben Wa, two of Hunter's oldest friends.

Hunter had been asleep for only an hour or so when his deep inner sense told him to wake up. The same extrasensory perceptive ability that made him the premier fighter pilot of his day worked when he was out of the cockpit as well. Now a vibration rising up inside him told him he had to get up, get alert. Trouble was on the way.

Sure enough, the intercom inside the crew compartment came on not two seconds later.

"Flight deck to Hunter," JT's very distinctive voice crackled. "You'd better get up here, Hawk, old boy, on the triple . . ."

It was a short float up from the crew compartment to the flight deck of the Zon.

Three days in space had acclimated Hunter and the others to the quirks of zero-gravity. Drifting along weightless was a very pleasant experience; it was almost like sex—Hunter just could not get rid of the feeling that this was how man was supposed to be.

But when you had to get somewhere in a hurry, you had to bring one of Isaac Newton's laws into play: once a body is in motion, it tends to stay in motion. It was amazing how little muscle power it took to propel oneself across the crew compartment or up to the Zon's flight deck. Hunter just gave himself a tap of the boots and he was spinning like a bullet toward the overhead hatch and the flight deck beyond. It was the slowing down part that could be painful. Usually a well-placed shoulder or even a preemptive kick of the boot would do the trick. Hit the right place on the ladder or the compartment wall and you had the equivalent of brakes. Miss it by a centimeter or two and you'd wind up with a space bruise, painful and long-lasting.

The urgent call from JT had woken them all. Now, as Hunter bounced his way up to the flight compartment, Elvis, Cook, and Geraci were right on his heels.

"What've you got?" Hunter asked, floating up and into the left-side commander's seat.

"Maybe trouble," JT replied. "Maybe with a capital T."

He was pointing to an object that appeared to be

about 20 miles straight ahead of them. It was white and twinkling, indicating that it was tumbling.

"That showed up on the radar about two minutes ago," Ben explained from the makeshift navigator's station.

"So?" Hunter asked. "We've seen a lot of junk up here."

"But the computer says this particular piece wasn't there when we came around last time," Ben replied. "Wasn't anywhere near here. I checked the radar's memory. It's a new object."

"You mean something that's been launched since we went around the last time?" Elvis asked.

Ben could only shrug. "Maybe . . ."

Hunter doubted this. His inner sense would have told him if it were so. Plus, they surely would have detected a new satellite's entry trail; the telltale stream of smoke and exhaust left behind by a payload's boosters was hard to miss.

Hunter pulled out the shuttle's extremely powerful bi-scopes, a kind of computer-driven set of binoculars. The radar on the Zon had been a hasty addition before take-off and Hunter knew better than to rely on it too closely. It was time to go with the naked eye.

He got the tumbling object within his sights and tried to study it. It appeared to be a piece of space trash, one of many thousands of objects floating around above the planet, the result of nearly 50 years of earth-launched space flights. But looking at things up here was different than down on earth. First of all, the Zon at the moment was streaking along at several miles a second. The trouble was, so was just about everything else around them, thus giving the illusion that everything was in fact standing still, and the earth below them was spinning around at a fantastic rate.

Second, just because they were in a stable orbit

didn't mean everything around them stayed in the same position in relation to them everytime around, especially in low-earth orbit. Space was not a static place, though it might look that way from the ground up. Actually, things were changing all the time.

This particular object was bothering Hunter. It had taken a marathon preflight session to figure out the Zon's rather primitive guidance computers and then link them up in such a way that they could keep track of the spacecraft's orbital path and avoid any collisions. Up here the tiniest screw spinning free from a deteriorating piece of space junk could prove fatal to something as big and as fast as the Zon.

Colliding with the object Hunter now had in the bi-scopes would prove catastrophic.

The reason they were up here was to apprehend Viktor II and drag him back to earth for trial and hopefully execution. When they realized he was not on the Zon when it was forced to land on Lolita Island, that left only one place he could still be: inside the old Russian-built Mir space station, a frequent destination of Viktor's previous orbital flights.

But finding the Mir was a task that stretched even Hunter's estimable talents to the limit. It could be anywhere in orbit—higher than the Zon's present path, or lower; hundreds of miles ahead, or a few miles behind. It could be on one station one day and move to another the next. It could be on the other side of the globe and by maintaining the proper speed and altitude, forever elude their searching.

But something inside Hunter's brain was buzzing, and it had to do with this mysterious object which had suddenly appeared in their vicinity.

"Is there anything in the computer memory that can ID this thing?" he asked JT.

The shuttle pilot began furiously punching buttons

on the main control panel. The small TV screen before him began generating long lists of known space junk on one side and two-dimensional stick-figure illustrations on the other. Both Elvis and Ben had bi-scopes and were studying the tumbling object, occasionally looking down at the computer readouts to see if there was anything similar.

About twenty seconds into this procedure, Elvis got a match.

"It looks like a Progress M-27 satellite, similar to the Cosmos series," he announced, keeping the object in view. "Same framework. Same mass and dimensions, according to the computer. Same . . ."

Suddenly, Hunter's psyche began vibrating madly.

"Jeezus . . ." he was just able to whisper. An instant later, the tumbling object blew up.

It was an amazing sight—for about three seconds. The explosion went off as if in slow motion. A bright flash, and then a billowing cloud of flame shooting out in all directions. There was no sound, but a concussion wave hit the Zon a few moments later. It shook the spacecraft from one end to the other.

And then it was gone. The flash, the flame, the sharp jolt. All that remained was the cloud of white specks— and that was the problem.

Before Hunter even knew it, he was deep into the pilot's seat and pushing buttons madly. He unlocked the Zon's main systems from the GPS-2 computer, essentially putting the shuttle into manual control. Then he voice-commanded the steering jets to prepare to be lit. Then he lit them.

Suddenly the Zon flipped on its side, which in the directionless environs of space meant it had changed its position relative to the earth. Hunter hit the steering jets again. Now the Zon began moving sideways, shuddering in protest at the violent action. Hunter hit the steering jets a third time. Now the Zon was suddenly standing on its tail and vibrating even worse than before.

Throughout all this, the other crew members held on for dear life, their mouths hanging open at Hunter's lightning-quick actions. They weren't quite sure why he had suddenly seen fit to throw the Zon all over the place.

The answer came a few seconds later.

For suddenly the cloud of debris from the explosion was on them. It went by like a thousand tiny missiles, still aglow from the tremendous blast. Hunter had managed to steer the Zon away from the bulk of it. Still dozens of small particles began slamming into the spacecraft, especially around the tail section and the right wing. An outer glass panel directly over their heads was smashed. A large chunk hit the nose of the spacecraft, too. The lights blinked; the computer screens went crazy. Three separate warning buzzers went off at once. Even the intercoms went to static.

But just as quickly as the debris cloud was on them it was gone. Its individual particles losing velocity by the second, it seemed to disappear as the Zon zoomed out of it. Elvis, JT, and Ben were pushing reset panels and hitting panic buttons, but in a relatively short time, the on-board main computers were telling them the damage to the Zon was slight and that all systems were still operating at high integrity.

They had dodged a mighty large bullet.

Finally Hunter pushed a series of buttons, putting the Zon back under control of the GPS-2, in effect, returning it to auto-pilot.

In all, the crisis had lasted less than thirty seconds.

"Christ, what the hell happened?" JT finally breathed. "One moment that thing is in our way, the next, it blows up and almost kills us."

"Some coincidence . . ." Ben gasped.

Hunter was already scanning space in front of him. The rock-hard features on his face were not good news to his colleagues. When Hunter looked concerned, it was usually timc to worry. And he looked very concerned right now.

"That was no coincidence," he said finally. "Someone sent that toward us intentionally. In the old days, they used to call it flak . . ."

Four

On the Jersey Shore

It had been a long year and a half for the members of NJ104.

The high-tech combat engineering unit had been involved in continuous military action since the beginning of the previous year. Commencing with the war against the Fourth Reich and its Norse allies, the specialized combat engineers—who were actually members of the pre–Big War 104th Engineering Battalion of the New Jersey National Guard—had fought against the Asian Mercenary Cult in the South Pacific, had then transited to Southeast Asia for the Second Vietnam War, and had then played a key role in the capturing of the Zon space shuttle on Lolita Island in the middle of the South China Sea.

In that time NJ104 had lost its air transport—a C-5 gunship specially outfitted for lugging the team's vast array of CE gear around—along with about 20 percent of its weaponry and nearly 30 percent of its manpower. Moreover, in those 18 months of combat, NJ104 hadn't had any R & R, vacation, or anything close to what could be considered a day off.

The unit was long overdue for a rest.

So this is what had brought it to the shore town of Surf City, New Jersey. The unit was now about 150 men strong, though just about everyone was nursing some kind of wound or ailment. Many men were suffering from simple exhaustion, others from dehydration and even malnutrition.

Surf City seemed to be just the place for the unit to heal its wounds, regain its strength, and catch its collective breath. The nearby beaches were pristine, the water clean, relatively warm, with high waves and plenty of bluefish and stripers. The town was full of saloons, eateries, gambling halls, and strip clubs. The old O'Keefe Naval Air Station was close by and here a new C-5 Galaxy gunship was being refitted for the combat engineers. A well-staffed medevac unit was also located on the base.

The unit and their families were billeted in a row of beachfront condominiums about a quarter mile south of Surf City, at a place called Ship Bottom Bay. One of the condos had been turned into a command post and chow hall. The hierarchy of the elite engineering unit was stationed here. The place was known simply as the Hut.

Unlike many UAAF-affiliated units, NJ104 was run by committee. Seven officers made up this command staff, all of them members of the original pre-war 104th Combat Engineering Battalion. They were Colonel Frank Geraci, Lieutenant Colonels Don Matus, Ray Palma, Roy Cerbasi, Nick Vittelo, and Frank DeLusso, and semi-retired General Tom McCaffery. Geraci was temporarily up in space. He'd left the command of the unit in the hands of his six colleagues.

These officers had set up the top floor of the Hut as their operations center. From here they could track the progress of their new airplane, the strength reports of the unit, and the recovery rates of their wounded troopers, as well as day-to-day business, such as the number of lobsters and steamers for the nightly clambake and the number of beer kegs the unit currently had under chill.

It was now close to noontime and the NJ104 officers were gathered around a huge radio set, awaiting the daily transmission from UAAF provisional headquarters at Cape Canaveral. The unit was officially on stand-down, and by orders of commander-in-chief and de facto president Dave Jones himself, NJ104 was to divorce itself from all UAAF activities until it was up to full strength again. The radio briefing at noon was Jones's only concession to the NJ104's officer staff, the daily fix the CE men needed to stay plugged in.

It was a daily event usually greeted with coffee and sandwiches and today was no different. The six men were lounging out on the top balcony of the Hut, gazing down on their men and their families as they fished, body-surfed the huge waves, or sunbathed on the ultra-white sand below. Some were straggling out of the chow hall three floors down, bringing their noontime meals to the shoreline. Others were preparing a squadron of windsurfers for the daily afternoon boat races. It was August first. The day was hot and breezy.

Matus had just poured out six cups of coffee when the CP radio crackled to life. A message was coming in. Automatically, Matus checked his watch. It was quarter to noon, still fifteen minutes away from the Cape Canaveral broadcast. Usually the CP radio set was inactive except for this daily radio briefing. Who would be calling them now?

Palma was the closest man to the set. He casually flipped down the scramble buttons and activated the initiate panel.

"This is NJ104-CP receiving," he spoke into the microphone. "Go ahead . . ."

"I will send a fire," a deep, echoing voice responded.

"And among them who dwell carelessly, I will bring it down upon them."

Palma looked over at the others who looked back as baffled as he. The CP radio was a secure set; it was almost impossible to use its frequencies without the proper security and scramble codes.

"Who is this?" Palma asked into the microphone.

"Behold, it has come," the eerie voice intoned. "The day whereof I have spoken is here . . ."

"Who the hell *is* that?" Cerbasi breathed.

"It sounds like God," Vittelo replied.

"God, hell," Palma snapped. "It's someone down at the Cape yanking us."

"Let me see it," Matus said.

Palma passed the mike over to NJ104's unofficial CO.

"This is radio station Delta Zebra," Matus said into the microphone, using NJ104's temporary call sign in measured, even tones. "Who is this, please?"

"All these things are the beginnings of sorrows," the voice replied. "Whosoever's name is not written in the book of life shall be cast into the lake of fire. This is the day whereof I spoke . . ."

And with that the radio went dead.

The six officers just stared at each other, coffee cups frozen in mid-sip, sandwiches in mid-bite. Palma tried to raise the voice again, but to no avail. The transmission was gone.

"Well, Christ, that was some joke . . ." McCaffery snorted. "Someone down at Cape Comm is in for a court martial, I would say."

The others would have agreed with him, but oddly, none of them could speak at the moment. The wind had suddenly kicked up, blowing some papers and empty coffee cups around the balcony.

"That was . . . very strange," Matus said, breaking the silence. "It was almost as if . . ."

But he never got to finish his sentence. Suddenly there was a loud noise at the other end of the CP. The main door flew open and two women came running in. They were wives of two troopers. Both were in tears and close to hysterics.

"The kids . . ." one of them kept repeating. "The kids!"

The six officers were on their feet and over to the women in a flash.

"What's the matter?" several of the men asked at once. "What happened?"

The women were crying so much it was hard for them to get the words out.

Finally, one of them grabbed Matus by the lapels. "The kids. Four of them. They're missing . . ." she cried. "You have to come. Right now!"

The six officers grabbed their sidearms and piled out the door and down the steps of the Hut.

It was 11:59 A.M.

When the daily broadcast from Cape Canaveral came on the radio a minute later, no one was in the NJ104 CP to hear it.

A group of children and family members from the NJ104 billet had taken a morning trip to a beach approximately two miles south of Ship Bottom Bay.

This place, known locally as the Dunes, was a deserted stretch of shoreline festooned with high, towering sand dunes and thick plumbush vegetation. It was a favorite spot of the billeted families, especially those with young children. The water was a little calmer here, and the dunes were a natural playground. Some were more than fifty feet high, and with the proper acceleration, some kids were able to fling themselves out twenty feet or more before falling to the soft sand below.

The party that had left for the Dunes earlier that day was made up of sixteen children and five adults, all women, two of whom were combat engineers. The group arrived around 8 A.M. and settled down into the shade of Big Two, one of the largest dunes in the area. The group of children then split. The seven boys, their ages ranging from eight to thirteen, went immediately to dune-jumping, while the nine slightly older girls chose to go swimming.

The next two hours passed without incident. Some of the girls retired to their blankets to sunbathe. The boys continued playing on the dunes, moving down to Big Three, probably the largest dune of them all. Sometime after 11 A.M., four of the girls told the adults they were going to Big Three to join the boys.

They never made it.

It took a while before anyone realized the girls were missing. Two of the boys, hungry and thirsty from two hours of dune-jumping, saw the girls climbing up the north side of Big Three just as they were climbing down, on the way back to the others. They said the girls had flirted and thrown sand at them as they passed. The boys continued on their way, last seeing the girls about twenty feet below the summit of Big Three.

It wasn't until these two boys ate a sandwich, drank some punch, took a swim, and then returned to Big Three that anyone knew something was wrong. They found the other five boys atop Big Three—but the girls were not there. Some more time passed before one of the two boys asked where the girls were and was told by the others that no one had come to the top of Big Three since they'd left.

One of the younger boys became concerned, as his sister was in the group of four girls. He ran back down to the others on the beach, and when he found the girls were not there either, the adults began looking for them. Thirty minutes went by, and still there was no sign of the girls. The adults, now joined by the other children, searched the dunes and the thick vegetation nearby. They scoured the shoreline in both directions. They even climbed to the top of the larger dunes and called the girls' names in unison. There was no response.

By this time, one of the adults was on a personal radiophone calling back to the Surf City billets, but as luck would have it, the radiophone was malfunctioning. All that could be heard were static and strange unintelligible voices. Finally, one of the women ran the two miles back to Ship Bottom Bay to alert the others. The first people she came upon were the mother and aunt of one of the missing girls.

These were the two women who had run to the top of the Hut to get the NJ104 staff officers.

By 1 P.M. there were 100 people swarming all over the dunes—CE troopers, women, and older children.

Two of NJ104's attack helicopters, AH-1 Cobras, had joined the search. Both had LANTIRN day-assisted radars able to see through the thickest underbrush. Two more helicopters, huge Chinooks, were dispatched from NAS O'Keefe, as were fifty additional SAR personnel.

This small army searched the Dunes for ten miles in both directions. All they found was the bathing suit top of the oldest girl hanging from a plumbush tree about two miles from Big Three, near an area known as the Crater. The search was then concentrated in this area, though it was beyond anyone's comprehension how the four girls, last seen just twenty feet from the summit of

Big Three, could have made it so far, over rough terrain, so quickly.

More troops arrived from O'Keefe around 3:30 P.M., ferried in by the big Chinooks. An OV-10A Bronco airsearch plane arrived from NAS Cape May around 4 P.M. It was equipped with highly sophisticated listening equipment used in covert operations, carried in a pod beneath its left wing. Around 5:15, the pilots thought they picked up sounds of a girl crying near the Crater; a similar report was heard at a location a mile to the south about 6 P.M.

But though both areas were scoured by nearly 200 combat-hardened troops and volunteers, as of nightfall, no further sign of the girls had been found.

For Don Matus and the other members of the NJ104 command staff, the search for the missing girls was a heart-wrenching experience.

Though none of the girls was directly related to any of the men, if there was a family-oriented combat unit anywhere in the world, it was NJ104. They were a clan. Everyone felt related to everyone else, and they were famous for looking out for their own. When trouble beset one member of this extended tree, it was felt by everyone.

With night falling, Matus had two patrol boats from NAS O'Keefe searching the nearby surf. The four choppers were still in the air, as was the Bronco. The combat engineers had established positions on every dune and were sweeping all the areas below with NightScopes and listening devices. The direct families of the missing girls were keeping vigil on the beach near Big Two. The unit's two chaplains were on hand, as was a padre from O'Keefe. Matus himself was manning the command post on Big Four. Palma and McCaffery were with him. Squads of search teams passed them regularly, some going into the search areas, others coming out for brief respites of coffee and food. Their faces looked more concerned, more pained, more agonized than at any time Matus had seen them in combat.

Night fell. The searchers now began encountering obstacles that in daylight were mere annoyances. Tree branches now became near-lethal weapons, sinkholes were like land mines. To make matters worse, a sudden storm blew up around 8:30 P.M., soaking sand and searchers alike. Still the members of NJ104 pressed on, covering and recovering their tracks, looking into each and every crevice, plumbush, crater, and sand hole they came to, urging each other on but finding nothing.

By 11 P.M., the Bronco had to depart; it was low on gas and its listening suite needed a recharge. The Chinooks left, too—Matus felt it best that the airspace above the ten-mile search area not be made more dangerous. Now only the Cobras were overflying the Dunes, and their pilots had been at their controls continuously for nearly 12 hours.

Finally, by a quarter to midnight, Matus had one of the AH-1s ferry him back to Surf City. Landing directly on top of the roof of the Hut, he went down one floor to the command center and sat down before the CP radio. Though he wasn't exactly sure why, he felt compelled to report the missing girls to UAAF provisional headquarters down at Cape Canaveral. Maybe someone down there would have some advice. Maybe an aircraft with powerful infrared capability could be dispatched to the area or more volunteers sent in from other UAAF bases nearby.

It was precisely one minute to midnight when Matus hit the power button on the radio set. Outside the wind was howling. There was a boom of thunder, followed by a crack of lightning. The storm was getting worse.

He picked up the microphone. But before he could say one word, there was a burst of static from the radio receiver and then the low-echoing voice of someone speaking.

"The day whereof I have spoken has arrived," the eerie voice intoned. "The days of many sufferings are at hand."

Matus was so stunned the microphone fell from his hand. The voice. It was the same one they'd heard on the radio earlier that day. With the events since, he'd almost forgotten about it. Now the words chilled him to the bone.

"Prepare, those of you who have dwelled carelessly." The words vibrated as they came out of the radio speakers. "The end is very near . . ."

Five

Free Territory of New York, The Next Day

There was another elite unit attached to the UAAF that was presently on standdown.

This was the famous JAWS outfit, the do-it-all/done-it-all special operations group whose nucleus had been formed several years after the Big War by a small police force in the upstate town of Johnstown, New York.

Named after the bastardization of their community's name—Jacktown—the "Jacks Are Wild" group was made up of eighty combat-hardened regulars. Like NJ104, the core command of JAWS consisted of a handful of men, all of them close personal friends of Hawk Hunter. They had been through many climactic battles with the Wingman, including those leading up to the freeing of the American continent, and the UAAF's more recent overseas actions as well.

Like NJ104, JAWS had lost their C-5 Galaxy gunship during the Second Vietnam War. Like NJ104, they had suffered nearly 30-percent casualties in Southeast Asia and in action in the South China Sea. Like NJ104, they hadn't had any substantial R & R in nearly 19 months.

But unlike NJ104, the members of JAWS were not taking their vacation at the shore. Instead, to relax, the JAWS command staff had gone mountain climbing.

Their intention was to scale Mount Chazy, also

known as "Crazy Chazy," a virtually uncharted peak at
the very northern tip of the Free Territory of New York,
not far west of Upper Lake Champlain. Chazy was 6001
feet high, an almost identical lookalike to Mount Washington, a few hundred miles to the southeast. Like
Mount Washington, Chazy was high enough to affect
the weather in the surrounding areas. The winds whip-
ping off Lake Ontario would buffet the western side of
the peak, condense, pick up speed and strength, and
rip over the top of Crazy Chazy so quickly, you could
sometimes hear the roar 50 miles away. Add a constant
cap of snow and ice at the peak, persistent reports that
a yeti-like creature inhabited the caves near the mountain's crown, and a fatality rate among climbers that
rivaled Mount McKinley's, and an adventure on top of
Mount Chazy was something to ponder a long time
before undertaking.

This was exactly the kind of adventure the JAWS
team craved. They'd *blown up* a mountain almost this
big on the island of Okinawa a year or so back, one
that contained several divisions of Asian Mercenary
Cult troops and an underground aircraft factory—and
this after fighting their way up the side of the thing.
They were highly trained in the arts of repelling, Alpine
warfare, difficult infiltrations, and quick getaways. For
unlike many postwar military units who tended to spe-
cialize in one thing or another, the JAWS team was
good at doing just about everything.

Climbing Mount Chazy would be a breeze for them.

But they weren't going to be stupid about it. The
climb team had come well prepared. They'd chop-
pered up from Jacktown the night before, setting up
camp at the base of Chazy on its somewhat protected
southern side. There were four of them: Mark Snyder
(now the team's unofficial leader, since Captain Jim
Cook was in space), Warren Maas, Sean Higgins, and

Clancy Miller. Two local men, Eddie Edson and Louis DeMarco, would serve as guides. Snyder and Higgins had once climbed K-2; they would be the climb leaders. Miller was a photo expert and would be carrying nearly 30 pounds of photo gear. Maas would be lugging most of the team's provisions. Edson and DeMarco would carry the emergency gear and the radio.

The plan was to leave at 6 A.M. and be at the top of Chazy peak by mid-afternoon.

The climbers got off to a good start.

The day dawned bright and sunny, and though it was August, the temperatures up in the northern Adirondacks promised to remain comfortable. The team found their main ascent trail right away, and by 8 A.M. they were up the first quarter of the mountain.

By 10, they'd reached the halfway point, an hour ahead of schedule. Now the trees were beginning to thin and the views were becoming spectacular. Looking to the right from the southern side, they could see clear into Old Vermont; to the left, the immense puddle of Lake Ontario. By looking straight up, they could see the snow-capped peak of Chazy itself. It looked cold and mysterious, especially in the warm summer sun. All four men had promised to bring snowballs from the summit back home for their kids.

They reached the top of the treeline just about noon, again ahead of schedule. They found a shaded, rocky area and decided they'd take a 20-minute meal break. Miller wandered off to snap some pictures; Maas heated water for mixing their MRE rations. Higgins and Snyder did stretching exercises to keep their hands and feet loose for the last part of the long climb. Edson and Demarco, the two guides, found another cliff nearby and lit up smokes.

The first sign of trouble came when Miller stumbled back into the small camp about two minutes later. He was as white as a sheet, his pile of expensive camera equipment nowhere to be seen.

He could barely talk; he was having trouble breathing. His colleagues gathered around and forced him to drink some water. Then they hustled him into the shade. It was a frightening moment. They'd never seen their friend like this.

"What is it, Clancy?" Snyder pressed him. "What the hell happened?"

But Miller could not speak. He could only point to a spot around the bend from where they party had made camp. He was gurgling and choking and trying like hell to say something. Finally they let him calm down, catch his breath, and take another long swig of water.

"Jeezus Christ," he gasped at last. "I just saw . . . Christ, I don't believe I'm going to say this . . ."

"Saw what," his friends urged him.

"It's the damnedest thing . . ." Miller went on wildly. "I saw them. This bunch of people. There right over that next bunch of rocks. They're . . . they're . . ."

"They're *what?*" the other three were yelling at him in unison.

"Christ, you guys," Miller finally gasped. "They look like frigging ghosts. There's bunch of them. Over there. They're building something. I saw them, and . . ."

Miller just about collapsed at this point. His friends poured an entire canteen of water over his head and urged him to cool down. They suspected that he was suffering from heat exhaustion, even though it really wasn't that hot.

Calling Edson and DeMarco back to the camp, Higgins, Snyder, and Maas grabbed their handguns and began climbing up the small cliff over which Miller had claimed to see the ghosts.

To their astonishment, they saw them, too.

There were about fifteen of them. They were in a shallow ravine, protected on three sides by sharp, sheer rocks.

These people, if that's what they were, were dressed very strangely; they were wearing dirty white tunics, crude sandals, and leather headbands. Their skin was a reddish copper color. They had very straight hair, very thin lips, and weirdly narrow faces. Their movements were, for lack of a better word, erratic. They seemed clumsy, uncoordinated.

They appeared to be building something. It looked like the beginnings of a tower, made of brick and mortar. And though at that moment the weather was fine, to look at these strange people, it was as if they were working out in the rain and wind. Indeed, their hair and clothes were being blown around mercilessly, even though where the three JAWS men were, the wind was gusting only up to five or six knots.

But the strangest thing of all was that one of these men was lashed to a crucifix-type structure about twenty feet from the main group. He'd been shot with many arrows, and he appeared to be dying. He was crying out at the top of his lungs, yet the others were doing nothing to help him. To the contrary, they were acting as though he wasn't really there.

The JAWS men could hear these strange people talking, too; they were chanting as they worked on this tower. The words were odd, yet somehow recognizable. From their hiding place about 30 feet away the JAWS men could hear words like *"Lehi," "Lamanite,"* and *"Jaredite."*

The three JAWS men were absolutely stunned by all this; now Miller's actions were more understandable.

But what were they looking at here? A vision? A mirage? *Ghosts?*

Being the combat veterans they were, the JAWS men decided to take a direct approach. They climbed down from their perch so they were level with this strange group. Then they began yelling at these people—but the people did not look up or show any reaction at all. Snyder pulled out his pistol and fired two shots into the air. Still the people did not look up.

"They're acting like we aren't even here," Higgins gasped.

But Maas was shaking his head.

"No, you got it backward," he said. "I think we're here . . . and *they're not.*"

Higgins saw something in a clump of bushes nearby. He carefully moved over to it and discovered it was Miller's camera bag, dropped when their friend had seen what they were now seeing.

Acting on impulse, he found Miller's Nikon and snapped off a half dozen photos. Then he took out his friend's small video camera and reeled off about a minute of videotape. Then he retrieved the rest of the bag's contents and crawled back over to his colleagues.

That's when they heard a noise behind them. They turned to see that DeMarco and Edson were climbing down. The pair of guides, curious because the group had been gone for so long, had decided to investigate. It turned out to be a fatal mistake.

Edson reached them first, and after indicating that he should keep quiet, they pointed in the direction of the strange group of people. The guide took one look and immediately soiled himself.

"Jeezus," he gasped. "It's the . . ."

"The what?" the three JAWS men asked at once.

DeMarco now took a look—and collapsed right on the spot. His eyes suddenly went up into his head. A white foam came shooting out of his mouth and he stopped breathing. The JAWS men tried to revive him, but his heart had stopped beating. Maas continued CPR on him, but it was no good. He was dead. In about ten seconds. Just like that.

Seeing his friend go so suddenly, and then looking up at the strange people, caused Edson to lose his faculties, too.

"They are Nephites. The ghosts of the people who lived up here thousands of years ago," he began crying. "They say if you see them, then you are about to die yourself."

With that, Edson jumped up and just started running. Away from the JAWS team, away from the strange people, he reached the edge of a sheer, steep cliff—and kept right on going. There was no scream, no final cry. He fell more than 500 feet to his death without ever uttering another sound.

The JAWS men rushed over to the cliff only to see Edson's broken body on the rocks below.

When they looked back into the rocky ravine, the strange people had disappeared.

It took them four hours to go back down the mountain.

It was a silent, dreadful trip, each man turning over in his mind what had happened near the peak, the sudden death of DeMarco, the silent, horrible death of Edson. The vision of the strange people.

Maas and Higgins carried DeMarco's body halfway down the mountain; Miller and Maas carried it the rest of the way to the base camp. Upon reaching their auxiliary radio, they called the local military police unit and requested a helicopter be sent to recover Edson's battered body. One was promised, but it would take at least until the next morning to get there.

The JAWS men were forced to spend the night at the bottom of what they now considered a haunted mountain. They did not sleep; they did not let go of their guns the entire night. They just stayed awake, stayed quiet, and prayed for the sun to come up again.

When it did, they packed up their gear and began the hour-long hike back down to the road where they would meet the rescue helicopter. Before leaving, Higgins took a chance and rewound the piece of videotape he'd shot during the incident the day before.

To no one's surprise, the tape was blank.

Six

Bajiib Baharushimina Sanagreshmeshmarogi had been crying for almost two days now.

The tears that stained his face had been so constant, and the weather outside so cold, that furrows had begun to form on his cheeks, curving in toward his thin nose, then across his even-thinner lips.

This was not the first time he'd cried like this. When he was fourteen and just initiated into the Be'hei-Sajetlamalla Order, he'd touched the robe of the famous Maharishi Hamijjib Mahaollaboola, the man who was famous for knowing 15,000 pages of sacred text from memory. After that, Bajiib had cried for eighteen hours. When he was 19, he'd broken his right big toe. He'd cried for about 90 minutes after that.

But now, two days of weeping—this was the longest ever. And he had no one but the girl named Chloe to blame.

Her dream had been told to him the morning after the winds had calmed. He'd heard it first from the two monks who had initially tried to comfort her and then, apparently, tried to have sex with her. Though their renditions lacked any of the subtlety needed for interpreting these things, there were enough clues to intrigue Bajiib and then frighten him.

He'd called for the girl. As head monk at the Be'hei Temple, he could order people here and there, request they do his bidding, all in the name of God, of course. Usually they came at his first beckoning.

But the girl Chloe had to be summoned three times over the course of an hour, a delay that would have infuriated Bajiib if he hadn't been such a holy man. When she finally did arrive at his residence, she was carrying a travel bag. Bajiib hastily dried his tears and refilled and lit his incense urn. It was just the two of them in his spartan quarters. She looked as beautiful as ever.

"How long have you been with us now?" Bajiib asked her, knowing it was best to attack the question of her travel bag from an unexpected direction.

Chloe had to think a moment.

"It seems like years," she finally replied, unconsciously tugging on her low-cut blouse. "But really, it's only been a month or so."

"You enjoy it here, I take it?" Bajiib asked. "You have found this to be an enlightening place? A worthwhile place?"

"Yes, it is," she replied, brushing back her blond hair and offering a half-smile. "It is surely one of the most wonderful places in the world. . . ."

"But?"

"But I must leave," she told him rather directly. "I think the sooner, the better."

Bajiib felt the tears coming on again. This was disastrous, for several reasons.

"May I ask why?"

Chloe lowered her head. She was about to cry, too. "You heard about my dream?"

Bajiib wiped away the first drop in what would be another assault of tears.

"I have," he replied. "It is very disturbing, on several

levels. Though I can't pretend to understand it completely. At least, not yet . . ."

"Nor do I," Chloe replied, dabbing her eyes with her hair. "All I know is that something terrible is going to happen—and I feel like I'm the only one who knows about it."

"We *both* know," he corrected her gently. "What happened in your dream was written down many years ago in one of our most ancient texts. I have read this text. Yesterday, and again today. The calmness the other night, and your dream—there is no doubt. It is all in there."

Chloe looked up at him, slightly confused.

"Are you saying what I saw in my dream was predicted?"

"Yes, many centuries ago," Bajiib replied. "It is in what the elders called *The Book of Thirteen*. It is, to us, what the Book of Revelation is to Judeo-Christians, or the *Tibetan Book of the Dead* to the Hindus. It is, quite frankly, the book depicting the end of the world and the destruction of all mankind."

Chloe's hand went up to her mouth. More tears appeared in her eyes.

"Yes, that's what I feel," she sobbed. "The end . . . it's coming."

Bajiib rose from his pillow and pulled his saffron robes away from his chest, exposing it. He'd been working out lately: secretly lifting weights and doing push-ups, decidedly unmonklike behavior.

"This is why I cry, too," he said, sitting even closer to her. "I fear for us. I fear for the whole world. Certainly something momentous will happen soon, if it hasn't already."

"I think people should be warned," Chloe said, unconsciously moving closer to him. "People must be told. The right people, I mean. Do you agree?"

Bajiib knew he would have to answer carefully. If the world was coming to an end, he wanted to taste this lotus flower before it did so.

"I agree that people should be warned," he replied calmly, inching closer to where she knelt. "But I also believe your dream needs more . . . how shall I say it? *Interpretation* . . ."

Chloe looked at him for a long time and then shrugged.

"But if you already know the dream, and you've read this *Book of Thirteen,* what more is needed?"

Bajiib moved even closer to her; their knees were touching.

"The book predicts many, many things," he began. "It tells of people disappearing. Here one moment, gone the next. It tells of strange voices in the sky. Of ghosts rising up to haunt the living. It tells of terrible visions, great wars, and suffering and death. It tells of a world gone mad. *Our* world. Wrapped in insanity before the end finally comes."

He rested a fatherly hand on her soft knee. His fingers were beginning to tremble.

"Some men will rise above all this," he went on. "Some women, too. Though the bravest will suffer the most sorrow; the most stable will go insane. The book tells of many great battles. One is fought near the Ladder into Heaven. The brave soldiers will fly out over the water and meet their enemy and surprise him and live, yet they, too, will be among those to be haunted. Others will see the past and not understand it, and they will almost go mad.

"But the book also says that a few will be chosen and they will see everything in their dreams. They will be compelled to go to a secret place and gather. I believe you are one of those the book speaks about. I think that's why you had the dream. But I think more study is needed."

His hand was now working its way up her thigh. It was time to make his move.

"How do you mean?" she asked him.

"I know only the conscious aspects of your dream," he replied, tripping slightly over the words "conscious aspects." "I think in a situation such as this, one that is admittedly very dire, we must explore the *un*conscious aspects of it as well. I think more truth, or perhaps even a *solution*, could be found in there . . ."

"In where?"

Bajiib looked at her. She was probably the most gorgeous creature ever born. And so sexy.

"Inside you, my dear," he finally breathed. "Like you, your dream has many layers. Like you, I think we must peel them back, like the petals of a flower, and search together for a hidden meaning. For the reason why you, above everyone else on this planet, were chosen to receive this dream."

Chloe pulled back a little. Another ocean of tears welled in Bajiib's eyes. He knew what was coming, knew what her dream meant. He just wanted his before the lights went out.

"Inside me?" she asked. "Do you mean sex?"

Bajiib nearly lost his breath. The tears began falling again, down his cheeks, in toward his nose, and across his lips to meet on his chin. He'd been celibate all his life. Fifty-three years. And for what?

"It is another means of exploration," he finally managed to gurgle.

"You could tell more about my dream if we have sex?" she asked him innocently.

Bajiib was blubbering like a baby now.

"It is possible," he replied. "But only if the mind is willing will the body go along . . ."

Chloe seemed to consider this, then looked back over at him and smiled weakly.

"If you think it will help . . ." she said.

With that, she began unbuttoning her blouse. Beneath she wore a white lace see-through bra. It barely held her small, yet pert breasts in check, and they both popped out when she unsnapped it. Then she reached behind her and undid the ties on her long, flowing dress, pulling it off in one swift motion. This revealed her shapely waist, her perfect rear, her hairless crotch, her beautiful legs.

She now knelt naked and vulnerable before the great Bajiib. He was staring back at her, tears falling to his newly redefined chest.

"Is it helping yet?" she asked him.

Bajiib closed his eyes, and to his great surprise, he began to see colors. Many different reds and blues and greens and yellows were racing toward him at the speed of light. It was both frightening and beautiful.

"More . . ." he gasped.

Chloe took his hand and laid it gently on her right breast. The nipple immediately became erect.

Now Bajiib could see nothing but a bright white light. It was bouncing off his retinas with such luminescence, he really didn't know if his eyes were open or not.

She moved his hand down past her abdomen to the area between her legs. It was already moist. Bajiib was now bathed in a glow, and in his ears a choir was singing. This was not what he'd expected, not exactly what he wanted. He'd simply wanted to get laid—once, in his lifetime. All that other stuff about revealing the unconscious and peeling back the flower was just a bunch of crap. There wasn't even such a thing as *The Book of Thirteen*. He'd made it all up. Or at least, he thought he had. Never did he think it would *really* be like this.

Chloe began moving his fingers back and forth across her genitalia, moaning in response. Bajiib was now hallucinating. He was looking at a man with a long flowing beard and bright white robes. His finger was pointing directly at Bajiib's skull. He seemed to be saying something . . .

Chloe reached over and touched the area between Bajiib's trembling legs. There was already a protrusion in his robes. Chloe began stroking. Bajiib was now face-to-face with the man in the white beard. He was whispering something in Bajiib's ear. Chloe began stroking harder. The two explosions came almost simultaneously. First, Bajiib's long overdue scrotum ruptured and emptied—and then so did his heart. And in its last beat, he knew the true meaning of the word ecstasy. He collapsed to the floor, gasping wildly. All blood flow to his organs had stopped. Only his brain remained in function, and that for only a few seconds more.

He managed to pull Chloe close to him and whisper in her ear just as the bearded man in the vision had whispered in his. He had to tell her the key to her dream before it was too late.

But he could only form one last word.

Her ear directly on his mouth, he drew one last breath.

"Hubble . . ." he gasped.

And then he died.

Seven

The British Aerospace S.Mk 2B Buccaneer fighter-bomber circled the fog-shrouded airfield once, then came in for a bumpy, rather ragged landing.

A small army of rescue vehicles surrounded the airplane as it screeched to a halt on the dark, wet runway. This was just a precaution—many terrible air crashes had taken place at Gander over the years. The rescue vehicles usually rolled out whenever an airplane touched down, especially one that came in as hard as this.

The imperfect touchdown could be excused, however. The man at the controls of the ancient airplane had been flying for nearly 16 hours straight. He could barely keep his eyes open. The man in the rear seat, the airplane's systems operator, was even more exhausted than the pilot. He'd been asleep for almost two hours.

Once the engines were cooled and secured, both men had to be helped from the cockpit. The systems operator came out first. His legs seemed permanently bent in the sitting position. The attending ground personnel wrapped him in a blanket, put him in a chair, and carried him down the access ladder in just that way. He was so cramped up, a severe muscle tear was a real possibility.

The pilot left under his own power, but he, too, was obviously expended. He was Major Ricard Frost, Free Canadian Air Force, and under more normal circumstances, first liaison officer between the Free Canadian government and the United American Armed Forces.

Like so many of the principal people connected to the UAAF, Frost had been given thirty days leave to recover from wounds suffered in the twin actions of the Pacific and Vietnam. Like so many others, though, he'd felt antsy after the first few days and had volunteered to spell some other pilots who needed time off even more.

The recipients of this gesture were the men of the joint FC-UAAF Maritime Patrol Service, a combined-forces air unit which patrolled the uneasy waters between the tip of the North American continent and the western reaches of the Icelandic floe. Using a variety of aircraft, many of them much older than the men who flew them, the MPS provided the thankless job of endlessly monitoring the main shipping lanes between Iceland and Newfoundland, keeping tabs on any suspicious-looking vessels and always being on the lookout for nefarious submarines.

MPS duty was unrelentingly routine—that was what made it so exhausting. While the service had certainly seen its share of harrowing incidents, especially in the first few years following the Big War, the dedicated pilots and technicians had not spotted an unfriendly vessel, either surface-riding or U-boat, in nearly eighteen months. This lack of action didn't mean the MPS was obsolete; just the opposite. The MPS was vital because it was so good and so meticulous. Any potential enemy from abroad would have to think twice before traveling the regular sealanes to get to North America.

Still, the airplanes the service operated were decidedly bottom-of-the-barrel. There were eleven of them based at Gander. Besides the Buccaneer, there were three Mk 3 BA Shackletons, four-engine, piston-driven maritime bombers that bore more than a passing resemblance to the B-24 Liberators of World War II fame and were almost as old. There was a quartet of Dassault-Breguet Alize antisub aircraft, bulbous little airplanes that somehow found room for a crew of three and a bomb-bay big enough to carry two torpedoes. Probably the oddest craft was the Embraer P-95 Bandeirulha, an old Brazilian design that looked more like a sporting plane than a military aircraft. For in-flight refueling of this plucky group, there was also a pair of BA "Victory" K.Mk 2 jet tankers.

Frost had been flying MPS for six days. This had been his first flight in the venerable Buccaneer, and as he had vowed many times in the last 16 hours, it would be his last. Easing himself into the waiting jeep now, he could hear his knee joints crackle and pop as he stretched them straight for the first time in more than a half a day.

"I might be getting too old for this," he thought, even though he was just a few weeks shy of his thirty-sixth birthday. "Either too old or too smart . . ."

Sensing his condition, the Jeep driver drove slowly, carefully, across the rough tarmac, depositing Frost without so much as a bump at the front door of his officers' billet. The driver promised to fetch Frost a hot meal from the chow hall and maybe a few cans of Mooselake ale, too. This cheered the pilot enough to will himself out of the Jeep and up the steps of his quarters. The Jeep driver gingerly turned his vehicle around and then roared off into the night and fog.

It was now close to 2 A.M. and in the background Frost could hear the heart-stopping growl of two Shackletons starting up their paleolithic engines. Behind them were a pair of Alizes, and behind them, adding its own primitive engines to the roar, one of the "Victory" refueling ships.

This meant just about all of the MPS pilots were either in the air or climbing up into it. When Frost came through the front door of the officers' billet, he was the only living soul around.

That was okay with him. The last thing he wanted to do now was to see anybody, talk to anybody, or have to interact in any way. All he wanted was a shower, a shave, his meal, a few ales, and then bed.

This plan began unfolding like clockwork. He reached his quarters, stripped, and showered in luxurious privacy. He had a quick towel-off, a quicker shave, and then there came a rapping on his door. It was the Jeep driver, carrying a tray holding an enormous bowl of stew, a basket of rolls, a tin of common crackers, and a small container of hot sauce. It was Frost's favorite meal! He gratefully accepted the tray only to find the man was also holding the promised six-pack of Mooselake ale. Exhausted and famished, Frost felt tears come to his eyes. He thanked the driver profusely, promised him a citation of some kind, then shooed him out. Returning to his billet, Frost opened the first beer, rustled up an old copy of *Air Progress*, and dived face first into the basin of stew.

It was hard to say what went down quicker, the heavily seasoned goulash or the first Mooselake ale. Either way, they were both gone inside of five minutes. Frost licked the bowl several times over, then poured the first few drops from beer number two into the vessel and drank the runoff. Once the rolls and crackers were gone, he got up from the table, staggered a bit, and collapsed onto his bed. It was almost 2:30.

Outside the wind was beginning to howl; a huge

storm was churning in the Atlantic. Frost and his back-seater had seen the massive clouds forming on the southern horizon all during their long flight. The weather service was predicting this storm would hit New England within hours and linger there indefinitely. Some forecasters were already speculating that it might be one of the largest storms to hit the East Coast in history; it was so big it was already affecting them way up here in Gander.

Yet now, looking up through the overhead window in his room, Frost could see a patch of sky, one which the howling winds had cleared of all fog, at least temporarily. Through it, Frost could see a bright patch of stars. They looked absolutely stunning at the moment, so much so that he raised himself up a bit just to get a better look. His view was somewhat limited, but he could still partially make out the Big Dipper and Orion.

Suddenly he spotted a small blinking light swiftly making its way across the sky. He knew immediately it was not an airplane; this object was traveling through space.

Could it be? he thought. Was there really any chance that the light was the Zon spacecraft, containing Hunter and his UAAF colleagues?

No, not really. As the flashing light passed from view, Frost was sure it was more likely to be a satellite or a piece of space junk than the captured space shuttle, especially at this latitude. Still, as Frost lay back on his bed, his thoughts went to his American allies and their continuous struggle to bring freedom and order to their very troubled land. Frost was a close personal friend of Hunter himself, having first met the Wingman several years ago at a place called the Pitt, once known as Pittsburgh. Frost had transported a cache of jewels for Hunter, who was working as a pilot-for-hire at the time. They'd been amigos ever since.

Frost ripped the cap off his third beer and drained it greedily. It felt like the high-alcohol-content lager was flowing directly into his tired veins, bypassing his stomach and liver entirely. Many things had happened since he'd linked up with the United Americans. The continent had been freed, invaded, and freed again. Major battles had been won in the Pacific and in Southeast Asia. Now Hunter and company were hunting for Viktor II in orbit. It seemed to be an appropriate culmination of all the hard-fought and hard-won victories. Where else should the climactic chase be, but in outer space? A pang of sadness went through Frost's tired chest. If only he was up there with them . . .

His fourth beer brought more memories. Sure, the key wars had been won, but many men had died as a result. Brave souls and close friends. Bull Dozer, the one-of-a-kind commander of the original 7th Cavalry, United America's first credible ground force. Dozer had been killed in a titanic last battle against the Russians in Washington, DC. Then there was Seth Jones, twin brother of Dave Jones, the C-in-C of the UAAF. Frost had never met the man, but from what he'd heard, he seemed to be nothing less than deserving of his reputation as the patron saint of the entire Free America movement.

There was Mike Fitzgerald, the godfather of the UAAF. Fitz had been a close friend of everyone in the UA inner circle, the kind of guy who'd made a million dollars no less than six months after the Big War had ended, only to give most of it away and join the UA freedom fighters. A ballsy pilot and an expert strategist, Fitzgerald had been killed preventing an enemy nuclear missile from obliterating Football City in the last stages of the war against the Fourth Reich.

Of all the men who'd passed on, Fitz was the one Frost, as well as everyone else, missed the most. Popping his fifth beer, Frost wondered what it would be like if Fitz were still alive; what he would think now that the American continent was finally free of all outside invaders. What he would think of Hunter's high-speed chase in outer space . . .

Sometime during draining his sixth and last beer, Frost finally fell asleep. Dreams flowed through his head like clouds whipped up by a storm. First, he was back at the controls of the antique Buccaneer, then he was swimming in the Caribbean, then he was a child again, playing hockey outside his family's home in Parry Sound, then he was back in the old Buck again.

It went on like this for sometime: Frost drifting in and out of montages of nonsensical dreams. Yet despite his depleted state and his belly full of beer, his instincts remained sharp, and somewhere in the midst of all his dreaming, he sensed that he was not alone in the room. The feeling grew stronger even as he dreamed he was up on a high, snow-capped mountain, looking down on a burning city below.

Finally, somehow, in some way, he was able to open his eyes. Vaguely, through the sleep and the faint light of his room, he saw that, indeed, he was *not* alone. There was a figure sitting in the chair directly across from his bed. It was a man. His legs and arms were crossed in a very familiar way. He was staring very intently at Frost, his features wrinkled in worry on his pudgy, Irish-red face.

Frost raised himself slowly and only then did he realize he could see right through the man.

"Hello there, Frostie," he heard the words echo in his room, the last one tinged with a definite brogue. "It's been a long time . . ."

Frost's eyes were now wide open. His jaw had dropped and he was trembling. He recognized the man and the voice immediately.

"Jeezus, Fitz!" he cried out. "Is it really you?"

The ghost of Mike Fitzgerald laughed once, then his face returned to its former frown.

"Yes, it's me, Frostie," he said sadly. "In the pink, if not the flesh . . ."

Eight

It was a gentle beeping that shook Jim Cook out of his zero-gravity slumber.

The commanding officer of the elite JAWS special operations team was floating in place down on the crew compartment level of the Zon, his shoulders and knees straining slightly against a pair of sleep tethers. Two bubbles of saliva were hovering approximately three inches from his nose. People tended to drool in space, especially when they were in a deep sleep. This particular pair of sputum had been floating in front of Cook for the past hour or so.

The beeping woke him not because of its soft volume, but because it was a sound he hadn't heard on the Zon before. It was a pulsing tone, a repetition of the slightly tense notes of A and G. It was not a warning buzzer per se. It was the spacecraft's earth-to-space radio, and this was the first time it had come alive since the Zon had reached orbit.

This mission into space was the most secret operation ever undertaken by the United Americans. "Top Secret" didn't come close to describing the security surrounding the Zon's launch and the ensuing space-chase. Any radio communication between the spacecraft and earth controllers ran the risk of exposing the whole operation. It had been agreed upon from the beginning that contact between earth and the Zon would be nonexistent. The spacecraft would be on its own, running silent as it pursued the supercriminal Viktor II. This blackout decree would be breached only in case of an extreme emergency on either side, and then they would speak only in code.

This is why hearing the sound of the radio come alive woke Cook so quickly.

He shook the sleep from his eyes, unlashed his tethers, and pushed himself across the compartment to the radio set. A gentle engagement of the receive button was rewarded with a violent burst of static.

"Behold a mystery," Cook heard a strangely echoing voice intone. "We shall not all sleep, but we shall all be changed. In a twinkling of an eye, a trumpet shall sound. And the dead shall be raised. And we shall be changed."

Still groggy, Cook thought at first he'd somehow broken into a stray radio or TV transmission from earth. Was this nonsense really originating from Mission Control at the Cape?

He quickly consulted a card listing all the emergency security phrases that was floating next to the radio set. None of them matched what he had just heard.

The radio began beeping again. He pushed the receive button and again was assaulted by a burst of static.

"We who are alive shall not prevent them who are asleep," the same voice began again. "The Lord Himself shall descend from heaven with a shout. And with the voice of an archangel, the dead shall rise first . . ."

Cook was now more confused than ever. If this was someone on the ground trying to tell him something in code, they were not reading from the same page. There was nothing on the security phrase list that even came close to what he was hearing.

"We who are alive will then be caught up together," the creepy voice came back on. "The dead shall rise and they will mock you. And then it will be your time to die."

With that, the transmission ended.

Cook tried for the next five minutes to regain the frequency of the strange broadcast, but to no avail. Whoever had sent the weird message was no longer on.

Confused and still punchy, Cook now faced another quandary. How should he report the odd incident? Normally, he would not have hesitated a bit. He would have floated up to the flight deck to tell those up there what had happened. But the way things were aboard the Zon lately, he knew they had enough problems to handle already.

Still, he pushed his way to the roof of the crew quarters and then over to the hatch, which led up to the flight compartment. Then he took a deep breath, undid the hatch lock, and drifted up.

The flight deck was dark and somber. The only light was coming from the green and red VDT screens; it cast an almost cartoonish glow on everybody and everything.

But what was happening up here was anything but humorous.

Hunter was sitting in the flight commander seat. His right hand was gripping the control stick so tightly, and had been doing so for so long, Cook believed he could see where it had actually bent a little.

Hunter was staring intently out the front windshield and into space beyond. His eyes were darting back and forth, up and down, this way and that. Like a human radar, he was sweeping the space in front of the speeding spacecraft, looking, searching . . .

JT was in the seat beside him. He, too, was gripping his control stick tightly, his eyes looking everywhere at once, though not as quickly as Hunter's. Ben was in the seat directly behind JT, Elvis was behind Hunter, Geraci was behind Elvis. They were studying space directly above the spacecraft, which, because the Zon was inverted at the moment, was actually straight down, toward the cool blue globe of Earth.

Cook quietly floated into the flight compartment and took his place behind Ben. Ever since spotting the first piece of exploding space junk, the crew of the Zon had been forced to maintain this tense, mind-numbing vigil. One wrong move, one missed unidentifiable object, and they could all go up in ball of flame. It was the equivalent of a ship trying to wind its way through a minefield—at 17,500 miles an hour.

They'd come across six of the space mines since the first one—each exploding once it had placed itself in an orbital path about five miles in front of the Zon. Only by quick action on Hunter's part had they been able to avoid the results of an explosion which created thousands of pieces of deadly space flak.

But the key to this defense was spotting the space mine before it could get into position and explode. And the only way to do this was to keep watching for the tumbling objects and get the Zon out of the way as quickly as possible. It had proved to be a stressful endeavor.

That these orbital bombs were being sent against them intentionally was no longer in dispute. It was obvious that someone somewhere was controlling the space mines simply because of the way they moved prior to detonation.

Because everything flying around in each orbital path was traveling at relatively the same speed, the space mines had to slow down in order to get into position to harm the Zon. There were a couple of different ways to do this: firing retrojets by remote control was one, sending a control message to the mine to start tumbling was another. Either way, the object's velocity would decay and slow it down. Either way, this had to be done on purpose, by a guiding human hand. There was no doubt in anyone's mind on board the Zon just whose hand was controlling these potentially disastrous weapons.

But they also knew that by sending these devices against the Zon, the same controlling hand was providing them with clues to its location.

Each time a space mine had been detected and avoided, Hunter and the others took note of its location, its estimated speed, and from which part of the sky it had come. The plots that resulted from this stressful tracking had pointed to one indisputable conclusion: whoever was dropping the space mines in the Zon's path was just up ahead, maybe as close as 230 miles, and traveling in an orbital path just slightly higher than that of the Zon.

If they could continue to pick their way through the minefield, they could follow the orbital bombs right to their source . . . if they could stay up that long. As it was, the Zon had only about six days of supplies and power left.

Cook finally got his straps around him and settled down into the extra seat in the rear. He would have to pick his spot carefully. He figured Ben Wa would be the guy to tell about the strange radio transmission. Ben was very wise in a quiet kind of way. He would know whether to bother Hunter with what might be an unimportant piece of . . .

"Jeezus, Hawk!" JT suddenly cried out.

"I see it!"

"Latitude is . . ."

"No, trajectory is . . ."

"There it goes!"

"Christ—hang on!"

The next thing Cook knew, he was upside down. Hunter and JT were pulling mightily on the control sticks at the same time Hunter was pushing the flight computer control panel with fingers moving at lightning speed, giving orders to the Zon's steering jets to fire in an exact sequence to get the spacecraft away. In the next instant, a tremendous light filled the flight compartment—to Cook's unadjusted eyes it seemed like the sun had exploded right inside their little cabin. He was blinded by it; it was so intense his eyeballs began to ache. Purely by reflex he raised his hands to his eyes to shield them from this awful illumination.

When Cook opened his eyes again, he was staring straight up, meaning the Zon's rear end was suddenly pointing back toward earth and it nose was pointing in the general direction of Alpha Centauri. Elvis went flying by him at this point, jolted in a kind of slow motion right out of his safety harness by the sudden violent maneuver.

Cook was forced to shift to his left to avoid a collision with Elvis's boot. Then he found himself looking straight down again—this time it appeared like the Zon itself was plummeting right back to earth. Before his brain had time to react to this heart-stopping prospect, the Zon was jerked around once more. After a few more seconds, it returned to what had been its previous position.

Now everyone else on the deck was crowded over Hunter's shoulder and looking out the window to his left. Cook floated up to join them and finally saw what they were looking at: the debris cloud, the powder puff of flak resulting from the mine's detonation, was passing just below them.

"Hang on," Hunter said. "Shock wave . . . right now!"

No sooner had the words left his mouth than the Zon was shaking violently once more. Everything began rattling, again in the slow, dull kind of way. The ship itself seemed to shudder right down to the heat tiles. How much of this could it take? But suddenly, in the next moment, all was calm. The control panels stopped flashing, the floor beneath Cook's feet stopped vibrating.

All was safe once more. They'd dodged another space mine.

"Tracking, JT!" Hunter immediately called out.

A second later, JT was pushing buttons on his navigation computer, reverse calculating, in numbers and oddly stick-like graphs, exactly where the space mine had come from. As JT was doing this, he was calling out long lists of numbers, which somehow seemed to make sense to Hunter, who, it appeared, was doing calculations in his head faster than JT was doing them on the navigation computer.

It was like a *ding!* went off in the cabin. Hunter had reached the solution seconds before the new computer had.

"Same place. Same velocity," he said bitterly. "They're about 210 miles ahead of us. Maybe closer. Maybe 7500 feet above. Just up a notch."

"They're throwing these things back at us blindly," Elvis said, finally settling in his seat again. "They're probably figuring that the more they launch, the better the chances they'll hit us . . ."

". . . Before we reach them first," JT finished the sentence for him.

"Well, don't worry," Hunter said quietly. "That won't be long now."

With that, he increased the Zon's throttles slightly. The spacecraft nudged itself forward in response.

Cook sat back, all thoughts of the strange radio transmission forgotten for now.

The idea, he knew, was to sneak up on them slowly. And that's what they were doing, bit by bit.

Nine

The huge United American seaplane was just beginning the fourth hour of its night patrol when it happened.

The flight, charged with keeping an eye on the straits separating the southern trip of UA Florida from lawless Cuba, had been progressing in a routine fashion so far. The crew members had already covered more than 900 miles, buzzing several suspicious vessels, but in all, they'd found nothing of any major concern.

It was a usual mission for an airplane that was actually quite unusual. The patrol craft was a one-of-a-kind XP6M-2 Seamaster, a gigantic jet-powered seaplane built back in the fifties and refurbished by the United Americans shortly after the so-called Circle War. The Seamaster had four huge engines mounted atop its slender boatlike fuselage at the point where its long, droopy wings met just aft of the cockpit. The Seamaster was not only the fastest seaplane ever built—it could reach .75 Mach easily—it also had a long-range capability, especially with the extra internal fuel tanks the UA engineers had installed inside its cargo bay.

It was heavily armed. Two radar-controlled miniguns dominated the nose of the seaplane, another pair guarded the rear. Slung under the long, slender wings were four hardpoints, two on each side, all capable of carrying a variety of weapons. This flight, the Seamaster was hauling two Harpoon antiship weapons and two AIM-9L Sidewinder air-to-air missiles, just in case.

Its speed, endurance, and sting made the Seamaster a formidable enemy to those brash enough—or stupid enough—to attempt an illegal entry across the Florida Straits. Every gun runner, drug smuggler, white slave trader, and moonshiner in the Caribbean knew about the so-called *Aero Carumba*. Since the Seamaster arrived on the scene about a year before, unlawful crossings, once a torrent, had slowed to a trickle.

On rare occasions, the big seaplane would detect an aerial target trying to dash across the 90-mile strait. In cases such as these, the big plane would give chase and begin tracking the interloper, AWACS-style, until fighter aircraft could be scrambled from the big UA naval air station on Key West. Only once in the past 12 months had the seajet been forced to use its own air-to-air weaponry. It had shot down a known drug-smuggling plane whose pilot had refused to heed all prior warnings. Never before had the Seamaster's radar detected more than three airplanes flying around the strait at one time. Usually it saw nothing at all.

This night though would be different.

It happened exactly at midnight. The Seamaster had been in the air three hours after sea-launching from Key West shortly after sundown. It had already completed three transits of its patrol pattern when suddenly its on-board long-range air defense radar went wild.

First one, then two, then four, then *ten* blips popped up on the screen, almost simultaneously. Even worse, the radar was telling the Seamaster crew that these unknowns were carrying aerial weapons which were just one step away from being fired at somebody or something.

The Seamaster flight commander immediately had the radio officer send a scrambled message back to Key West, telling them what they'd detected. The 10 airplanes were approximately 35 miles south of the Seamaster's position, which was about 65 miles southeast of Key West itself. They were flying in a staggered-V formation, cruising at 270 knots and heading due north. With their weapons systems lit, they appeared to be heading for a combat-imminent situation.

The urgent message was received at Key West, and four UA combat fighters—old and creaking F-106 Delta Darts—were dispatched in short order. Five additional aircraft, A-7K Strikefighters in the air already, were vectored toward the Seamaster's position, as were two A-6P armed electronic warfare aircraft, who happened to be returning from a training sortie out over the Lower Bahamas. These 11 airplanes, plus the Seamaster itself, would present a counterforce to the ten bogies, whoever they were and whatever their intentions.

Then ten more mystery airplanes showed up.

Like the first group, they simply popped up on the Seamaster's radar screen as if they'd materialized out of thin air. They were hard on the heels of the first group and they, too, appeared to be carrying weapons ready to be fired.

Just as the crew of the Seamaster was absorbing this new information, *another* ten aircraft suddenly appeared, right behind the second group. The UA airplanes streaking toward the location now were facing 3-to-1 odds. And still they had no idea what the intention of the mystery airplanes might be.

The Seamaster got the first visual sighting on the lead wedge of intruders. Because of the location of its engines and several other factors, such as radar-absorbing paint, the Seamaster had a certain amount of stealth capability. It encountered the lead chevron of

trespassers at a position about sixty-two miles due south
of Key West, picking them up on its long-range LAN-
TIRN scope, while staying undetected for the moment.

What the radar officer saw in this NightVision-type
device were ten white jet fighters, wings bulging with
missiles and bombs, flying a course that would bring
them right to Key West, now just a few minutes' flying
time away. But what was even more startling was the
type of airplane these were: not the B-list jets that the
majority of air units in the UAAF flew. These were F/A-18
Hornets, top-of-the-line naval fighter attack craft, the likes
of which had not been seen in the postwar world ever
since . . . well, ever since the Fourth Reich had invaded
North America nearly three years before.

When the Seamaster's radar officer zoomed in on
the lead airplane, the first thing he saw were the blood-
red swastikas emblazoned on the Hornets' wings and
fuselage.

"Son of a bitch," the radar officer breathed into his
microphone. "The goddamn Nazis are back . . ."

It was just pure good luck that another UA fighter
diverted toward the oncoming strike force was being
flown by Captain John O'Malley, former president and
CEO of the Ace Wrecking Company, sometime business
partner of space traveler Elvis Q, and now in possession
of the hottest warplane this side of Hawk Hunter's own
F-16XL.

Having lost his much beloved F-4X Super Phantom
during the battle for Lolita Island, Crunch had acquired a new, even ballsier airplane. It was an F-101X
Super Voodoo, a reconditioned, kick-ass Century
fighter with a massive GE 404 engine under the hood
and every new air-combat gadget known to man
crammed into its cockpit.

Crunch had spent his R & R time following the action in the South China Sea fixing up the elderly airplane, which he'd purchased for a song from the infamous used-airplane salesman Roy from Troy. Crunch and his new airplane just happened to be on a layover at Key West on their way to Cape Canaveral, which was the main provisional headquarters of the United American Armed Forces these days. When the call came in about the strike force of 30 jets heading toward UA territory, Crunch was in the air not five minutes after the F-106 Delta Darts had been scrambled. Crunch's new airplane had not been tested in combat yet. He figured this was as good a time as any.

There was no dispute that the Super Voodoo was the quickest thing in the air at the moment—it was much faster than the F-106s Darts or the Strikefighters. So when Crunch heard a Mayday call from the big Seamaster, he opened up the afterburner in his enormous power plant, threw it into fifth gear, and rocketed away to the south. He had the big seaplane on his radar screen less than ninety seconds later.

He hadn't arrived a moment too soon. The oncoming Nazi Hornets had spotted the big seajet by now, and four of them had peeled off to engage it with their nose cannons, two from the front, two from the back. It was only through the Seamaster's incredible speed and surprising maneuverability, that the big amphibian hadn't been shot down already. Still, the quartet of agile Hornets were obviously closing in for the kill, while the rest of the Nazi strike force continued north toward Key West.

Crunch came upon this one-sided engagement and immediately took steps to even the odds. He was lugging four Sidewinders under his wings, plus a dual M-61-A1 rotary cannon pod attached to the belly. The two Hornets attacking the Seamaster's rear had just peeled off, scoring a few hits on the seaplane's high-tail. Crunch voice-commanded his weapons systems to lock onto the trailing Hornet—and nothing else. At such close quarters, he couldn't risk his own missile being sucked up by the Seamaster's huge wing-mounted engines.

The Super Voodoo's target acquisition computer locked onto the unsuspecting Hornet a few seconds later. Crunch was still ten miles away from the battle and about a half mile above it. Like any pilot in the heat of aerial combat, the Hornet driver was not watching his own six o'clock. He was too busy ganging up on the big seaplane.

It would be a fatal mistake.

Crunch's first Sidewinder went off the rail three seconds later. It stayed true to the course the weapons' radar had proposed for it, quickly locking on to the F/A-18's hot exhaust. The missile slammed into the Nazi's left-side pipe, slicing the extended tail off the attack plane and putting it into an instantaneous spiral. The left wing broke off a second later, Crunch could see it clearly in the bright flash resulting from the plane's fuel tank going up. The Hornet went ass over and began the long plunge down to the sea. It hit with another large explosion and quickly sank beneath the waves. There was no parachute. In all, the Super Voodoo's opening attack had taken less than 15 seconds.

One A-hole down, Crunch thought. Three to go . . .

He'd dipped down to 7,500 altitude by this time and was now just a few hundred feet above and six miles behind the air action. The big Seamaster was still in desperate straits; the three Hornets, afraid to use their own Sidewinders in such close quarters, were now screaming in for murderous cross-fuselage cannon runs. The seaplane had no defense for attacks on its flanks. Its pilots could do only one thing in this case:

they booted their throttles and headed down to the wet deck.

Crunch followed them down, closing to within two miles of the big seaplane. The Hornets went down, too, sending streams of ugly tracer fire into the amphib's midsection. Crunch could hear the Seamaster's radio man desperately calling out their ever-changing position—if they were going down, they wanted rescue forces to know where to look.

But Crunch didn't want the Seamaster to go into the drink. It was much too nice a plane for that—and besides, the chances were good that he knew some of the guys on board. He kicked in his afterburner once again and felt the jolt as gallons of raw fuel were dumped directly into his engine's exhaust flue. Inside of ten seconds, he was right on the trailing Hornet's tail.

It took a squeeze, a jink, and another squeeze of his cannon trigger to shred this pussy's tail. True to form, the Nazi pilot ejected even before his ass got hot. The F/A-18 did a slow twist and then went nose down, exploding about two hundred feet above the water.

The remaining Hornets now knew that Crunch was there, and more out of anger than anything, they peeled off the Seamaster's tail and turned their sights on him—a foolish thing to do. Not only did it give the Seamaster extra time to get down near the deck, it put the Hornet pilots in the position of trying to find a smaller target in what had suddenly become a very large and empty sky.

Crunch yanked up on his stick, booted his throttle again, and put the F-101 on its tail. The Super Voodoo had outstanding climb characteristics, especially straight up, which it could do at Mach 1.2 without breathing hard. The Hornets, on the other hand, weren't such great tree-climbers. Because the F/A-18 was half-fighter, half-attack craft, things such as climb rate, turn rate, acceleration, and speedy AOA had been compromised to some degree. The Nazi birds had to huff and puff it to catch up to Crunch—which was exactly what he wanted them to do.

All this was taking place in the dead of night, and against a moonless sky. The Hornet had some night-fighting capability, but it was more on the rudimentary scale, maybe enough to keep its pilots out of trouble, but not much more. Crunch, on the other hand, had a ton of nocturnal combat crap stuffed into his super-plane. Two AWG-9 radars slaved to a main on-board computer. A LANTIRN see-in-the-dark pod. Plus a NightVision capability built into his HUD. Crunch was like a cat in the dark. The pair of F/A-18s—well, they were like a couple of puppies.

It was a classic rule of dogfighting that you never, ever, put yourself in a position that makes it easy for your opponent to get on your tail. Yet this was exactly what the pair of Hornets did. When they broke through a cloud layer at 27,000 feet and found Crunch was not there, they leveled off and began searching for him with their acquisition radars. Crunch in the meantime had broken through the clouds not fifteen seconds ear-lier and had performed a classic loop, turning the Su-per Voodoo on its nose, pitching back down through the clouds just as the Nazis were coming up and poking through again once they'd leveled off. That's when he switched on all his night-fight gear, getting images of both 'Nets just as if it was daytime. Before the Huns knew it, he was delivering an AIM-9 right up the tail-pipe of the trailing F/A-18 and into its reserve fuel tank. The explosion was so huge, it lit up the sky for miles.

This left just Crunch and the lone Ratzi, and not to Crunch's surprise, the Hornet decided to run. It was also a classic rule of dogfighting that if an opponent decided to beat it, it was probably wise to let him go. But Crunch was never one for this page of the book. He hated Nazis, hated everything about them. And even though the chances were good that these guys were actually mercenaries simply flying for some Nazi cell, just the fact that they would climb into a plane lugging a swastika was enough for Crunch to want to kill them.

So he took off after the Hornet. Booting up his huge engine and keeping his eye on the prize despite the darkness, he was on this guy in less than a minute. But it appeared that the Hornet was trying to flee south toward Cuba, and not to some aircraft carrier from which Crunch had just assumed it had come.

Now *this* came as a surprise to Crunch—one that was big enough to make him change his tactics.

Maybe it would be wiser just to follow this guy for a little while, he thought.

To see exactly which hole he was heading back to crawl into.

The wounded Seamaster had made it down to the watery deck.

It was flying so low at the moment, the crew was amazed that they were still airborne.

This was just the thing to do though. Stay down, stay hidden, and try to put as much distance between yourself and the people who were trying like crazy to shoot you down.

The damage sustained in the Hornet attacks had been extensive, however. One crewman, a gunner's mate, had been killed, and three others had been wounded, including the co-pilot. The plane was now running on three engines, and the way number four outboard was smoking, the pilot knew he'd have to shut it down soon, too. The guidance systems and the long-range radar had been destroyed. There was a large hole in the starboard wing, and gas was flowing out of it like a body wound. The primary electrical systems were kaput, and the backups were functioning at only fifty percent. Their weapons systems were all okay, though, if low on ammo, and their radios, both primary and backups, were still functioning.

Still, the Seamaster was in a tight fix. It was heading southeast and really didn't have the strength or fuel to get back up to a reasonable altitude, turn around, and dash home to Key West. The only option left was to get to another friendly base before the Nazis spotted it again. And in this area, there was only one place like that: a UA radar station set up on a small island about halfway between Florida and Cuba called Double Shot Rocks.

Navigating by starlight, the pilot figured they were about thirty-five miles west of Double Shot. Though they were now flying on only two engines, he was fairly confident they could make it—*if* they could find the island. One doodad that could help them do this was the LANTIRN set, a kind of electronic see-in-the-dark device more at home on night fighters. The pilot had switched it on earlier simply because the plane was flying so low. He was legitimately concerned they might run into a ship mast or even a particularly high outcropping of rocks.

When the device finally warmed up to maximum power and the first long-range images became clear, the pilot and crew knew that running into some rocks was suddenly the least of their problems.

The Seamaster crew saw a line of warships that stretched literally from one end of the horizon to the other. It didn't take an expert to know exactly what kind of vessels there were. Long, with low bows; massive superstructures with enormous guns both fore and aft.

"*Battleships* . . ." the pilot breathed.

"There's got to be at least a dozen of them," the radar officer gasped.

The crew of the Seamaster knew that these days battleships could mean only one thing: the Asian Mercenary Cult. It was the only force in the world at present that could float such an armada. But previously the Cult had operated only in the Pacific Rim area. Never had they been spotted this close to the East Coast of America.

But here they were, not five miles ahead of the struggling seaplane, and obviously heading north, toward UA Florida.

The pilot breathed the fears of everyone on board.

"Nazi warplanes, Cult battleships," he said, almost in a whisper. "What the hell is going on here?"

The moment of astonishment quickly passed. Now the Seamaster crew knew they had to swing into action. It was obvious that their coming upon the huge flotilla was an enormous fluke—from all indications the battleships were running without any air defense radar illuminated, a necessary tactic if surprise was their ultimate goal. The crew of the big seaplane could see them, but as of yet, they had not been seen.

This was an opportunity the Seamaster could not pass up. Battered though it was, it had obviously stumbled upon a golden opportunity.

The pilot didn't even have to order his crew to combat stations; they were already scrambling to them. The forward gunnery officer was quickly line-sighting a battleship that was riding slightly off flank from the rest of the fleet. The offensive weapons officer had already acquired this same vessel's bridge and communications deck on his Harpoon missile system's passive radar.

Even the defensive systems officer was searching for something hot at which to send his pair of Sidewinder missiles.

By the time the Seamaster was within two miles of the unsuspecting battleship, all of these weapons were ready to fire.

The pilot had shut down the seaplane's outboard four engine long ago, but now he needed some kick and the wounded engine would have to come back on-line. He had the banged-up co-pilot douse the power plant with the built-in fire extinguishers and then they lit it again. It exploded to life with a flare that would have been seen for miles had they not been flying so low. The engine coughed twice, then began providing thrust, though only about half its normal output.

That was okay, though. They only needed the bum engine for a few seconds.

They were now about a mile out. The pilot did one last check of his systems, and everything that was working was performing within tolerable limits. A quick check of the radar told him that the battleship now looming large in the cockpit windshield had no idea what was about to happen. The seajet crew collectively held its breath as the pilot slowed the plane's speed down to an 80-mph crawl, just barely enough to keep them airborne.

On the count of three, he whispered three words into the plane's on-board intercom: *"Fire at will . . ."*

There would be some discussion later as to exactly which weapons got off first. The pair of Harpoons were certainly the first to actually ignite their engines, but the two Sidewinders were probably off their rails before the antiship missiles launched. The quartet of missiles hit the battleship *Somumi* at approximately the same instant. The heat-seeking air-to-airs impacted on the red-hot stack just aft of the superstructure, caving it in and destroying four of the six boilers below. The first Harpoon nailed the double-bridge dead-on, killing everyone on both decks. The second anti-shipper went through mid-mast and down two levels before exploding not 15 feet from the auxiliary magazine. This started a fire that would take exactly 30 seconds to reach the main bomb storage area.

The Seamaster's forward mini-guns were opened up at 1000 feet out; by this time they were firing into a growing maelstrom of smoke, flame, and exploding shells. The big seaplane went up and over the *Somumi* just as the fire finally touched off the magazine. The concussion from this explosion lifted the Seamaster 200 feet in the air, searing its tail to the point of melting one of the rear turret mini-guns. The pilot recovered only to find himself heading straight for the *Somumi*'s sister ship, the delicately named *Mimosa*. The forward gunnery officer never stopped firing. The rounds from his pair of mini-guns tore up this ship's bridge and communications mast before the pilot was able to lift the big plane up once again and clear the enemy ship by a matter of inches.

At this point, they saw the crackle of AAA fire start to rise up from nearby ships. But this was automatic, triggered by the attack on the *Somumi,* and as such, poorly aimed and completely ineffective. The Seamaster settled down to 50 feet in altitude once more, its forward guns peppering the battleship *Basami* before elevating a third time and then finally passing over the fleet altogether.

A few token AAA shells followed it as it disappeared into the night, but these fell way short of hitting the big seaplane, its two and a half working engines giving it just enough power to escape unscathed.

In its wake, it left one battleship sinking, another taking on water and its crew jumping over the sides,

and a third with a growing fire on its bridge and second
turret. In all, the seaplane's attack had lasted twenty
seconds.

Turning due west, it would reach safe harbor at Double Shot Rocks less than 30 minutes later.

The air raid sirens began wailing across Key West
Naval Air Station at exactly 0015 hours.

The base was well drilled in these things. They were
on the frontier of UA territory and had practiced extensively against any number of attack scenarios. Whenever the practice sirens went off, base personnel
scrambled to their assigned defensive positions while
dependents headed for the bomb shelters. The entire
base would be blacked out, all electronics would be
shut down, and a series of radio-jammers would be
turned on. The nearby civilian settlement of Old Town
would go dark and button up, too, with most of the
citizens heading for their cellars or the community
bomb shelter. The civilians and the base personnel had
practiced these procedures so many times, they could
do them in their sleep.

But this time it was not a drill. The base radar had
picked up the large concentration of attack planes approaching from the southeast. Air raid sirens were now
wailing across the entire key. Even as the UA jets scrambled earlier were engaging this oncoming strike force,
some of the attackers were breaking away and pressing
on toward the air base itself.

NAS Key West had a typical "three-in" defensive system. The base's scramble jets represented the outer
ring. The middle ring was a line of SAM sites—Hawk
II batteries, mostly—in place around the runways, as
well as on the outskirts of Old Town. The third ring,

the inner ring, comprised anti-aircraft batteries, both in static emplacements and mobile guns.

It was these mobile AA guns that represented the joker in the deck. They were made up of twenty-four separate units, three-quarters of which were M163 Vulcans, fast APCs armed with six-barrel multifiring guns. The rest consisted of odds and ends, including several German-built Krauss-Maffei "Wildcats" and even a few Russian-designed ZSU-23-4 "Carmens."

Many of these mobile units were now dashing through the streets of Old Town, hiding in the back-yards and alleyways of the resort area, keeping low and staying quiet. Waiting for the storm . . .

The first wave of Nazi attack aircraft was spotted off to the south at 0025 hours. The Hawk batteries began launching a few moments later. Hawk missiles were known for their reliability and accuracy, and despite the awesome size of the enemy force, the attackers had no electronic warfare or jamming planes with them. Inside of twenty seconds of the initial Hawk firings, three of the attacking planes fell burning into the sea.

The first wave of enemy planes was now about two miles from Key West. Another line of Hawks went up. Two more planes fell. Then the second enemy wave appeared over the horizon. The UA F-106 interceptors and the A-7K Strikefighters were firing into the rear of this line, knocking down two more Hornets. But now the Delta Darts, just about depleted of weapons stores, had to back off for fear of being hit by the Hawk missiles. The A-7s were running low on both fuel and ammo; they were forced to evacuate the area, too.

At 0032 hours, the first wave of attackers roared over South Beach on Key West. They came in two at a time, engines screeching ferociously. The first bombs hit at 0033. They were MK82 500-pounders, deep-penetration weapons that burrowed into the asphalt of the base's main runway, blowing out craters six feet deep and 20 feet across. Eighteen of these blockbuster bombs smashed into the main runway, with one stray shot hitting the base water tower. In less than 60 seconds, the first wave had come and gone.

The second wave of enemy airplanes were now a mile off shore. They were F-14s adapted for ground attack, and therein lay a handicap. Tomcats were superb aerial fighters, but close to the ground, they could be sluggish and had a tendency to stick together a little too closely. Even before they came over the beach, the hidden UA mobile AA batteries opened up on them. Though scattered throughout the old city, the AA guns were all pointing in more or less the same direction. They created a wall of anti-aircraft fire that appeared so suddenly, the first line of Nazi F-14s had no choice but to run right through it. Three attackers went down almost immediately, crashing on to the wide South Beach. Another had its right wing perforated, tried to turn, couldn't, and plowed into the center of Old Town. A fifth overshot the target and crashed into the swamps beyond.

Six F-14s made it through though, and now they bore down on the operations buildings attached to the base. They were carrying one MK84 2000-pound bomb each, massive weapons with four times the destructive power of the runway busters. The first of these bombs came down right on the main aircraft maintenance hangar and obliterated the huge structure. Another skipped across the main parking lot and into the base fixed-ops building, destroying it in an incredible explosion. A third boomer took out the control tower and the radar house next door. A fourth hit the main fuel depot. When that went up, it looked like nothing less than the end of the world. A huge bluish-orange flame rose high into the sky, shaping itself into a monstrous mushroom cloud which spread out and covered the entire key. More than 20,000 gallons of aviation fuel went up in the explosion.

As the second wave of attackers scattered, the third wave arrived. They were a combined wing of Tomcats and Hornets, but beneath their wings were neither 500-pound runway bombs or 2000-pound boomers. These airplanes were carrying more sinister weapons. Strung out so thick on their underwings that the planes were forced to fly incredibly low and incredibly slow were hundreds of pounds of napalm.

Napalm was essentially jellied gasoline in a can. When dropped from an airplane, the canister explodes and a flood of sticky, searing flame is dispersed over an area the size of a football field, immolating everything within. This kind of weapon was so insidious, the pre–Big War armies of the sixties and seventies actually stopped using it. Napalm really wasn't a military weapon at all; it was used strictly as a terrorizing agent. Its objective was to burn everything it touched: buildings, landscapes, human beings. Even in the savage conflicts that had raged in the post–Big War years, napalm use had been kept to a minimum by all parties.

But now, here were a dozen attacking planes loaded down with so much of the stuff, their pilots were practically begging the defensive forces to shoot them down.

Most of these fire-bombers came right in over the settlement of Old Town itself. Canister after canister of the jelly gas began falling on the quaint seaside homes and cottages, obliterating them in waves of blue and green flame. There were no real explosions from these bombs; instead, they produced a horrific *whooshing* sound whenever they hit, followed by the sickening loud crackle of flames consuming everything in their path. In less than a minute, more than a hundred na-

palm canisters had fallen on both Old Town and the
devastated air base. This conflagration rose up into a
single nightmarish flame. It would be later reported
that the glow from this gigantic fire could be seen in
Miami, some 150 miles away.

All the while the mobile guns were firing at the slowly
attacking Tomcats, even as their pilots were doing their
fire-bombing runs. One F-14 was caught by a triple barrage right on its tail, blowing it in two and sending
fiery pieces of wreckage into the air base's chow hall
and chapel. Another 'Cat was caught by a ZSU-23-4
barrage just as its pilot was pulling up from bomb release. The AA shells went right through the cockpit,
killing both the pilot and the rear seat weapons officer.
The F-14 spiraled wildly as the pilot's dead body fell
heavy on the control stick. The plane pitched up, then
down, then up again, before finally turning over and
crashing into the east beach. Two more attackers were
hit even before they reached their bomb release points.
They exploded in mid-air, further lighting up the skies
with tremendous flashes of napalm-induced flames.

Once the fire-bombing aircraft departed, only a trailing wave of follow-up attackers—two Hornets and a single F-14—remained. The pair of Hornets roared in
side-by-side, each carrying a 500-pound bomb. But
whether they mistook their drop point or they got nervous or confused with all the flak and fire flying around
them, both planes overshot the runway and wound up
releasing their payloads over the swamps beyond,
where they exploded harmlessly. A M163 Vulcan gun
caught both these planes right after they dropped,
shredding their tails and immediately igniting them.
Already shaken, the pilots panicked on cue, turned as
one, and being too low to eject, lowered the wheels,
and *landed* on the right side auxiliary runway, touching
down and skidding into the soft earth beyond.

Strangely, the lone trailing F/A-18 practically dupli-
cated the Tomcats' actions, dropping its bombs way out
beyond the landing strip, before getting his ass shot up
and coming in for an ugly but successful touchdown
on the heavily cratered main landing strip.

The air raid continued for about five more minutes
as a handful of the first- and second-wave attackers
came in again, dropping whatever ordnance they had
left and then quickly exiting the area.

By 0055, the last enemy aircraft had dropped its last
bombs on the base's water supply. A trail of AA fire
followed this airplane into the night, and then, finally,
the guns fell silent. The all-clear sounded at 0105. The
survivors began filing out of the shelters a few minutes
later.

What they found was a scene of utter and complete
destruction.

For all intents and purposes, the Key West air base
was gone. Five of its six major structures were in smoky
ruins; its main runway was cratered beyond repair. Fires
were raging out of control just about everywhere on
the base. And while the majority of personnel had escaped injury by staying in the well-fortified bomb shelter, 23 defenders had been killed and 55 wounded in
the attack. The base was so roundly devastated that the
scramble jets were forced to fly to another UA field
further up the coast in order to land.

The settlement of Old Town had also disappeared.
Flames had literally consumed the settlement and now
nothing over five feet tall was left standing. Here the
death toll would be astronomical: 735 civilians killed,
210 more missing. The wounded would number only
26, proving the napalm had done its job all too well.

However, in this catastrophe, there was still a silver
lining. For even though NAS Key West had just been
bombed out of existence and Old Town burned to the

ground, sitting astride the air base's cratered runways were two F-14 Tomcats and an F/A-18 Hornet.

And now in the custody of the base's security personnel were the five pilots who had landed them there.

Ten

It was extremely cloudy when Crunch arrived over the northern edge of Cuba.

He wasn't really surprised that the F/A-18 he'd wounded had led him here. The large concentration of unfriendly fighters that had been converging on Key West had to have come from somewhere. And if there wasn't an aircraft carrier or two about, then Cuba was the most likely spot.

Lawless, corrupt, and filled with terrorists, criminals, drug runners and spies, present-day Cuba wasn't that much different from the pre–Big War version. With its hundreds of miles of rugged coastline, thick jungles, and vast mountainous regions, Cuba was a natural safe haven for some of the world's more nefarious types. More than once in the top-secret meetings of the United American Armed Forces Security Council the subject of invading Cuba had come up. Such an action would have eliminated not only the misery of several million civilians still stuck on the island nation, it also would have secured the UA's southeastern flank.

But such an idea was always voted down simply because an invasion of Cuba would cost too many lives, both in UA troops and civvies on the ground. It would soon be evident to Crunch, though, what the price of that decision might be.

His Super Voodoo had a certain amount of stealth

capability, and its high-speed and high-altitude operating characteristics made it a hard target to detect. He crossed over the edge of Cuba right at Matanzas, about 50 miles east of Havana. The lights from the notorious place were quite evident off to Crunch's left. Green, yellow, and neon blue, they gave the impression that one big festival was in progress just over the horizon.

The F/A-18 pilot, his left wing smoking badly, still wasn't aware that Crunch was trailing him. It was obvious that the Nazi flier was concentrating all his efforts into getting back to where he'd come from and setting down safely. Looking in his rearview mirror for anyone on his tail certainly wasn't foremost in his mind.

The Hornet finally began descending about ten minutes after Crunch made landfall. The pilot was turning slightly to the left and heading for what looked to be a fog-enshrouded valley surrounded by mountains and high ridges on all sides.

Once Crunch saw the Hornet pilot commit to a landing approach in this valley, he yanked back on his stick and was soon traveling straight up again. At last he knew where the Nazi F/A-18 was going—now he wanted to find out why.

Within forty-five seconds, the Super Voodoo was doing a long, looping orbit nearly thirteen miles above this mysterious valley. Crunch had spent the first couple of minutes of this high-flight checking his instruments and making sure that his airplane would be able to stand the nose-bleeding altitude. But everything seemed to be green, so he clicked open his lookdown IF radar set and took a peek.

What he saw chilled him.

The valley housed a huge military base, one that had somehow gone undetected by the routine recon flights the UA flew over Cuba. This base had no less than a dozen runways, several control towers, two dozen large aircraft hangars, and rings upon rings of SAM sites and AA guns protecting it all.

The place was enormous and obviously well equipped. But once he got over the initial shock, the surprise wore off pretty quickly. To find a secret air base in the middle of the Cuban wilderness was only mildly astonishing. As the United Americans had grown in strength and projected power, their various enemies had excelled in building secret bases. It was almost like a game: the UA's enemies concentrating on getting as close as possible to the land of milk and honey, and usually the UA discovering these hidden places and taking them out.

So this place in the Cuban mountains was just another example, though its size was certainly larger than those bases found in the past. Crunch opened up the small but powerful recon camera he kept in the nose of his airplane and snapped off a roll of IR photos. He saw the wounded F/A-18 land on the base's northernmost runway and the small army of crash trucks that had come out to meet it. He also saw at least another dozen or so Hornets out on the flight line along with a dozen or so medium-sized bombers. They looked like Ilyushin IL-28 Beagles, formidable if ancient airplanes, capable of bombing any number of targets in the southeastern part of America.

Crunch did another sweep over the base, he wanted to make sure he was getting an accurate account of the surrounding AA emplacements. After what had happened earlier in the Florida Straits, he was anticipating that the UA would have to hit this place someday soon, and finding out what the ground opposition was going to be was very important.

After about two more minutes of selective picture-taking, Crunch checked his fuel load and decided it was time to start thinking about returning to base. He would do one more go-around, and then scoot. If everything went okay, he could be back in UA airspace inside 15 minutes.

Then something strange happened. Whether it was because of a brisk wind or that the ground temperatures were suddenly changing, the fog was lifting slightly around the hidden base, giving Crunch a much better view than before. For the first time, he realized that there were actually two valleys down there, hidden by the high mountains, one sitting right next to the big air base. Inside this new place, Crunch spotted more military installations.

But they weren't SAM emplacements or aircraft revetments or AA sites. Nor were there runways or hangars or fuel depots. Inside this valley next door were roadways that, from Crunch's tremendous height, looked like dozens of figure-eights carved into the rugged, if flat, terrain. Inside these looping thoroughfares he saw hundreds of cylindrical objects, some long, some short, many apparently still inside packing crates and poorly camouflaged with netting and jungle flora. All of this was contained inside a miles-long extremely high fence.

Even for a veteran like Crunch, it took a few moments for him to realize exactly what he was looking at. The curly-Q roads, the large number of thin tubes, the crude attempts at camouflage—this was a weapons storage area he was looking down on. But it was not a typical one; it was one that seemed sinister by virtue of its rather elementary layout.

"Jeezus," he breathed, "Can it be?"

Crunch desperately put his airplane into yet another orbit, now concentrating on the second hidden valley. Looking down through the dissipating mists and the moonless night, he switched on a device that had come already installed inside the Super Voodoo. It was an

ACQ-167YV radiation threat detector, literally an aerial Geiger counter.

No sooner had he powered up this doodad when he heard a high-pitched series of staccato electrical bursts. The volume grew and grew until Crunch had to reach over and turn the amplication down and then finally off completely. Still his ears rang from the frightening sound for several seconds; it was echoing back and forth, up and down, as if it were bouncing around inside his skull and couldn't get out.

Then he felt as if a giant hand had taken him by the chest and was beginning to squeeze him tightly. The ACQ-167YV had confirmed his worst fears. The weapons storage yard below was generating tremendously high amounts of low-yield radiation.

In other words, it was filled with nuclear weapons.

Crunch's fuel bingo light popped on a second later, but he hardly noticed it. His heart was beating faster than he could ever remember. He was taking gulps of oxygen so deep, his eyes began to ache.

He suddenly felt as if he'd been transported back in time to the cockpit of a spy plane overflying Cuba more than forty years before—and finding just about the same thing below. The 1962 Cuban Missile Crisis had transformed the world, had brought it to the brink, and had run up the collective anxieties of just about everyone on the planet. Many wars had been fought since then, and more than once the earth had felt the nuclear glow.

But because they were so expensive and so hard to maintain, nukes were very rare these days—or at least, everyone thought they were. The UAAF had a stockpile of less than three dozen. The UA's various enemies combined had fewer than that, or so the current intelligence said.

But right now, right below him, within about a square

mile area, were at least forty nuclear warheads of all shapes and sizes, many more than he or anyone else in the UAAF thought still existed on earth.

The most frightening part was, all these nukes were just 90 miles from the American mainland.

Eleven

It was called the VAB.

The letters stood for "Vehicle Assembly Building," but this did not come anywhere near to describing what the building actually looked like. Many people called it the VBFB—"Very Big Fucking Building"—and that was much closer to what it was: the largest freestanding one-room structure on the planet. Its front door was so monstrous, an entire space shuttle and its movable launch pad could fit through it with room to spare. It was by far the biggest structure among the vast expanse of buildings, roadways, and wetlands that made up the Kennedy Space Center.

The VAB also had an extensive underground section, and it was here that the United American Armed Forces command had set up temporary headquarters.

The only reason the UAAF was located at the Kennedy Space Center was that the Zon shuttle had blasted off from here and it was here that it was expected to return, with the supercriminal Viktor II in custody. The entire command staff of the UAAF had taken over the sub-basement of the VAB, a bunkerlike affair which gave them plenty of room to move around and install their communications gear.

General Dave Jones, commander-in-chief of the

UAAF and the de facto president of United America, had brought his office here, too. For the past few weeks, in tandem with the UA's infant space program, he'd been running the country from a small suite located in the deepest part of the VAB. Because of the quick move to the Kennedy Space Center, there were only about 800 UAAF personnel at the base at present, most of them technical support people. Only about 200 were combat soldiers. This number was low for two reasons: the UA command didn't expect to stay at the KSC for very long, and moving a large number of UA troops to the KSC didn't seem necessary because no one was expecting any trouble from any outside forces.

As it turned out, that had been an incorrect assumption.

The disturbing news about the brutal firebombing attack on Key West and the sighting of the battleship flotilla in the Florida Straits reached the VAB command bunker at about 0430 hours.

General Jones immediately called an emergency meeting of his command staff; they were all gathered in the VAB situation room by 0500. Every one of the officers was astounded at the reports of enemy activity off the south Florida coast, Jones included. There had not been a substantial attack on American soil in nearly a year, not even a threat of one. The UAAF reconnaisance and intelligence services were the best in the world. Neither of them had foreseen any kind of unfriendly activity on any potential front around the UA's borders.

It was obvious now that strong naval elements of the Asian Mercenary Cult had made a long, covert transglobal trip to show up off the American East Coast. Even worse, at least three squadrons of swastika-adorned warplanes were operating somewhere in the Carribean, too. These, Jones and his officers feared, might actually be remnants of the Fourth Reich, the Nazi-led mercenary army that had invaded America several years before only to be thrown out after a series of titanic battles.

Jones and his men spent the next few hours hunkered down in the command bunker, poring over a huge lighted situation board currently projecting a map of the south Florida region. UAAF reinforcements were already rushing to the area. A company of the famous Football City Special Forces, UAAF's version of a rapid deployment force, was presently en route to the Kennedy Space Center. Six UA C-5 gunships, monstrously armed aerial weapons platforms, were also on the wing, heading down from their base at the former Andrews Air Force Base in Maryland. Advance elements of the UAAF's 1st Airborne Division Reserve, presently headquartered near Fort Hood, Free Texas, would also be at the Cape by dawn.

There was some cold comfort in the fact that though the sneak attacks had destroyed the Key West base, the quick action of the scramble planes and especially the crew of the Seamaster had forestalled what probably was intended to be a follow-up bombardment on another target and possibly even an armed landing by Cult troops aboard the battleships. And the UA did have three high-tech jets and five prisoners to show for their defense of the doomed air station. Still, the unexpected action cast a gloom over Jones and the two dozen or so men crammed into the VAB situation room. What they'd heard about Key West was apparently part of a trend that was actually developing worldwide.

During the past 12 hours, reports had been flooding into the VAB bunker concerning conflicts that had sud-

denly popped up all around the world. Using the few
spy satellites it had at its disposal, plus intelligence from
various radio monitoring assets and the old reliable
"Hum-Int," the UA command staff had been besieged
with communiqués of wars suddenly breaking out in
many parts of the world, especially in the Balkans, the
Middle East, and South and East Africa. A full-scale
conflict had apparently erupted between what was once
China and what was once India; enormous bombings
and missile attacks were reportedly going on between
the Kingdom of Brazil and the so-called Glorious Empire of Argentina. Dispatches telling of battles big and
small were coming in from just about every point on
the globe. Even a war between Iceland and Greenland
had apparently broken out, prompting one UA staff
officer to ask: "What the hell are those guys fighting
over? Ice?"

It seemed like the world had suddenly gone mad.
Anyone anywhere who had a gripe against his neighbor
had suddenly decided now was the time to do something about it.

"We live in very scary times," Jones had told his command staff, as they'd worked ferverishly to pull UA
combat units from all over the continent and get them
to the crisis zone. "Every day, every hour, we still do
not know what the next will bring . . ."

No sooner were those words out of his mouth than
a radiophone on Jones's desk began beeping.

On the other end was John O'Malley, Captain
Crunch himself.

He'd just returned from his overflight of Cuba—and
he had some rather disturbing news to tell.

Twelve

Chloe appeared before the gates of Rangoon City just as the sun was coming up over the titanic mountains to the east.

It was just as she remembered it—yet different, too. The huge air base, the rows of shiny jet fighters, tanks, and other military equipment, were displayed like the toys of the richest child in the world, which was exactly what they were. The streets were lined with old-fashioned American-style billboards. The glittering spiral palace rose above it all.

This was the center of the kingdom of the place once known as Burma. Its ruler was a thirteen-year-old boy referred to by everyone as the Kid King.

Chloe knew this place, and its adolescent monarch, very intimately. During the transglobal dash to keep Viktor II's space shuttle from landing except where they wanted it to land, Hunter and Chloe had come here to Rangoon, and after a bit of subterfuge and intrigue, had convinced the Kid King to deny his huge base and its ultralong runway to the orbiting superterrorist. This act set up the final battle on the South China Sea island of Lolita and resulted in the United Americans' capture of the Zon spacecraft.

Though Hunter had moved on to this final confron-

tation, Chloe had chosen to stay behind in Rangoon.
It was from here that she eventually traveled up to the
high mountains where the temples were. At the time,
she believed that she would stay up there forever, or at
least, until Hunter came to get her.

But now she had returned to the city, to the place
where it had all started. It had taken her just two days
to get here—coming down off the mountain, the trip
south on the Irrawaddy River, hitching a ride down to
the Imperial City. None of it was any problem. Chloe
was so beautiful that getting people to help her had
always been easy. But the dream that had woken her
up at the temple had stayed with her throughout the
journey; even in the daytime it was always there, in the
back of her mind, its vision haunting her, especially the
horror of the gigantic hand and the sound of someone
laughing from very far away.

She knew she had to do something about it, knew
she had somehow to warn people—the *right* people—
about the writings in *The Book of Thirteen*. That quest
had to begin here, oddly enough, at the palace of the
Kid King.

To her amazement, the guards at the entrance to the
palace recognized her right away. They fell to their
knees in tribute, an action which lasted for an embar-
rassing length of time. They remembered her as the
beautiful woman from whom their king had finally
found his first manhood, an outstanding national
event. In the short time she'd been gone, her image
had been ingrained in their minds as some mystical
entity, both real and unreal at the same time. Indeed,
a myth had risen up around her, fueled by the Kid King
himself. Completely without her knowledge, Chloe was
in the process of being deified in Rangoon. For her to
suddenly show up at the palace gates like this was the
equivalent of the guards witnessing a vision of the

Blessed Virgin Mary. No wonder they'd remained prostrate until Chloe gently nudged them back to their feet.

Once the commander of the guard was called and he recovered from his shock, Chloe was whisked to the palace. Word had already spread by this time, and the Kid King, anxious and yearning, was waiting for her as soon as she arrived inside the Imperial Hall. He yelped when he first saw her, literally running down the steps from his throne and embracing her lustily. She had facilitated his journey from virginity to adulthood, so far the biggest event in the Kid King's life. To see her now again, so soon, was like a dream come true for him. He immediately began leading her to the royal bedroom.

But Chloe had to gently stop him and request they speak privately, while remaining vertical. The King reluctantly agreed and they retired to the royal drawing room instead. Fresh melons and a pitcher of ice-water awaited them there. A luxurious foldaway bed dominated one corner.

"I need your help," Chloe told him, watching his pudgy, dark features rise and fall on her every word. "And I need it badly."

"I am your servant," the King replied, even as his eyes feasted on her delicate features, her blond hair, her pert breasts poking through her nearly transparent white silk gown. "If your desire is to own the world, then I shall get it for you . . ."

Chloe smiled for the first time in many days. She was not that much older than the Kid King, yet eons separated them in maturity. Still, there was a warm place in her heart for him.

"My desire is to save the world, not own it," she told him.

He stared back at her and began to laugh. "Save the

world?" he asked. "That's a tall order for someone like you, is it not?"

Chloe nodded and smiled again. She realized how strange it had sounded as soon as the words left her lips. But they were true. She believed nothing less than the fate of the planet rested with her, and the words she knew from the swami and *The Book of Thirteen*.

"I must go on a long journey," she began again, knowing it would be best to keep it simple at this point. "I must get to the other side of the world very quickly. I believe there are people there who can help me . . . help us all. I have information that they must know. And only I can tell it to them."

The Kid King's face screwed up into an expression of confusion and disappointment. "You mean you are not here to stay?" he asked, his voice cracking a little.

Chloe shook her head no.

"I have to get to America," she told him again. "As soon as possible. That's why I have come. I know you of all people, would help. And that you have the means to help."

"You need an airplane," the Kid King said, after allowing it all to sink in. "A fast one, yet one that can make the journey with few stops, or without any stops at all."

"Yes, yes," Chloe said, her hand inadvertently landing on his knee.

The Kid King's face lit up like he'd just been plugged into an electrical outlet.

"And you will need someone to fly this plane for you," he continued, his voice cracking for other reasons now. "Someone who is trustworthy and brave."

"Yes," Chloe said, intentionally moving her hand upward from his knee now. "Do you have such a plane? One that will go fast and get me to America quickly? And a pilot to bring me?"

The Kid King gasped at her hand movement.

"Yes, I do," he said quickly.

Her hand moved higher.

"Can I leave right away? Is this pilot available?"

The Kid King felt like he was about to explode. These things happened very quickly and without much stimulation.

"Yes, the plane . . . can be . . . made ready," he groaned. "And the pilot. He is my second cousin. He will be able to . . . my God, I'm going to make a mess!"

The Kid King exploded a moment later. His eyes closed at the intensity of it. He shuddered once, twice, a third time. Then it was over. Chloe's hand never made it halfway up his thigh. It didn't have to.

"I must leave now," she whispered to him as he floated back down to earth. "Every minute counts . . ."

He finally caught his breath and opened his eyes again.

"Yes, of course," he replied, his voice deeper than just a moment before. "I will make the necessary preparations. You can leave within the hour."

Exactly fifty-five minutes later, Chloe and the Kid King arrived at the huge imperial airport, riding in one of the teenager's sleek Rolls Royces, accompanied by an armed escort and palace entourage that numbered in the hundreds.

It was still early morning and the last of the fog had yet to lift from the air base or the five-mile-long runway it boasted as its centerpiece. In this part of Asia, as well as around the world, length was everything. The Rangoonese were extremely proud of their runway, claiming that it was the longest in the world, and not being too far off. Whenever the long runway was to be used, it served as a kind of instant national holiday. This is why many of the civilian population was on hand, too.

At the far end of the base, past the rows of MIGs, Alpha Jets, Mirages, and Jaguars that the Kid King had collected as his own, there was a huge flight hangar surrounded by a veritable forest of SAM positions. This place was the equivalent of the Kid King's top-secret toybox. Inside were his most prized aerial possessions, aircraft that even the closest members of his family and imperial staff rarely got to see. The hangar was quite nearly a sacred place in the city; ordinary citizens were warned not to even look in its direction without permission. No surprise, then, that it was probably the most-guarded place in the country.

But now, on this day, the doors to the hangar were open, and a great beam of light was flowing out from the inside. To mark the honor of the occasion of Chloe's return to the city, the Kid King was about to reveal his latest prize possession, an aircraft that was at once very rare, very expensive, yet capable of flying very fast, very far, without the need for refueling. It was, in effect, the answer to Chloe's prayers.

It was a B-58G Hustler, an enormous supersonic jet bomber that had first flown back in the mid-1950s. The Hustler was the fastest bomber ever built. With its delta-wing design, its four huge underwing engines, its needle nose, and its extremely high tail, it looked like a stretched-out, pumped-up fighter plane, which, in reality, it was. When it was first designed, the Cold War creators of the Hustler needed an airframe that could go fast with a heavy load of bombs. Instead of starting from scratch, they took portions of designs from existing jet fighters, expanded them to twice or three times their normal size, added more power and more fuel capacity, and came up with the B-58. On its worst day, the Hustler could do 1600 mph, nearly two-and-a-half times the speed of sound.

On a good day, it could book at Mach 3.3.

This was the Kid King's favorite toy, and if anyone other than Chloe had asked for its use, they would probably have been beheaded. But she was the spiritual mistress of Rangoon these crazy days, garnering equal to, or even surprassing, the respect given the Kid King's overbearing mother. Chloe could have asked for the Kid King's entire collection of fighter jets *and* the Hustler and gotten them all. That was the power of giving someone his first taste of sex.

The huge bomber was towed out to the end of the long runway; no less than six APCs were needed to do the job. Riding in the entourage behind the Kid King's Rolls was a small car bearing his second cousin, a man nicknamed Budda-Budda. He was considered the best pilot in the kingdom and the man who flight-tested and supervised all of the aircraft acquisitions for his cousin the King. He was also a eunuch, a sacrifice he'd made years before as a sign of loyalty to his royal cousin.

Now Budda-Budda emerged from his car and walked to the ladder set up beside the cockpit of the B-58. The Kid King and Chloe alighted from the Rolls and met the pilot at the bottom of the steps. The crowd cheered at this, and a seven-gun salute was heard in the background. The mistress Chloe was leaving on a mission to the other side of the globe, the purpose of which was no less than saving the entire human race. And the Kid King's own cousin, the much-beloved Budda-Budda would be taking her on this most important journey in the King's most precious airplane. What a glorious day for Rangoon! The fate of all civilization now lay in their hands.

But for royal second cousin Budda-Budda, other

things were taking precedent. His eyes, having first fallen on Chloe, now would not let go. He'd never seen such a beautiful creature. Even in her bulky flight suit, the curves of her body, the porcelain quality to her skin, her luminescent hair—it was all quite apparent, quite real. Budda-Budda barely listened as his cousin the King introduced her to him and explained what Budda-Budda must now do.

"Take her where ever she wants to go," the Kid King was explaining to him. "Protect her. Keep her safe. Lay down your life for her, if need be."

Budda-Budda still could not pull his eyes away. She smiled at him and he glowed. Quite impossibly, he felt a stiffening between his legs.

"I will do all that and more, my King," he was finally able to gasp.

The Kid King reached out and put his hand on Budda-Budda's shoulder. The crowd, now swelled to several thousand, let out an enormous cheer.

As if in response, the Kid King leaned in and whispered something else in his cousin's ear: "Take good care of my airplane, too . . ."

Ten minutes later, the huge B-58 was at the opposite end of the extra-long runway, its four enormous 16,000-pound-thrust engines screaming with power and creating a hurricane of smoke and exhaust in their wake. The crowd never stopped cheering as the big plane began its take-off roll, the smoke behind it so thick now, it all but obscured the picturesque view of the grand mountain ranges beyond.

About halfway down the strip, Budda-Budda hit the throttles to max. The huge jet bomber suddenly leapt into the sky, the roar of its engines completely drowning out the cheers of the crowd and the ongoing cannon salutes. The big plane rose straight up, almost like a rocketship on its way to the stars, finally disappearing into the clouds at 20,000 feet.

Still, it wasn't until five long minutes later that the roar of its engines completely faded away.

Thirteen

The bright yellow Grumman J4F-1 seaplane came in for a very bumpy landing on the very choppy seas.

Though the small amphibian was more than 60 years old, it held its own against the high waves, rolling with the big ones and going through the small. Inside, the pilot tried to steer the one-man seaplane toward the beach, barely visible in the windy murk about 150 feet away. He hoped he could make the shoreline without destroying the precious little airplane. But if not, then that was how it would have to be.

At the moment, saving the classic Grumman was the least of his concerns.

It was now close to midnight and the tide was running extremely high here off Nauset Beach. The gigantic storm churning up the Atlantic was drawing closer to land by the hour, and the growing waves were just a small precursor of things to come. The wind was up to 40 knots and blowing out of the east, a most unusual direction for this time of year. The gale would not make the job of getting the small J4F-1 in to shore any easier.

It was not the typical coastline facing the sputtering airplane, either. For the most part, Cape Cod was flat, if irregular. From the Canal all the way up the crooked arm to P-town, the highest things were the dunes and the occasional steep hill. But here, at Nauset, there was a ridgeline that soared over everything else. They called it the Heights, and it was the highest point on the entire cape; as a result, the view of the Atlantic was spectacular. From here, the old-timers used to say, you could see France on a clear day.

But awe-inspiring and fanciful views were not on the mind of the Grumman's pilot, either. At that moment, all he was concerned with was getting to dry land in one piece.

He steered the old seaplane to a course roughly parallel with the pounding surf. He was now about 100 feet out from the beach; a dangerous-looking jetty was nearby. There were only two ways he could do this: Pick a wave, ride it in, and hope for the best, or . . .

He didn't even think much about the second option. He instinctively gunned his engines, twisted the nose of the seaplane directly toward the ocean shoreline, and pushed to full throttle. The wave that came along was a big one. It lifted the tiny seaplane up, its wings caught the roaring mist of the wave's chicane, and the aircraft went into a brief, stuttering hover. Finally the engines kicked in and with one last burst of power, lifted the seaplane up and over the crashing surf.

It came down hard just a few seconds later and began skidding wildly on the soft white sand. The pilot quickly killed the engines, shutting down all power even before the plane stopped bouncing. The propellers fluttered as the seaplane lurched to the left and commenced to dig its portside wingtip into the ground. Around and around it went, once, twice, three times, and almost a fourth before finally coming to a stop in a cloud of smoke, exhaust, and billowing sand. Finally it lay still.

The abrupt touchdown had given a nasty crack to the head of the pilot, but he hardly felt it. The first part of his strange mission had been accomplished. He'd made it onto Nauset Beach alive.

Now for part two.

He popped the canopy door and climbed out onto the wing and down into the blowing sand. He was instantly soaked by the spray from the raging surf only about 20 feet away—but again, he hardly noticed it. Using a tie line, he secured the plane as best he could to the nearby jetty. Then he looked to the south, where the land rose up dramatically into a long line of heavily-vegetated bluffs called the Heights.

If he started running now, he thought, he could probably reach the top in less than an hour.

The long strands of salt hay billowed in the brisk wind like waves on the stormy ocean.

There were four and a half acres of hayfields in all; the northern edge of the largest one ran right up against the peak of Nauset Heights. From there, it was a sharp drop to the rocky beach some 500 feet below. The wind was always the strongest here.

In the middle of the hayfield was a small farmhouse. It was rustic, weatherbeaten to a picture-perfect pitch. A porch ran all the way around it; a set of creaky wooden steps led up to the front door. It was dark inside, except for the light from a candle. The wind, traveling through a porous section of the ancient chimney, gave off an eerie whistling sound. Somewhere off in the distance, an animal was howling.

Or at least, it sounded like an animal. . . .

It was now about 45 minutes after his dramatic beach landing and the pilot was exhausted. The climb up to the Heights had been much harder than expected, even though he'd found a helpful path early on. He hadn't slept in nearly two days, and this hadn't helped his ordeal any. Nor had he eaten or taken any fluids. So intense was his desire to come to this place, all thoughts of food and drink had vanished.

But now, finally, he was here.

He reached the gate of the rickety fence that ringed the small farm and paused at the sign that hung flaking and crooked to one side.

It read, *Skyfire.*

The pilot took a deep breath and then walked the 50 feet to the front steps of the farmhouse. The wind was blowing even harder now, and the waves crashing on to the shore at the bottom of the bluffs sounded like cannonfire coming from very far away. He was crazy for coming here, he knew—crazy that he would think the answers to a slew of unanswerable questions might be found at this place.

He went up the stairs nevertheless; unbalanced or not, he had to go through with this. He cringed at each squeak of the porch boards but was finally an arm's length from the door. Another gust of wind, another deep breath. Then he reached out and knocked twice.

There was no answer. He knocked again, this time a little harder. Again, no response. He rapped a third time, stronger, louder. At last he heard a stirring inside. A fourth and final knock.

That's when the door finally opened and a beautiful blond vision appeared inside.

"Hello, Dominique . . ." he said with a weary smile.

"My God . . . Frost? Is that really you?"

Yes, it was him, and yes, he was insane—this he was sure of at that moment. He'd left his post up in Gander nearly 48 hours before, practically stealing the little seaplane to fly down here, in the worsening bad weather. And for what? To find out if he was really seeing ghosts?

"Frost . . . are you all right?" Dominique asked him;

it was evident she was as surprised to see him as he was
to be here.

"Yes, I'm all right," he finally answered. "At least, I
think so."

She led him inside and eased him into the nearest
chair. One small candle illuminated the room, though
the embers in the fireplace were still aglow. The house
smelled of cedar and hay and salt air. Crystal seemed
to be sparkling from everywhere. Outside, the wind was
picking up again.

Dominique went to her knees in front of him and
took his hands in hers. A look of horror came across
her face.

"My God, it's not Hawk, is it? Is he . . . dead?"

Frost hastened to reassure her. "No, no, not at all.
That's not why I'm here . . ."

A wave of relief washed through the room.
Dominique disappeared only to return a few moments
later with a bottle of brandy and a larger candle. She
poured a huge glass for Frost then lit the candlewick
with a straw from the fireplace. Frost drained the
brandy before she could put the candle on the table.
She poured him another.

"So, then," she asked, "to what do I owe this occasion?"

Frost smiled wanly and shifted in his seat. This was
the part he'd been dreading. It seemed a dream to him
now. Here he was, in Hawk Hunter's house, talking to
his beautiful girlfriend, and still he did not quite know
why.

"It's going to sound very crazy," he stuttered.

Dominique tapped him lightly on the knee.

"Nothing could be crazier than what's happening
here," she said. "Please, tell me . . ."

Frost sucked in another deep breath.

"We've known each other a long time," he began. "True?"

"Yes, of course . . ."

"And have you ever known me to be—how shall I say it?—not *normal?*"

Dominique shook her head, her long blond hair swishing beautifully as she did so.

"You are one of the sanest people I know, Frost," she replied.

He gulped down some more brandy.

"I know you've studied the mystics," he began again. "I know you've searched for truths among all the nonsense."

Dominique gave a little shrug. It was true. The house at Skyfire was filled with books on mysticism, magic, the supernatural, and the paranormal. She'd been reading about such things ever since coming here. Not because she believed in all of it—much of it was pure bunk. What she was looking for, what she was hoping to find, were instances of legitimate extraordinary events. Just one piece of proof would, in effect, make it all true.

"I've read about a lot of things," she finally replied. "But why do you ask this? Did you come all the way here just because . . ."

Frost held up his hand and gently interrupted her.

"Have you ever seen any proof of the actual existence of ghosts?" he asked her starkly.

A sudden chill went through the room. The wind picked up outside. Dominique gathered her shawl around her.

"You've . . . you've seen a ghost?" she asked him.

Frost looked up at her, his eyes beginning to glisten in the soft light of the candles. He slowly nodded.

"Not just any ghost," he said, in a voice barely above a whisper. "Mike Fitzgerald's ghost . . ."

Dominique stared back at him. She would have thought this was some kind of joke if Frost didn't look so serious.

"It's true," he went on, after another greedy sip of brandy. "It happened the other night. Right after I came back from a patrol up at Gander. He was there, right in my quarters, as plain as day. He spoke to me. Just like he'd spoken to me a thousand times before. The only difference was, I could see right through the bastard!"

Dominique reached over to the cupboard and retrieved another glass. This one she used to pour some brandy for herself.

"I'd give anything to believe that this was nothing but a dream," Frost went on. "At least then I'd know for sure that I wasn't going insane."

He looked up at Dominique. His eyes were glistening even more than before.

"But I was awake," he said finally. "And Fitz was there. Right in my room."

A sudden gust shook the old farmhouse from the roof to the cellar and back again. The two candles nearly went out. Once again, the embers in the fireplace stirred themselves back to life.

"He told me he had to come back," Frost went on after another gulp of brandy. "He had to come back— though it was very hard to do. He had to come back because he had to tell us—his friends—that something very terrible is about to happen. To us. To the entire world. He knew of this thing, but he could not tell me what it was directly. He said there are signs of this thing—*this awful thing*—everywhere these days. He told me we should all be looking. The signs will become more obvious as each day goes on. Even the fact that he was able to come to me was a sign of what's coming . . ."

Frost bowed his head again, too distraught even to sip from his glass anymore.

"It was all just too unbelievable." He finally began sobbing. "Too crazy."

Dominique laid her hand on his knee again.

"No, it isn't," she said.

"But I really don't even know why I'm here," he told her, just barely getting the words out. "I just felt . . . like I *had* to."

She calmly got to her feet.

"Come," she said. "I must show you something."

Taking one of the candles, she led him out of the living room and into the hallway. Slowly, cautiously, they made their way up the darkened stairway to the second floor. In front of them now was the door to the master bedroom. Dominique looked over at Frost for a long moment. Then, slowly, she opened the bedroom door.

Inside, four young girls were sitting on the bed, staring out the window to the growing storm beyond. The oldest was no more than fifteen. They were all wearing bathing suits; they all looked to be a long way from home. They did not move in any way when the door opened; in fact, they were sitting incredibly still, almost like statues. And a strange glow seemed to be all around them. It was the same aura that Frost had seen around Fitz.

Frost looked over at Dominique, his mouth open, more bewildered than ever.

"They don't know why they're here, either," she told him.

PART 2

Fourteen

The first sign of trouble around the defense perimeter of the Kennedy Space Center came in the form of a bird.

It was an estrich, a rare, gangling, cranelike bird that inhabited the marshes around the space complex. Shy, if imposing, the estrich came out only in the very early morning hours to feed on small fish in the many tidal pools north of the complex. It was almost never seen once the sun was up, and never, ever at night.

But now, an advance party of Football City Special Forces scouts saw one of the huge birds fly over their heads, its great wings making a distinct whooshing as it passed. A brief rustling had proceeded this strange event, and now the FCSF troopers, hugging the damp smelly ground about 200 yards north of the main defense line, were quickly putting two and two together.

Beyond them was a line of bullrushes, and beyond that, the beginning of an almost impenetrable tract of swampland that stretched all the way from the far banks of the Banana River. It was from here that the estrich had fled. Each trooper in the eight-man squad reached the same conclusion simultaneously. Somebody—or something—was out there, either in the bullrushes or in the swamp beyond.

The Football City troopers were experts at this sort of thing. This was why they were patrolling beyond the defense perimeter in the first place. Still, it was rather unnerving to detect possible infiltrators along this part of the defense line. The terrain was extremely inhospitable, full of sinkholes and deep streams; the only solid ground was marshland, some of it wet enough to take a man down to his ankles or more. Maybe it had been another animal that had frightened the estrich. A gator, or even a fox, something with four legs and a snout, out looking for a midnight snack.

But with everything and everybody on high alert since recent events down around the Keys, the troopers knew they couldn't take any chances. Quickly, silently, seven of them began digging into the soft, mucky soil.

The eighth man radioed back to the base.

Colonel Donn Kurjan, aka "Lazarus," took the call from the Football City troopers.

Kurjan was commanding the forward defense bunker on the north side of the Kennedy Space Complex. Located in an abandoned "fire hole," a place where space workers could seek shelter in case of an accident on the pad, the bunker was filled with communications gear, NightScope screens, motion-detection equipment, and ultrasensitive listening devices. From here, Kurjan could direct the battalion of mixed troops that held positions all along the left-handed arc that stretched from the Atlantic to the lower Banana River and crowned the top of the huge rejuvenated space complex.

Solid and wiry, with a penchant for plain, black combat utilities, Kurjan was one of the most respected officers in the UAAF hierarchy and a member of the inner circle. He'd been skiing in the territory that had been Utah when the trouble had erupted off the Florida Keys and was rushed to Kennedy to coordinate the crash program of heightened defensive awareness. They didn't call Kurjan "Lazarus" for nothing—he'd been in many tight spots, in many covert actions, and many times behind enemy lines, given up for dead, only to reemerge intact and with his mission accomplished. Like a cat, Kurjan seemed to have at least nine lives, maybe more.

On this night, he would use up another of them.

The call from the Football City radioman came at exactly five minutes after midnight. Speaking in code, he gave his position and then went onto a scramble frequency. This was Kurjan's first clue that something big might be up. He immediately beeped the radio shack back at the UAAF main combat center beneath the VAB, telling the officers on duty there to stand by.

He went on the scramble line with the FBSF radioman. The trooper told him of the patrol's suspicions that all was not right in the north swamp, adding the part about the estrich. Kurjan quickly signaled his technicians to activate the sight/sound/motion gear in the direction of the swamp. Then he turned back to the scramble phone to talk to the FBSF radioman again.

But the line had gone dead.

Kurjan heard the first explosion just a second later. It sounded like a big *whomp!*, and it shook the fire hole even though the bunker was made of 12-foot concrete blocks held together with two-inch reenforced steel girders. This was followed by two more tremendous explosions, and then a third and a fourth. Kurjan still had the scramble phone in his hand and was trying desperately to raise the FBSF troopers, but there was no reply. It would later be determined that the first explosion—a Katyusha rocket containing a warhead filled with high-explosive—had landed right on top of

the Football City troopers' position, killing all of them
instantly.

They heard the trumpets next. Whether it was a hundred or possibly a few blowing some kind of amplifica-
tion device, their sudden blaring shook the concrete
bunker almost as violently as the first barrage of
Katyusha rockets. The trumpets were so loud, two technicians manning the listening devices had their eardrums blown out. Another found his nose had started
bleeding. Alarmed, Kurjan ordered the listening posts
to shut down and bumped up the NightScope monitors
instead.

What he and the others inside the fire hole saw was
a scene from a nightmare. Hundreds, possibly thousands, of armed men were swarming out of the swamp
through the marshes, heading for the northern defense line. These men were like something from another time. They had long beards, woolen clothes, and
steel helmets with horns. Each man was carrying at
least two weapons: a rifle or machine gun of some kind
in one hand, and an ax, a long sword, or in some cases,
a spear, in the other.

Every TV monitor was showing the swarm of armed
men sloshing through the muck and mud, explosions
going off all around them. There were more rockets
and what appeared to be artillery shells going off amid
the attackers. But they weren't coming from the defense forces; rather, they were being fired by the attacking side itself.

It was a pattern Kurjan had seen before. He quickly
leapt to the hotline phone and called back to the VAB.
There was no time for the niceties of coded messages
now. He simply yelled, "Attack on the north line! Near
penetration on the wire!" twice into the radiophone
before tossing it away and retrieving his M-16.

At the rate the attackers were advancing, they'd reach the first defense line in less than two minutes.

The alert horn went off at the emergency UAAF air base inside the Kennedy Space Complex at exactly 12:07.

The temporary base, set up on the extremely long runway previously used for the American space shuttle landings, had just been established earlier in the day, as part of a hurry-up contingency plan to protect the complex. As such, it had a wild variety of aircraft on hand, all of them from units that had been called on to send aircraft from various parts of the country as quickly as possible.

On hand were a half-dozen reconditioned F-86 Sabre jets recently purchased from the Central Empire of Peru; a single TA-4K two-seat Skyhawk; two P-2H Lockheed Neptune antisubmarine ships converted as light bombers; a single F-105 Thunderchief; and an A-37 Dragonfly light attack plane. The big daddies of this motley crew, however, dwarfed the mélange. Three massive C-5 gunships, the monstrous aerial workhorses of the United American Armed Forces, had arrived late that afternoon. They were, specifically, *Bozo 2*, *Football One*, and *Spock's Dream*. Part of a massive reconditioning program started the year before, these Galaxies were just three of the two dozen C-5s either presently in operation or being reconfigured out at Edwards Air Force Base in California. Each of these frightful aerial platforms carried a vast array of weapons sticking out of portholes on the left side. Anything from Gatling guns to multiple-rocket launchers to howitzers could be carried aboard these flying behemoths, their design being a nightmarish extension of the C-47 Spooky gunship idea born many years ago during the First Vietnam

War. These Galaxies had quickly gained a reputation around the world as the worst things short of a nuclear bomb that any attacking ground force could come up against. All three were now being hot-started and rolled out onto the ultralong airstrip.

As with the airplanes, there was a vast array of UA personnel manning them. Two of the C-5 gunships were carrying ground personnel filling in for regular crew members. Aircraft mechanics, maintenance workers, even some spacecraft technicians had been pressed into service for the emergency.

But probably no one was more out of place than the man strapped into the co-pilot's seat of the first C-5 gunship to get into take-off position, *Bozo 2*.

His name was Stan Yastrewski. He was by training a Navy man. He'd served on a Trident submarine during the Big War and on several other combat vessels in the postwar years, including the UA's first aircraft carrier, the *USS Mike Fitzgerald*. Known to everyone as "Yaz," Yastrewski most recently had been serving as General Dave Jones's chief of staff. He, too, was a close friend of Hawk Hunter.

Though a highly valued member of the UAAF command structure, Yaz had the perverse ability to find himself in the middle of the most unusual predicaments. Short of being captured by aliens, just about everything that could happen to a person both in and out of a combat situation had happened to him. (Being the love slave of the beautiful yet highly unbalanced terrorist queen Elizabeth Sandlake was probably the pinnacle so far of his unusual career.) It was a lot he'd finally come to accept in this crazy, upside-down world: if something strange was going to happen to someone, Yaz just assumed that it was going to happen to him.

Just how he got to be sitting in the co-pilot's seat of the massive C-5 gunship was yet another example of this. He'd been visiting his family in Maine when the first reports of trouble in Florida had come in. He made it to Boston within a few hours and caught the first available UAAF flight south. It happened to be the massive gunship *Bozo 2*. On the way, the Galaxy received a message that a provisional fighter-bomber squadron was being formed at the old Langley Air Force Base in Virginia, and that the C-5's co-pilot, a guy named Raycroft, had been drafted into it.

Because Yaz had actually spent some time behind the controls of some smaller UA aircraft, though as a co-pilot only, he was asked to come up and sit in the second-banana seat for the rest of the trip down to the KSC. The airplane had been on the ground no more than a few hours when this alert horn went off, not nearly long enough for a regular C-5 co-pilot to get to Canaveral. So Yaz was strapped into the number-two seat instead.

The guy actually flying the gigantic airplane was named Vogel, an Air Force pilot from way back. In the back were 17 men pressed into service as gunners and loaders. *Bozo 2* was one of the "kitchen sink" Galaxy gunships. Like its namesake, *Bozo 1,* which was destroyed in Vietnam, *Bozo 2* carried any and every gun and weapon its designers could fit into it. There were 21 gun ports on its left-hand side. Eight were filled with Phalanx Gatling guns, four at each end of the fuselage, each one capable of firing 300 uranium-depleted rounds *a second.* Six more gunports had M102 105-mm howitzers sticking out of them; these more or less centered in the middle of airplane. Filling the gap forward of the howitzers and before the big Gats were three Kongsberg FK 20-mm single-barrel anti-aircraft guns, specialized weapons built for firing a variety of high-explosive shells. In the four remaining rear ports, the designers had somehow crammed into place a pair of ZSU-23 SO23mm quadruple anti-aircraft guns, a single Bofors 40L70 40-mm AA gun, and, outrageously, an Israeli-designed IMI MAR-290 multiple-rocket launcher.

The ammunition and power systems for all this took up nearly 80 percent of the Galaxy's lifting capacity—but that was one thing about one of these monsters going into combat: the load got progressively lighter the more the weapons were fired. The shorter the distance between base and the combat area, the more the C-5 could lug into the air. In this case, the distance from base to the northern defense line was only three miles.

Vogel turned *Bozo 2* out toward the head of the runway, right behind one of the P-2 Neptunes. The Nep would be serving as a light ship. It not only carried a full load of star flares, but a powerful array of halogen lights had been attached to its belly via the service pod connectors. Its armament would be only a single M60 gun in the nose and another in the tail.

Off in the distance, Yaz could see the glow of flames and gunfire rising from the swamps on the north end of the space complex. His headphones were filled with a cacophony of voices, a direct line from the command bunker beneath the VAB, in which the various defense forces were being rushed into position to repel the sudden onslaught. Just the pitch of the voices in this tense choir told Yaz the surprise attack was large and serious. From the sounds of it, a division-sized attack force was trying to break through on the north side.

There was no time for procedures such as take-off clearances and weather checks; as soon as the Neptune lightship was airborne, Vogel gunned the C-5's quartet of engines. Though he was no expert in aeronautics, Yaz knew the giant gunship would need every foot of take-off space it could get. Overloaded as it was, and with its engines hot-started and not yet up to proper trim, it seemed like a small miracle would be needed just to get them off the ground.

But Vogel was a pro—and he knew he had some gas to waste. So he simply ran all four engines up to peak and got the gunship quickly screaming down the runway. Yaz was yelling out the airspeed to him, the minimum take-off speed, he guessed, was at least 110 mph. But somehow, Vogel managed to coax the big ship into the air at around 97-plus. One moment they were rumbling along the ground, the C-5 shaking like every lock washer and tie-rod was coming undone, the next, the big plane had groaned itself into the sky and everything had become incredibly smooth again.

Vogel got barely 1000 feet of air underneath her when he turned toward the combat area.

Already the fight was ten minutes old.

The Neptune lightship was the first UA aircraft to reach the battle scene.

The crew was shocked by what it saw. Swarming through the marshes and swampland in front of the first UA defense line were not hundreds but thousands of attackers. Many had already breached the first line of defense and were now blowing holes through the seven rows of concertina wire separating them from the second defense line. Just as the defense procedure dictated, the UA forces had pulled back to an area between the second and third defense perimeter, a kind of no-man's-land pockmarked with small bunkers, concrete firing positions, and time-delayed mines. Behind this was the main defense line—known as the Three Wire—and beyond that, a last-ditch position known simply as Four-Four. After that, it was a clear run of about a mile to the outer reaches of the space complex itself.

The crew of the P-2 was so stunned by the size of the
attacking force, its front and rear gunners opened up
without even waiting for an order to do so. The Neptune pilot put the airplane into a long, low orbit and
quickly illuminated his halogen array. Suddenly night
was turned into day. The halogen arc stretched for a
quarter mile in all directions. In full luminescence, it
showed the area between the swampland and the second defense line was absolutely covered with attackers.

Oddly still, artillery and rockets were landing among
these armed men as well as in front and behind them.
Many were being killed by this wildly-inaccurate fire.
But those still able kept plunging through the difficult
terrain, hell bent on getting into the barbed wire and
to the second defense line beyond.

Now some UA artillery shells were falling among the
attackers, too. Fired from beyond Four-four, the fragmentation shells were bursting just above the heads of
the invaders, slaying dozens of them with every explosion. Combined with the shells and rockets coming
from the opposite direction, a horrible toll was being
taken on the army of attackers. But still they kept coming.

The Neptune was now in its assigned position, its two
gunners continuing to add their own fire to the fray.
Then, from above the battle scene, a new sound was
heard. High-pitched. Searing. *Frightening.* It was the un-
mistakable whine of a Galaxy gunship.

Kurjan heard the C-5 coming.

Instantly, he knew what it was, knew what it meant.

He and his men—what was left of them—were
locked in battle just behind the second wire. Kurjan
had ordered the line abandoned due to the sheer force
of the onslaught. Fifty yards ahead of him, the myste-

rious attackers were swarming all over the barbed-wire barriers, plunging through holes left by artillery fire from both sides, and in some grisly instances, running up the backs of comrades who had thrown themselves onto the razor-sharp concertina and were alternately being bled and stomped to death.

Kurjan's men were simply firing into this mass. Up, down, this way and that, aiming was not a necessity in this battle. Any projectile fired in the general direction of the attackers hit somebody or something. The gunfire was so fierce, the barrels of some of the defense force's weapons, notably the pair of .50-caliber mgs mounted on their Humvees, were glowing white hot and were actually beginning to melt around the muzzles.

Kurjan's sapper unit had just set off a row of time-delayed mines when he heard the C-5 approach. There was no time to dawdle now. Kurjan grabbed the nearest three guys and ordered them to run down the line to the right flank and tell the UA forces to retreat. Then he grabbed two more men and ran to the left himself. Soon they were all screaming at the top of their lungs for the UA troops to fall back, beyond the Three Line and even behind Four-Four. Kurjan had seen many times what an attack by a C-5 gunship could do. He didn't want to be anywhere near this one once it began.

Though some of the enemy soldiers were just 200 feet away now, the UA retreat was as orderly as could be expected. The Neptune lightship was still maintaining its position, directing many of its beams to the rear and aiding the defense forces to pick their way through the marshy riverlets and concrete obstructions. The attackers' artillery was now falling all around them, but the thick, soggy ground, and many misfused shells, held casualties down to a minimum. Kurjan picked up one trooper struck in the leg by shell fragments, slung him over his shoulder, and began running. In his ears the sound of the huge C-5 gunship was growing louder with each second.

Out of the corner of one eye, Kurjan could see that his right flank was now entirely cleared back to the beyond Four-Four. On his left, the retreating defense forces were just scrambling over the larger bunkers of Line Three. Inside thirty seconds, they'd all be out of harm's way and the approaching C-5 could do its job.

He readjusted the guy on his shoulder. He had just one more riverlet to cross, and then . . .

Whump!

The next thing Kurjan knew, he was flying through the air—upside down. It was an odd sensation, one that lasted but a second, though it seemed more like a minute. While he was inverted and airborne, he saw many things: the horde of attackers charging over the Third Wire. The Neptune lightship, flying much lower than he'd thought possible. The small stream in which he'd just been wading when whatever happened to him happened. The guy who he'd been carrying on his back was now spinning through the air right next to him. Above it all, he saw the ominous shadow of the C-5 gunship, getting closer.

Kurjan landed on his left shoulder, the perilous fall cushioned by a clump of soggy eelweed, but not by much. He came down with so much force, his utility belt snapped itself off and his M-16 fired an unguided three-round burst. The guy he'd been carrying landed on top of him in a heap not a second later. His face buried in the mud and weed up to his ears, Kurjan nevertheless heard a distinctive huff when the trooper hit the ground. Kurjan pulled his own face out of the muck and then turned the man over. He was headless. His left arm and leg were gone, too. Their empty sockets were still smoking, as was the man's uniform.

Only then did Kurjan realize what had happened.

An artillery shell—one of theirs, most likely—had come down right on top of him. If he hadn't been carrying the guy with the leg wound, he, too, would now be without his head. This ghastly realization sank in damn quickly. Kurjan kicked the corpse away from him; it fell like a doll into the muddy water below. He grabbed his M-16 by the muzzle, burning his hand severely, and began climbing up the stream's slimy bank. There was still gunfire all around him. The night was filled with tracers going in both directions. The clanking of the P-2's engines was now rising in his ears. Why was that damn plane flying so damn low? he wondered, as if such a thing should be a concern to him now.

He somehow reached the top of the bank—and only then did he stop to check that he had all his fingers and toes. He was covered with mud, blood and for some reason, motor oil, but he was still intact. At least for the moment.

Catching his breath, the reality of the situation began to take hold. Kurjan looked to the south, back toward the complex, and saw the last of his soldiers just reaching the Four-Four line, now about 500 yards from him. He looked to his right and left and saw nothing but smoking shell holes and dead bodies. Then he looked over his shoulder, and at that instant he was aware of a tremendous roar filling his eardrums.

Not 25 feet away, on the other side of the bank of the stream he'd just sailed over, were several thousand armed, wild-eyed attackers.

They were heading right for him.

The *Bozo 2* gunship took up station over the battlefield at exactly 12:17 A.M.

It had been a short, bumpy ride from the improvised air strip to the scene of the fighting. Vogel, the pilot, needed no FAC information to locate the trouble area. A fiery glow caused by the savage fighting was lighting up the entire northern horizon.

Still strapped tightly into his co-pilot's seat, Yaz was craning his neck to see the battlefield over the Galaxy's bulbous nose. Even with this obstructed view, his jaw hit his chest. There were swarms of armed men below them—clearly they'd already overrun the first two defense lines and were quickly approaching the third. At their present rate of advance, they would very soon be onto the fourth.

"Jeezus, who the hell are these guys?" Yaz exclaimed involuntarily. "There's so many of them. Where did they come from?"

If Vogel had a guess, he didn't offer it. He was too busy yanking the huge gunship around the battlefield to get it into its proper firing profile.

"Christ, these A-holes will be in our pants in five minutes," the pilot cursed, watching the steady progression of the horde. He flipped a radio switch which connected him to the VAB main command bunker.

"Is the fire zone clear of friendlies?" he screamed into his microphone.

"Thy wrath will set a hundred fires to burning . . ." came the unexpected reply. "And these fires will consume your friends . . ."

"Who the *fuck* is that?" Vogel and Yaz yelled at once.

"Main CP!" Yaz now began calling. "Is fire zone clear? Come on!"

"Fire Zone clear . . ." came the calm if tense voice of an unseen comm tech back at the VAB bunker.

That's all Vogel needed. He'd maneuvered the huge gunship over the center of the Three Line, now covered by thousands of the attackers illuminated by the Neptune lightship flying directly across from the C-5 in a complementary orbit.

"Are they ready back there?" Vogel yelled over to Yaz, as he put the big gunship further on its left wing.

Yaz punched in the internal intercom radio.

"Gunnery officer, what's your situation?"

"We're up to eighty percent," came the crisp reply. This meant about 16 of the Galaxy's 21 weapons were ready to fire. "Everything will be on line in about thirty seconds . . ."

"We ain't got thirty seconds," Vogel yelled into his intercom mic. "We're going in now."

With that, he yanked the huge airplane nearly over completely on the left wing. Yaz was suddenly thankful for his tight seat harness.

"How's the electrical?" Vogel yelled. Nothing would work if they didn't have enough juice.

"One hundred and ten percent," Yaz yelled back, reading the numbers of the airplane's fire control display. "Can't get better."

"OK," Vogel said, flipping the microphone away from his face. "Here we go . . ."

The way it was supposed to work was that the smaller weapons sticking out of the C-5—the Gatling guns— would fire off first. Then, gradually, as the main fire control computer began absorbing information, the larger weapons would start discharging, all the way up to the huge Israeli rocket launcher. This incremental process could take anywhere between 15 and 30 seconds.

But Vogel knew they had no time to go by the book— and Yaz agreed. The attacking force 1000 feet below them looked like a swarm of bugs—dark, massive, unstoppable, and intent on getting into the inner reaches of the space complex. If that happened, it would be all over very quickly for the UA side.

"We're going with everything," the pilot yelled to Yaz. "Right . . . now!"

No sooner were the words out of his mouth than Yaz hit all 10 fire control buttons at once. There was a frightening roar; it was so loud it drowned out the scream of the C-5's four massive engines. A huge ball of flame and smoke enveloped the left side of the airplane—Yaz was certain the left wing had been blown off. Then the huge plane began vibrating so badly, Yaz's seat-harness snapped off. He managed to turn himself to the left and saw the tremendous broadside of bullets, rockets, and AA shells pouring out of the side of the airplane and down onto the attackers below. It looked like nothing less than a fiery waterfall. It was so bright, it dwarfed the Neptune lightship's halogen array many times over.

"Jeezus Christ!" Yaz yelled, jaw still agape at the frightening display. "No one will live through that!"

"That's the main idea," Vogel replied grimly.

Donn Kurjan was in hell.

All around him was fire. And smoke. And bodies. And in his ears were screams, and the sound of flesh crackling, blood boiling, and bones vaporizing.

The narrow stream in front of him was sizzling now; it looked like a long ribbon of liquid fire. Flowing rapidly by were the remains of the dead and dying. The attackers, their hair and beards on fire, many missing arms and legs, some cut in two yet somehow still alive, they were all tumbling down the suddenly violent river as the tremendous wall of fire continued to rain down upon them. Even their swords and guns and helmets were melting, so intense was the heat. Their mouths were open in gut screams that sounded too much like laughter. Above it all, the shadow of death, the one everyone always talked about, flew in the shape of a C-5 Galaxy gunship. It was like a huge bird, vomiting

fire and brimstone. This was death, Kurjan knew. This
was Azael. The King of Terrors. The Dissolution.

Smoke. Fire. Screams. Kurjan could hear and see
them all. Right above him, a second monstrous shadow:
another gigantic gunship, spewing terror and death
from its body, was flying overhead, and another was
right behind it. The streaks of light coming from the
three gunships went round and round in a carousel of
death. Smaller airplanes roared by, adding dozens of
fire bombs to the conflagration. Helicopters appeared,
their blades coughing as they chopped through the
smoke to drop thousands of sparklets of fire. It went
on like this forever. Smoke. Fire. Screams. Death.

No one could live through this . . .

No one except a guy nicknamed Lazarus.

They found him the next morning.

He was lying in a pool of brackish water, tinged to
pink with blood, beneath a thick layer of low fog. All
around him were human remains. Not bodies; they
could not be accurately described as that. These were
skeletons, and in some cases, simply lines of ash laid
out in the form of what was once a human being.

There were swords and helmets and rifles and axes
and pieces of body armor lying around him, too. Much
of it had melted into the soft earth; some of it was still
sizzling and hot to the touch. In his right hand, his
rifle had melted into the ground. The rubber had
melted off his boots. The starburst major's pin had
melted through his lapel and into the skin of his neck,
permanently scarring him.

But he was alive. When the soldiers found him lying
in the bloody water, he looked up at them and blinked
and joked that they certainly didn't look like angels,
but that they didn't look like devils, either. They eased

him onto a stretcher, astonished that he had somehow made it through the nightmarish battle, and carried him to a waiting helicopter. This flew him the two miles back to the center of the space complex, the field hospital, where the doctors and nurses and his fellow officers and friends marveled that he had somehow beaten the odds again.

When General Dave Jones arrived, accompanied by Yaz and the pilot Vogel, the UA commander-in-chief was almost overcome with emotion.

"What's the secret?" he asked Kurjan, who was still sore, still singed, and still slightly in shock. "Why does this always happen to you?"

Kurjan could only look up at the CIC; he felt tears well in his eyes.

"I don't know," he said finally. "But maybe it's time I found out."

The morning mist which had obscured most of the battlefield finally lifted about an hour after dawn.

Only then did the true scope of what had happened become apparent. A division-strength force of about 12,000 men, apparently hidden in the swamplands north of the space complex, had attacked the UA defense lines. They'd been armed with light weapons and some artillery and Katyusha rockets. They'd rushed the defense line at exactly midnight. Not one of them made it beyond Four-Four or into the space base itself. The combined attack from the three C-5 gunships and the smaller UA aircraft had seen to that.

Even stranger, it looked like none of the mysterious attackers had survived. As UA security troops surveyed the battle area within the four defense lines, several patrols of Football City Special Forces troops went through the thick marsh and into the swampland using motorboats and rubber rafts. With helicopter gunships providing cover, the FBSF troopers searched every piece of dry land inside the heavily layered thick-treed swamp. They found some evidence of the attackers' forward assembly area—empty ammunition boxes and the like—and clues that the attackers had moved into the swampland only recently.

But they found no survivors. Even at the half dozen artillery emplacements, set up on nipples of high ground beyond the treeline, there was nothing but dead bodies. Apparently sensing defeat of their massive attack, the artillerymen either had killed each other or had killed themselves. At each of the six gun sites, the FBSF troopers found only corpses, many with bullets in their heads or swords in their chests.

But the dead left some clues, and when they were combined with their actions of the night before, a frightening if familiar profile of the attackers emerged. The horde had used brute force and not any kind of stealth or tactics in trying to reach their objective. They'd advanced under an artillery barrage that was laid down with absolutely no regard for their own safety—indeed, the attackers' shellfire had killed nearly 20 percent of their own men. And when it appeared that the battle had been lost, many of the attackers had taken their own lives in lieu of retreat or surrender.

When all this was taken into consideration, the conclusion was that these mysterious attackers were not so mysterious at all. The entire East Coast of the American continent had been terrorized by them just two short years before. They were Norsemen, modern-day Vikings from lawless, war-ravaged northern Europe who'd sailed to the American shores in slapdash troop-carrying submarines and quite nearly come close to establishing a foothold on America, just as their ancestors had done centuries earlier, before being destroyed by the combined United American armies.

Somehow, a division of these fierce fighters had infiltrated the swamplands north of the Kennedy complex and launched the murderous attack on the space center. Only the delaying tactics of the defense forces and the massive firepower brought to bear by the Galaxy gunships and the other aircraft had prevented a disaster of catastrophic proportions.

As it was, more than 120 UA soldiers had been killed, including the eight Football City Special Forces troopers who'd died in that first rocket attack. More than 85 were still missing and almost 300 wounded. The battlefield, nearly two miles long and about a quarter mile deep, held the remains of most of the attackers. They would be burned and their ashes covered with lime later in the day.

Then, only two baffling questions would remain: how had so many Norsemen been able to get so close the space complex in the first place, especially since it was thought their armies had been wiped out in America a long time before?

But second and more important, under whose direction had these fierce warriors launched their attack?

Fifteen

In Orbit

Frank Geraci was alone in the Zon's crew compartment when the radio began beeping this time.

The NJ104 officer-turned-astronaut was not sleeping. Rather, he was doing his hourly check of the Zon's chaotic internal systems diagnostics. While the Russian-built spacecraft bore a striking resemblance on the outside to the U.S. space shuttle, it was nothing like the American version on the inside.

Where the old NASA designers and engineers had used the latest in microtechnology to construct and power the shuttles, the ham-handed Zon designers had used everything from standard-gauge fray-happy electrical wire to antique vacuum tubes to get their baby into space. Where the Americans had built in a micro-processor-based triple-plus redundancy system to make sure the shuttle was as fail-safe as could be, the Zon's builders had simply double-wired everything and let it go at that. Even such things as quadruple-layered pressurization seals—needed to keep all the valuable oxygen in—had been glossed over. Whenever they came to a particularly irregular or hard-to-access construction point, the Zon builders had simply *painted* the oxygen seal on, using a highly reflective polymer-based goop that was full of trapped oxygen bubbles, and therefore porous and dangerously brittle.

A testament to bravery or stupidity or both, the Zon was amazing in that it was so obviously thrown together by unenlightened or unconcerned engineers, yet it was still able to fly in space.

Keeping it together was Geraci's job. He was, after all, the engineer of the UA crew. But he felt more like a train engineer than someone who was responsible for keeping the spacecraft intact as it sped along at seven miles a second. A seam could bust at any moment, and Geraci would have little else but a roll of duct tape and a bucket of the Russian goop to make the patch. Should any of the electrical systems go, he would have exactly six replacement parts to work with.

And if something cropped up with the main engines? Well, it would be a long, cold night, because there was nothing on board with which he could repair them.

Geraci was in the midst of soldering a particularly scary-looking wire bus—it contained many yellow, green, red, and blue leads, all of which seemed to be going everywhere and nowhere at the same time— when he heard the radio softly beeping.

The sound startled him at first. He knew well the intense restrictions on communications between the Zon and Earth. Security being what it was, contact was supposed to be nonexistent. He hadn't even heard the radio call signal before this.

So why was it beeping now?

Geraci glided over to the radio set and contemplated it for a moment. The laminated list of code-phrases was floating nearby. If Geraci understood the procedure correctly, to answer the radio call, he would have to push in the receive panel, activate the scramble mode, push the power button twice, and then wait. But should he do it? Cook had told him something about hearing a strange transmission on the radio earlier—it was unclear exactly what happened as the Zon had been dodging space mines virtually nonstop ever since.

Maybe this was another one of those crazy calls . . .

Or maybe it was an actual radio transmission from Cape Canaveral.

Geraci finally pushed the receive panel, simultaneously punching the scramble button. The speaker exploded in a storm of static. He quickly hit the power button once. Twice. Then he released the receive switch and waited.

At first the voice sounded very strange. Distorted. Eerie. But then Geraci pushed a couple of filter buttons on and the words cleared up immediately.

"A low front expected tonight along the eastern seaboard," the voice intoned in obvious code. "Tides will be running much higher than expected."

It was the Cape!

Geraci quickly retrieved the floating code-phrase card and ran his finger down the list. He was startled by what he found. "Low-front" was code for a major military action was in the offing. Any indication of "high tides" meant the situation was extremely serious and ongoing.

"Damn," Geraci breathed. Something big must be happening below.

At that moment, JT floated down into the crew compartment. He looked worn-out and tense after manning the co-pilot's seat for the past two days straight. Still, Geraci was relieved to see him.

"We've got a problem," he told JT, indicating the flashing radio light.

JT was beside him in a second. He, too, was amazed that the radio had suddenly come alive.

"*Shit,*" JT cursed. "This is going to be bad. I can just *feel* it."

He finally pushed in the scramble panel and kept it in. A moment later they were talking to Yaz, duly scrambled and unfettered. All radio protocol was quickly dismissed with.

"We've got to make this brief," Yaz began.

"What's the occasion?" JT asked his friend. "Something big?"

"Would you believe World War Four, maybe?" was Yaz's reply.

For the next ten minutes, using a calm if deadly serious tone, Yaz recounted the specifics of how the world had suddenly gone crazy—or better put, *crazier*—since the Zon had left. Reports were flowing in from all over, telling of major wars erupting, old conflicts flaring up, and nasty sneak attacks and counterattacks. Yaz gave a soberingly detailed account of the firebombing of Key West, the results of Crunch's Cuba overflight, and the recent attack on the Kennedy Space Center.

"And you're sure those guys were Norsemen?" was the first question JT asked him. "I thought we greased all those A-holes a long time ago."

"I saw the helmets and swords myself," Yaz replied. "They were the genuine item. How so many of them got there, no one knows. Maybe they all swam over from Norway or wherever the hell they came from. I mean, it's as crazy as all the other shit that's going on."

"And is everyone really sure those were Fourth Reich flyboys who took out Key West? And that the Cult is involved?"

"Sure as the swastikas on their little bitty heads," Yaz answered. "As for the Cult—who else would be able to float around in so many battleships? It's the fact that these guys have access to so many nukes that scares the shit out of me."

"Jeezus," JT breathed into the microphone, "what next? Mid-Aks?"

"It's as if everyone has suddenly flipped out," Yaz concluded. "Bottom line, Jonesie thought we should call because we don't know what will be happening by the time you guys get back."

"*If* we get back," JT told him.

Now it was his turn. He quickly detailed the ordeal the Zon had been going through with the space mines, and the wear and tear in both spacecraft and crew as a result of trying to avoid the deadly orbital bombs.

"We're like a B-17 on our way to Stuttgart," JT told Yaz. "We're full of holes, and the next one could be the last. But we're getting closer to the target . . ."

A burst of static interrupted Yaz's next transmission briefly.

"Well, whatever you find up there, I'll bet it has something to do with what's going on down here . . ."

"Just keep it together," JT told him. "You never know what's going to happen . . ."

"Exactly," Yaz concluded. "That's the problem."

With that, he broke off the transmission.

JT and Geraci just stared at each other as the radio died again. Both were weary, stressed out, and now, extremely concerned.

"I know it sounds crazy, but I think the wildest thing is this attack on the Cape," Geraci said finally. "I mean, the Cult battleships are in the area. Apparently, so are some high-tech Fourth Reich aircraft. And if they're working together, then they have access to a pile of nukes. Why, then, would they send in a very low-tech army to destroy the space center?"

JT just shook his head.

"Maybe because they weren't looking to destroy it," he replied. "Not completely, anyway."

"You mean, they sent in the goons to *capture* it?" Geraci asked. "That's not really their style, is it? I mean, those Norse guys are pretty low on the food chain. They fight for booze to get drunk and ammo so they can fight again. I think that's about as elaborate as their military strategy goes."

"True," JT conceded. "But maybe they were sent in just to fuck us up a little. Like throwing in the fodder first. Bump our defenses before the real attack. I mean, let's face it: one or two battleships could stand twenty-four miles offshore and with a five-minute barrage wreck everything at KSC. I don't think that's what's going on here."

"So if they don't want to destroy it . . . what *do* they want?" Geraci asked.

"Maybe they want to use it," JT said with a zero-g shrug.

"You mean, to launch something?" Geraci gasped. "Something of their own?"

JT just shook his head.

"Well," he said, "that would be a party, wouldn't it?"

A minute later, Geraci and JT had floated back up to the flight deck.

As usual, it was dark and tense there. At last count, they had encounted 16 space mines, the latest just an hour before. This one was probably the most powerful yet; its explosion had been incredibly bright and the resulting shock waves so violent they'd sent the Zon up on its tail even before Hunter had had a chance to steer the spacecraft completely out of the way. The close call only added to the frayed nerves aboard the increasingly dented and battered Zon.

But as before, each explosion also put them closer to the source of the space mines. Ben Wa had been manning the navigation computer when the latest one had gone off. Despite the jarring that resulted in the space bomb's wake, he'd been able to get a good retro-track on its position prior to its detonation. By triangulating backward, Ben determined that whoever was leaving the trail of space mines was now just 35 to 40 miles ahead and maybe a couple of miles above them.

JT now steered himself over to the space next to the command pilot's seat and knocked twice on Hunter's helmet.

"Can you talk for a moment?" he asked the Wingman.

Hunter flipped up his visor and took a deep breath of the stale cabin air. He was tired, hungry, and more than a little stressed out—three things that rarely entered his personal repertoire, and never all at once. Something was definitely wrong here. He'd faced larger challenges than this. In the past, he'd gone days without sleep, days without food and hadn't felt this miserable. He'd fought air battles with the odds a hundred to one against him and still had not felt this uptight.

What was it, then? He'd thought flying in space was going to be the gas of his life, the realization of his long-held dream. But since they'd begun encountering the space mines, it had been one long, harrowing, uncomfortable, and nerve-frazzling ordeal. He'd always wanted to go into space—and now he was here, and for the most part, the trip had sucked so far.

Maybe there was something in that old saying: be careful what you wish for, it might come true someday . . .

Hunter took in another deep breath, then turned to JT.

"What are you going to tell me?" he asked his friend. "That this is all just a bad dream?"

JT hesitated a moment, then slowly nodded.

"Well, yes," he replied. With that, he quickly briefed Hunter and the others on what he and Geraci had just heard via the radio call from Yaz. The world below had suddenly gone crazy. Wars and titanic battles were breaking out all over, not the least of which was on the Florida Keys and around the Kennedy Space Center. There were nukes in Cuba. The Cult battleships had been spotted. The long-missing remnants of the Fourth Reich Air Force had reemerged, and even the heathen Norsemen had somehow returned.

Hunter and the others listened to the report with open mouths and sinking spirits.

"None of this makes sense," Hunter finally said. "If someone wanted to destroy the space complex, the last thing they would do is send in an army of drunken slobs . . ."

"That's exactly what we thought," JT told him. "I'll bet they're trying to capture it, not destroy it . . . maybe to launch something of their own."

This sent a chill down everyone's spine. While supporting control from the space complex would be crucial for the Zon's eventual reentry, Hunter was confident he could set the spacecraft down somewhere if the complex was no longer in friendly hands. But should that be the case, it would mean that the lives of a lot of his friends and colleagues—not to mention the heart of the UAAF command—would be in peril or even dead, and that the UA's infant space program might end with exactly one flight.

"Who knows what those A-holes might be planning," JT went on. "Maybe they've been able to get into a stockpile of Arienes or . . ."

But Hunter wasn't listening anymore. His body had suddenly commenced vibrating. Somewhere in the depths of his extraordinary inner being, a message was coming through.

JT was staring at him intently—everyone on board the Zon was. They'd seen him like this before.

"Jeezus, what is it, Hawk?" JT asked him. "Another space bomb?"

Hunter slowly shook his head.

"No, not exactly," he replied.

Ben did a quick check of the forward radar set. He didn't see anything unusual—at least, not at first.

Hunter leaned forward in his seat and stared up through the Zon's top window. Way up into the perpetual dark night, he saw a tiny greenish speck of light twinkling among the stars.

"Son of gun," he whispered to himself. "Will you look at that . . ."

Inside of 30 minutes, Hunter had maneuvered the Zon to a position about 32 miles above their former orbital path.

The small green twinkling light he'd spotted was now just a mile in front of them. Everyone in the Zon had his nose pressed up against the front windshield, trying to get a better look at the strange object.

It was bulbous yet cylindrical—and as battered as the Zon, even more so. There was a miniature light on the ass end, blinking intermittently. The object was tumbling in such a way that the light caused streaks to reflect off the Zon's windshield.

"Is that what I think it is?" Elvis asked, verbalizing what the rest of the crew suspected.

"It's an old Soyuz," Hunter confirmed. "Looks like something from the seventies—or even earlier."

The Soyuz was a Russian equivalent to a cross between NASA's old Gemini capsules and the later space shuttles. Big enough to carry just two or three crew members, the Soyuz crafts were more like space taxis. In the later years, they were the means by which the

Russians sent supplies and replacement crews up to the orbiting Mir space station.

But what was this one doing up here, tumbling and obviously out of control? Something inside Hunter was telling him he should find out.

"Anyone up for stretching their legs?" he asked, unstrapping himself from his seat for the first time in more than two days.

The five other crew men looked at each other and then back at Hunter.

"You mean you're going over to that thing?" JT asked him. "How come?"

Hunter just shrugged.

"If we're going to be up here a while," he said. "I think we should get to know the neighborhood."

An hour later, Hunter and Geraci were inside two of the Zon's half-dozen EVA suits.

Bulky yet tight, the suits made them look more like deep-sea divers than two humans ready to make a space walk. Like everything else aboard the Zon, the "outdoor" spacesuits were crude and uncomfortable, and patched in more than a few places.

Geraci went through the pressure lock first. In its present state, the Zon was equipped to handle only one spacewalker at a time. Hunter waited patiently as Geraci depressurized the lock and slowly opened the hatch to space beyond. He floated away almost immediately, reappearing once he'd reached the end of his lifetether. A wave and a thumbs-up indicated everything was working.

Now it was Hunter's turn.

He slipped into the pressure lock and secured the door behind him. Working the controls from the other side, Cook and Ben set the depressurization process in

motion. Hunter could feel a slightly deflating effect on
his suit as all the air left the chamber. Then he gave a
thumbs-up to his colleagues, opened the outer hatch,
and joined Geraci in space.

Wow . . .

Now *this* was something. He was floating—though
floating wasn't really the word. He was flying, too—
though flying wasn't the right word, either. What was
it, then? He had to think about it for a moment. Then
it came to him. It sounded crazy, but he felt like he
was just another body in the universe, revolving, spinning, moving in unison with the zillion other objects
in the cosmos. A whole world unto himself.

Christ, what a feeling it was!

Almost good enough for him to forget what a miserable experience the spaceflight had been so far . . .

Geraci's somewhat frantic signaling broke Hunter
out of his self-induced space rapture.

Hunter's tether was slowly becoming entangled in
one of the many unsightly projections hanging off the
blunderbusslike Zon. He was able to retrieve the slack
before any real trouble could occur, knocking himself
upside the head twice for letting his inner senses get
the best of him.

He joined Geraci at the edge of what passed for the
Zon's payload bay. It was about two-thirds the size of
its American shuttle counterpart and much narrower.
The hardest thing in getting the Zon launchworthy after the UA captured it was getting the two big doors
of the payload bay to close and seal properly. Geraci's
engineers finally solved the problem, shaving a few
inches off the end of each door. Once closed, no one
connected with the Zon's flight wanted anything to do
with opening them up again. Hunter and Geraci had

exited through a smaller bay just forward of the unusable larger one.

Both of them had zip guns—these were the small, gas-powered, dual-jet devices that looked like elaborate coat hangers. One squeeze of the trigger expelled a stream of gas which served to propel the user along in the vacuum of space. As far as technology went, these things were old back in the 1970s. But again, the Zon experience was one of settling and using whatever resources one had at hand.

Slowly, carefully, Hunter and Geraci began their short hop over to the tumbling Soyuz, now about 500 feet away. Hunter was glad when Geraci volunteered to take this trip with him. Like the others aboard the Zon, Geraci was reliable, quick, and fearless. The added bonus was that he was also an engineer—and engineers thought differently than other humans. Hunter knew his help in getting the Soyuz to stop tumbling would be invaluable.

Using information transmitted over their helmet radios by Elvis and JT, Hunter and Geraci glided over to the spinning Russian space capsule without incident. Hunter found himself fighting off the euphoria which had gripped him when he'd first emerged from the Zon. There was business to be done here—he couldn't let anything interfere with the matter at hand, even if it was something as cool as walking in space.

They both pulled their tethers to a halt about 20 feet in front of the Soyuz. Now it was time for the real fun to begin. Geraci unhooked his lifeline and used his zip gun to get within a few meters of the Soyuz. With the NJ104 officer now so close to it, Hunter got his first good indication of the size of the space capsule. It was actually much larger than he'd thought, probably about the length of a city bus, but much thinner. It was painted lime green, with absolutely no streamlining. Up close, it looked like a Klingon warship.

Geraci pumped his zip gun again and now he was within arm's reach of the spacecraft. Another shot of jet-gas and he began spinning almost at the same pitch as the ancient Russian spacecraft. Hunter could only shake his head in admiration for the engineer. It was the old "if you can't beat 'em, join 'em" response to problem solving.

Geraci gave his zip gun one more short burst and was now spinning in synch with the Soyuz. He reached out with his left hand and grabbed hold of an antenna mount. Then his right toe snapped an equipment bay latch. In one quick motion the engineer lodged his left toe under a porthole frame and fired the zip gun once, twice, and then a third time.

Amazingly, the Soyuz stopped spinning.

But it was still a little wobbly. Hunter immediately jetted himself over to Geraci and rehooked the engineer's tether. Then, together, they pulled the huge but weightless Soyuz toward them. The resulting jerk served to stabilize the spacecraft. Soon it was floating along as evenly as they were.

Each took a deep gulp from the oxygen supply. They'd corraled the old Soyuz easily enough. Now what?

"Let's get inside," Hunter radioed over to Geraci.

They found the main door latch after about a minute of looking. Geraci ran his finger along the seal and found that it was broken. The door into the capsule was not secured. Getting in would be no problem.

Hunter radioed their intentions back to the Zon; JT and Elvis, now sitting in the one-two seats, were on guard for more space mines. Ben and Cook were still acting as the ETA coordinators.

"Whatever you do, you've got to make it quick," Ben

told them. "My flowchart tells me we can expect another bomb to go off within the next twenty minutes."

Sufficiently warned, Hunter and Geraci used pure muscle power to pry open the main hatch to the capsule. All the tumbling had bent it to the degree that its hinges no longer wanted to work. They were able to get it open wide enough for them to slip through. Taking a few moments to tie their tether lines to the nose of the capsule about six feet away, they guided themselves back to the open hatchway and prepared to go inside.

Geraci went first. It took him a few seconds to set himself correctly, but he quickly found some handholds and began climbing inside headfirst. He had to maneuver himself through the small airlock, then pass through a kind of safety tube in order to reach the crew cabin. This journey would take about two minutes in all, Hunter guessed. He began counting off the seconds as Geraci's boots disappeared from view.

Just as he reached 1:59, his headphone exploded in static.

"Jeezus, I'm here," he heard Geraci exclaim. "And wait 'til you see this . . ."

Now Hunter propelled himself inside the Soyuz, through the tiny airlock and into the safety tube. The interior looked like nothing less than the set to a science-fiction movie, and not a particularly expensive one, either.

It was very dark inside the airless space capsule. There were no interior lights or reflective material of any kind. A kind of greenish-blue powder covered everything. Hunter touched a panel with his glove and found the dust to be extremely sticky. Had smoke filled the capsule at one time, causing the odd coating? He didn't know. What was obvious was how very cluttered it was inside; all kinds of space junk was hanging from the walls, making it very cramped and hard to maneuver around. Still, Hunter pressed on.

He could see Geraci's boots suspended beneath the porthole which led up to the Soyuz flight compartment. Hunter inched his way up to them, feeling more uncomfortable with each passing second. Should an emergency arise—like a space mine going off nearby, or if the Soyuz began tumbling again—this was not the place to be. It was an odd sensation, being claustrophobic in outer space. But that's exactly how Hunter felt.

It took him at least another minute to claw his way through the safety tube, but at last Hunter found himself climbing up into the flight compartment. That's when he saw what had caused Geraci to call out.

Skeletons. There were three of them. They were still in their space suits, still strapped into their seats. But the faces behind the glass of the helmets were devoid of skin and muscles, leaving only skull and bones and teeth. They looked like they'd been picked clean by some kind of flesh-eating scavenger, but the more likely explanation was that a lack of oxygen inside the capsule had caused their skin to dry up and turn into minute specks of powder which were somehow dispersed in every direction around the capsule. This, Hunter was sure, explained the presence of the ghastly dust everywhere.

"Hell of a way to go," Geraci said. "However they went, that is . . ."

Hunter could only agree. One man's hands were grasping his throat; another's were cemented to his air supply regulator. Clues, Hunter surmised, that a sudden, unexpected depressurization had caused the demise of the three nameless spacemen.

"But when?" Geraci asked, reading his mind.

It was a good question—and one that was difficult to answer. Soyuz capsules began service decades before.

For all they knew, this incident could have taken place back in the sixties or seventies, a space flight that went bad and was covered up by the Russian government. Then again, these cosmonauts could have died the day before, or the day before that. The whole concept of time, aging, and decomposition did not apply in the same way out here in space. Whether this happened recently or back more than 30 years ago, the capsule and the stiffs would still look pretty much the same.

Hunter reached over and unstrapped one of the dead spacemen, allowing the weightless corpse to float free. Beneath his seat was a radio device which Hunter retrieved and studied. It looked to be something made during the 1930s, and not in any era of spaceflight. It was a tantalizing piece of equipment, but it gave them no clue as to when the spacemen had died—or under what circumstances.

There was still a little bit of electricity aboard the spacecraft—the tiny light on its rear end was still blinking. But again, this did not provide anything. Fuel cells could go on for years, especially if they were maintaining a small load. But juice on the inside might mean that some of the other instruments could be brought back to life and possibly salvaged to help maintain the Zon.

Hunter was about to push the flight computer power panel when suddenly he felt a familiar vibration rise up inside him.

"Damn," he whispered. "This is not a good time . . ."

Their helmet radios crackled to life an instant later. Cook was on the line.

"You guys better get your rear ends back here now," he told them. "JT just spotted another mine . . ."

* * *

As it turned out, JT had discovered not one but two space mines.

One was orbiting in approximately the same flight path as the Zon had been before moving up 30 miles to inspect the Soyuz. But the second mine was perilously close—less than a half mile below their present position.

Hunter and Geraci scrambled out of the Soyuz as fast they could, all curiosity as to how the spacecraft came to be tumbling out here with its ghoulish cargo now forgotten. Cook gave them continual radio updates on the location of both space mines even as they emerged from the hatch and began undoing one of the tethers from the Russian spacecraft. The lower mine would probably pass by without affecting them. But the upper bomb—well, that would be a different story.

"We read it as coming into a complementary orbit in less than four minutes," Cook was telling them urgently. "Better speed it up, guys . . ."

Hunter and Geraci needed no prompting. To save time, they left one tether tied to the Soyuz and shared the other to make their way back to the Zon. They were now streaking toward the mother ship as fast as their zip guns would carry them.

"Three minutes," Cook said, as they arrived back at the Zon. "Two and fifty-five . . . hurry!"

But moving quickly in space was impossible. Hunter and Geraci had reached the Zon's hatchway, all right, but now the simple task of undoing the tether and getting the pressure lock to work seemed to take hours, with every moment performed in painfully slow motion.

"We'll be in its track in one minute, fifty seconds," Cook was telling them as the bawky hatch finally snapped open. "One minute forty-five . . ."

Hunter had to practically shove Geraci inside the air-lock; it would hold only one person at a time. The engineer reluctantly went in, headfirst—and then had to stay that way for a long agonizing minute as the primitive pressurization system slowly filled the lock with oxygen.

Hunter, meanwhile, was turned somersaults just outside the hatchway, trying to position his body this way and that in order to get a visual track on the space mine. He finally did catch a glimpse of it. It was indeed about a half mile below them and maybe two miles out. Like everything else around him, it was moving slowly, but spinning in such a way as to deteriorate its orbit—and get closer to the Zon.

"You got about one minute, Hawk," Cook's voice told him, just as the pressurization seal light came on. Now, at least Geraci was inside. But how could Hunter get into the pressure lock, wait for it to repressurize, then get into the Zon itself, climb out of his ETA suit, get up to the flight deck, take over the controls, and get them away from the space mine all before it went off?

The answer was, he couldn't. There just wouldn't be enough time.

On this one, the evasive maneuvers would have to be done by someone else.

It was Elvis in the commander's seat when the light flashed on the control panel indicating that Hunter was inside the pressure lock and that the hatch was locked and sealed behind him.

Well, at least Hunter was safe, he thought. But now they had less than 30 seconds to evade the oncoming space mine. That was not enough time for any of the elaborate, ballet-like maneuvers that Hunter had instituted when encountering the previous orbital bombs. Those precise movements had been choreographed in such a way as not to call attention to the Zon while maintaining their orbital path. But now, with every second important, Elvis knew only blunt, evasive action could save them.

Luckily for them, he was the man to do it.

Elvis had been at the controls of the Zon spacecraft for its five previous flights, all of which had been taken under duress at the hands of Viktor and his minions. As such, he knew how to finesse the creaking spaceship and how to kick it in the ass. Right now, it was the latter that was needed.

So as soon as he knew Hunter was safely on-board, Elvis fired the Zon's main engine, and at the same time, commanded the steering jets to point the spacecraft's nose straight up. There was a tremendous burst of power felt by everyone on-board. There was also a disturbing buckling sound—once again, it felt like the whole spacecraft was about to come apart at the seams.

But Elvis stayed with it, slowly backing off the throttles as the Zon zoomed away from the orbital bomb. A few seconds later, the mine went off, not a kilometer away from where the Zon had been just moments before. The shock wave hit the spacecraft five seconds later, shaking it from nose to stern and back again. The electricity failed; then the computers crashed. The vibrations got so bad, the zero-gravity toilet flushed itself. But finally the violent rattling died away. The electricity blinked back on. The computers regained their previous whir. Everyone breathed a sigh of relief. They had survived yet another space blast.

JT and Geraci immediately hurried aft to get Hunter out of the pressure lock. Elvis and Cook righted the Zon again as Ben began backtracking the space bomb's orbital path. He noticed something odd on the radar.

Somehow the Soyuz space capsule had followed them up their escape route and was now tumbling dangerously close to their nose.

"Jeezus, look at that!" Cook yelled, as the oddly-shaped green spacecraft came back into view.

The Soyuz was spinning in such a way that everything not strapped down inside it was now spewing out into space. This included one of the cosmonaut's skeletal bodies which was suddenly ejected through the main hatchway.

As they all watched in horror, the dead cosmonaut suddenly became entangled in the tether line Hunter and Geraci had left tied to the Soyuz—so that's how the Russian capsule had followed them up! But now, with uncanny movements, the ghostly spacemen began climbing up the lifeline right toward the Zon itself.

"God damn," Elvis breathed. "This is too much . . ."

It took only a few seconds for the skeleton to make its way up the tether and bump against the front of the Zon. The force of that collision then caused it to topple over the snout and lodge right up against the front window.

Suddenly, the dead cosmonaut was staring right in at them.

"God damn!" Elvis cried again. "Damn, this is *way* too much!"

The cosmonaut's mask was open and his teeth were bared. He was jiggling in such a way, it appeared as if he was laughing hysterically at them.

"Do something!" Ben yelled over at Elvis—but the pilot was already taking action. He fired a side maneuvering jet and the sudden movement dislodged the body and sent it spinning off into space forever. One second it was there, the next it was gone.

Elvis, Ben, and Cook just stared at each other in disbelief. It was as if they'd all just shared the same nightmare.

The words Cook had heard on the strange radio broadcast the day before came back to him.

"The dead shall rise and they will mock you," the voice had said. "And then it will be your time to die . . ."

Sixteen

There was still a column of ugly black smoke rising above the northern end of the Kennedy Space Center when the six F-86 Sabre jets pulled on to the main runway and prepared to take-off.

Despite the pall from the previous night's battle, it was a crystal-clear morning; the sun was about 20 minutes from rising and the sky was brightening quickly. The half-dozen Sabre jets, their engines now at full growl, were about to embark on a recon flight which would take them down to the southern tip of UA Florida and back to Cape Canaveral again. Their mission: to look for signs of any "belligerent naval activity" moving toward the KSC from the south. The Sabres were being sent out to search for any Cult battleships that might be in the area.

A recent acquisition from the Empire of Peru, the Sabres had been extensively refurbished by Jeff and George Kephart of Sky High Spies Inc., the same company that operated the world's last remaining SR-71 hypersonic spy plane. Instead of the antique J47-GE-17 power plant originally installed on the Sabres, the Kepharts put a balls-out J79-GE-11A 15,000-pound thrust afterburner engine in each F-86, the same power plant found on the old yet speedy F-104 Starfighter.

These engines gave the Sabres speed and power their original designers could only have dreamed about. Also removed were the airplanes' inadequate armaments. Instead of a single .50 nose-mounted machine gun, the Sabres were given two M60 aerial cannons attached by pods to the underbelly. Hard points were also installed on the reinforced underwings, allowing the F-86s to carry a variety of ordnance, including antiship, anti-tank and air-to-air anti-aircraft missiles.

Once their equipment rehab was completed, the Sabres were painted in bright silver with red trim and detailing around the nose intake and rear stabilizer. When finished, the six jets looked like aerial hot rods. The Kepharts sold them to the UAAF for a song. Their only request was that the Sabres be handled by a specialist maintenance crew and that the Kepharts themselves be allowed to fly them once in a while. The UAAF high command readily agreed.

The first action the Sabres saw was during the mass suicide attack by the mysterious army of Norsemen the previous night. Loaded with full cannon pods and a wide array of ground ordnance, the F-86s had bombed and strafed the attackers on the fringes of the battlefield while the three huge C-5 gunships concentrated on the main enemy force in the middle. Despite their small role, the rehabbed Sabres had given a good accounting of themselves, proving an airplane could look sharp and still perform well in combat.

This recon mission out over the Atlantic would be a little less strenuous on the Sabre jets and their pilots—or so it was hoped. Ever since the fleet of Asian Mercenary Cult battleships had been spotted off the Florida Keys, the UA command had been garnering all its recce elements in an attempt to locate the elusive enemy fleet. Because of the attack the night before, this effort was redoubled since a follow-up Cult attack

on the KSC seemed like a real possibility. And though
the Sabres were not your typical recon plane, the way
things were going, every little bit would help.

For this mission, the Sabre flight would first head
east out over the Atlantic, then turn south over Grand
Bahama Island, then southwest to an area off Key
Largo. Once there, they would land and refuel at an
auxilliary UAAF naval station, then make the return
flight to Cape Canaveral. In all, the entire mission
would cover just 320 miles. For radio purposes, the collection of Sabres would be known as Flight 19.5.

Two of the airplanes were fitted with dual seats and
dual controls; these planes also carried extra navigation
equipment on board. The other four Sabres were hauling heavy weapons, including one Harpoon antiship
missile apiece. Leading the flight in one of the two-
seaters was a UAAF lieutenant named Taylor
"Chuckie" Charles. A veteran of the war against the
Fourth Reich and a pilot in the UAAF's 1st Aerial Expeditionary Force, which had deployed to Vietnam the
year before, Charles was known as a level-headed, com-
petent officer and an extraordinary flyer. He was due
for a promotion to Captain as soon as this mission was
completed.

The six airplanes took off without incident. The
weather was surprisingly crisp for August, and the worst
of the heat had yet to hit the Florida coastline. The
flight reached its first vector point just 13 minutes after
take-off. Because the armed recon mission was being
undertaken in strict security, a near-total radio blackout
was mandatory. Still, as per the mission paper, Charles's
back-seat systems man sent a brief message to Kennedy
Control that the six Sabres had reached their first objective and were now turning south.

The radio blackout was reimposed, to be broken only
after Flight 19.5 reached its second objective, the

northwestern tip of Grand Bahama Island, or if it spotted any sign of the Cult battleships.

But shortly after the radio man reported this first position check, another message came in from Flight 19.5. It was received by air controllers both in the Kennedy Space Center main control tower and the tower at the old Banana River Naval Air Station nearby.

The radio message was unclear and broken up in transmission—this was the first sign of trouble. Though garbled, it sounded like the radio man was saying, "We seem to be off course. We cannot see land. Repeat: we cannot see land . . ."

This was very strange. If Flight 19.5 was following its flight plan correctly, none of its pilots would be *expected* to see land, as they would be flying too low and too far out to sea. Also disturbing was the fact that the second radio transmission had been sent unscrambled and on the Sabre flight's main frequency, not its emergency one.

Both control towers attempted to send a coded message back to the Sabre jets telling them in effect to shut up and go on a scramble line if they had to talk to the base control. Whether these messages were simply ignored by Flight 19.5 or not received at all, would never be determined. The only thing for certain was the radio man continued broadcasting on an open and unscrambled line.

"We are not sure of our position," came his second message from Flight 19.5. "We cannot be sure of where we are. We seem to be lost . . ."

At this point, air traffic controllers at both the space center and Banana River were beginning to think they were being targeted for some monstrous practical joke. It was nearly impossible for Flight 19.5 to be lost—they were just 20 minutes' flying time from the coast, 10 minutes or less if they all went to afterburners. Plus it was still a clear morning; the sun was obviously still rising in the east. Even if every one of their navigation devices went wrong, the Sabre pilots could simply position themselves with the sun on their left and then fly to the right and reach land. But even this simple solution to their problem seem to elude them.

"Everything is wrong," said the third transmission from Flight 19.5's radioman. "Everything is strange. We are not sure of any direction. Even the ocean doesn't look as it should."

At this moment, another UA aircraft was landing at Banana River. Its pilot happened to be a friend of Charles, the Flight 19.5 flight leader, and he'd overheard the Sabre jets' trouble calls.

Breaking in on the unscrambled line, this pilot radioed a message directly to Charles. "Give me your altitude," he said. "I'll fly south and meet you . . ."

This should have been a welcome message for Charles and the Sabre jets, yet it was not answered for five minutes. When the helpful UA pilot, who was presently flying in a C-130 cargo plane, sent the message again, a person that many people would come to believe was Charles himself came on the line. He said: "Don't come after me. They look like . . ."

Then there was nothing but silence.

By this time, 6:40 A.M., the KSC controllers had notified UA command of the problem with Flight 19.5. When apprised of the peculiar situation, the first thought in many minds was that the radio transmissions were actually coming from an enemy source, in an effort to have the UA reveal its coding procedures. This was a long shot, though—how would the Cult or any other potential enemy know exactly where and when the Sabres were going or that the UA would fall for such an obvious ploy, unless there was an enemy spy at the space complex, a highly unlikely possibility.

And if a spy *was* the culprit and the enemy *had* penetrated the UA's multilevel security apparatus, then learning something like the standard combat mission radio codes would seem like small potatoes.

What was happening with Flight 19.5?

The last transmission from the Sabre jets came at 6:53 A.M., less than an hour after they took off. The tapes revealed the voice of Lieutenant Charles, apparently speaking to the other pilots in the flight.

"All planes close up tight," Charles was heard saying. "If we don't see landfall in thirty minutes, we'll be forced to ditch . . ."

This message set off bells at KSC control tower. Had the level-headed Charles suddenly gone mad? Ditch six of the most valuable jets in the UA arsonnel? For what?

The controllers knew immediately that some kind of rescue plane had to be dispatched and had to reach the lost Sabre flight. Just the plane to do such a job and do it quickly was anchored off the Banana River station. It was the jet-powered Seamaster flying boat, all fixed and patched after its scary encounter off the Florida Keys.

But who would fly it? This mission called for someone who could gather a crew, get out to where the Sabres supposedly were, and lead them back to base safely, and under the highest security conditions. And do it damn quickly.

That's why when the KSC controllers asked UA command who they should send, the UA command suggested they sent Lieutenant Stan Yastrewski, the guy everyone called "Yaz."

He was asleep when he got the call.

Having spent the night before flying shotgun in the huge Galaxy gunship and then all of the next day in post-battle debriefings, Yaz was worn out by the time his head hit the pillow on the bunk in his VAB office just a few short hours before.

The buzzing of the radiophone next to his cot intermingled with a dream he was having about watching huge waves hit a beach he'd seen many times before but whose name he could not remember. The waves were landing with mighty crashing sounds until one came in and buzzed when it hit. Then another. And another.

By the fourth one, Yaz was aware and fumbling for the phone.

It was General Jones himself on the other end. His voice sounded tired and weary—he too had been up for the past 48 hours, once again trying to stage-manage the UAAF's latest crisis. He quickly explained the situation to Yaz, who, while still drowsy, thought for a moment that he was back in his dream. Six Sabre jets missing? Only 50 miles or so offshore? Can't get them on the radio? Why weren't they listening?

"Our rear ends are up to it, as usual," Jones told him. "And you're my best go-to guy. So get a crew together, get that flying ocean liner in the air, and find those guys—quick."

And with that, Jones hung up.

It took Yaz exactly two minutes to climb into his flight uniform, call over to base ops, and get an air crew together. He spent another three driving like a wild man over to Banana River, where the immense Seamaster was waiting.

Six minutes after getting the call from Jones, he was standing on the dock next to the huge seaplane. Yaz was somewhat familiar with the big amphibian; he'd flown on one of its sea trials after it had been refurbished the first time. It really was a beautiful airplane, the early morning sun gleaming off its dark blue paint job as it bobbed in the choppy waters of the Banana estuary. There were many red-paint patches apparent on the fuselage, though, and especially up and down the gangling wings and around the cockpit. The Seamaster had survived its encounter down around the Florida Keys several days before in relatively good shape, considering its advanced age. However, Yaz could not get over the impression that the red paint patches looked like gunshot wounds that were still bleeding.

The crew was already aboard when he climbed through the top hatch. It would be a skeleton one at that. Just a pilot—a guy named Burns—a navigator and flight engineer. All high-tech weaponry had been removed from its flight compartment, most of it had been destroyed in the battle off the Keys. This made the cockpit seem almost too big, too comfortable. A small but visible swatch of dried blood was still evident on the flight deck floor, a reminder that one man had died and two were seriously injured on-board the plane just a few days ago.

The Seamaster's jets were already purring when Yaz appeared; Burns had the big plane taxiing out onto the Banana even before Yaz climbed into the copilot's chair. The seat was obviously older and less comfortable than the one he'd ridden for seven hours the night before inside the Galaxy gunship. Hopefully he wouldn't be strapped into this one quite so long.

Burns had the seaplane up to speed and off the water within 30 seconds, a remarkable job, considering he'd only flown the big jet once before, and that had been several months ago. The huge airplane bullied its way into the sky, its long wings flapping with amazing flexibility as it clawed for altitude, its shoulder-mounted engines screaming.

No sooner were they up when Burns put the plane

on its left wing and pointed the nose out toward the ocean. A quick radio report back to base ops told the air controllers that everything aboard the big plane was working perfectly.

It was now 7:05 A.M.

In addition to the huge Seamaster, there were several seaborne UAAF units looking for the missing Sabre jets.

One of these was the USS *Marconi*, a counterintelligence radio ship transitting down to the troubled UA Florida area from the Chesapeake Bay. Actually a converted fishing trawler with a reinforced hull and an elevated superstructure, the *Marconi* was bristling with radio antennas, satellite dishes, and deck weapons, including a Harpoon antiship missile launcher. The *Marconi* was in essence a spy vessel. Its communications gear could not only send strong, clear messages from anywhere in the world, it could also listen in on radio transmissions, pull down unfriendly TV broadcasts, and, under the right conditions, decipher scrambled enemy codes on the spot. Its crew of 34 were highly trained, highly motivated members of the SSSQ, the UAAF's version of the old Navy SEALS. Some of them had been involved in combat situations dating back to the UA's wars against the Mid-Aks and the supercriminals of the Family of Chicago. They were considered to be among the best of the many elite units within the UAAF.

Strange, then, what happened when they joined the search for the lost Sabre flight.

The *Marconi* was about 62 miles off the coast of Cape Canaveral when the Sabre jets made their last message to the Kennedy Space Center air controllers. The spy ship was in the middle of an extensive equipment test-out before moving further south to the Florida Keys and beyond. All its radio receivers and sending gear were in perfect working condition. All of the crew were on duty and at their posts.

Because the *Marconi* was the UA vessel closest to the last reported position of the Sabre jets, the KSC air controllers made contact with the spy ship and asked for its help in locating the wayward airplanes. Had the *Marconi* seen the Sabre jets? Yes, they had. The six airplanes had shown up on the ship's air-search radar about 15 minutes before. At that time they were heading east, further out into the Atlantic, rather than south, as they were supposed to. Had they made radio contact with the airplanes? Again, they had. The *Marconi* had sent a routine radio check to the jet fighters, scambled and coded, and the flight leader had returned the call.

He'd reported all was proceeding normally.

This was baffling to the KSC controllers because when the *Marconi* said they'd talked with the Sabre jets, the six airplanes had already been "missing" for nearly 10 minutes, when they'd had their last radio transmission to the KSC controllers. The Sabre jets were obviously off course, yet they told the spy ship that everything was fine.

Even more puzzling was a radio transmission the *Marconi* intercepted about five minutes after their encounter with the Sabre jets. It was an order from the Sabre jet flight leader to his men to "arm all weapons immediately, form up, and descend gradually toward the target . . ."

So now a new twist had been added. The Sabre jets had spotted something. Something big. Big enough for the flight leader to get his men to quickly arm all weapons and go into an attack mode.

But what could it have been? What would cause the

Sabre jet flight leader to do all this without even attempting to call someone, whether it be the controllers
at KSC or anyone else, to report his actions?

There really was only one earthly explanation: the
Sabre jets had spotted one of the Cult battleships.

It was now 7:25 A.M.

At the request of the Kennedy Space Center air controllers, the USS *Marconi* began steaming east toward
the last reported position of the Sabre jets. Meanwhile,
the huge Seamaster flying boat was heading for the
same area at full throttle. The KSC controllers provided
a secure channel through which the aerial amphibian
and the spy ship could communicate. They'd made
their first contact at 7:22.

The Seamaster was still about 30 miles west of the
Marconi when Yaz reached the spy ship's communications officer. After double-scrambling the line, the ship
officer told Yaz about the last report from the Sabre
jets, and how the aircraft had been ordered into an
attack mode by their flight leader. The theory that the
Sabres had spotted a Cult battleship was discussed
briefly. Yaz was convinced that was exactly what had
happened; the *Marconi*'s communications officer wasn't
so sure. If something as immense as a battleship was
within 100 miles of the *Marconi*, surely its powerful,
over-the-horizon, sea-search radar would have picked it
up. At the very least, something in its array of sound
detection gear would have been tripped. These were
devices that could "hear" an unamplified conversation
from 250 miles away under the right conditions. Something as noisy as a 55,000-ton battleship would certainly
have been detected.

But nothing had been.

By 7:40, the Seamaster was in sight of the *Marconi*.

Many members of the crew took a moment to go up on deck to see the huge flying jet boat pass over. Even among to the SSSQ combat veterans aboard the spy ship, this was a first. To a man they stood, mouths open in awe, as the immense aircraft streaked over, engines roaring, not 500 feet above them. It wagged its wings once and continued east into a thick cloud bank that had suddenly materialized out on the horizon.

It would be the last time anyone would see the huge Seamaster again.

What would be the last series of radio calls from the flying boat reached the *Marconi* at 7:55, about 15 minutes after the Seamaster had passed over the ship.

The big seajet had reached the area where the Sabre jets had reportedly been preparing to attack something on the surface. After the Seamaster had broken through some low weather, they too reported spotting a huge vessel.

"It's enormous," came the report from the flying boat. "It's got to be at least nine hundred feet long. Twin stacks. With a lot of rigging on the foredeck and midships . . ."

The description sent the radio men aboard the *Marconi* scrambling through the computer files. The spy ship had a profile of just about every ship roaming the seas these days, including all the Cult battleships and attending vessels. But the report of this ship spotted by the Seamaster must have been in error, at least with regard to its length. Nine hundred feet was much too long for any current vessel; even the largest Cult battleship was only about 750 feet long. And what was all that about rigging and twin stacks?

"We're in orbit at fifteen hundred feet above this vessel now," came the next report from the Seamaster.

"Previous length estimate might be a little off, but this ship is very large. Very long, with what looks to be steel girder scaffolding running about two-thirds its length. It has twin stacks far aft and an odd superstructure far forward. It appears to be very old . . ."

By this time, the intelligence officers aboard the *Marconi* had already completed a speed search of their computer files and had found nothing anywhere near the description they were hearing from the Seamaster. Baffled, they began a manual search, typing in bits of information they were receiving from the flying boat and hoping that their powerful computer would soon find a match. But after two minutes of this, still nothing came up.

"This vessel is heading north at twenty-two knots," came the third radio message from the Seamaster. "We have attempted radio contact with it but have received no reply. We cannot see any evidence of Flight nineteen-point-five. No oil slicks, no sign that any combat took place here. We are continuing to circle and maintain observation . . ."

At this point, one of the radio officers aboard the *Marconi* made contact with the KSC air controllers and filled them in on what they were hearing from the Seamaster. The KSC men told the *Marconi* that they had lost all contact with the flying boat about 20 minutes before, or just after it had passed over the spy ship. They then asked if the *Marconi* had picked up this mysterious ship on its radar or sound-detection systems. The *Marconi* replied that it had not.

That's when the last radio call from the Seamaster reached the spy ship.

"This vessel is acting in a very odd fashion," it began. "We can see crewmen on the deck, we are flying very low now, at five hundred feet, and they don't seem to see or recognize us. We are hailing them with navigation lights, but there is no response. Ship is flying an old American flag. Repeat. Ship is under sail with old American stars-and-stripes. It doesn't look like a fifty-star field, either . . ."

Then, finally, "We're going in further, to get a closer look. Stand by . . ."

Then all contact with the Seamaster was lost.

The radio officers aboard the *Marconi* tried frantically for the next 30 minutes to raise the flying boat, to no avail. Even when air controllers at KSC joined in, hailing the Seamaster on a number of open frequencies, there was no response. It was numbing experience and more than a little frightening. In the course of 90 minutes, seven UAAF aircraft had been lost in clear weather under very mysterious circumstances.

When the *Marconi* finally reached the area where both the Seamaster and Flight 19.5 had made their last reports, it could find no evidence of any of the aircraft—or of the mysterious ship that they both must have seen.

The spy ship would stay on station for the next two hours. Seven more search and rescue aircraft were dispatched from Banana River, but none found any trace of the Sabres or the huge flying boat.

Word of the bizarre disappearances swept the KSC very quickly. Shock and dismay followed. All UA military facilities up and down the East Coast were put on alert. The loss of all the pilots, and especially Yaz, was taken very hard at UA joint command. General Jones, in particular, was devastated.

Only later would he receive a top-secret report generated from the maritime files kept aboard the USS *Marconi*. Its search computer had finally found a match based on the description of the mysterious ship given in the last reports from the Seamaster.

The computer identified it as the USS *Cyclops,* a U.S. Navy collier, a ship designed to carry coal.

It had left Barbados with a load of manganese ore in March of 1918—and was never seen again.

Seventeen

Cape Cod

The storm raging off Nauset Beach had reached a new level of ferocity by midnight.

It had been determined by the UAAF weather station up in Boston that the powerful hurricane that had swept the mid-Atlantic had suddenly stopped and was now swirling in place about 150 miles off the coast of southern Massachusetts.

This lack of movement was called the "Felix Effect," after a similar hurricane of that name had parked itself off the American East Coast for several days years ago before finally moving off and dissipating. Knowing that opposing high and low pressure fronts were responsible for stalling the storm, the UA weathermen were at a loss as to how long the hurricane would be battering Cape Cod and the nearby islands. In any case, they didn't expect any significant change in the next 48 to 72 hours.

The storm had already blacked out most of Cape Cod. The electrical service, never the most stable to begin with, had failed up and down the peninsula a long time before. Now the only lights seen through the wind and rain were those being powered by emergency generators inside the handful of coastal military installations. Everyone else was relying on candlepower or nothing at all.

It was particularly dark inside Skyfire, the farmhouse atop Nauset Heights.

The lights had failed completely around dusk after a long windy, rainy day in which the electricity had been blinking on and off intermittently. Frost was sitting on the overstuffed couch in the tiny front room, his knees shaking, his stomach aching from indigestion, dehydration, and stress. He was holding a lit candle, his fingers cupped around it, trying to keep the flame alive in the drafts blowing through the porous farmhouse.

Outside the wind was howling, the rain fierce. The lightning and thunder had been constant since morning. There were at least five other people in the house, but Frost wasn't too sure exactly where any of them was. He'd been spooked ever since his ethereal encounter up in Gander, and with the long trip down here and the strange events since—well, he felt lucky just to be sitting here, breathing normally and thinking in a somewhat rational way.

His knees were shaking, though, and that had never happened to him before. He'd been in air combat many times; he'd faced down some of the most bloodthirsty air pirates during his days as a Sky Marshal; he'd survived the siege and battle at Khe Sanh during the most recent war in Vietnam. During all that and more, his knees had never shaken. Oddly, this bothered him the most.

He was a professional soldier, and as such, he knew when adversity struck it was always best to consider what the hell was wrong and then lay out contingencies to fix the problem.

What was wrong?

He was sitting in a haunted house, that's what was

wrong. Upstairs, in the main bedroom, were four ghosts. Or at least, Frost thought they were ghosts. Actually, they were the four young girls Dominique had first shown him shortly after his arrival. How did they get to Skyfire? They didn't know. Where did they come from? They weren't sure of that either. Only the oldest girl had talked, and that was briefly to Dominique, after she'd discovered the four sitting in the bedroom. This girl, who was missing part of her bathing suit at the time, told Dominique that she and her friends had been playing on a beach somewhere when suddenly, they woke up to find themselves inside the bedroom, crying, sunburned, and very lost. They had said nothing ever since.

And now Frost was sitting here, trying to keep the candle going and think about something other than the thunder and lightning and wind and the girls upstairs and his own frightening experience that had caused him to come here in the first place. He could only wish this was all a dream and that he would soon wake up in his bed up at Gander and he could blame the meal brought to him by the overly helpful enlisted man. But even then, Frost knew he would have a problem. If this was a dream and he was dreaming of the children upstairs, then that meant a maelstrom of bad luck would soon be coming his way. His grandmother had told him years ago that it was bad luck to dream about children, especially young girls. Either way, Frost had decided, he was in for some bad times.

There was another thing his grandmother had told him, suspicious old windbag that she was. But this one had stuck with Frost, too, mostly because his grandfather, a stately man of regal European stock, had concurred when he'd told him about it. The world will go a little crazy just before it comes to an end, Grandma had said. Things will go just a little off-kilter; Nature will short-circuit a bit before the Final Day. This way, she'd claimed, everyone who'd been good enough to get into heaven could start packing their spiritual bags for the trip. In fact, these good souls would begin disappearing even before Doomsday arrived. Yes, that will be a nightmare for the missing persons bureau! Grandpa had said.

And what will happen to the rest of the people, Granny? What will happen to the ones who weren't so good, the ones left behind while all the true believers suddenly started disappearing? Granny had put it this way: where they were going, there would be no need to pack a bag.

These were the disturbing retrograde thoughts that were flying around in Frost's head. The candle kept teasing him, seemingly going out, only to flare up briefly just as soon as he'd begin to panic. The wind grew worse, if that was possible, as did the rain. The old house was creaking so much now, Frost's ears were beginning to sting. Christ, didn't Hunter do *any* work on this place while he was here?

Apparently not.

There was a crack of lightning followed by a particularly sharp crash of thunder. It sounded like a small nuclear device going off. This time Frost's candle did go out for good, leaving him alone in the suddenly dark room. Now it was more than his knees that were shaking. From above he heard another crash, as if someone had just fallen. Then, more pounding and tumbling sounds from upstairs.

Where was Dominique? She'd left the house sometime before—to get candles, he thought. Or was it to take in the hay? Had she returned? Frost wasn't sure.

Another crash from upstairs; another bolt of lightning, illuminating everything outside and nothing inside. What was going on upstairs? Were those ghostly kids still up there? Were they in trouble? A shiver the likes of which he'd never felt before went through Frost. He heard a scream—high, short, shrill. It was one of the kids. They *were* in some kind of trouble. And that meant he would have to go up those stairs and try to help them.

He stood up, surprised he could, his legs were shaking so much. He had no weapon, no gun or even a knife, to take with him. All those things had been left back in Gander. Whatever he was about to do, he would have to do it unarmed.

He took a few tentative steps toward the stairway— that's when heard another scream, followed by some whimpering. Something bad was happening up there, Frost knew. Despite his almost pathetic condition, he knew he had to get up there and see what it was.

Somehow, he found the gumption to put his foot on the first stair and start climbing. It was pitch black at the top of the stairs, and Frost couldn't get over the dreadful feeling that he was really ascending into some kind of black hole, a void from which nothing could escape, not even light.

He stopped about halfway up, using the excuse that he should allow his eyes to adapt to the darkness. But in the next short breath he knew this was bullshit: he'd been sitting in the near-dark for hours, and this was as good as his eyes were ever going to get.

Still, he stayed frozen on the fifth creaky step, wondering just when the hell it was that he lost his manhood. Where did the courage to drive a jet fighter through the sky in pursuit of some dangerous enemy go? What happened to the balls he'd needed to stick it out under the falling shells at Khe Sanh? Now he couldn't even walk up the stairs in the dark.

Another tiny scream. And now more crying, somewhat muffled. Frost sucked it up and went up the last five stairs as fast as he could, which was still somewhat slow. Finally he reached the landing and was confronted with the closed door which led into the bedroom where the mysterious children had first appeared.

Sure, all the goody-two-shoes will start disappearing from the face of the Earth and they will ride up into the clouds—but what the hell had Granny told him about people suddenly disappearing and popping up in other places? Nothing that he could recall. With a shaking hand, Frost reached out and nudged the door open. The whimpering got a little louder.

The four girls were sitting on the bed in the exact same positions as when he'd last seen them. Only one of them, the oldest, looked up at him. The others seemed to be terrified and mesmerized at the same time, their eyes glued on the closet door, which was just an arm's reach away from the foot of the old four-poster bed.

Two of these girls were crying; the third, who was the youngest, was in such a state, she was having a hard time just catching her breath. Frost was beyond trembling at this point. He'd never been so scared in his life. Another bolt of lightning. Another crash of thunder outside. All four girls jumped at the tremendous sound. But this is not what was scaring them.

Whatever was doing that, was behind the closet door.

Frost looked at the older girl and she pointed first to the door and then, to the floor at the bottom of it. A puddle of water was forming under the door itself. Something inside the closet was dripping wet.

Frost took two very small steps into the room and found himself within reach of the door. This was the moment of truth. These kids looked as if the devil was in the closet, and now Frost had taken it upon himself to find out exactly what it was and do battle with it, if necessary.

Maybe he hadn't lost all his courage after all, he thought, as his shaking right hand grabbed hold of the doorknob.

He gave it a twist even as he caught a whiff of seawater in his nose. Then he pulled it open . . .

Suddenly he found himself letting out a little yelp. There was a man inside the closet. He was dripping wet. His eyes were closed, yet his mouth was moving. He was dressed in a soaking flight suit and still had a radio wire and an oxygen mask draped across his chest.

Frost felt his eyes go wide and his jaw drop. He was certain he was inside a nightmare now because he recognized the man in the closet even as he fell forward into his shaking arms.

It was Yaz.

Eighteen

It was on the thirteenth orbit of the fourth day in space when the Zon's first and second GPC computers finally failed.

It was not an unexpected event. Just 20 inches long and about 10 inches high and wide, the 60-pound GPCs (general purpose computers) were the brains of the Zon's operations. They were the reason the spacecraft could launch, get into orbit, stay there, and, if everything was still together, reenter the atmosphere and return to earth. They were, in effect, the remote control unit for the spacecraft, the highly advanced autopilot.

But the GPCs had been working on overload ever since the flight had begun. With all the violent maneuvering to avoid the space mines, and the constant need to switch back and forth between automatic and manual control, GPC 1 and 2 just couldn't take the strain. Like endlessly turning a light bulb on and off, the wear and tear finally got the best of them.

They blinked out just as the Zon had come around from the dark side of the planet on 13-4. A warning buzzer came on momentarily, followed by two flashing panels on the main control board. Geraci was up on the flight deck at the time. He pushed the flashing panels to off and reset the warning buzzer. There were five GPCs on-board the Zon; 3 and 4 were primarys, 5 was the back-up. Theoretically, the spacecraft could run on just one—but that was a situation no one wanted to face.

Failing computers were not the only problem facing the Zon crew. Two maneuvering jets, both on the right side of the spacecraft, had also failed; either they were clogged with frozen fuel residue, or all the wild maneuvering had killed them, too. Then there were the warning lights that kept popping concerning the integrity of the main engine systems—these were the things of nightmares. Everything else aboard the battered spacecraft could be working perfectly, but if the main engines didn't fire when they were supposed to, then the Zon and everyone on board would be stuck in space forever.

Oddly, though, Geraci and the others had come to view these main engine warning lights as glitches—each time one came on, Geraci would run a diagnostic program on the main engines and everything would come back green. The only logical conclusion was that the problem lay inside the warning lights. But no one wanted to go in and start pulling them apart. What would happen if one of *them* broke? So they lived with nagging blinking lights—and the frightening possibility that at any time the warning light might be true and the heart of the Zon might indeed fail, condemning them all to a slow, gruesome, airless death.

They had just completed 13-4 and were moving into 14-4 when they finally saw it.

Elvis was in the jumpseat; Hunter was at the controls. Ben had just completed another in what seemed like a never-ending series of probability/location profiles

on the space mines when his navigation computer began blinking. He looked over at JT, who was fretting
in the seat next to him, and they in turn looked at
Hunter.

For the first time in a long time, the Wingman had
a smile on his face.

"Son of a bitch," he was whispering, "There it
is . . ."

Way off in the distance, almost hidden in the haze
of stars about 40 miles ahead and several orbital layers
above, was a long, irregular-shaped object that looked
like a huge mechanical multilegged spaceborne water-
bug. It was much larger than any previous space junk
that they'd encountered. It was larger than the haunted
Soyuz capsule and even the Zon itself. As soon as they
saw it, they all knew exactly what it was.

It was the Mir space station, the entity they believed
housed Viktor and was responsible for sowing all the
murderous space mines.

At last they had found it.

"God, it's an ugly-looking thing," Cook said, straining to get a glimpse of the spacecraft through the front
windshield.

"Yeah, but ugly don't make a difference up here,"
Elvis replied.

Everyone knew exactly what Elvis meant. On earth,
there was an old saying regarding airplanes: if it looks
good, it flies good. Of course the kernel of truth in
this was that aerodynamic lines usually had a design
element to them—sometimes the more dramatic the
element, the better.

But up in space, there was no need for smooth corners and trim edges. There was no air, therefore no
resistance and no need to build in any cool curves or
swept-back wings. Just as long as the thing could survive

the many hazards of space, what it looked like had no bearing on its operation or success as a spacecraft.

But the Mir looked particularly unattractive, as if some giant hand had simply stuck this here and that there and declared it a spacecraft. Of course, that wasn't too far from the actual story. The Mir had been cobbled together from separate parts flown up by the Russians in the course of two decades. It was a like a mobile home that had sat in the same place for 20 years or more, getting the latest in mobile home technology—awnings, room extensions, bigger windows, a porch—but still basically a trailer.

"Well, this is what we've been waiting for," Hunter said, powering up the Zon's remaining maneuver jets. "We'll only have one chance, so let's do it by the book . . ."

"You mean if there *is* a book on something like this," JT replied.

One hour and twenty minutes later, they had maneuvered the Zon to within a mile of the Mir.

The space station was much larger than it appeared when they first spotted it. It was apparent that since Viktor had appropriated the place, he and his minions had added some new modules. Now the Mir had so many extensions—at least two dozen solar panels for power, several additional docking rings to accept Soyuz capsules, plus two large cylindrical objects, stuck on the southern portion of the complex—that it looked like something from a Rube Goldberg nightmare. But this wasn't about being pretty. It was about staying alive in space.

The space station seemed eerily serene as Hunter closed to within a mile of it. It appeared to be powered up. There were two sets of navigation lights on its most far-flung extensions: a pair of red lights at the end of the foremost solar panel, and a couple of green lights flashing at the end of the cylindrical capsule on its bottom tier. Both sets were blinking rapidly. There were several portholes visible from the Zon's current angle, and dim, bluish lights could be seen within them.

Still, they were getting no reaction at all as they slowly moved in. But what did they expect? What does one do if the space station is about to be intruded upon? It's not like they could just fire a burst from their cannons and then run away or escape into a convenient cloud bank, like during a high-speed dogfight down on earth.

No—in space, everything was different.

It was no easier for Hunter to climb into the EVA suit a second time than it had been the first.

The damn things were bulky and uncomfortable and made in such a crude way that they never felt like they fit right in all places everytime. They were tight where they should have been loose, loose where they should have been tight. Add the fact that climbing into one in zero-gravity was like trying to wrestle underwater, a truly miserable experience.

Yet Hunter proceeded to pour himself into the suit with a kind of grim determination. It seemed like he'd spent most of his adult life chasing Viktor—whether the real one or the fake—and now, at last, he was certain he had the supercriminal dead to rights. Unlike their previous confrontations in the desert, above the ocean, or through holographs or proxies, there really was no place Viktor could hide this time, now that Hunter had found the Mir. They were in space; there was nowhere else to go but down, and Viktor's only ability to do that was the Zon, and Hunter and Company had taken that away from him. Now, it seemed like only a matter of apprehending the much-hated terrorist and dragging him back to earth for a quick trial and, it was hoped, an even quicker execution.

And then, maybe Hunter and the rest of the world could finally get some peace.

Elvis was right beside him, struggling to get into his ETA suit. There had been no need to ask for volunteers to go on this particular excursion. Of them all, Elvis probably had the most personal debt to settle with Viktor. The supercriminal might have robbed the earth of many years of what could have been restablization, but he'd robbed Elvis of many years of his life. During the time under his capture, Elvis had been beaten, brainwashed, and beaten again so many times, he wasn't even sure who he was. Only after the Zon was captured by the UAAF on Lolita Island did Elvis begin to emerge from the fog of his nasty experience.

With each passing minute, the ex-fighter pilot and member of the Ace Wrecking Company grew more determined in his quest to make Viktor pay—and pay big someday.

From all appearances, that day was today.

JT and Ben were now strapped into the Zon's flying seats. Cook was in the jumpseat, helping them look for any rogue space mines which would absolutely fuck up the upcoming EVA. Geraci was down in the crew compartment, trying to assist Hunter and Elvis into their suits and get their admittedly crude weaponry and communications equipment to work.

When this Zon flight was first planned, one question that arose was what weapons, if any, the crew should take into orbit. It wasn't as if standard military firearms would be of any use. And the UAAF didn't have any ray guns or destructo beams in its arsonnels. There was really only one weapon anyone could think of that might be effective in outer space. This was the taser, the police-issued stun gun first popularized in the 1970s. The Zon crew had brought ten with them. Each one could deliver a whopping 50,000-volt jolt, enough to knock a person unconscious, at least on the ground. Truth was, Hunter had no idea exactly how they would work in space, if at all.

In any case, he and Elvis were now packing two tasers apiece, each carrying a full charge. They also had two radios sewn into their suits. One was a NASA-issued so-called "local communicator" of the same type used in the early shuttle days. Their back-up would be a Russian-designed two-way radio that looked liked it had been assembled by elves up at the North Pole. It was so tinny and toyish, no one believed it could work, or if it did, for very long.

Finally, they were set to go into space. On Hunter's word, JT and Ben had maneuvered the Zon to within 1500 feet of the Mir, specifically, the space station's lower left side. Here, Elvis knew of a rudimentary emergency hatch which led into a pressure lock which could be operated manually from the outside; he'd used the hatchway several times during his days in Viktor's capture. Through this, he was sure, he could get them into the Mir, and possibly without anyone inside knowing exactly what they were up to.

Though they were in space and were about to go into what amounted to hostile territory, the plan was fairly simple: gain entrance to the Mir, eliminate any opposition, search for Viktor, and then take him back—and hope he had a spacesuit that fit. The search and the chase were over; now all that remained was the capture.

One last call up to the flight deck revealed no problems. The Mir was still blinking passively, now but 1200 feet away and there wasn't a space mine in sight.

Hunter and Elvis did one last pressure check on their suits and Geraci did a green test on the external chamber-lock. Everything was working as well as could be expected.

Hunter and Elvis shook hands with Geraci and then each other. Then they went out the door.

It took exactly eight minutes for them to get out into space. The depressurization chamber seemed to take longer every time they used it. But finally they were free of the Zon and untangling their lifeline tethers.

Elvis was particularly eager to get going. He didn't even bother to test his zipgun, the gas-powered steering device which would propel them over to Mir. He attached his tether and gave his zip a long, powerful press. The next moment he was speeding away from Hunter and toward the spaceship looming off the nose of the Zon.

Hunter, once again caught up in the absolute beauty and freedom of walking in space, now hastened to join his colleague. He gave his own zipgun a long pull and was soon horizontal and nearly colliding with the bottoms of Elvis's space boots.

It was very strange to be out here, though; this thought could not escape Hunter's mind no matter what the circumstances. The whole when-an-object-is-in-motion-it-tends-to-stay-in-motion thing had an absolutely entirely different meaning up in orbit. With no atmosphere, gravity, or external means of friction to slow you down, once you got up a head of steam, you kept it unless you took it upon yourself to slow down. It was this external aspect of being in space that made Hunter the most excited. The great blue earth, spinning so tremendously fast directly below him, seemed to be the one out of place up here. Space—cold, dead, dark, and yet magnificant—was now the norm. Life on Earth, the air, the water, the people and the plants, seemed the aberration.

And above him, billions of stars, billions of galaxies, worlds of untold tales. Life, or what might pass for life, swirling around within the cold, pale light of the stars. Spinning in what might be . . .

A sudden jerk on his helmet knocked Hunter out of his latest daydream. It was Elvis. He'd kicked both of them to a stop about two-thirds of the way across the void to the Mir. Hunter looked up at him and saw he was gesturing frantically. But what was wrong? The Mir was still there, unmoving, though its velocity was nearly seven miles a second. His spacesuit seemed to be working okay, no leaks that he could see. The same with Elvis's suit.

"What's the problem?" he called over to Elvis.

Of course, the reply was broken up with static.

"Six o'clock . . . look . . . just about . . . six . . ."

He was pointing to a spot at the bottom of the Mir, which corresponded roughly with six o'clock low. The glare from the earthglow made it hard to see at first— but then Hunter finally got it.

"Damn," he whispered into his microphone.

Two tiny figures, clad in black spacesuits, had come out of the Mir and were heading right for them.

What followed was the first fistfight in outer space.

The pair of men in the black spacesuits were also equipped with zipguns. One push on their triggers and they were suddenly looming large in Hunter's face plate.

"Split up!" someone yelled into his headphones. It could have been Elvis, or maybe JT, back on the Zon. But whoever was giving the order, it was good advice.

Hunter and Elvis quickly separated via a quick punch
from the zipguns. Within a few seconds they were 50
feet apart but still barreling in on the Mir.

Their two oncoming opponents also split up. The
one on the left was now heading right for Hunter, the
other for Elvis. Both appeared to be carrying long,
thin, dark twisted tubes, possibly some kind of space
tool, but bearing a remarkable resemblance to a crowbar. Obviously these were intended to be used as weapons. But again, this seemed crazy. They were in space.
Essentially, nothing had any weight, only mass. What
happens when you get hit with a crowbar that is weightless while you are weightless as well?

Hunter was certain that the man heading for him in
this weird kind of speeded-up slow motion was bent on
finding out.

His potential opponent was now but 50 feet from
him. Arms outstretched, bar in one hand, zipgun in
the other, he certainly looked menacing, not unlike a
MIG or some other enemy airplane zooming in on
Hunter, hoping for a quick kill.

There was no way the guy in the black spacesuit
could know what a big mistake that was . . .

Once the enemy spaceman had reached a point
about 20 feet in front of him, Hunter turned his zipgun
forward and gave it a half-second burst. This was
enough to stop him completely. He then turned the
zipper to the left and gave it an even shorter burst.
This moved him just enough out of the way to allow
the spaceman to rocket by him. Hunter could see the
look of complete surprise on the guy's face as he
zoomed by, flailing his weapon, but just out of reach.
He also saw the man was badly in need of a shave and
some dental work. A number of crudely healed scars
across his cheeks and nose confirmed that he was in-

deed one of Viktor's goon boys, sent to do their boss's dirty work.

Hunter zipped again, rotating his entire body like a cartwheel, then pushing himself forward about 10 feet. The spaceman had stopped himself by this time, and by slowly turning on his back, was now zipping back toward Hunter headfirst. Hunter pulled his zipgun trigger again, banking left as the space thug flew by and catching him with a solid punch right to the face plate. The goon was instantly knocked off at a sharp angle and began tumbling out of control from the sudden exertion of external force.

Predictably, Hunter went flying in the other direction—it was that every-action-causes-an-equal-but-opposite-reaction thing again. But unlike the spacethug, he was prepared for it. A short burst from the zipgun slowed him down completely; another got him moving forward again. His opponent was getting pissed by this time—which was exactly what Hunter wanted. He came right at Hunter a third time, trying to swing the pipe while keeping his zipgun all the way open. Hunter put his own zipper behind his back and squeezed off a one-second burst. This got him rotating on his backside, and as the thug roared by, he was able to hit him three times—twice with is fists, landing blows on top of his head and in his chest, and once with his left boot, which connected solidly with the man's groin.

Hunter imagined he could hear the grunt as the spaceman doubled up and went tumbling back toward the Mir. Hunter's maneuver had worked perfectly.

But now it was time to stop fooling around.

He twisted himself to the horizontal and gave his zipgun a long, hard squeeze. In the next instant he was rocketing toward the space thug even as the man was recovering from his triple whammy. He saw Hunter coming and manage to stop spinning just as the Wingman's right fist connected with his neck. Caught completely flatfooted and unprepared, the thug began tumbling in place once again, no doubt expending what was left of his energy. Hunter reached out, pulled the pipe from his hand, did a quick calculation, and then drove his fist squarely into the guy's stomach. The combination of this force and the man's tumbling combined to both knock him unconscious and propel him in a downward trajectory. Within seconds he was spinning out of sight, falling toward earth with a quickening velocity and a fatal burn-up on reentry.

"Next time, don't skip physics class," Hunter bade him as he plunged toward the upper atmosphere.

Hunter turned himself around to find that Elvis and the other remaining spaceman were locked in a titanic struggle up against the Mir. Just how his friend had got himself into this position, Hunter didn't know—and there was certainly no time to find out. One squeeze of his zipgun and he was rocketing to Elvis's aid.

But in that short span of time, the Mir spaceman had been able to lodge the zipgun out of Elvis's hand, just as Elvis had managed to pull the weapon from his opponent. Now Elvis was trying to batter the enemy spacewalker with the crowbar-like device even as the man was spraying the zipgun gas in his face. Blinded and disoriented, Elvis took a massive punch from his opponent and went sailing off in the opposite direction. Somewhat aghast, Hunter did a quick plot on Elvis's tumbling trajectory and determined that his friend would be lost forever if he didn't get to him inside of 17 seconds.

Hunter squeezed his zipgun trigger, and though it was now dangerously low on fuel, was able to get a good burst and a quick velocity. He went right by the Mir spaceman and was able to swipe him once on the head with his first opponent's crowbar. The action served to cut the man's external oxygen hose. He grabbed his throat and began struggling, but the end came quickly. The man was dead and falling back to earth inside of two seconds.

Now Hunter's headphones were filled with concern from JT and Ben back in the Zon. They'd been watching the entire encounter and now realized the fix Elvis was in. But even if they got the Zon started up again and went after their tumbling colleague it would probably be too late to do any good.

If Elvis was going to be saved, it was up to Hunter to do it.

By this time, Elvis had tumbled far beyond the top of the Mir. The last gasps from Hunter's zipgun now sent him rocketing by the tip of the space station and into the deep black void beyond. It was imperative that he keep Elvis in sight, catch him, and figure out how to get back later. To this end, Hunter unconsciously put his hands back to his side and closed his boots together. Like an F-14 or an F-111 going to full-swept wing, he streaked toward his tumbling friend, finally gaining on him, catching the heel of his boot about 15 seconds after the punch that had put him in this position.

Now all Hunter's brainpower would have to come into play. He didn't so much grab Elvis as he redirected his trajectory. Like hitting a cue ball, which in turn hits the next ball and the next, Hunter's action sent Elvis heading straight down, still out of control, but at least not on a path to Jupiter or out of the solar system.

Hunter squeezed his zipgun again; there was just about enough gas to slow his own trajectory, with maybe one last burst to spare. Standing on his head, he gave the zipgun trigger that one last pull. Slowly but surely, the weak stream of gas spilled out and he found himself following Elvis back down toward the Mir.

It was here he would have to get lucky. He'd hoped
to push Elvis in such a way that he would—for lack of
a better word—*collide* with the Russian space station.
And that's exactly what happened. Elvis went into a
docking ring at the top of the MIR headfirst, hitting it
hard enough to stop his flight path, but not enough
to ricochet him off in another unpredictable direction.
Out of gas and fairly out of control, Hunter slammed
into the same docking ring just a few seconds later.
Somehow, he was able to grab a hand hold on the Mir
and catch Elvis's right arm at the same time. He pulled
his colleague over to him and rapped twice on his helmet.

Groggy, confused, and damn dizzy, Elvis finally responded with a shaky thumbs-up. He was okay.

Compared to the fistfight in space, getting into the
Mir was a breeze.

The emergency entryway was exactly where Elvis had
remembered it. And just as he predicted, the hatchway
could be operated from the outside and was functioning. It took them a few moments to figure exactly how
the thing worked, though. It was jerry-rigged to some
degree, no surprise, considering the same people who
had built the Mir had built the Zon. But finally Hunter
figured out that of the three twist-and-dog locks on the
outside of the hatchway, two turned clockwise, while
the third went counterclockwise. He pulled the hatchway open with a mighty heave that almost sent him off
on his own fatal trajectory. Only the smallest puff of
air came out, leftover, no doubt, from the last time the
hatch was used, which appeared to be some time ago.

Hunter went in first. Elvis, still punchy from his experience, brought up the rear. Both of them had their
tasers out and ready; though powerful, these weapons

had only a limited power supply, which was why they
didn't use them during the astral fistfight. They were
both able to squeeze into the pressurization chamber;
it was tight, but a marked improvement over the Zon's,
which was barely large enough to fit one person. The
pressurization itself went much quicker than they were
used to. Within 30 seconds, they were able to open the
inner hatchway and step inside the Mir.

If anything, it was darker inside the station than in
the haunted Soyuz. What light there was came in the
form of tiny blue bulbs strung almost like Christmas
ornaments along the entrance corridor. They had entered this long hallway about halfway between two large
hatchways. These obviously led into the main interiors
of the station. One was to the left, the other directly
above them.

But which way should they go? To their left was the
part of the station where most of the docking rings
were. Did this mean a kind of unimportant cargo area
lay close by? Maybe. In any case, when Elvis pointed
straight up, making a suggestion on which direction
they should travel, Hunter quickly agreed.

They floated up, tasers ready, not quite knowing what
to expect. Just because only two gorillas came out after
them didn't mean there weren't more inside. They had
to be ready for anything.

They reached the end of the upper passageway and
spun the hatchway lock. It was already unlocked. With
Elvis holding his taser out as far as possible, Hunter
pulled the doorway back.

They found themselves staring into a larger, darker
cylindrical tube. This was obviously one of the living
modules. By this time, both Hunter and Elvis had gone
off their internal oxygen supply and were breathing
the station's air through their open face plates. They
say that your sensory organs are heightened in space,

where there is no gravity to affect the molecules of an odor or a sound. And are they right!

The inside of this module smelled like the worst barroom either one had ever been in. It was a sickly combination of spilled whiskey, sticky beer, cigarette and/or cigar smoke (who the hell would smoke in space?), and body odor. Also present in this free-floating malodorous cloud were thousands of tiny white specks. They looked like household dust, but when Hunter wet his finger and caught a few dozen, he knew immediately they were more than just some ordinary dirt sprinkles floating around due to some sloppy housekeeping.

"Let me guess," Elvis said, studying the legion of white specks which had adhered to Hunter's finger. "Cocaine or heroin?"

Hunter gave it a taste test.

"Both," he declared. "With maybe a little PCP and other crap thrown in, too."

Elvis just shook his head.

"Whenever I was up here, it was Party Central," he sighed. "You'd think being a hundred miles up and going seven miles a second would be high enough and fast enough for these guys."

Hunter wiped off his finger in disgust.

"These guys wouldn't know a good buzz if it came up and bit them on the ass."

They floated on, past a debris cloud made up of plastic containers which had previously held beer, extinguished cigarette butts, bottle caps, and expended matches. The last item of litter was the most frightening for Hunter. Obviously the Mir was not pumped up with 100-percent oxygen. If that were the case, one strike of flame, one tiny spark, and the whole kit-and-kaboodle would have gone up like a bomb.

This was because oxygen was very flammable. The

earth's atmosphere was made up mostly of nitrogen; otherwise, everything would have burned up long ago. But inside most spaceships, the oxygen content was much higher, to aid in respiration as well as simplicity in pressurization and filtering. So how much pure O did the artificial atmosphere inside the Mir have? Just how much of an ignition point would be needed to set the whole place up? It couldn't be much more than it already was, and that's why Hunter shuddered to think of anyone actually lighting up a tobacco stick inside.

They reached the next hatchway and were forced to fool with its lock for more than five minutes. There was a corked cap stuck in its gearbox and the door would not budge until Hunter and Elvis were able to cut it away. They finally achieved this with the help of their helmet antennas, and with some more pushing and shoving, were able to pull the hatch open.

It led to another tubelike corridor, which in turn served as the entrance for a second cylindrical living module. Getting into this one was no problem—but the smell inside was even worse than before—booze, smoke, a fog of coke and smack particles. Hunter found the whole thing appalling. Viktor and his gang had achieved space flight, one of the grandest accomplishments of human history, yet they were defiling it like it was nothing but another place to get high, get drunk, and get stupid.

So much for that giant leap for mankind.

There was one further item floating around in this weightless flotsam. It was a female's bathing-suit top. Elvis snagged it with his index finger about halfway through the smelly module. It appeared small. Hunter couldn't venture to guess what it was doing here, or who'd left it behind. Keeping it as evidence, though, he and Elvis pressed on.

The next hallway was even darker than the first two.

The string of blue lights were ragged and many of the bulbs were burnt out. Up ahead, they thought they could hear a slight pounding noise. Irregular and at a different volume than the low hum of everything else aboard the Mir, this indicated the first sign of human activity might be straight ahead. Tasers primed and ready, they reached the next hatchway and began to open the dog-locked door.

Hunter was getting the distinct impression that he was floating through a space-borne version of Führerbunker, the underground hiding place Hitler had chosen for his grave in the last mad days of the Third Reich. What would lay inside this, the third and last living module? Dead bodies, full of self-inflicted wounds? More skeletons? Or were these simply ghosts they were hearing, lost souls trying like hell to get off the smelly space station as well?

However superintuitive he was, Hunter's musings weren't even close to what they found inside the third capsule.

It was better lit than the first two, and unlike them, it was crammed with communications, navigation, and life-support gear. However, it was in an even further advanced stage of decay—and it smelled worse, too.

There were two people inside. Two scantily clad young girls, mere teenagers, were floating around the cabin, eyes drawn, bodies deflated, mouths open, and tongues stuck out, attempting to catch as much of the free-floating cocaine and heroin as they could.

Tasers up and ready, Hunter and Elvis stared at them as they floated by, trying their best to be human vacuum cleaners. One was topless and a sure bet to be the owner of the article of clothing they'd found next door. A quick visual check of the rest of the capsule showed no one else was here, just the two girls, apparently the playthings of the pair of spacemen Hunter and Elvis had just eliminated.

"Where is Viktor?" Elvis asked them harshly.

The two young girls ignored him.

"Where the hell *is* he?" Elvis demanded.

The pair just kept swimming through the cabin, snagging bits of drug crystals like fish trying to capture smaller prey. Either they didn't hear him or they weren't interested in talking.

Finally Elvis reached up and grabbed the topless one by the leg, pulling her down in front of them. She stared back with a mixture of horror and confusion. It really did look like she was noticing them for the first time.

Hunter was at eye-level with her. She was pretty, but obviously ill from drug use and malnutrition.

"What's your name?" he asked her.

The girl had to think a moment.

"I . . . I really don't know," she finally replied unconsciously rubbing her smallish breasts.

"How about your friend?" Hunter asked, indicating the other girl, who was floating directly above their heads at the moment. "What's *her* name?"

The first girl had to think a bit. Finally she shook her head again. Tears were beginning to form in her eyes.

"I used to know," she whispered. "But now . . ."

She began crying, treating Hunter and Elvis to the odd spectacle of tears coming from her eyes—and floating away.

Hunter reached into his pocket and came up with the bathing suit top. He gave it to the girl and she obligingly put it on. Then Elvis pulled the other girl down and rested her beside the first.

"How about Viktor?" Hunter asked both of them as calmly as possible. "Do you remember who he is?"

Surprisingly, both girls laughed a little.

"Of course we do," the first girl said. "He's the A-hole who brought us up here in the first place . . ."

Elvis leaned forward—he was obviously more personally involved in this little discussion.

"Okay, then you know who he is," he said, through gritted teeth. "Now, tell us *where* he is . . ."

Again, both girls laughed, this time somewhat grimly.

"Where is Viktor?" the first girl said. "How should we know?"

Both Hunter and Elvis were stunned.

"What do you mean?" they both asked at once.

The first girl laughed again.

"Jesus, get with it, man," she said. "Don't you get it?"

"Get what?" Hunter asked them.

"We're the last ones left," the second girl explained. "Viktor left a long time ago . . ."

PART 3

Nineteen

The pair of CH-53E Sea Stallions circled the small island from about 1000 feet up, their engines rumbling in the warm, breezy Caribbean night.

It was close to 0100 hours, and the seas all around the quarter-mile square island were eerily calm despite the growing tide. The moon was three-quarters full, providing enough light to feed the NightScopes being used by the helicopter pilots. It was very important that they were able see exactly what they were doing and where they were going. One wrong move and disaster would be the result.

Finally, the first Sea Stallion set down onto the hard rock beach on the north end of the island. The second chopper came in about 10 seconds later. Both pilots quickly killed their engines and reengaged their noise dampeners. The Sea Stallion was a great aircraft, but it could make a commotion when landing. The special mufflers cut that racket by about two-thirds.

Thirty seconds after landing, all was quiet again. Slowly the side doors on both choppers slid open and a small legion of dark figures came pouring out. There were three dozen inside each chopper. As they jumped out onto the beach, half of them went immediately to defensive positions around each Sea Stallion; the other half went plunging into the thick jungle which made up the rest of the tiny island.

They were looking for gasoline.

Key Lime was one of the smallest and southern most specks in the string of islands known as the Florida Keys. It was slightly out of position, about 28 miles southwest of Big Pine Key and therefore not really a part of the main archipelago. But this made it a perfect launching point for special operations, especially ones in which absolute stealth was needed. That was definitely the case for this particular night.

Earlier in the day, two similar helicopters had visited Key Lime. They were aerial cargo trucks as opposed to troop carriers, and in their holds were two fuel bladders, each containing about 1000 gallons of aviation gas. They'd dropped the fuel into the deepest part of the jungle and their crews had camouflaged it as best they could. Now, nearly 24 hours later, three dozen soldiers, all dressed in black, were looking for this precious gasoline.

About five minutes into the search, they found it— and this came as a welcome relief for Major Mark Snyder, the XO of the famous JAWS team. It was his men who were now on the ground on Key Lime, getting ready to attempt one of the most treacherous yet important missions in their history. The gasoline found here in the jungle would fuel the two big choppers for the next leg of this jump. Had the gas not been there, or had it leaked or been discovered by unfriendlies, then the JAWS team would have would up high, dry, and very exposed on the tiny island out in the middle of nowhere.

But the celebration in finding the fuel was a short-lived one. Now they had to get the gas into the choppers, top off the tanks, and get the hell going. They were still on their mission schedule for the moment.

But every second would be precious when the real work began.

The JAWS team quickly laid out six hoses and began hand pumping the gas into the Sea Stallions' bottom-mounted fuel tanks. The whole refueling operation had to be pulled off in 12 minutes in order to stay on time. Snyder was intent on getting it done in under 10 minutes.

The first five minutes of the gas-up went well. While three dozen JAWS troopers provided the muscle power to move the gas through the hoses to the choppers, the other three squads maintained the defensive integrity of the island. Captain Warren Maas was in charge of the 12-man unit watching the southern tip of the tiny island. His squad was equipped with a long-range IR/Nightscope capable of seeing more than 15 miles away. Two of his men had their eyes glued to this device, searching the southern horizon for any sign of activity, either on the surface or in the air.

Six minutes into the refueling operation, their scope picked up something.

It was just a tiny blurb of heat spotted due south of Key Lime, way out on the cloudless horizon. At first the men on the long-range NightScope feared it might be an incoming missile, an Exocet or even a Harpoon-like weapon. This initial apprehension drained away after they intensified their heat filter and discovered that the source was not moving fast enough to be a missile. And it wasn't coming toward the island, but moving parallel to it.

But then another heat blurb was detected. Then another—and another. Maas himself got on the scope and after further refinement of the image discovered the heat sources were actually small patrol boats. He called his intelligence guys up and had them take a look. The first thing they did was declare the vessels not to be of friendly origin—they were not a kind or class found in the arsonnel of the UAAF or any of its immediate allies.

This racheted the tension up a notch or two. Maas told the intell men to make a definite ID on the four ships, now moving in a line about 12 miles off the southern tip of the island. They began pumping all the data from the NightScope into their IFF-AQ computers, devices which were able to identify just about any weapons system currently in vogue around the world. The IFF-AQs chewed over the information for about 30 seconds and then popped out an answer. The ghostly forms the JAWS team had detected were *Sparvieros*, small, speedy hydrofoil vessels that usually carried a vast array of weapons, including ultradeadly surface-to-surface Styx missiles.

This was not good news. If fully armed, a single "Sparvee" could unload about a third of its weapons stores and wipe Key Lime and everyone on it off the map. Four of them could take out a fair-sized city. Maas called back to Snyder, who'd set up a temporary CP outside the first Sea Stallion helicopter. A quartet of Sparvees was out there, but they were not heading toward them—not yet, anyway. Though they had no idea who the deadly ships belonged to, Maas suggested they get the refueling operation done as quickly as possible.

It was a suggestion that Snyder really didn't need to hear. He'd been urging his men to get the gas through the hoses and into the helicopters as quickly as humanly possible. At that moment they were about 65-percent done; 1300 hundred gallons had been transferred. Snyder knew they could go with 1500 gallons and leave the rest behind. But in missions like the one facing them, fuel was usually the most precious resource. He really wanted to get as much gas on-board as possible before lifting off.

But about a half minute later, Snyder heard another piece of bad news. This came from the patrol watching the western horizon. They'd picked up a disturbing indication, too. Captain Sean Higgins was the CO of this unit. His intell guys had identified no less than 16 aircraft moving in a circular fashion about 12 miles due west of Key Lime.

The airplanes were identified as Ilyushin Il-28 "Beagles." A favorite of air mercenaries, the specialty of these two-engine, light-strike jet bombers in the post–Big War world was the sneak attack on poorly defended targets, such as advance airfields or unsuspecting population centers. The Beagles could get in quick, usually under radar, drop nearly four tons of high explosives, and exit, all in a matter of seconds.

These sixteen airplanes were either gathering for an operation or flying a pre-mission pattern, a practice run for a later bombing strike. Either way, should they detect what was going on on Key Lime, a two-second pass by just one aircraft could sink the whole island.

Snyder checked his watch. The pumping operation was now eight minutes old. They'd crossed the magic 1500-gallon mark; the remaining 500 gallons were gravy. What to do? Take off now and go into the mission flight? Or risk another few minutes and take on the extra gas? Just as he was weighing these options, he received a third report, this one from the patrol watching the eastern side of the key, a unit under the command of Major Clancy Miller. Their long scopes had found something even more disturbing breaking the surface of the water not two miles offshore: a periscope.

Snyder quickly ordered Clancy to get an ID on the device. Clancy's reply came back exactly 20 seconds later. The scope belonged to a Enrico Toti-class submarine, a conventionally powered U-boat known for its

ability to operate in very shallow water and launch surprise "pop-up" attacks with its unique surface-to-air-to-
surface "Popeye" torpedoes. Each of these weapons
could carry a 150-pound warhead. In the past few
months, UAAF intelligence had heard that some of
these flying torpedoes had been adapted to carry nerve
agents, poison gas, or even small tactical nuclear weapons.

That was enough for Snyder. He immediately cut off
the refueling operation and ordered all units back to
the helicopters. They'd selected Key Lime for this sensitive fueling operation because of its isolation. Yet they'd
unwittingly set down in the middle of a hornet's nest of
military activity, all of it unfriendly and most probably
gearing up for an attack on the American mainland. Yet
due to the highly sensitive nature of this operation, Snyder could not call back to base ops at KSC and sound a
warning. He would just have to hope that other UA units
would detect the enemy forces in time.

Still, though he was hardly one for superstition, Snyder couldn't help feeling that all this was a bad omen
for the rather scary mission he and his men were about
to attempt.

All of the troops were back on their respective choppers within two minutes of Snyder's order. Their sound
dampeners clamped down as tight as possible, the pilots started up the pair of Sea Stallions and lifted off
the second they were airworthy.

Getting down very close to the surface of the water,
the pair of big troop-laden choppers immediately
turned due south, their noses pointing directly into the
heart of Cuba, now just 62 miles away.

Behind them on Key Lime, they'd left a total of 400
gallons of precious gasoline.

* * *

The pair of Sea Stallion choppers made landfall over Cuba at exactly 0150 hours.

Remarkably, they were still on schedule, despite the hasty departure from Key Lime and a couple of squall lines through which they'd been forced to fly.

Now, as they crossed over the island at the point near Matanzas, their engine dampeners became their most important weapon. The Sea Stallions were covered with black, radar-absorbing paint to ward off roving radar sweeps. Their power plants were sealed in heat-absorbing material to deflect any heat-seeking weapons. But they had to be quiet, too, or the whole game would be blown. Luckily, the mufflers on both choppers were working up to snuff.

They were heading for the Jovellanos region, the fog-enshrouded valley where Crunch had found the mysterious dual air base, redesignated the rather ironic "Double-Trouble" by the UAAF intelligence corps. A subsequent series of U-2 overflights had confirmed the existence of the huge twin bases, as well as the presence of nuclear weapons on-site. But intensive analysis of photos taken by these spy flights had also raised several baffling questions.

There were a total of 44 nuclear warheads in storage at the base; this was confirmed either by normal photography or images taken by infrared, radiation-sensitive cameras. One odd thing was that the weapons were not all the same size, shape, or capacity. Some nukes were blockbusters—25-megaton hydrogen bombs many times more powerful than the weapon dropped on Hiroshima so long ago. Others were battlefield nukes, mortar-round-sized warheads that could fit in a toolbox and whose capacity was measured in low-range kilotons. Still others appeared to have been taken from nuclear-tipped torpedoes, nuclear-tipped artillery shells, antiship missiles, even Russian-built cruise missiles.

So what Crunch had discovered was not exactly a replay of the 1962 Cuban Missile Crisis, in which much of the American continent was at risk for sudden and indefensible nuclear bombardment. Very few of these nukes were adaptable for launching aboard medium-range missiles.

What were they doing here, then? Why were the forces unfriendly to the United Americans stockpiling such a hodge-podge of atomic weapons so close to the American mainland?

That was what the JAWS team was going in to find out.

They found the site covered with a thick mist; and with a cloud cover above, no moonlight shone through. This was perfect for the JAWS team. For this operation, the darker, the better.

The pair of choppers avoided the west end of the base, where the landing strips and the attack fighters were. Instead, the Sea Stallions stayed as low to the treetops as possible and skirted to the northern edge of the site, where the nukes were being stored.

Using maps generated from the U-2 photos, they quickly found a flattened hilltop about 600 feet from the outer perimeter of the weapons stockyard. The pair of copters set down, quietly and unseen, and disgorged 72 troops.

Now came the hard part.

The JAWS team was not here to destroy the nuclear weapons. That was way too risky. If the UA's initial intent was to blow up the nuclear stockpile, any number of preemptive air strikes could have been launched. The problem was, the UA had no idea as to the stability of the nuclear weapons. Were some or all of them fused? Were they prefused? Were they "clean" or "dirty" bombs? An air raid might very well take out the whole stockpile in one fell swoop, but the result might also be the triggering of a massive chain reaction of nuclear explosions that would vaporize Cuba and most of the Caribbean—and possibly half the planet as well.

Thus was the need to get some hard, human intelligence on the ground.

As before, the unit broke into four components upon landing. Team Clancy took the southern flank; Team Maas went north. Higgins and his patrol took the center; Snyder and his men set up a defensive perimeter around the choppers and established the command post.

Higgins and crew would move first. Once the others were in place, the 12-man patrol wormed its way down a series of vine-encased slopes, reaching the edge of the nuke junkyard in a matter of minutes. Each of Higgins's men was equipped with an M-16-663D, complete with three-dimensional target acquisition sight, muzzle-loaded flash suppressors, and extra-long ammo clips. Each man also had an emergency radio, an IF video camera, and a small, lip-mike-mounted tape recorder. The JAWS team was famous for its ability to take on a hardened target, usually against overwhelming odds, destroying said target, making a lot of noise, and then getting the hell out.

This night, however, their mission was more subtle. They were to infiltrate the nuclear stockyard, take photos and record audio versions of what they could, and then get out—all without making a sound. When you came down to it, blowing up things was a lot easier.

Higgins and his men had moved right up to the stockyard fence by 0215. Another strange thing about the nuke pile was the lack of security surrounding it. While the air base nearby was covered with guard towers, AAA guns, and SAM sites, the perimeter of the nuke pile consisted of an elderly chain-link fence and four guard towers, one at each corner of the 125-acre lot. There were no motion detectors, no listening posts, no IF cameras or NightVision huts. The greatest massing of nuclear weapons since the end of the Big War was being protected by less than a dozen individuals spread out so far apart they could barely see each other. This told the JAWS team two things: first, the nuclear stockpile was probably so much of a secret that very few people within the coalition of unfriendly groups knew of its existence. And second, the peons watching over it probably had no idea what the hell they were actually guarding.

This would make it even easier for Higgins's men to infiltrate—almost too easy. They made short work of the chain-link fence; it was neither electrified nor wired with sensing devices. They cut four holes about 10 feet apart in the barrier, and after leaving one man to guard each entryway, they quickly penetrated the interior of the stockyard.

Higgins was at the lead of this 8-man group; he quickly had his men spread out and start recording anything and everything. What lay before them were dozens of canvas-covered objects ranging from six to 20 feet high. They were arranged in irregular rows and separated by artificial alleyways, each about six feet wide. Higgins selected a group of objects and sent a man into each alley. He took the northernmost pathway, the one closest to the nearest guard tower.

Getting down on his hands and knees, he activated both his video camera and his audio recorder. The camera lens fit conveniently on the snout of his rifle, so anywhere he pointed his weapon, he got a video image as well. Moving swiftly, he scurried up against the first object and lifted its canvas covering as if it were a lady's skirt.

Underneath he found exactly what they'd come here to look for: a clear plastic crate containing a nuclear device inside. This particular weapon seemed to be a STB-350, intell-speak for the standard-sized Russian-built 350-kiloton tactical nuclear weapon. This one was in the form of an air-dropped parachute-release gravity bomb, the sort that would be carried on a Russian-built fighter-bomber or attack aircraft. On its case was a mouthful of Germanic writing, plus a line of swastikas. This left no doubt as to who owned all this megatonnage, not that anybody needed any further confirmation. Higgins got full footage of the weapon and then moved on.

The next weapon was a same-sized warhead; this one looked like it had come off a nuclear mine. It was lying in the same kind of swastika-happy plastic coffin, a small, very rinky-dink cooling apparatus attached to it. Higgins got footage of the length of it twice and continued on.

In his headphones he could hear the activity of the other infiltration units. Clancy's men were already inside the north end of the stockyard; Maas and his guys were just going through the fence to the south. At this rate, and with no problems, they would have the place taped and covered inside of 10 minutes. Then it would be a quick withdrawal, a short run back to the choppers, and the ride back home. If everything went right, they could be eating breakfast at the KSC by sunup.

Higgins got great footage of the third weapon's coffin—an air-dropped nuke similar to the first—and then moved on. Unlike the others, the fourth weapons crate was made of wood, old pine that was still sticky in some spots. Higgins considered passing it by—videotaping the weapons through the clear plastic cases was no problem. Fucking around with a wooden sarcophagus might be more trouble than it was worth. But Higgins wasn't in JAWS to have things go easy. He knew that it was important that each and every weapon be chronicled if they were to discover exactly why the weapons were being kept here.

So he put down his gun/camera, unstrapped his utility belt, and dug out his old-fashioned jackknife. It took him about a half-minute to work the six nails holding the top of wooden crate on. He was becoming increasingly aware of a strange odor emanating from the box. Higgins knew he had to be careful here—he had to make sure he left the crate as undisturbed as possible once he'd taken his pictures. Anything he moved he'd have to put back. Even losing one nail could be disastrous.

Finally he was able to wiggle all six nails out of the top. Now, using the butt end of the knife as a hammer, he pushed the lid up and over to one side. Suddenly, he was overcome with the most putrid of smells.

And something began moving inside the box.

To Higgins's absolute astonishment, a man sat up from inside the crate.

He was old, bearded, and covered with blood. He had hideous wounds on his face, neck, and arms. Most of his shoulder looked as if it had been bitten away by some kind of animal, maybe a shark. He was missing his left ear and part of his skull. Higgins nearly vomited at the sight of him. What the hell was happening here? This man not only looked like he should be dead—he looked and smelled like he *was* dead.

"Hey, there, how are you doing?" the bloody ghost asked him. "My name is Pooch. What's yours?"

At the other end of the nuclear stockyard, Warren Maas and his men had come upon something other than clear plastic caskets holding nuclear weapons.

Both Crunch and the U-2 spy photos had indicated that a separate holding area inside the stockyard was at the northern end of the bin. Instead of lines of different-sized containers, this area held just a handful of covered objects, these being huge in comparison to the weapons yard. Some of them were more than 100 feet long and 20 feet wide. What could be inside these containers? It was up to Maas and his men to find out.

Because of the prepositioning planning, when the Maas squad came through the fence, they were the unit closest to a guard station. The 25-foot tower was darkened, though a .50-caliber machine gun could be seen hanging off its edge. Maas had his NightScope guy sweep the guardhouse with his IR and heat-seeking equipment. Two heat blurs came back on this man's scope. At least two people were definitely inside the guardhouse, but luckily for the raiders, they were probably asleep.

Maas and his men stealthily moved through the stockyard, keeping low to the ground and making no noise whatsoever. They reached the inner containment area inside a minute and quickly went under its even older chain-link fence. Maas was almost overwhelmed by the size of the objects he'd been sent to identify. They looked much bigger than they appeared on the U-2 photos, much bigger than they looked when he'd first seen them from the hill. The thinking back at UA Command was that these hidden objects might actually be ICBMs, long-range missiles that could reach the other side of the globe.

But Maas knew a thing or two about long-range weapons systems. He knew right away that these were not ICBMs.

Maas stationed six of his men at the entranceway they'd made under the inner fence and then proceeded with the second half-dozen inside the corral itself. The objects they were looking up at were at least the size of an airliner, sans wings and tail. There were four large ones and two smaller ones. They were shrink-wrapped in white plastic and whenever a slight breeze blew through the fog-enshrouded area, the rippling was enough to send shivers up the spine.

Maas faced an interesting problem here: unlike his colleagues, he couldn't lift up a canvas covering and videotape whatever the hell was inside. The shrink wrap would have to be peeled away for him to reveal this secret. His solution was found in the cigarette lighter one of his men was carrying with him. They could peel back the shrink wrap, take a peek underneath, then maybe melt the stuff back on.

It sounded like a good idea, so Maas carefully began unsticking the taut white plastic from underneath the largest object. He was immediately hit with a smell that seemed to be a combination of things: kerosene, engine igniter, plain old motor oil, and scorched metal. It was an odor he'd encountered many times recently. It was the prevailing smell back at the Kennedy Space Center.

More intrigued than ever, Maas dislocated about thirty feet of the shrink wrap and then climbed underneath the massive object. It was being suspended about five feet off the ground by a series of concrete and metal supports. The smell under here was almost too much. Maas had to retrieve his bandanna and quickly tie it around his nose and mouth just to breathe, the fumes were so bad.

Finally he got to a point where he could lie down and shine his flashlight up and under the object and see most of its length. He did just that—and was astonished at what he saw. This was indeed a missile he'd crammed himself beneath; that was the reason for the overwhelming fumes reminiscent of the KSC. But as he'd previous divined, it was not an ICBM; it was much too big for that.

No, what the object was was an immense *Energia* booster rocket, a Russian-built behemoth used to lift thousands of pounds of cargo into outer space. And that was when it all started to come together for Maas. The booster rockets, the collection of nuclear weapons, big and small.

There really was only one conclusion . . .

They found Higgins crawling along the inside of the chain-link fence.

He was about 55 feet south of where he should have been. His rifle and video camera were gone, as were his utility belt, radio, and helmet. He was dazed, to say the least. He looked like he'd been drugged or gassed. He was incoherent when the men watching the southern hole in the fence discovered him. He was shimmying along on his hands and knees, babbling incoherent nonsense. His face was wet with some kind of gooey substance, as were his hands and neck.

At first they thought he'd been in a fight with one of the unfriendlies—what other explanation could there be? When they radioed this information back to Snyder at the CP, he sent in his reserve squad and then prepared to transmit a coded radio scramble back to KSC Command, telling them the mission had probably been compromised and they might need air support to get out.

Snyder then slid down the hill to the fence and, with Clancy Miller's help, dragged Higgins through the hole under the wire and back up to the helicopter. Now every JAWS guy inside the stockyard was ready to do battle—the problem was, there was no one to fight. A quick check of the guardhouses told of people still inside, snoring away. A quick IR sweep of the weapons depot showed no heat sources anywhere inside or around the immediate perimeter.

What *had* happened to Higgins? What had caused him to abandon his weapon and gear and wind up crawling along the fence?

It was a question that would have to wait for an answer. Snyder and Miller had a quick conversation and then decided it was best to sedate their colleague and ask questions later. They had one of the medics pump him with 20 cc's of morphine and then loaded him aboard one of the helicopters. Then Snyder put out the recall order to the remaining JAWS members inside the weapons yard. They'd been on the ground now for 20 minutes. It was time to get going.

Maas and his men came scrambling up the hill soon thereafter; one of them was carrying Higgins's gear. They found it piled neatly beside their entry point in the fence, almost as if someone had stacked it there just so they would see it. This was as baffling as Higgins's disturbing condition, but it was also a stroke of luck for the JAWS team, as it meant they would not be leaving any evidence of their daring recon mission behind.

The Sea Stallions started their engines at exactly 0205 hours, just five minutes off their schedule. Both aircraft took off just three minutes later, with all men accounted for and a wealth of video and audio information in their possession. The command officers of the team all rode back in the same helicopter.

Snyder, Maas, and Miller sat with their sedated colleague and held a whispered conversation, just low enough so the rest of the troopers could not hear. Their concern about Higgins was somewhat overwhelming, especially after their shared experience up on Chazy Mountain.

But they also had the operational situation to discuss. Despite the spookiness, their mission had been a success; they'd infiltrated the nuclear weapons storage yard and had come back with some hard intelligence.

But what had they discovered, exactly? They'd known going in that the weapons were probably not the type to affix to medium-range missiles, and therefore the southern part of the American continent was not in imminent danger of a sneak nuking—at least, not from these weapons.

No, it was what Maas had found that held the key. Energia rockets were like the tugboats of space. Their sole function was to boost heavy loads into orbit. The JAWS officers agreed that the presence of the big rockets—there were four in all—in the same storage area as the hodgepodge of nuclear weapons was probably not a coincidence.

So the bottom line was this: there were missiles here at the Double-Trouble site. But they weren't the kind that could be used to carry the various warheads to targets.

Rather, they were superboosters, rockets that could be used to carry all those nuclear warheads out of the atmosphere and put them into outer space.

Twenty

The formation of I1-28 Beagle bombers was first picked up on the Kennedy Space Center long-range radar net shortly after 0500 hours.

The initial indication was that 16 of the small two-engine jet bombers were circling out about 42 miles off the coast of Cape Canaveral. Their speed was pegged by KSC radar at about 110 knots, dangerously slow for the usually speedy airplane, and a clue that the potential attackers might actually be loitering, possibly in wait of a second force.

Discovering the flight of Beagles was a stroke of luck for the UAAF commanders. An ancient C-119 Flying Boxcar, serving as a radar picket aircraft, had first gained the Beagles on its radar scope just as it was returning from a routine patrol around the Keys. Once the bombers were bumped up to the main tactical situation screen in the VAB bunker, the C-119 was told to back off and continue monitoring the bombers for as long as possible. Then all UA radar units up and down the eastern Florida coast were made aware of the situation.

What the UAAF command staff was looking at now was a bomber force that could seriously damage, if not outright destroy, the Kennedy Space Center—and take only a minute or two to do so. But the command staff also faced a monumental problem. Because of the urgency of the nature of the UAAF's space program, the defensive aspects around the KSC were nowhere near complete. It was wholly ironic that the massive ground attack by the Norsemen two nights before had been staged against the space center's northern flank, the only section of the vast perimeter to have been finished. Had the Norsemen hit from the west or the south, the outcome could have been entirely different.

The same was true for the space center's air defenses. On hand were barely a dozen Patriot antiaircraft launchers, and four squads of 1st Airborne Division reserve troops equipped with portable Stinger missiles. That was it. All to protect a base that spanned 20 square miles and currently had nearly 1,000 highly skilled people on hand, along with a treasure trove of high technology.

Then there was the hodgepodge of aircraft currently operating from the five-mile shuttle runway. These were now a half-dozen C-5 gunships, so useless against a bomber attack that the UAAF commanders had sent an order to their crews to take off immediately and head west, away from the coast and any impending trouble. The same order was given for the Neptune lightships, the handful of troop carriers and unarmed cargo planes. Like ships leaving harbor before the storm, the airplanes were quickly being scrambled and flown out of harm's way, leaving behind a depleted and vulnerable base.

With the mysterious disappearance of the six Sabre jets, the only air defense fighters at KSC at the moment were a pair of old F-105 Thunderchiefs—technically a fighter bomber—and a single F-106 Delta Dart, a refugee from the destroyed Key West base. To make matters worse, the fuel situation was very low at the shuttle run-

way airstrip. Most of the gas had been given over to
the big gunships so they could get away. The Thunderchiefs and the Dart had about a full tank between
them. A quick calculation by the KSC intell section determined all three airplanes could stay in the air for
about six minutes each and no more.

There was, however, a joker in the deck—three of
them, in fact. They were sitting 300 miles away on the
pockmarked runway at Key West.

They were the pair of F-14 Tomcats and the single
F/A-18 Hornet captured during the bombardment of
the naval air station. Earlier that day, a small group of
pilots and air intelligence officers, using information
gained from interrogations of the Nazi pilots, had finally cracked security codes unlocking the flight control computers on the Hornet and one of the F-14s.
They had started the F/A-18 earlier in the day and had
reported all its flight systems up and working.

But what good could these airplanes do as far as the
impending action up at KSC? Nothing, so far as the
UAAF staff was concerned. But they made a quick
scrambled flash to Key West anyway, informing them
of the enemy bomber force forming off the eastern
Florida coast.

At the time, it seemed like the prudent thing to do.

This is not to say that there weren't *any* defenses
being prepared around the KSC.

On the contrary, the building of fortifications, bomb
shelters, defense lines, aircraft revetments, and AAA
sites had been proceeding at a feverish pace, even more
so since the events down in the Keys and in the aftermath of the Norse attack.

The morning before, the entire complement of the
104th New Jersey National Guard Combat Engineering

battalion had been secretly airlifted out of their R & R area on the Jersey shore and rushed down to the KSC, two weeks ahead of schedule. With all the strangeness that had been happening with the unit in Surf City—as far as they knew, their girls were still missing—to a man, everyone in the unit looked forward to the change in scenery.

In the 24 hours they'd been on the ground, the defensive face of the KSC had begun to take shape. Two 24-man units were immediately sent to repair the damage on the northern defensive line; bulldozed slit trenches, reenforced with concrete and steel, now made up the bulk of the perimeter. Another team was sent to shore up the southern end of the vast space center, laying down minefields whereever they could and installing everything from bunji-stake pits to "foo lines," trenches filled with natural gas piping to be ignited in case of attack.

The rest of the CE unit had begun work on setting up the Patriot antiaircraft missile emplacements, many of which had been flown in the day before the Norse attack. These SAM batteries were operational, but they'd been dispersed in a temporary fashion. The NJ104 engineers quickly set about moving them around to get the best in area defense from the 24 launchers on hand.

It had been a long, hard, strenuous job, but by midnight, 18 of the Patriot batteries were in their proper places. Ten had been arrayed in a wide semicircle to protect the VAB and the main KSC control buildings. Three had been set up to protect the small but important Banana River station. Three more had been installed around the complex's huge fuel storage area. This left only two for protection of the makeshift shuttle-strip airport. The plans for the next day were to install four more of the anti-aircraft launchers around the runway, making its defensive alignment complete and leaving two in reserve.

But for what was coming, this was a case of everything being just a day short.

For Don Matus, acting CO of NJ104, the first news about the gathering of Beagles came in a phone call from General Jones.

Matus and the other staff officers of NJ104—Vittelo, Palma, Cerbasi, DeLusso, and McCaffery—had been working nonstop since their arrival at the space center, typically down in the trenches with their troops, manning shovels and picks, trying to get the impossible done ahead of schedule.

Matus and McCaffery had worked the past 20 hours setting up the Patriots around the VAB. Both men had collapsed and were out cold when the phone rang inside the battalion bivouac at 0505 hours. Coincidently, their barracks were shaking as the huge C-5s were taking off to make good their escape, flying low and slow over the empty administration building the engineers had taken as their own.

Matus was surprised to hear the voice of General Jones. The general's friendly drawl sounded very tense—and thick with concern. He quickly briefed Matus on the situation and asked him to get his men back to the main part of the base as quickly as possible.

If and when the Ilyushins attacked, the men of NJ104 would be pressed into service—not as engineers, but as the manpower needed to work the Patriot batteries, something none of them had ever done before.

There was an art to firing a Patriot antiaircraft battery. The acquisition radar was probably the best ever built; it could spot and paint targets flying many miles up and more than 40 miles away. The tracking systems were also superb—once the Patriot began following an intruder, it was almost impossible for that intruder to break the lock. While a battery of microprocessors and minicomputers actually ran the show from the moment the enemy aircraft was sighted, there was a manual override built into the UA's version of the Patriot, just in case the operator wanted to launch against something coming in particularly low and particularly fast.

Something like an Ilyushin Beagle bomber.

By the time the NJ104 engineers made it to the area around the VAB bunker, the force of Beagle bombers off the coast had grown to 28. Even worse, a small flotilla of Sparviero missile boats had been picked up on surface radar, heading north up the coast. There was also a report from a UA spotter unit that maybe as many as three Enrico Toti submarines had been detected moving in the shallow waters off Vero Beach, also heading north.

This was highly disturbing news for the UAAF command staff. A massive attack was coming and the Kennedy Space Center was its intended target. By 0515 hours, every available man at the sprawling base had been mustered and sent to a defensive position. Many were directed to the beaches as the UA command feared that an armed landing might also accompany the attack or occur soon afterward. Others were put into trenches and behind defensive barriers dug the day before around the KSC's most important buildings.

For Don Matus and two squads of his NJ104 engineers, the positioning would be a bit higher. They were assigned to a Patriot missile battery that had been airlifted to the top of the massive VAB by one of the base's CH-54 Flying Crane helicopters. Two smaller Huey choppers were presently ferrying men from the ground to the top of the building. Matus went up on one of these flights, a short hop that took 60 seconds to complete and could be compared to flying up the side of an enormous concrete and steel mountain.

The top of the VAB was so high, the men who'd been placed there could already see the sun, slowly rising out of the ocean beyond the horizon. Matus and two of his electrical techs immediately went to work checking the power lines running into the Patriot missile battery. Though no one in the NJ104 team had ever worked a Patriot before, the computers inside the firing hut seemed fairly user-friendly. Once they'd determined that the antiaircraft system had enough electricity to operate, Matus and the techs sat down at the firing station and ran a quick diagnostic and training program through the system.

In clear, concise, and amazingly lifelike fashion, the computer ran a 3-D simulation on what it took to fire a Patriot. Basically it meant identifying the enemy aircraft, making sure all the systems were locked on it and then sitting back to let the software do its work. If everything went as it should, the missile would launch automatically when the bogey reached the outer portion of a 15-mile threat threshold and destroy the incoming aircraft about 35 seconds later.

But in combat, few things rarely went as they should—and no one knew that better than the men of NJ104.

Also positioned along the edge of VAB were four infantry teams carrying Stinger missiles, the smaller, portable, less powerful, but still dangerous antiaircraft weapons. These men were attached to the 1st Airborne Division Reserve, and as such, were probably among the most experienced regular combat troops at the KSC. They also had two .50-caliber machine guns set up, plus a small SBAT-127 multiple-rocket launcher which the Airborne troopers had captured in their travels.

Matus left the Patriot control hut and walked to the southeastern edge of the VAB; he needed to stretch some of the kinks out of his tired, lanky body. The waters of the Atlantic looked deceptively calm and sparkling in the growing dawn; it was hard to believe that anything other than the rising sun was waiting for them out beyond the horizon. The beaches, too, appeared to be eerily sane and inviting, despite the frentic activity as hundreds of UA troops rushed to their makeshift positions. It was the beginning of a perfect beach day. The waves looked high and clean and great for swimming. The nearby dunes and scrub trees would provide shade once the sun became too hot. A little lunch. Maybe a cooler of beer. Matus wiped a bead of sweat from his brow. If only we could take the day off, he thought . . .

But then more sobering notions came flooding in. Matus couldn't help but think about what had happened at Surf City and the strangeness surrounding the disappearance of the four young girls. Though the townspeople were still looking for them, few had any hope they'd ever be found. He stared into the unfolding dawn now, removing his Fritz helmet and rubbing his tired neck. A rare wave of philosophical feelings washed over him. He was hardly a religious man, but he did recall some Bible training from when he was a boy . . . something about how the faithful and the innocent would be lifted up into the heavens before the final battle between good and evil heralded the end of the world.

At that moment he looked straight up into the brightening sky and saw that it was turning the color of blood. From one dark horizon to the other, the sky was becoming a bright, deep crimson, as vivid as a sunset, yet just minutes from the dawn. Matus felt a chill go right through him. He'd never seen anything like this before.

Then it hit him: maybe today *was* Doomsday and the end *was* near. After all, the signs were everywhere. The red sky. The eerie calm. A world gone completely insane. Wars raging full tilt around the globe, the fighting worse since the Big War. Maybe this *was* all part of one big cosmic conclusion. Maybe the four missing girls were in a vanguard of innocents that the cosmos had decided to spare, a divine evacuation before Armageddon arrived.

Matus shook his head. It all seemed to make so much sense under this blood-red sky. And yet, deep down, he realized these apocalyptic musings actually made him feel better.

Maybe those who had disappeared were the lucky ones, he thought finally. Maybe they'd be spared the glimpse of hell that might soon come . . .

He was broken out of these deep thoughts by an urgent cry from one of his electrical techs. Matus raced back to the Patriot command hut where a message from the bunker below the VAB was waiting.

"Click on your long-range imaging radar," one of the command officers told him. "And get everyone up there ready for action."

Matus did as he'd been told and soon punched up the Patriot's powerful acquisition radar. To his astonishment, he found himself looking at a long-range live TV feed that showed a formation of at least two dozen small jet bombers apparently heading right toward them. The Patriot's threat-archive screens were identifying them as Ilyushin-28s. The targeting radar said they were now 31 miles off the coast and coming on fast. Matus called back down to the bunker, reported what he saw, and asked for further instructions.

The reply was curt and brief.

"Start firing," the anonymous bunker officer told him, adding rather ominously, "and you can start praying, too."

The first Patriot missile went up from the roof of the VAB 15 seconds later.

The 17-foot rocket whooshed away from its launcher at an incredibly high speed, leaving behind a trail of white, almost luminescent smoke as it turned over and disappeared beyond the horizon.

Matus was seated in the Patriot management center's main control chair, astonished as he watched the missile approach the oncoming bomber formation on the live TV feed. The imaging was so clear he could clearly see the bombs hanging from the lead Beagle's wings, the airplane's slapdash blue and white camouflage scheme, and even the two pilots ensconced inside the aircraft nose.

Then, just like that, the bomber was gone, replaced by a flash of light and then a ball of flame. Their first Patriot had hit its mark. A chorus of buzzers and flashing lights on the control panel confirmed this.

But just as soon as this plane vanished, another one came up to take its place. And then another behind that, and another behind that. Now the forward Patriot batteries were firing, as well as those arrayed on the ground around the VAB. Matus somehow found the button which gave his TV screen a long range. Within seconds he was looking at the entire formation of Ilyushins again, this time as the waves of Patriots were cutting into them.

His battery locked onto another target and automatically fired its second missile. A third target was acquired seconds later, and the third missile went up in

a flash. Matus was astounded. Never had he seen combat played out so quickly, so up-close and violent. It
was like watching a movie. The planes dropping from
the TV screen looked like products of a special-effects
team; the people inside them did, too. Everything
looked so real, it seemed *un*real.

But the racket coming from outside the hut dragged
him back to reality quickly enough. The whooshing of
Patriot missiles going off was nearly deafening now.
Somewhere, air raid sirens were wailing. Big guns could
be heard, though Matus had no idea who was firing
them or at what targets.

The VAB-rooftop Patriot battery fired its fourth and
fifth missile a few seconds later. Both left in a hurricane
of smoke and exhaust, heading up into the dreadful
red sky and quickly disappearing over the horizon.
Equally fascinated and horrified, Matus watched them
take out two more bombers on the wide screen, destroying them utterly with their high-explosive fragmentation warheads, setting off the underwing
weapons even as the doomed pilots tried desperately
to unload them.

The rooftop launcher fired its sixth and final missile
about 10 seconds later. Matus chose not to stay and
watch this one go up. He left the command chair and
ran back out to the rooftop. The Beagle formation, or
what was left of it, was now 12 miles away. He was sure
he'd be able to get a visual on them very soon.

The scene that greeted him on the outside was like
something from a Bosch nightmare. Missiles were going off all around him. The crimson sky above the KSC
was crisscrossed with contrails, seemingly hundreds of
them. Off in the distance, he could hear many violent
explosions; it was like the air was vibrating with incredible shock waves. With each successive blast, his ears

began to ache a little more. It was getting so loud, so fast, he was sure they'd start bleeding soon.

Strangely, though, the beaches below him still looked tranquil, peaceful, inviting. He couldn't stop thinking about how warm the water must be, how high the waves were, and how much he would have liked swimming around in them, just as he'd done so many times before as a kid . . .

Another loud explosion shook him back to real time. This one was not up in the clouds somewhere, but very, very close. He turned to see an enormous geyser of smoke and flame rising up from the main communications building about a half-mile north of the VAB. The smoke was quickly blown away to reveal the place had been vaporized. There was nothing left—no building, no antennas, no satellite dishes. Nothing but a hole and a huge ring of fire around it.

Matus knew instantly what had happened. He pulled out his long-range binoculars and trained them out on the eastern horizon. Sure enough, he could see a handful of bluish specks out there, each of them kicking up a geyser of smoke and water behind it. They were the Sparviero fast-attack boats. One of them had just fired a Styx missile at the KSC and had destroyed the comm shack.

Now three more Styx had been launched. Matus could see their fiery trails coming out of the water and right toward him at incredible speed. He had just enough time to shout a warning to the troops on top of the VAB when the trio of missiles went over their heads, emitting an ear-piercing screech as they streaked by. An instant later, all three came down, not on any KCS building, but out on the shuttle runway behind the base. There were three enormous explosions—they were so powerful, Matus imagined he could feel the VAB actually shaking. When the smoke and fire cleared, it revealed three gigantic holes in the middle of the very long airstrip.

A series of shouts brought his attention back to the front of the building. Three I1-28 Beagles were roaring in right over the beach. They were so low, Matus was actually looking down on them. They were also flying so close together, they seemed like one aircraft.

Matus didn't even have to yell out a command. Suddenly everyone on the rooftop was firing at the three bombers. The 1st Airborne guys opened up with their own twin big fifties. At least two Stingers went off. Even some of his own engineers were firing down on the jet bombers with their M-16s.

But the Ilyushins were way too fast for any of this fire to do any good. They streaked by the VAB in a flash, somehow got even closer to the ground, turned slightly to the right, and as one, unloaded their weapons on the cratered shuttle runway. Then, in a combined scream of exhaust and power, they pulled up slightly and disappeared over the western horizon.

Suddenly the firing from the top of the VAB started up again. Another trio of Beagles was roaring in. The next thing he knew, Matus found himself on the railing, too, firing his M-16 at the oncoming jet bombers. They rocketed by so close to them, Matus imagined he could see his own stream of bullets pinging off the left wing of the nearest bomber. A Stinger went right over his head and began a high-speed chase of the three airplanes. Once again, all three airplanes headed for the shuttle runway. Once again, they dropped their loads in a precise bombing pattern. Once again, a series of enormous blasts shook the VAB and everything around it.

The Stinger finally caught up with the attackers. It clipped the tail section of the middle airplane, blowing it off the bomber and causing the attacker to spiral

first up and then straight down. The Beagle hit with
the impact of a Styx, exploding on contact and blowing
yet another hole in the already battered runway. The
two surviving aircraft streaked away.

There were cheers coming up from the troopers on
the roof, but Matus knew better. It was obvious now
that the attackers were intent on destroying the shuttle
runway—and doing a good job of it. As if to emphasize
this, three more Styx missiles went overhead, slamming
down onto a trio of temporary support buildings lining
the temporary air base.

Three more Beagles were coming over the beach.
Furious, Matus threw a new clip into his rifle and began
firing again. In his scope he could see the lead bomber,
oddly framed against the aquablue sea and luxurious-
looking waves. Two Stingers went shooting off the
rooftop; somewhere below, a Patriot rose up to meet
the trio of attackers. Suddenly the sound of firing and
missile engines mixing with the roar of the oncoming
jets reached a crescendo. Matus had never seen combat
this intense, this desperate, this insane.

Yes, the world had gone crazy, he decided in this split
second, the sky in front of him actually crowded with
bombers, missiles, and tracer fire. Yes, the missing girls
had been taken to spare them what was to come. These
were the opening shots of some final battle—all of this
seemed frighteningly clear to Matus at this point.

As the Beagles streaked by, one of them was caught
simultaneously by a Patriot and a Stinger. It immediately slammed into the plane next to it and both blew
up not 200 feet in front of Matus's eyes. He could feel
the heat on his face; the terrible noise rose in his ears.
Yes, this was madness, he could see it, hear it, and taste
it.

Then came a scream. He turned to see a huge streak
of fire in the red sky overhead, coming straight at him.

It was a Styx missile, either fired directly at the VAB or falling short of its target on the runway. It slammed into the roof of the VAB a split second later, exploding with a might crash and taking out the northeast corner of the building.

Don Matus found himself flying. He was heading out to sea. Below him was the beach he'd been admiring, and the blue water and those great waves. They would be the last thing he remembered as he was blown off the building and out onto the ocean.

Those waves . . . they looked even better from up here.

It was one of those flukes of combat—a pinprick of light amid the fog of war—that the two helicopters carrying the JAWS infiltration teams arrived back in the vicinity of the Kennedy Space Center shortly after the beginning of the murderous attack.

Though under orders to maintain strict radio silence throughout the entire mission, including the ride home, the JAWS members were nevertheless able to listen in on the emergency frequencies coming out of the space center and thus were aware that their home base was being bombarded by both aircraft and Styx missiles.

They could tell by the frantic radio calls going back and forth between the UA command staff and the defense forces that the attackers were concentrating on the makeshift air base and its communications capabilities—and studiously leaving alone the space center's launch facilities and support buildings.

This only lent more credence to the conclusion made by the JAWS team that the attackers didn't want to destroy KSC as much as they wanted to capture it in order to launch the Energia rockets and their nuclear payloads into space. By the way things seemed to be deteriorating for the UA forces, how to prevent the enemy from doing just that seemed like an impossible task—short of destroying the space center.

The pair of Sea Stallions came upon the frightening attack about ten minutes in. What greeted them were columns of smoke rising high into the red morning sky, sheets of flames from the destroyed communications buildings, a firestorm over the long, perforated shuttle runway, and the air filled with Beagle bombers and expended missile contrails. Offshore, the four small Sparvee rocket boats were maneuvering in closer to the beach in anticipation of launching another barrage.

Further out on the horizon was a new, even greater threat. Six battleships belonging to the Asian Mercenary Cult were steaming toward the action. Now the role of the Toti submarines became clear—they'd been employed not to attack the KSC, but to check the depth of the bay leading into the space complex. Was it deep enough to support six huge battleships? Unfortunately for the UAAF, it was.

It didn't take a military genius to figure out the battleships were probably stocked to the gills with troops, a common practice of the Cult. In the past, the Cult had carried as many as 1,000 marines per battleship. This meant a potential landing force of 6,000 men was offshore, waiting for the softening up of the KSC defenses to finish before they attempted a landing.

With barely 1000 people defending the space center, how could that landing be anything but successful?

As it turned out, the fact that all of the JAWS officers were riding on the same helicopter was fortuitous. This way they were able to assess the situation in a more or less secure environment. But what should they do, exactly? It would have been acceptable for them to fly to an area unaffected by the battle and set down to wait until things were all clear. This course of action would have been perfectly understandable—after all, the JAWS team was returning from an combat-intensive in-filtration mission. Many of the men had been up for at least 24 hours and after the long flight were probably depleted.

But sitting on the sidelines just because you were a little tired was not the style of the UAAF and definitely not the style of the guys from JAWS.

They knew they had to do something—something big and dramatic; nothing less would do. But there were a few problems. First, both choppers were run-ning dangerously low on fuel. Second, two helicopters flying around low and slow in the middle of the attack would make inviting targets for the gunners aboard the battleships and the Ilyushins. Not to mention the dan-ger of getting hit by friendly fire.

After a quick discussion, the JAWS officers decided they should head in the opposite direction.

With little fanfare, they directed the pilots of the two Sea Stallions to head further out to sea.

The Sparvee fast-attack boat was a strange little weapon.

It was no bigger than a speedboat, so small it could barely hold its crew of ten. Many of its surface materials were made of plastic and aluminum, none of them strong enough to stop a bullet. Because the boat re-quired an inordinate amount of gasoline to get from one place to another, it carried several large reserve fuel tanks at its rear. Unprotected and vulnerable to the slightest spark, Sparvees were known to become completely engulfed in flames within 30 seconds of a fuel-tank rupture and sink in less than a minute, usually with all hands still aboard.

But there was an upside to these dangerous little boats. They packed more firepower than some ships ten times their size. In reality, a Sparvee was less a boat and more like a floating missile launcher, especially ones readapted after the Big War. Gone were the front-mounted 5-inch naval guns. Now most Sparvees carried four Styx missile launchers, each capable of firing a semiguided SSM weapon carrying a warhead packed with several hundred pounds of highly explosive fragmentation bombs. One of these missiles hitting the right place on a heavy cruiser, a battleship, or even an aircraft carrier could probably sink that ship. Four missiles in the right place would destroy it utterly. It was the ultimate naval version of David and Goliath. And the Styx missiles worked just as well on land targets.

The Sparvees were also hydrofoils, and as such, they could reach speeds as high as 50 knots. This was great for maneuvering as well as getting away once their missile loads were expended. But there was a downside to this above-the-water capability: it was very noisy at full throttle, so noisy that every man aboard a Sparvee had to wear a radio headset just to communicate with the man standing next to him. So noisy that sometimes the crew was unable to hear the loudest noises of a battle raging around them.

So noisy it could drown out the racket of an approaching helicopter . . .

Ernesto Sparviero had served aboard the noisy fast-attack boats for so long he'd taken the vessel's name as his own.

Ernesto's squadron of four boats, known as *Elixo,* made up part of a naval mercenary team originally out of Genoa, Italy. They'd seen almost continuous action in the five years since the Big War, mostly around the Mediterranean or in the Arabian Gulf, but with forays as far away as the Indian Ocean and the Malay Peninsula.

This job to the American continent was the longest and most enduring ever for the *Elixo* squadron. The trip over from Europe had been stormy and plagued with mechanical problems. Once in place near an isolated chain of islands in the northern Bahamas, the *Elixo* fleet had to wait for two months until the people who had hired them—their identities were unknown to Ernesto and his mates at the time—got their battle plans in order.

More bad weather and a number of false starts delayed their seeing action even further. At one point, the four attack boats had to retreat to the islands south of Cuba after the mighty hurricane now battering the northeastern part of America had come too close to their Upper Caribbean hiding places.

But finally, all of the attack elements came into place. While massing off northern Cuba a week ago, Ernesto and his men saw for the first time the Beagle bombers and the Toti submarines and knew that they were about to become engaged in a major action.

But it wasn't until they saw the flotilla of battleships—they looked like ghosts on the misty horizon that foggy morning seven days ago—and the squadrons of swastika-adorned F-18s and F-14s flying overhead that they realized exactly who their employers were. And that's when it all began to make some rather frightening sense. They were working for two of the most ruthless, feared entities on earth: the Asian Mercenary Cult and the Fourth Reich. Their opponent would be the United Americans, undoubtedly the most respected.

This revelation put fear into the hearts of Ernesto and his comrades. True, they were mercenaries, and by definition, they fought for the highest bidder. But even in their cold hearts they knew that getting in league with the Fourth Reich and the Cult would probably lead only to misery and despair, especially if they believed, as most people in the Old World did, that these two forces were actually just military fronts for a far more nefarious entity: Viktor II, the devil himself.

All this made Ernesto and his mates very uneasy, and the night before they sailed from Cuba, they all took a vote to renege on their contract and return to Europe. Word of this reached one of the Cult's low commanders, who sent two representatives to discuss the action with Ernesto's immediate superior, a captain named Bilbaldi.

The next morning, Bilbaldi's head was found attached to a spike on the quarterdeck of Sparvee number 1. After that, the rest of the *Elixo* fleet reconsidered its decision to bolt.

When the rest of the attacking force sailed north toward UA Florida, the Spavees of *Elixo* squadron sailed with them.

Now Ernesto and his men were in the thick of it— and so far, things weren't going that badly.

The Beagle bombers were plastering the objective— which Ernesto and his crew thought was just a large American air base—and their Styx missiles had destroyed three of the four targets they'd been assigned, communications huts apparently vital to the UA's operations. Further out to sea, the gang of Cult battleships was waiting, their holds filled with bloodthirsty marines just itching to get ashore and kill. From Ernesto's point of view, standing on the bridge of *Elixo*

2, the action could be wrapped up by noontime. The Cult would have destroyed the UA air base and then invaded and killed whatever survivors were left. Then Ernesto and his colleagues could collect their money and start the long voyage home.

So maybe their initial fears had been unnecessary, he kept telling himself. Maybe they could make a lot of money here and get out with their lives.

But then again, maybe not.

Ernesto's men were loading and arming Styx launcher number 4 when he heard the strange sound.

The years of working on the Sparvee boats had damaged his own hearing considerably—this was an occupational hazard they all endured—and at first he ignored the high-pitched whine that was somehow leaking through his headphones and into his dirty ears. He was maneuvering the boat in further toward the shoreline—the last missile shot was their furthest, a huge igloo-like communications building located about three kilometers in, and therefore isolated from the rest of the squadron. The Styx missile was originally built for ship-to-ship combat; firing one at a land target took a little more finesse. Ernesto knew the closer he could get to the shoreline, the better the chances of hitting the target. As their eventual pay would be based on the number of assigned objectives they actually destroyed, he was determined to put the last missile right on the money.

He'd moved the boat to a position just slightly more than a mile offshore. From here, the columns of smoke and flame rising from the American position were so evident, Ernesto imagined he could feel the heat from the battle zone. He was quick to dismiss this as a figment of his imagination—just like the strange whining noise in his ears.

His headset crackled once; it was a report from his first missile officer. Launcher number 4 was ready to fire. Ernesto did one last check of his position and radioed the helmsman, who was standing right next to him, to reduce speed and prepare to fire.

Oddly, the helmsman did not respond. Ernesto repeated the order, then looked over at the man, who was looking straight back at him, a silent scream etched on his face. A gush of blood suddenly cascaded out of his mouth and nose. He fell forward, landing on the throttles, unluckily for Ernesto and the rest of the crew, stalling the engines at the worst possible time. The man then slumped to the deck. For the first time, Ernesto realized he had a hole in his back the size of a bocci ball.

Startled and more than a little confused—Ernesto was certain that a stray shell from one of the other boats had killed his helmsman—he quickly spun around expecting to see another of the Sparvee boats right on his tail. What he found instead was a monstrous black helicopter hovering off the bow not 20 feet away from him, its open left door filled with heavily armed men firing their weapons down at him. The strange noise he'd heard but ignored had been the helicopter's huge engines, unmuffled and straining, as they'd come closer to his speeding boat.

Now Ernesto realized that three more of the crew were lying on the deck behind him, bleeding heavily, their bodies riddled with bullets, that the number 2 launcher was engulfed in flames, and that soldiers were jumping out of the unstable helicopter and onto his deck, firing their weapons in every direction but his own.

What is this? These words echoed in Ernesto's ears.

His first thought, irrational and panicked, was that the Cult had sent these soldiers to kill him and his crew because of some transgression they'd committed. It wouldn't be the first time a mercenary's employer had decided to kill the hired help rather than pay them.

But in the next moment, Ernesto realized these heavily armed men jumping onto his swift little boat were not Cult soldiers or anyone in their employ. They didn't move like Cult warriors and they seemed more determined than mercenaries. That's when Ernesto finally reached the only other logical conclusion.

These soldiers were Americans, and they were here to capture his boat.

Trying to fight them was futile. In the few seconds since Ernesto realized what was going on, more than 20 American soldiers had jumped to his deck, an action made infinitely easier since the boat's powerful engines had stalled. Ernesto screamed an order into his microphone, telling his crew not to resist, to let the invaders have their way and maybe they would get out of this with their lives.

But when Ernesto looked around and began counting the bodies on the boat's tiny deck, there were nine, each one wearing the distinctive blue striped jersey of the *Elixo* squadron. Ernesto realized he had no more crew. They were all dead. He was the only one left—and now the Americans were climbing up to the bridge to get him.

A few prayers ran through his mind in the seconds it took for the fierce troopers to reach him. They seemed awfully big to him; he was a slight Mediterranean type. They seemed to be in possession of more weapons, utilities, ammo belts, and combat gear than any one person could possibly carry. The first man to reach him slammed his fist into Ernesto's jaw, then knocked him across the control column. Another kicked him hard twice in the seat of his pants. Another drew out a frighteningly sharp serrated knife and put it across Ernesto's unprotected neck. The steel of the blade was so cold it seemed blazing hot to Ernesto. He was certain he would die in the next second.

But the man with the knife bent down close to his ear, so close Ernesto thought he was going to bite it off. The man had a question for him. His voice gruff, his tone leaving no doubt that he would just as soon slit Ernesto's throat as to save it, he asked him in very broken Italian: *How many missiles do you have left on board?*

Ever the diplomat, Ernesto gave the exact answer the American wanted to hear: *As many as you want.*

Mark Snyder was holding on for dear life.

The acting JAWS CO was hanging halfway out of the open door of the Sea Stallion helicopter, an enormous .50-caliber machine gun between his legs, a series of safety harnesses lashed tightly around the rest of his body, trying to shout orders down to his men on the deck of the captured Sparvee missile boat just 20 feet below.

It was a hard thing to do, though. The commotion around them was deafening. The racket of the helicopter, its noise dampeners long ago blown out, the sound of the missile boat's engines, now restarted and screaming, and the roar of the battle still going on all around them combined to make any conversation, real or amplified, virtually impossible.

So Snyder just gave up. The two squads of men on the missile boat knew what they had to do. He gave a thumbs-up to the pilot of his chopper, and slowly the huge flying beast finally moved away. A Beagle bomber suddenly flashed overhead and was met with a barrage of machine gun fire from the second Sea Stallion hov-

ering right next to Snyder's. The wall of tracer fire rising up toward the Ilyushin was more than enough to
chase the bomber away. It was clear its crew wanted no
part of whatever was happening on the water's surface
below.

From Snyder's vantage point now, he saw the tiny
attack boat stop almost dead in the water, turn 180
degrees to its left, and then start moving again, this
time straight out to sea. Another Beagle went over, its
pilots too intent on getting out of the battle zone to
pay attention to the attack boat or the pair of choppers
hovering nearby. The sky was still filled with exploding
AAA fire as well as Stinger missile bursts. It really was
no place for an airplane to be.

However, one of the other *Elixo* boats did take notice.
Their squadron commander's boat was apparently leaving the field of battle and they wanted to know why.
Plagued with the same noise problem as all the other
attack boats, this particular vessel took off in pursuit of
Elixo 2. If the lead ship was hightailing it out of there,
then the last thing they wanted was to be left behind.

Watching from the JAWS chopper, Snyder knew this
added a complication to what was already a tenuous
plan. The second boat had to be dealt with. Using hand
signals, he conveyed this to the other JAWS chopper
and together they swooped down on the unsuspecting
Sparvee.

For the crew of this boat, the end came quickly. The
lead JAWS chopper came up behind it, turned slightly
to the left, and with as many troopers as could fit in
the open doorway, laid a barrage of automatic weapons
fire onto the boat's pair of reserve fuel tanks left so
woefully unprotected on the bow. Meanwhile, Snyder's
copter blindsided the boat from the left, mimicking
the other JAWS aircraft and sending a fusillade into
the control house. The combined aerial assault paid

off at almost the exact same moment. The bridge house went up with a great *whopp!* just as the fuel tanks at the rear of the vessel exploded. The pair of attacking helicopters got out of the way before the remaining Styx missiles blew up, spraying thousands of deadly exploding bomblets all over the area.

There was one great explosion now as everything flammable and combustible aboard the small ship erupted at once. When the smoke finally cleared, nothing was left but an oil spot and a few pieces of charred and burning flotsam.

In the meantime, *Elixo* 2 was three miles from its last position, the JAWS troopers on board demanding that the swift little boat's engines be locked on full throttle. If anyone else still involved in the battle took notice, they didn't act upon it. The pair of remaining Sparvees continued launching Styx missiles into the KSC and the third and final flight of Beagles was about halfway through their bombing run. All that remained now was for the six Cult battleships to begin moving in for the anticipated landing and the carnage that would undoubtably follow.

But there was a glitch in this plan: It was the newly commandeered *Elixo* 2.

The Cult battleship *Miajappe* was serving as the command ship for this operation.

On-board was a clique of Cult naval officers known as The Far-Away Boys, warriors who specialized in military campaigns far from the Japanese Home Islands, which served as home base for the Asian Mercenary Cult. These men were regarded as much for their brutality as for their far-flung military adventures. Their reputation was so bad, they were feared even at home in Japan, which was why the Cult hierarchy allowed them to sail to all parts of the world killing, terrorizing, and otherwise satiating their bloodlust as far away from their own shores as possible.

This, their attack on the East Coast of America, was their crowning achievement—more so, as their every move had been transmitted back to Japan and was being followed by the millions of Cult followers on the Home Islands. A successful completion of this campaign could mean only good things for the Far-Away Boys. They would be further lionized in the eyes of their people, further feared in the eyes of their enemies, and further ingratiated into the good graces of Viktor II, the person they wanted to please most of all.

To ensure success, the Far-Away Boys had sailed from Japan with a division of "specialty troops" in the holds of their vast battleships. These soldiers, all of them veterans of earlier Cult terror campaigns, had been selected not so much for their skill and combat experience as for their demonstrated killing capacities, their absolute lack of human feelings, and their willingness to inflict pain on anyone at any time for any purpose.

The bloodlust of these troops was at such a high level that during the six-week voyage to the Atlantic, the ships had been forced to stop at several spots in the Indian Ocean, near the tip of Africa, and in Dominica. At each stop, special landing parties had gone ashore and rounded up several dozen local residents, mostly girls and young women, but also some mature men and boys. These poor souls were then literally fed to the Cult specialty troops below decks, none of whom had seen the light of day, or any light at all, for a month and a half. These human sacrifices were torn apart as if they'd been thrown to a pack of wild dogs. In some cases, their bodies were eaten, in others, mutilated to the point of being unrecognizable. All this was done to keep the "specialty troops" in the right frame of mind for their eventual landing on the Florida coast.

Now it appeared like this perverted dream was about to come true. In the hold of the *Miajappe*, the specialty troops had been given their combat gear and had been issued rifles, ammunition, a liquor ration, a dozen pep pills, and two machetes apiece. Even over the growl of the battleship's massive engines, haunting war chants, along with yelps, shrieks, and screams, could be heard coming from deep below. From all appearances, the battle to soften up the KSC was going well, especially as it was being viewed from the bridge of the *Miajappe*. The dozens of columns of smoke alone seemed to prove that the hired Beagle bombers had done their selective job adequately, as had the Sparvee missile boats. The Far-Away Boys planned to slaughter every-one left alive in these two mercenary groups—but that wouldn't be until the victory party. What would come first was the landing of their bloodthirsty troops and the orgasmic slaughter of the Americans inside the space center.

Because this was such a special moment, all six of the Far-Away Boys had gathered on the bridge of the *Miajappe*. The honor of giving the formal order for the six battleships to move into shore was presented to the oldest member of their group, Admiral Kurasawa Kiamoto. With great fanfare, the admiral growled an order into the ship's intercom, commanding the en-gine room to increase speed by two thirds and bring the great ship into the bay. Behind the *Miajappe*, the five other battle wagons would follow suit. The landings would begin within 15 minutes.

Watching from the bridge of their command ship, the Far-Away Boys decided it was time to pose for a photo. After all, this was an historic occasion. The ship's photographer was called for, and once it was set up, he had the six officers stand side by side on the bow of the ship, just below the Imperial War Flag.

"Tojerki!" the photographer called out, asking the six men for the Cult version of a smile. The men complied and the photographer snapped his one and only picture.

Had it been developed, this photo would have revealed the six smiling officers, their uniforms rippling slightly, their pants bulging in anticipation of the savagery to come.

But in the upper left-hand corner, the photo would have shown something else: an incoming Styx missile, its warhead filled with 500 pounds of high explosive, heading right for the bridge of the battleship *Miajappe.*

Clancy Miller saw the Styx missile strike the deck of the huge battleship even as he was trying to keep his balance and prevent himself from falling out of the Sea Stallion helicopter.

The JAWS officer was part of a human chain that was attempting to lower a rope ladder down to the JAWS commandos still on the Sparvee fast-attack boat and lift them to safety.

It was apparent from the get-go, however, that this would be a difficult thing to do. The missile boat's engines was locked into full throttle when the Styx finally fired at the *Miajappe,* but the resulting backfire seared the control cables to the engines below. Thus the power plants were stuck open and could not be slowed down.

This meant that the hovering JAWS helicopters would have to attempt to pluck the dozen or so JAWS troopers still aboard the fast-attack boat from its decks even as it was traveling along the surface at speeds upward of 50 knots.

Still, Miller found himself looking up at the battleship as the huge missile struck it square on the bridge. The warhead exploded just a split second later, long enough, though, for the missile to drive itself down three decks and hit the ship's auxiliary magazine. There was a second, even bigger explosion just moments after the first as tons of cannon shells and incendiary bombs began blowing up.

Not five seconds later came an enormous third explosion. This one was so powerful, it lifted the huge battleship right out of the water, breaking it in two and sending it back to the surface, where the two halves quickly sank between the waves. Debris from the explosion carried to nearly a half mile away, much of it slamming into the forecastle and rear turret of the next-in-line battleship, the older, slightly smaller *Nomisti*. This caused one of the ship's rear guns to discharge, sending a mammoth one-ton shell right into the hull of the third-in-line battleship, the newer, stainless steel *Argohrra*. Two more secondary explosions occurred as the shell hit the main boiler room. In seconds, this battleship's midsection was ablaze.

Mouth agape, not quite believing what he was seeing, Clancy Miller managed to let out a long, low whistle. All of this happened in less than 15 seconds, an incredible chain of events that sank one large battleship and set two others aflame.

The JAWS team wanted to do something dramatic, and on this count, at least, they'd fulfilled that desire.

"What would have happened," Miller wondered aloud, "if we'd fired two missiles?"

Miller was snapped back to the reality of the moment, the attempt to retrieve the JAWS troopers still stuck on the out-of-control attack boat.

Two men had been able to clasp the hand of the man who was hanging onto the feet of the man Clancy himself was hanging onto. How these two soldiers were able to scramble up and into the helicopter to safety he would never know.

But there were still 10 men on the attack boat and the vessel itself was smoking badly from the rear, its engines were pitched so high. No one on-board either chopper had to be told what would happen to the Sparvee if a heat source reached the two unprotected fuel tanks on its bow. Just like the *Miajappe* battleship they'd just greased, there'd be nothing left but an oil slick.

There was an added peril. The three remaining battleships, the captains obviously catching on to what was happening in the bay, were steaming right toward the runaway Sparvee, their big guns turning to register on the speeding attack craft. Even worse, two Beagles had apparently been ordered back to the battle scene and were now circling angrily overhead. Though the jet bombers had unleashed all of their underwing weapons, they were still armed with lethal cannons in the nose and tail.

Clancy Miller was taking all of this in, even as a third JAWS trooper managed to scramble up the human ladder to the safety of the helicopter. But this would be the last soldier they'd be able to rescue this way. For at that very moment, a Beagle was peeling off and heading down the gullet at them, its nose guns blazing away.

Miller imagined seeing the Sea Stallion disintegrate around him, and then having himself fall into the sea. The Beagle was moving too fast and its dive had been too shallow to get an accurate burst anywhere near the Sea Stallion. The two-engine aircraft streaked overhead, its tail gunner firing randomly down on the chopper, an action that was answered with some valiant but equally off-the-mark firing from the soldiers in both Sea Stallions.

The Beagle's pass forced the choppers to move away from the speeding attack boat. Now the Sparvee was heading right into the flames left behind by the *Mia-jappe*'s sinking. Somehow, someone on the boat was able at least to get control of the steering column. As the rest of the JAWS team watched in a mixture of hope and horror, the boat skimmed up and over the worst of the fire and managed to go around the largest pieces of floating wreckage.

But this action caused it to come under the guns of the fourth battleship, the enormous *Itibiti*. In a flash, the ship let loose with a massive barrage from the trio of 16-inch guns on its front turret. The three gigantic shells streaked across the bay and over the runaway attack boat by a margin of 40 feet or more. When they hit the water, it was like three watery volcanos had suddenly erupted. The spray alone nearly swamped the speeding attack boat.

By this time, the second Beagle had swooped down and was now heading for Clancy's chopper. It was going much slower than its predecessor and had begun its firing run further out in order to be more accurate. Clancy was still hanging out of the open cargo door; he'd finally pulled in the last man in the human chain. Now he was living a moment of frightening déjà vu: a Beagle bomber, its nose aglow with cannon fire, was bearing right down on him.

This time he knew there would be no errors in speed or aiming. He could already see the cannon shells streaking overhead, just a few feet from the helicopter's twirling rotors. In that moment Clancy saw part of his life pass before his eyes. He was a kid again, cramming for some big exam in high school, not having the time or the right materials with which to study. To flunk meant summer school or repeating a grade. He remembered turning on his radio and by mistake, passing by a 24-hour-a-day religious station. The preacher, screaming at the top of his lungs, was bellowing, "Expect a miracle, you heathen lamb!" Clancy took the advice to heart and the next day went to school to learn his teacher had been arrested the night before for pandering and the test was indefinitely postponed.

But what kind of miracle could get him out of this one? he wondered desperately, as his mind flashed back to the present and the reality of the Beagle's front guns carving into him at any moment.

He got his answer a moment later.

As he would recall it, the Beagle was about 200 feet out, its guns still blazing, when suddenly it was gone. No smoke. No fire. Just gone.

The plane hadn't simply vanished—though in these particular times and in this particular area, that wouldn't have been an impossibility. This miracle had a more earthly basis to it. The bomber had been blown out of the sky, shot to pieces so completely that it broke up and fell into the ocean so quickly as to give the appearance to someone looking down its gun barrels that it had vaporized.

The vehicle of this odd deliverance was something of a miracle in itself, and Clancy still didn't understand it until he saw the flash of silver and gray and the great twin streams of smoke and exhaust streak by him.

Only then did he realize it was an F-14 Tomcat which had destroyed the Beagle, one which was now painted, if crudely, in the blue and white colors of the UAAF, one of the trio of airplanes captured after the devastating attack on Key West just a few days before. Somehow the three supersonic airplanes—two Tomcats and the single F/A-18 Hornet—had arrived just in the nick of time to save the JAWS chopper and everyone on board.

"You heathen lamb," Clancy Miller whispered to himself, as the Hornet and the second Tomcat streaked right by him as well. "Your sorry ass has been saved again . . ."

At just about the same time Miller was having his epiphany, Warren Maas was watching a very odd scene out the portside window of the Sea Stallion.

Three airplanes were swooping down on the fifth-in-line battleship, the all-black and menacing-looking *Okido*. The lead airplane was the F/A-18, its wings sagging with the weight of bombs hanging from its hard points. Behind it was one of the KSC's ancient F-105 Thunderchiefs, an airplane that was old when it fought in the First Vietnam War, back in the 1960s. Behind it was an equally elderly F-106 Delta Dart, an airplane that defined the term "interceptor"—as opposed to "fighter"—and really had no business diving in on a naval target, never mind one so formidable and well armed as the *Okido*.

As Maas watched, jaw agape, at the unusual scene, the trio of unlikely airplanes got themselves down to wavetop height and began a long run toward the fierce battlewagon. The ship's gunners immediately opened up on the troika of attacking airplanes. There were no radar-guided weapons or heat-seeking AA missiles scouring the skies here. The weapons being fired at the three airplanes were old-fashioned five-inch guns, and plenty of them. The three jets showed their mettle as they began swaying in the low, thick air, making themselves a harder target for the Cult gunners but not wavering a bit from the bombing run.

But now, as the three planes reached the halfway

point, Maas was horrified to see the out-of-control
Sparvee fast-attack boat come right into their line of
sight. Instantly a number of nightmare scenarios went
through his mind. At the very least, the speeding boat
would wind up in the middle of the wall of AA fire
being thrown up at the attacking airplanes. Those
three planes were so low at the moment, he feared one
of them might collide with the vessel and gruesomely
end the lives of those troopers still stuck on board, as
well as the courageous pilot.

Worst of all, Maas felt helpless to do anything. The
Sea Stallions were about a mile from the action, having
completed a long sweep out from the place were the
Miajappe had sunk and the second and third battleships
were still burning. Like Clancy before him, Maas knew
that only an act of divine intervention could save the
troopers stuck on the fast-attack boat now. It seemed
more like a matter of time before something tragic and
unavoidable happened.

Suddenly, Maas noticed something. The Sparvee had
been heading right into harm's way at 50 knots—but
now it seemed to be rapidly slowing down. There was
no longer a large plume of smoke left by its overheated
engines behind it, nor the roostertail of water thrown
high in the air from its uncontrollable wake. Was this
just an illusion? An example of mind over matter, mul-
tiplied by a bad case of wishful thinking?

It was neither. The runaway boat was definitely slowing down. At the moment it was barely moving at all.
The three jets streaked right by it, the AA fire following
them and straying away from the attack boat.

What had spared the troopers on board the Sparvee
from such an untimely fate? The finger of God? Another example of the strangeness that had enveloped
the area?

No—it was something a little more down-to-earth

than that: what had happened was the small-attack boat, known for its notorious rate of fuel use, had run out of gas.

But now another peril was evident, and Maas could see it right before his eyes. The fast-attack boat was suddenly drifting right into the sights of the sixth-in-line battleship, the fearsome *Nori*.

The next thing Maas knew, he was scrambling up to the front of the big helicopter. He quickly directed the pilot's attention away from the sky full of AA fire and missiles and down to the surface, where the attack boat was now heading right toward the sixth battleship. The pilot turned the Sea Stallion over in a second, sending everything that wasn't tied down flying all over the cabin. Right beside them, the second chopper had performed the same gut-wrenching maneuver.

The AA gunners on the sixth battleship saw them coming and began opening up. Huge five-inch shells were now rocketing past the Sea Stallions as they drew closer and lower to the drifting Sparvee. The troopers on the attack boat were firing back at the battleship with their small weapons, an uneven match if ever there was one. Incredibly, some of the rifle fire hit home, killing several of the battleship's deck gunners, now just 200 yards away.

By this time, the first Sea Stallion was in position over the fast-attack boat. Hovering just 10 feet above the rear end, some of the troopers were able to climb up onto the depleted fuel tanks and make the leap into the open door. The first chopper took on six men and then backed away, its cargo hold full.

Now the chopper carrying Maas and the other JAWS officers came in. By this time, the gunners on the *Nori* had registered their guns and were barreling in on the desperate rescue operation. Maas was hanging onto Snyder, who was hanging on to Miller, who was literally lifting the troopers off the bridge of the foundering attack boat and throwing them into the chopper. During this time, enemy fire was exploding all around them. It seemed impossible that a shell hadn't hit them yet. To make matters worse, the attack boat had caught fire, either because the engines had finally melted down or an enemy incendiary round had hit it. Flames were soon leaping from the rear end and quickly working their way forward.

Clancy had just lifted the last guy from the attack boat when suddenly a huge explosion went off. It was so violent, the last JAWS soldier nearly lost his grip and fell back into the fiery sea. But somehow, all three JAWS officers managed to hang on to him. They started yelling for the pilot to move off, and their cries soon brought results. Slowly, gradually, the big Sea Stallion began moving away from the Sparvee. The attack boat quickly became engulfed in flames. There was another explosion—the lubricating oil tank had probably gone up—and then the small boat finally slipped beneath the waves.

The Sea Stallion by this time had turned a 180 and was heading in toward shore. Now all those aboard could see what had caused the huge explosion just seconds earlier. The fourth battleship was now engulfed in flames and smoke and smaller explosions. The F-14s and the ancient Delta Dart were flying around its mast, dropping bombs and strafing it from stem to stern. The water all around the battleship was covered with oil and flames—and bodies. The holds of the immense vessel had been full of the Cult's "specialty troops," and now these soldiers were the water.

Here was the strangest, most disturbing sight of the entire battle: many of these specialty troops were so close to shore, they could probably have swum to safety. Others could have conceivably grabbed some floating

wreckage and held on until a rescue. But none of the
troops had. Instead, many were killing themselves—
either by purposely drowning, or by slitting their
throats or stomachs. But even more disturbing, they
were killing each other. The JAWS men could clearly
see the soldiers from their helicopter, fighting in the
water among themselves, stabbing, slashing, trying to
hold one another's heads under water.

Why were they doing this? The only answer was that
the specialty troops had been so keyed up for killing
that when the opportunity was lost and they were
thrown into the water, they had no choice but to start
killing either each other or themselves. The madness
that had boiled up inside them wound up providing
their own demise. The sight of these specialty troops
meeting their ends in such a fashion was upsetting to
the point of inducing nausea.

But soon, the minds of the JAWS officers were on
other things. There was yet another crisis looming: the
dangerously low fuel tanks of their helicopter. The first
Sea Stallion had already made it to shore, but just
barely. It had come down in a controlled crash at the
water's edge, not far from the UAAF's first defense line.

Now the second chopper was absolutely out of fuel,
both main tanks and reserves. The pilots were shouting
at everyone on-board to get strapped down or at the
very least hold on to something—already the big rotors
were fluttering.

Maas looked out the cargo hatch to see they were
still a quarter mile from the beach. The water below
was littered with flaming wreckage and bleeding bodies. It offered no hope for any kind of safe landing.
The copter was filled with wounded and depleted
troopers—plus Sean Higgins, who was still in a state of
shock and under the influence of the massive dose of
morphine given to him at the conclusion of the recon

raid, back in Cuba. How would he be able to make it to shore if they set down in the dangerous waters?

The big copter began shuddering now, the engine was starting to melt down. The electrical wires began crackling and burning, and now a toxic cloud filled the hold. Outside, the sky was still thick with flames and smoke and the crashing of shellfire and the whooshing of missiles. The JAWS officers, crowded around the comatose Higgins, just looked at each other, the same thought on all their minds: was this the end? After everything they'd gone through, would they meet their demise simply because of a few gallons of fuel? Gas they could have taken on-board during the refueling on Key Lime?

As it turned out, the answer to all their questions was no. From somewhere, a great gust of wind came off the ocean and pushed the stricken helicopter the last 500 feet toward the beach. The pilots let out one last wail for everyone to hold on. The next thing the JAWS men knew, they were flying around the cabin, almost weightless.

Then, finally, the helicopter came down—hard, and with a crash—but in one piece, in about two feet of water, just off the main beach. Incredibly, everyone on board had made it.

They began falling out of the cargo door, some on their own, others needing help. The waves and lapping water made evacuating the aircraft somewhat difficult, but the copter was empty inside of two minutes. The last to come off was Higgins. He was lowered on a stretcher into the waiting arms of the ablest troopers and carried further up the beach, just beyond the high tide mark. Above them, the battle was at last winding down. There were no more Beagles fouling the air, no more Styx missiles racing overhead. The bay was now the graveyard for five battleships. One had sunk, four others were burning and going down, and the sixth was speeding away, still under attack by the F-14s and the Delta Dart.

Behind them, many parts of the KSC were in flames. All of the communications buildings had been destroyed, along with the shuttle runway and the temporary aircraft housing. The VAB was smoking mightily on its southeast corner. One quarter of the immense building was either missing or obscured by smoke. Sirens still wailed across the vast UA complex, the sound of medevac choppers filled the air. It was still only 0745; the battle had lasted less than two hours. But in that time, more than 7,000 men had been killed—the vast majority of them Cult sailors and specialty troops. Still, UAAF casualties had been high, especially among the defenders around the VAB and in the AAA emplacements on the beach. Among the hardest hit were the NJ104 combat engineers.

Now the tide was rising and the wreckage and bodies from the battle were coming ashore. The JAWS medics attempted to revive Higgins with injections of adrenaline. It took a few heart-stopping moments, but finally the stricken JAWS officer came around. He opened his eyes to see a huge crowd of troopers staring down at him. A cheer went up as his face and eyes showed the first signs of revitalization. He had made it—and so had they. Somehow, they had accomplished their grand aim and still survived the the brutal battle.

Higgins jumped to his feet. To the astonishment of all, he pushed his way through the crowd of troopers and began running toward the water. It took a few seconds for the other JAWS men to react. Then they started chasing him, calling after him to come back.

Higgins reached the waterline and dived in and began swimming frantically out to sea. Those closest to him heard him shouting, "There's one left! There's one left!'' A dozen JAWS men dived into the surf to pursue him, but Higgins, apparently fueled by the double dose of adrenaline and morphine, was swimming like a madman.

He swam about 100 yards out—and then stopped. It appeared that he'd either run out of energy or had simply given up. But just as it seemed he was about to slip beneath the waves, he suddenly grabbed onto something and began swimming back.

The other troopers finally reached him and saw that he had retrieved a body—one that appeared quite dead, yet was still bubbling air from its mouth. The JAWS troopers managed to pull both of them back out of the water and soon began working CPR on them.

Higgins was easily revived. He jumped up and joined the effort to resurrect the man he'd dragged to shore.

"I was dreaming that I saw him flying through the air,'' he was saying, as the JAWS medics began performing artificial respiration on the man. "A voice—a woman's voice—told me I had to save him if I could . . .''

The man coughed up a stomach full of seawater and began breathing on his own. Another cheer went up, though Higgins's odd rescue had been downright eerie.

And who was the man whose life he'd so dramatically saved?

The answer was on the name tag of the man's extremely scarred and burnt uniform. Above the left pocket, still visible, was the patch of the NJ104 Combat Engineers. Below it was the officer's name: Lieutenant Colonel Don Matus, the man who'd been blown off the top of the VAB in the opening minutes of the battle.

Twenty-one

Major Donn Kurjan, aka "Lazarus," did not fight in the "doomsday" battle for the Kennedy Space Center.

He'd left the morning before. Catching a ride on a cargo plane heading for Boston, he'd been forced to get off at the Newark military air station because the airplane could go no further north.

The reason was the atrocious weather that had been battering most of New England for nearly a week. A major hurricane, unnamed, its strength at the top end of the scale, had been parked off the northeast coast for six days. During that time, winds in excess of 110 mph had shorn whole forests along the Maine coast. Tides running more than 30 feet above the norm had flooded large sections of lower Connecticut and Rhode Island. Mid-sized tornadoes, spawned by the massive storm system, had torn up sections of New Hampshire and Vermont.

Electricity, phone lines, and water systems, shaky in the area since the Big War, were now nonexistent. Disaster relief forces from neighboring states were having a hard time just communicating with each other, never mind with victims caught in the storm's gigantic swirl. Worst hit was Cape Cod. Here the winds were the highest and the rain the heaviest. Waves the size of tsunamis had been battering the fragile beaches for five days nonstop. Those caught on the Cape and the nearby islands could not get out, just as those who sought to bring relief to them could not get in. Most disheartening of all, UA military weather forecasters could see no end in sight to the massive tempest; indeed, the hurricane was actually gaining strength as the hours went by and not depleting itself, as storms of its ilk usually do.

A search of memories and the record books confirmed it: there had never been a storm quite like this.

So Kurjan's airplane had been forced to set down at Newark; this was as far north as any UA military airplane dared to travel. Kurjan used his UAAF staff connections to secure an ancient military jeep from the airport security detachment. Once he'd been able to wrangle a tank full of gas, he headed out through New York City, up the rain-slicked highway into Connecticut, over several swaying bridges into Rhode Island, finally reaching the approaches of Cape Cod. The trip, normally a 5- or 6-hour affair, took Kurjan nearly 24, the conditions were that bad.

But this did not deter him. Something deep inside him, the same thing that had somehow graced him with the longevity of a cat and plain old good luck in his military adventures, was now compelling him to get to the Cape at all costs, not matter what. His trip had taken on a surreal edge. He'd somehow survived the night in the swamp during the Norse attack and remained unharmed as the C-5 gunship rained hell down upon earth. Yet in his brief recuperation, all he could think about was how he could get to Cape Code by the quickest means possible. How strong was this attraction, that he would risk life and limb to obey it? What outside forces were drawing him toward the center of the worst storm ever imagined?

Kurjan didn't know—and the truth was, he didn't really think about it very much.

He just kept on driving.

* * *

It was close to midnight when he began coaxing the Jeep up the long, winding road that led to Nauset Heights.

The rain was absolutely fierce, the thunder and lightning so constant, the night seemed as bright as day. The wind was blowing at such a constant gale, the sand and water spray made it difficult to see even a few feet in front of him.

Finally, he reached the top of the heights, just as the old Jeep's engine gave out for lack of fuel and initative. Kurjan was forced to abandon it at the slight bend in the road which led to the farmhouse at the edge of the heights. Only by the crack of lightning could he make out the name on the signpost swinging mightily in the supersonic breeze: *Skyfire*.

Kurjan had been here several times before, back in happier days, when Hawk Hunter was repairing the place, living out his days in contentment and semiretirement. Kurjan's fondest memories of Skyfire were the nonstop sunny days and cool, star-filled nights, when he, as a guest of Hunter and Dominique, would sit with them on the creaky porch and talk away the hours, sipping spiked lemonade and eating plump, sinfully juicy lobster. Kurjan recalled thinking back then that even though days like these were few and far between, sometimes the cosmos does reward those who are patient enough a little glimpse of heaven. He could still close his eyes and feel the warm sun heating his face. Never had he felt so content.

But now, in the scary winds and pounding rain, the little farmhouse looked like something from a horror movie. Dark, wet, and forbidding, it seemed like a place that had been abandoned for years. The waves of hay, long unkempt and uncut, were blowing so hard in the gale, they combined to emit a kind of screech, a sound that went right to the bone.

There was no soul here anymore, Kurjan thought, looking at the ethereal setting. No life. Or at least, life as the place had known so many times in the past.

Still, he unclasped the gate and walked down the flooded, sandy path. A particularly nasty crack of lightning hit just as he reached the first step, the thunder that followed a second later loud enough to make him jump. The same compelling feeling which had led him to this place at this time was now telling him to avoid the front door. He wisely chose to follow the advice. Moving his head down against the wind, he stumbled to the rear of the house and let himself in through the back door.

The kitchen was dark and smelled of salt and spilled oil. An old wick lamp, its glass container cracked and leaking kerosene, was sitting in the sink. Several candles, their wicks long ago soaked and useless, lay scattered on the table. Long strings of herbs and bulbs, hung from the ceiling rafters to dry, were now broken and ruined, littering the cabinets and the floor. The ancient icebox, which Hunter'd once stocked with dozens of bottles of the local brew, was alone in one corner, its door hanging off the hinges, its shelves bare and stained. Kurjan put his hand inside and was disheartened to find it had been warm for a long, long time.

He moved through the pantry, to the swinging door he knew led to the small dining room. He pushed the door open slowly, his massive .357 Magnum up and ready for anything. Inside he found a single candle burning on the dining room table. Caught in its bare illumination was the face of a young girl.

She looked up at Kurjan as he came through the door, tears rolling down her cheeks. She was wearing a bathing suit and was probably no more than 12 or 13 years old. The wind was blowing through the cracked window next to her chair, but she seemed unaffected by it. He stared back at her, not quite believing she was there. Pale and fragile, she looked like a ghost.

He stepped up to her, lowering his gun to his side.

"Who are you?" he asked. "Who else is here with you?"

The girl turned her eyes toward him, but he got the distinct impression that she could not see. Rather, she seemed to be looking right through him, just as he imagined he could see right through her.

"Who are you?" he asked her a second time—but again, there was no reply. The girl simply turned away and resumed staring at the barely lit candle. Her sobs sounded like they were being emitted through an echo box. Kurjan raised his gun and moved on.

He stepped into the living room and here he found another girl, wrapped up protectively in the arms of an older man. Kurjan could not see his face in the dark, but when he moved closer and a crack of lightning lit the room, he was astonished to see the man was someone he knew quite well.

"*Frost?*" he asked increduously. "Is that really you?"

Frost looked up at him; his face, too, was pale and almost transparent in the eerie light.

"I . . . don't know," he whispered back to Kurjan. "I'm really not sure."

Startled and very spooked now, Kurjan backed away from his friend and found himself at the bottom of the rickety stairs, which led up to the second floor. An uncharacteristic tremor went through him. He'd been in combat many, many times; he'd faced death and had survived on more occasions than he cared to remember. But never had he felt so rattled as he did at this moment.

Somehow, he found the strength to begin climbing the stairs.

At the top was a hallway with four doors. The first he knew led to the master bedroom, the one next to it was the same room in which he'd slept many times before this place had become haunted. He toed open the door to the master bedroom, expecting to see nothing less that a gateway to hell on the other side. Instead, he found two more girls in bathing suits, sitting on opposite sides of the old brass fourposter. There was an unmoving figure lying beneath the covers of the bed; the pair of young girls seemed to be tending to it.

Kurjan stepped forward and pulled the covers down a bit. Instantly he fell back in horror and astonishment. Lying on the bed, ghost white and unmoving, was Stan Yastrweski, the man everyone called Yaz.

"My God . . ." Kurjan gasped, confused and shaking at this assault on his good senses. "Is he . . . is he dead?"

The two girls looked up at him, and then they began to cry, too.

"Not yet," they answered, in unnerving unison.

His mind reeling, his stomach suddenly turning, Kurjan backed out of the room and stumbled down the stairs. He didn't even look to see if Frost was still on the couch nearby. He headed for the front door instead, intent on leaving this place before he became a prisoner of its peculiar horror.

With shaking hands he opened the front door. A crack of lightning revealed a face looking in at him. He jumped back once again, his heart pounding as if it would leap out of his chest. His gun dropped to the floor. His hands were shaking so badly now he could no longer hold it.

That's when he realized that the face looking in at him belonged to Dominique.

Her hair flowing weirdly in the strong winds, her skin dry despite the driving rain, she beckoned to him to come out onto the porch with her.

Somehow, Kurjan found the gumption to comply.

"I am not surprised you are here, Major," she told him, her voice audible in the gale, though she sounded like she was just barely whispering. "You have always been gifted in matters such as this . . ."

Kurjan just stared back at her. With her long, flowing white robes and beautiful hair, she looked more like an angel than a ghost.

"Dominique," he was finally able to gasp. "What is happening? What are you doing out here?"

She shook her head, turned, and sat back down on the same battered couch he and Hunter had shared with her during those long, lazy, perfect days so long ago.

"I am waiting," she finally replied, her voice drenched in sadness and grief, "for someone *else* to arrive and tell us all."

Twenty-two

In Orbit

It was now very crowded in the crew compartment of the Zon spacecraft.

Jammed in between all the clutter and instruments and wires and trash were Cook, Elvis, Geraci, and the two teenage girls taken off the abandoned Mir space station. Everyone was asleep, victims of exhaustion and a filtering system which was releasing much more carbon dioxide into the spacecraft's atmosphere than would be considered normal. The craft's back-up filters were working overtime, trying to keep the CO_2 below a dangerous level—and right now, they were doing the job. But as with everything aboard the crude spacecraft, the crew knew the filters could fail at any moment. Then they'd really be in a fix.

Floating above them all was Hawk Hunter. He, too, was asleep, but for reasons other than tiredness or low oxygen in the blood. Hunter was getting his first real sleep in nearly 72 hours because his powerful inner psyche was telling him this was what he should do.

The events of the past 24 hours had been significant. If Viktor was not aboard the Mir, then he must be somewhere else, somewhere bigger and better defended. Somewhere secretly located in orbit, because aside from the Mir and Zon, there wasn't supposed to be any other place up here where humans could survive, nor was there any way they knew of for Viktor to get back down to earth.

Just as they had set out to find the Mir, now they had to find this new place. This secret place.

Hunter was sleeping to recharge his batteries. Before he drifted off, after leaving the Zon in the capable hands of Ben and JT, Hunter had set his mind into a kind of automatic review mode, a recalling of all significant events which had happened before and during the trip so far which might lead them to the secret place in orbit.

There were few clues. During his days in Viktor's capture, Elvis had flown five Zon flights. Carried inside the cargo bay during these trips, Elvis recalled seeing materials and tools, battery packs and oxygen tanks. Each time he gained orbit, the cargo bay was unloaded out of his sight, however; in his rather prolonged and dazed state, he'd simply assumed these materials were being hauled into orbit in order to fix the Mir.

But their examination of that orbiting antique had proved this assumption to be wrong. The Mir hadn't had any kind of refurbishing or revitalization in a long, long time. The place was basically a shell inside by the time they got aboard her. A shell with minimum power and just enough oxygen being pumped and repumped to keep four people alive. Those four were the two teenage girls and the two spacemen Hunter and Elvis had fought outside the space station. In subsequent interrogation of the girls, Hunter and the others had learned that they'd been aboard the Mir for at least four months.

They had originally come aboard as part of Elvis's fourth space flight, though he'd not seen them en route. Their role in space had mirrored their role on earth. Orphaned and addicted, the girls had provided

Viktor II with hours of perverse sexual amusement and drug-taking, a kind of time-killing hobby he'd acquired while his minions did his bidding up here in the zero-gravity environs of space. But some time in the recent past, the superterrorist had either tired of all this or had gotten scared. The girls said they'd come to after a particularly heavy night of *fricking* and snorting to find Viktor and most of his people gone from the Mir. That was about six weeks before, coinciding with the UAAF's capture of the Zon on Lolita Island in the South China Sea.

Only two guards remained on the Mir and the girls said they'd fucked them strictly out of boredom. When Hunter and Elvis informed the girls that the guards were now gone, they were overjoyed.

Now these girls were part of the crowd on the Zon, and while it did cut down on the living space for everyone else, no one had yet complained. Floating around in the Zon was always a matter of bumping into things: overhanging equipment, hatchways, door locks, and especially, fellow crewmen. Bumping into one of the young, beautiful girls made the crowded conditions bearable, especially since they insisted on staying topless, and when sleeping, cuddling up together in a still life of living, breathing, and floating zero-gravity erotic art.

These thoughts, too, wafted through Hunter's mind as he drifted off to sleep. Once deep into REM however, his brain shifted into overdrive. His dreams, complicated and highly detailed, passed before his eyes like the episodes of an old movie serial. Here he was, chasing Viktor across the frozen wastes of eastern Europe. Here he was, on top of a Swiss alp, watching the Zon go over and plotting its eventual reentry path. Now he was fighting the hordes of airplanes sent by Viktor to protect the last runway on earth capable of landing the Zon; now he was shooting down all those airplanes.

Visions of wild sex now enter Hunter's dreams: a blonde, thrashing this way and that, in a darkened room that is both hot and cold. She is denying him and satisfying him at the same time. She is laughing, then crying. A bare candle lights her face. The sound of the wind rages in the background. A huge, fiery snowball is falling out of the sky. Hunter is suddenly home, back on the Cape, at Skyfire. The blonde is smiling down at him. He opens his eyes, expecting to see Dominique's face, only to find it is Chloe, the girl he met while chasing down Viktor—the girl he'd fallen head over heels for, the girl he'd left atop the sacred peak in the Himalayas, the girl he'd promised to return to, once this space flight was over. . . .

Yes, his dreams were about secrets, and secrets usually led to questions. Could he find Viktor's secret hiding place? Should he leave Dominique for Chloe? What could be more important than those two things right now? How about this one: exactly how much longer did he have to live?

That last thought had the potential to turn this dream into a nightmare—and only JT's shaking him awake saved him from that fate.

"Hawk! Hawker, old buddy," JT was yelling at him. "Wake up! You ain't going to believe this . . ."

One minute later, Hunter was awake and up on the flight deck, staring out the front windshield in disbelief.

They had found Viktor's hiding place—that much, at least, was certain. At the same time, they'd finally discovered how the space mines had been laid out for them.

But still, looking out the window, his mouth hanging open in astonishment, Hunter couldn't believe what his eyes were telling him. Was he still dreaming? Was this real? *Could* a huge snowball really catch fire and fly through outer space?

What he saw hanging in space about 15 miles away was nothing less than a gigantic swastika. It was on a virtually identical orbit path as the Zon and turning slowly on the spokes of its twisted cross. It looked monstrous and overwhelming—and completely unreal.

"Christ, where did that come from?" Hunter gasped. He'd never been quite so astounded.

JT and Ben felt the same way.

" 'When' might be the better question," Ben replied. He handed Hunter the long-range binoculars. "Take a closer look," he urged.

Hunter did, and immediately he knew what Ben was getting at. The space station was made not of lightweight aluminum or thin stainless steel, as one might expect. It appeared to be constructed of heavy metal sections, hundreds if not thousands of them, quite clearly welded into place, like the plates on a battleship. In fact, that was exactly what the overall construction reminded Hunter of—a battleship, in space, something built circa 1940. Even in the middle of the twisted extensions, there was a large observation-deck structure that looked very much like the bridge of a World War II–era ship. The gaggle of antennas and receivers and space periscopes looked very much like what would be found on the *Graf Spee* or the *Bismarck*.

Hunter took his eyes off the binoculars and looked over at his two colleagues.

"This is happening, right?" he asked them, just to make sure. "We're not dreaming or having hallucinations because of high CO_2?"

"It looks real to me . . ." JT breathed, taking the

spyglasses and zooming in on the strange structure again. "Damn real . . ."

"It's registering on the radar," Ben offered. "Coming back like it weighs a thousand tons."

Hunter turned back and just stared out at the monstrosity. Ben was right: the question wasn't really how, but when.

The truth of it was, this thing looked like it had been up here in orbit for many, many years.

"Can we really believe," Ben began saying, "that . . . Werner Von Braun and those cats were able to put something this big into space—back in the 1940s?"

"And it stayed a secret," JT added, "for this long?"

Hunter shook his head, mesmerized by the gigantic rotating swastika. It did seem impossible. Even if by some wild leap of the imagination the World War II–era Nazis—the Third Reich, Hitler and his gang—had been able to lift all these materials into orbit, using secret, more powerful boosters than the V-2s, how could this thing have possibly been flying up here all this time and stay hidden? How did none of the old NASA astronauts see it? Or the Russians cosmonauts? Or the hundreds of telescopes, big and small, and their astronomers, professionals and amateurs, back on earth?

No, these things were impossible, just like a giant fiery snowball flying through the heavens. There had to be some other explanation.

But what could it be?

Hunter looked at his two friends and they stared back at him. He didn't even have to ask the question.

"It beats me," Ben said. "It would have been the biggest and most well-kept secret of all time if this thing has been up here for more than fifty years. Even if they were somehow able to mask it from appearing from earth—which is impossible, in my opinion—the conspiracy to keep it quiet would have to be huge, carrying over several generations, and I just can't imagine everyone involved—astronauts, military types, politicians, or whatever—keeping quiet about it all those years."

"But the damn thing looks so . . . so *fucking* old," JT blurted out, in characteristic abruptness.

Ben went below and roused the others. Soon the flight deck was crowded with five other people: Cook, Geraci, Elvis, and the two girls, who everyone had taken to calling Six and Eight.

Geraci above all just couldn't believe what he was seeing. The engineer in him wouldn't let the reality of the situation sink in.

"It's got to be a prop, or something," he kept saying over and over. "A fake, put up here to confuse us."

"Well, it's doing a good job of that," Cook chimed in.

Hunter let Elvis take his place close to the front windshield.

"What do say, King?" he asked him. "Ever see it up here before?"

Elvis was shaking his head slowly from side to side.

"Not in a million years," he finally replied. "That I would have remembered."

Hunter passed the binoculars to him. "Recognize any of that stuff?" he asked. "The steel plates? The bolts? The girders?"

But Elvis never stopped shaking his head.

"I doubt if I ever lifted any of that stuff up here," he said. "It all looks so heavy, it would have taken hundreds of NASA shuttle flights to lift it all. Certainly not in the five missions I flew in this piece of crap . . ."

Everyone moved aside and allowed the girls to get a better view.

"How about it, ladies?" Hunter asked them. "Ever see it before?"

Both teenagers shook their heads.

"You mean we were living in that crummy tin can and everyone else was floating around in that?" Eight said indignantly. "It looks like an old hotel—up here in space!"

"I agree with the G-man," Six said, taking a long look through the binoculars. "I think it's a fake. No one ever mentioned this to us before . . ."

Hunter retrieved the spyglasses and trained them on one of the twisted appendages. Sure enough, there was a crowd of space junk lashed to the sides of the last module. Old satellites, discarded booster rockets, even a couple of old NASA capsules, unmanned experimental prototypes launched into orbit before the human astronauts began coming up. Now it was clear they were being swept up by the huge space station and converted into orbiting space mines.

In contrast to the huge revolving swastika as a whole, this little operation looked very real.

"Do you think they know we're out here?" Ben asked. "I mean, if we can see them, they can see us, no?"

"Probably," JT replied. "But what can they do? It ain't like they can come out after us or shoot at us or anything. Can they?"

But suddenly Hunter felt his inner psyche start vibrating.

"We might have spoken too soon," he said, retrieving the spyglasses again.

Sure enough, a hatchway on one of the modules at the end of another twisted arm had opened, and now small objects were drifting out of it. Hunter zoomed the electronic glasses up to full power—and nearly dropped them, again so surprised by what he saw.

Without a word he passed the glasses to Ben, who took a look and had the same reaction.

"You've got to be kidding me," Ben said. "Now I know this *has* to be a joke . . ."

Busting at the seams, JT yanked the glasses away from Ben and took a look for himself.

"You've got to be shitting me," he breathed. "Komets?"

That's exactly what they looked like: Messerschmitt Me-163 Komets, a type of German wonder-weapon rocket plane used by the Third Reich at the tail end of World War II. Incredibly, they appeared to have been adapted for space use.

"This is just too much," Ben was saying. "Those things were barely able to fly during the war. How in hell could they get way up here?"

There was no easy answer for that one. The only thing that was certain was that six of the stubby, rocket-powered fighter planes had just come out of the module, each one carrying some kind of large muzzle-heavy weapon under its wings.

And now they were heading right for the Zon.

Hans Schikell was sick and tired of being in orbit.

He hated the food, hated the air, hated being weightless all the fucking time. He was German and by blood this meant he didn't enjoy the same things other people did. But for Schikell, all this flying in outer space stuff was for the birds.

He especially hated flying inside the cramped little Komet 363, but that's what he was doing. He was the flight leader for the half dozen Komets sent out to investigate the large spacecraft which had been spotted approaching the *Himmel-zwischenraum-Rang*, which was the grandiose name for the huge, spinning swastika and could be loosely translated into "Heavenly Space Station."

Schikell had spent most of the past 20 hours supervising the layout of more than two dozen space mines, a pain-in-the-*Esel* job if there ever was one. Like the Komets and the *Himmel-zwischenraum-Rang* itself, the tools and machinery used to convert the free-floating pieces of space junk into orbital bombs was old, unreliable, and poorly made in the first place. That was another reason Schikell hated being in space. He had a hard time living with the fact that at any minute an oxygen seal could burst or an electrical bus could melt and everything—the Komets, the space mines, the Heavenly Space Station, and everyone inside it—could go up and be gone, in less than a second.

But the pay was good, and as far as the politics went, Schikell was a Nazi, just like his father before him and his father before him. Besides, he was due to go back to earth sometime soon, and when he did, he would collect his wages and disappear—and never go into space again.

Schikell looked around him and saw the five other Komets were in their proper positions. The precision was as surprising as it was admirable. Of the six pilots in his squadron, Schikell was the only one with more than 200 hours of spacetime; the others were jet pilots hired back on earth and given crash courses in how to fly the Komet 363. This took more than a little doing; the whole relative-speed thing could be very disconcerting to someone who was used to whacking a jet into afterburner and getting an immediate kick-in-the-*damenschlupfer* result. These men were getting to know the ropes about flying in space in a machine that was designed by someone old enough to be their great-great-grandfather—and so far, they'd been doing a pretty good job of it.

It would take them five minutes to reach the vicinity of the intruding spacecraft. Though Schikell was not privy to exactly who was flying inside the interloping ship—not officially, anyway—he knew this was the one and only Zon they'd been sent out to intercept. It was hard not to recognize it. Not only had just about all of them on board the Heavenly Space Station come into orbit aboard the Zon, it was, to his knowledge, anyhow, the only other spacecraft from earth capable of operating in space.

Rumors had abounded aboard the *Himmel-zwischen-raum-Rang* that the Zon had been captured by the United Americans after its last reentry and that no less a figure than Hawk Hunter, the *Flugelmensch* himself, had engineered the seizure. If this was true, and if the further rumors that Hunter was now in space and coming to kick ass on anyone up here were too, well, then, Hans Schikell *did* want to get back to earth. In a hurry.

But Schikell couldn't worry about that now. His orders, direct from the *Stationsvorsteher,* demanded he intercept this spacecraft, no matter who was driving it, and "hold" it in place. Being a good German, he knew it was best to follow orders.

His flight was about halfway to the spacecraft now, and only an idiot would disagree that this was not the infamous flying rattletrap called the Zon. But whoever was behind its controls was certainly acting in an odd fashion. They weren't trying to evade the oncoming flight of Komets or change their orbital path. Schikell could see no evidence of steering jets being employed or main engine start-up. The Zon was just sitting there, drifting along in space, almost as if no one was aboard it. Schikell felt a chill go through him, even though he was typically roasting inside his spacesuit. Who was flying this thing? Ghosts? He chuckled a little, knowing it was an action akin to whistling by the graveyard. Were there ghosts in space? he wondered. Could the unsettled souls of the quickly departed actually attain escape velocity to haunt those who'd left earth's untidy bonds? Schikell shook off another chill. He really did have to get back to earth.

He took a deep gulp of oxygen and ordered his mind to get back to the matter at hand. The fact that the Zon was not moving was actually a good thing for him and his men. Like their earthly predecessors, the Komets were shitty when it came to fuel. They could carry only tiny amounts of the highly unstable chemicals T-stoff and S-stoff, the combining of which produced a highly explosive reaction, which in turn produced thrust, which in turn propelled the Space Komet. But once their dual tanks were dry, there was no reserve, no alternate way of producing that all-important *stob*.

Get caught out here with no T-stoff or S-stoff and you were *fricken*. And no one aboard the *Himmel-zwischenraum-Rang* would risk his life to come out to get you, either. In fact, they would be too busy dividing up your personal belongings.

So fuel was important and so was electrical power—to run the Komet and its weapon—but this, too, was a precious resource chronically in short supply. Actually, the controls in the cramped cabin were pretty rudimentary and took only about 25 percent of the juice on a typical flight. It was the weapon that drained all the power. It was known as a *Elektrischgewehr,* roughly "electric gun," or more crudely, the "juzegun." It was a long metal stem wrapped in copper wire with a sleeve of thick rubber insulation running about three quarters of its six-foot length. At its tip was an aluminum flare studded with copper spokes. By pushing a lever forward, a Komet pilot could send a direct current of electricity through the wand and out to the copper spokes, charging it up to 80,000 volts. Should the juzegun's victim be a working, fully-charged piece of space machinery, like a drifting satellite, the jolt would set up an opposing polarity—and kill all power inside the target. And out in space, no power was as good as a knife in the heart.

Schikell and his men had previously used the electric guns almost exclusively on space junk, the nuts and bolts of their orbital mines. Though most of it had been inactive for years, some space trash still carried electrical charges powerful enough to zap a man into the next orbital path if he touched them wrong. The juzegun neutralized that effect and allowed safe reclamation of the high-flying trash.

But should the *Elektrischgewehr*'s victim be a human, the 80,000-volt charge would undoubtably kill him, this Schikell and his men knew from experience. Several months earlier, two workers aboard the Heavenly Space Station had been caught committing a minor offense. They were quickly tried and convicted to several months in the brig. The stationmaster, however, decided that as a deterent, the men should be executed. They were set adrift in spacesuits and two Komets were dispatched to chase them down. Once caught, they were zapped with the juzegun. Both died instantly.

Now Schikell and his men were charged with intercepting and holding the Zon. Before embarking, the stationmaster had told Schikell directly that if the Zon tried in any way to avoid their capture, they should zap it with the juzeguns.

If any of the Zon's occupants should venture outside the spacecraft in a bid to ward off the Komets, then they should be zapped as well.

Back aboard the Zon, the equivalent of a call to battle stations had been sounded.

The flight deck was crowded once more. Hunter was

at the main controls, Elvis was at shotgun. JT and Ben
were in the jump seats, Cook and Geraci were behind
them. The girls were tucked in behind them. Everyone
was in his space suit.

The notion that the Zon was dead and drifting was
not entirely inaccurate. Hunter had directed the spacecraft to power down shortly after the Komets were first
spotted approaching. Hunter knew exactly what the
small, rather inconceivable spaceships were up to; their
glowing wands gave them dead away. They were
charged with so much electricity, the radar beams were
bouncing back over six bands, so thick was the inter-
ference. Just like the small tasers they had carried during their foray into the ghostly Mir, electricity was the
only real weapon one could use in space.

And the more of it one had in his possession, the
more powerful he could be.

So Hunter had ordered the Zon to go dark, and inside a minute their electricity usage was down to the
slightest of drains—just enough to keep the three surviving GPCs awake, the cabin pressurized and the air
filters working; everything else had been cut down or
off completely. Without the customary whir of the con-
trol-board computers, the navigation system, the intercom, and a million other things, it was strangely quiet
inside the spacecraft now.

Hands tense, more than a few beads of sweat popping up on the brows and lips, they waited for the six
Komets to get closer.

Hans Schikell was sweating, too.

He wasn't nervous per se; it was the temperature inside the Komet 363. It was now approaching 85 degrees
Fahrenheit, and that was damn hot for someone
wrapped inside a heavy rubber spacesuit sitting in a

tiny lead-lined cockpit. It was the combining of the T-stoff and S-stoff that caused all the residue heat. Once the two dangerous chemicals were fed together, they produced temperatures upwards of 12,000 degrees—all this no more than seven feet behind where Schikell sat. Just like its ancestor, the Me-163, the Komet wasn't known for its pilot amenities.

Besides, if there wasn't so much heat in the cockpit, he'd probably be complaining about the bitter cold.

They were now about a half mile away from the Zon, Schikell and his wingman in the lead, the other four Space Komets forming a chevron right behind them. They were drawing up to the Zon cautiously—Schikell had expected some kind of reaction by now. But the spaceship looked absolutely *in extremis.*

He really was wondering now if the thing had anybody aboard it or not.

But then it moved.

Just a little, and almost imperceptively, but it did move; Schikell saw it. It had moved slightly away from them. He immediately reached forward in the cockpit and hit the small red light on a strip of four on a bar up near the support beam for his canopy. The Space Komets did not have radios within them—they interfered with the juzegun's operation. There was no way then to communicate between the Komets except by this—signals by colored lights. Yellow meant status quo. Orange meant get ready and stop or go. Green meant return to base. Red meant expect trouble. Combinations of these lights meant different things, with a quick flashing of the red bulb meaning something was very wrong.

Schikell was flicking the red light madly now—he was certain that he saw the Zon move. But a quick glance at the rest of his men around him showed no red lights in return.

He did see the Zon move, didn't he?

Schikell reached up and flicked his orange light twice. This meant squadron halt. He gladly reached over and pulled the lever which stopped the T-stoff/S-stoff reaction, releasing a blast of compressed air from two nozzles in the nose for braking at the same time and feeling a remarkable difference in the cockpit temperature almost immediately.

Now, with the six Space Komets lined abreast, they were suspended about 100 yards away from the nose of the somnambulent Zon. Schikell was trying to figure out how he could communicate via the colored lights with the others to ask the question "Anyone see it move?" when, a moment later, the Zon moved again.

He definitely saw it this time. The big spacecraft shifted about five yards to the left and away from the idling squad of Space Komets. Again Schikell's hand was flicking wildly on the red light button, but to no response from the others. His wingman flicked three yellow, then an orange. It was the equivalent of "What's the matter?"

Schikell returned the query with a long, long sequence of red. This meant approximately *'Fuck you and pay attention.'*

When Schikell looked up again, the Zon had moved once more, this time at least ten yards to the left and away from the squadron. Now he felt a little shiver go through him.

The Zon *was* moving, wasn't it? Or was *he* moving and it just seemed like it? He didn't know and for a moment panicked slightly, applying a minute amount of compressed air brake and suddenly finding himself going backward at a high rate of speed. Flustered now, he hit the T-stoff/S-stoff throttle again, initiated the chemical reaction, felt the mild yet substantial kick in the ass, and then quickly cut off the dual fuel flow.

After all that, he wound up in approximately the same position as before, supremely embarrassed and that much lower on fuel.

The Zon moved again.

That was it for Schikell; the time to go in for the kill was now.

He began flicking his orange and red lights. At last his men knew what he meant. The two flankers applied throttle and began moving slowly toward the wings of the Zon. The pair of inner rooks did the same thing, inching their way down to a slightly lower orbit, intent on coming up behind the big spacecraft. Meanwhile, Schikell and his lieutenant carefully applied power and moved slowly up toward the nose.

It took about five minutes for all this shifting about; no maneuver, large or small, was easy in space. Everything was so exact that the room for error built in for the atmosphere and gravity on earth didn't come into play up here. To move an inch, sometimes you had to move a mile. Sometimes two. Or even three. Or four . . .

It would take Schikell the longest to get into the pre-juzegun position. His attitude was slightly askew from his jittery offside earlier, and he had to work harder and longer at getting into the proper alignment. The squadron was going to stick the Zon with six wands all at once, like harpoons to a whale. It was extremely important that they all move in and make contact simultaneously. If not, the connection might not take and the majority of the charge could dissipate without bringing much harm to the Zon.

As it was on earth, it was in space: timing was everything.

So Schikell fiddled and faddled, applied power, then braking, then more power, then more braking, at the same time trying to keep everyone else in sight in case they began signaling him about a problem.

Finally, he was in position, and so was everybody else. Schikell settled down a bit and took a long gulp of oxygen. At last they were all in place. That's when he turned in the cockpit, curious to see if anyone aboard the space station was watching them—and got the shock of his life.

The Heavenly Space Station was so far in front of them, he could barely see it. It was passing into night, fading into the earth's shadow. Schikell froze, absolutely *froze*—in his seat. *How did this happen?*

He turned back to the Zon and saw the answer. As the squadron was moving, the big dumb spacecraft had been moving, too. No one in the squadron had realized it because somehow, the Zon had moved in exact relation to them, making it appear like it wasn't really moving at all, when in reality, they were all moving away from the space station. *Far* away.

Schikell began flicking his lights madly once more, but it was an effort quite wasted. The others had already realized what had happened—they'd been suckered big time. And now they were reacting in a panicky mode. A *very* panicky mode.

One of the flankers turned 180 degrees and began a mad dash back toward the space station, already fading completely from view as it went into the earth's shadow. The other five Komet pilots watched their comrade's desperate attempt with a mixture of hope and horror. The Komets never strayed more than two miles from the Heavenly Space Station; they just weren't built for it, fuelwise. Now the station seemed like it was 100 miles away. Did they have enough fuel to get all the way back? Their colleague's reckless action would tell the tale.

It took only about a minute to get the answer. They

could barely see his taillight now as the gray-green plane ran out of chemicals and had an engine shutdown. It didn't take an astrophysicist to figure out the lone Komet had fallen way short of the mark. The flanker didn't make it back more than one-fifth of the way before he drained all his Stoff.

Now his engine had gone silent and so had his power, and soon he would begin to freeze and die. It would take anywhere from a minute to 48 hours. After that, he would plunge back into the atmosphere and burn to a crisp.

That was the fate that awaited the rest of the squadron, too. And all of them knew it.

Still Schikell wanted to spear the beast, the last defiant act of a desperate man, but even this would be denied him. The Zon was moving again, this time with a great amount of power. Its main engines had been lit and suddenly its cockpit was alive with light and movement. In that glow, Schikell through he saw the profile of a man he'd only heard about, one he wished he'd never have to come up against. The handsome features, the eagle nose. The too-long, slightly unkempt hair sticking out of his crash helmet. This was the famous Hawk Hunter, Schikell was certain of it now. Who else could have engineered such an illusion to trap them out here? Deep down inside, where all pain from embarrassment came from, Schikell felt like someone had kicked him about a dozen times. It was not the most unpleasant feeling though. If he was to die at the hands of the famous Hawk Hunter, he thought grimly, at least he'd been bested by the best.

The big Zon spaceship began moving even quicker now, away from Schikell and his men, leaving them in the depths of space. As it rode by, Schikell saw two more faces appear at the forward cockpit window. They belonged to a pair of young females; he recognized them as the "comfort girls" everyone used to *frick* inside the Mir before it was abandoned.

Both girls were laughing as they passed by. And both were displaying their middle fingers to him.

Twenty-three

Cape Cod

The wind was howling so loudly outside the headquarters of the Southern Massachusetts Home Guard that no one on duty inside heard the radiophone beeping at first.

For five days the tremendous storm had been battering Cape Cod and the members of small citizen military unit had been performing search-and-rescue duty nonstop for the past 100 hours. They were in the right place for it: their base was near Chatham Light, on the elbow on the Cape. In some places nearby, the tides were running so high, the waves were going across the peninsula and dumping into Cape Cod Bay several miles on the other side, washing out a number of roads and at least one major highway. This flooding had isolated large pockets of the upper Cape, cutting off all electricity and phone lines and trapping hundreds of people as well.

Because they were so close to the water, the SMH Guardsmen had been called on to save many foundering boats and dozens people stuck in flooded areas. But the ranks were now stretched extremely thin. Of the 200 or so civilian troopers, more than two-thirds were currently off on rescue missions, and the rest were at the Chatham barracks, exhausted, hungry, dirty, tired, and in many cases, uncertain about the fates of their families and loved ones.

When the call was finally answered and it turned out to be a report that several people had seen a "huge thing with wings" drop out of the sky up near Bassing Harbor, the number of guardsmen available to go check it out was small. And the enthusiasm among those who could go was pretty far down the scale, too.

But this was understandable; the report didn't make a whole lot of sense. What was this "thing with wings" these people had seen? An airplane? What would an airplane be doing, flying around in this weather? The winds outside were gusting at 120 miles an hour, the rain was coming down at a rate of an inch every 10 minutes. Why would anyone fly through such conditions?

There were no answers to these questions, only a follow-up report from the local police force over in Chatham Port that a "huge silver flying craft" had been seen cutting through the stormclouds, its wings on fire and its wheels down. An explosion was heard by people near the small village of South Neponset and two witnesses said they saw something fall into the woods about a mile away.

This put the possible crash site just 11 miles from the Home Guard barracks. Sense of duty and the vicinity of the incident finally compelled a squad of six very weary troopers to jump into their ancient APC and investigate.

It would turn out to be a long journey. It took them nearly a half hour just to find a fordable entrance to Route 28, the thoroughfare which would bring them up to the scene of the reported crash. They wound up crossing a marsh on the edge of Oyster Pond and proceeding through a series of flooded bogs which somehow supported the weight of APC, gaining the highway six miles south of their base.

Then it took them two more hours just to travel four miles north. By the time they reached the village of South Neponset, it was growing dark, though the truth was, in the wind and rain, it was already difficult to tell the difference between night and day.

The troopers picked up the local fire chief at his house and with him now squeezed into the old military vehicle they headed up the road that led to the woods behind the small village. The only conversation during this trip was centered on the severity of the weather and the fact that they were probably on a wild goose chase, a sentiment with which the fire chief of South Neponset heartily agreed.

They finally reached the high point of the woods, a small lookout post which at one time had served as a fire watchtower. From this vantage point, the Guardsmen had the ability to see the village below, the miles of swamped cranberry bogs, the roaring ocean, and the western part of the woods. To their astonishment, down in a hollow about a mile and a half from this position, they could see outline of an enormous silver craft resting among the thick pines.

Whether it was the weather or their exhaustion or the never-ending intensity of the storm, they would never know, but at first, none of the guardsmen or the fire chief wanted to go down to the wreck. It just seemed too strange, too eerie down there. The wreck was glowing with an odd orange light, and clouds of smoke and steam were covering the surrounding areas with a disturbing, yellowish fog. The craft itself didn't look like an airplane. It seemed too big, too stream-lined to be any kind of aircraft they were familiar with.

Though they felt foolish at the time, the Guardsmen wondered openly if this thing down in the woods was even of earthly origin. After all, what kind of an airplane *could* possible fly in this weather? And what kind of a pilot would want to if he could?

But finally a sense of duty prevailed—and a bit of morbid curiosity, too. The guardsmen drove the APC to the point closest to the wreck, a gully which looked down on a raging stream, which in turn ran into the hollow where craft had come down. From here they climbed down on ropes and chains, finally reaching the overflowing stream bed and eventually the northern end of the hollow itself.

It was quite dark by this time and the rain and wind had not let up. Using powerful lights, the six guardsmen and the fire chief inched their way along the overflowing stream's ridge, finally reaching a thicket of pines all of whose tops had been sheared off.

Once through these trees, they came upon an odd, open area, a swath of land where the trees had not only been knocked down but seemingly vaporized. Beyond this lay the wreckage of the strange craft.

The guardsmen had their weapons out now; even the fire chief had drawn a small pistol. They crept through the yellow fog, trying to make out the lines of the enormous craft. It was silver in color and its power plants seemed gigantic. It had come down on its belly after lopping off about a half mile's worth of trees, and as a result, its wings were bent in very bizarre contortions. Its extremely sharp nose, also battered and punctured, lay in the raging stream. An incredible stink of burnt rubber and some kind of fuel was thick in the air.

Most astonshing of all, there was a man sitting on the edge of one wing, his head down, crying uncontrollably.

The small party of seven men approached him carefully. When he finally peeked up at them, he seemed not at all surprised or impressed. Instead, he eyed their weapons and began pleading: "Shoot me. Please. Do it. I have failed terribly. My only recourse is to die . . ."

The guardsmen and the fire chief now lowered their weapons and drew closer. A first sergeant named Boutwell was the highest-ranking member of the group; he stepped forward, reaching a point about six feet off the crumpled wing and 10 feet from the weeping man.

"What's going on here, pal?" Boutwell asked. "Are you okay?"

"I will never by okay," the man on the wing answered in thickly accented broken English, not looking up. "I have failed. And failure means death. I have lost her, so I have lost myself. Please, then, shoot me and get it over with."

"We ain't going to shoot you," Sergeant Boutwell replied. "So you knock that off."

They all took another quick look around. It was amazing that the man had survived the crash. But a quick study of the cockpit showed that it had been designed to hold two.

"Was someone else with you?" Boutwell asked him. "Where are they?"

" 'They' is a 'she,' and she is gone," the man on the wing said, still not lifting his head, almost as if it was too heavy, so constant was his flow of tears.

" 'Gone' as in dead?' " the sergeant asked.

The man just shook his head. "No, 'gone' as in, she's left the area. An hour ago. She's gone and she's left me behind . . ."

"What's her name?" Boutwell asked, strictly for lack of a better question.

"She is the mistress of the stars," the man replied with a shrill voice. "A goddess of the clouds. No woman could do what she did for me, or what she could do for you. And I have lost her. To this storm. To the rain.

And this wind. You see, I don't deserve to live. I have failed my king and my country—and the only woman I could have ever loved."

Sergeant Boutwell looked back at his men and the fire chief and just shrugged. The last thing they expected to find down here was a pilot with a broken heart. Or one suffering from delusions.

"I'll tell you what, pal," Boutwell said finally, drawing a bit closer. "Why don't we carry you out of here. Fix you up. Get you warm and dry and fed and bandaged—and then we'll help you look for your lady friend. How's that?"

For the first time the man looked up and the guardsmen were surprised to see that he had Asian features. His teary eyes were suddenly wide with expectation.

"You will help me do this?" he asked. "You will help me look for her?"

"Sure we will," Boutwell said, giving the high sign to the others. "I mean, how far can she have gone?"

"She can move in very mysterious ways," the pilot replied. "I will need all the help I can get."

"Well, that's what we do," Boutwell replied with a weary sigh. "So come on, climb down off there, and we'll get you fixed up."

The pilot thought about this for a moment and finally did start to climb down off the wing. The wind was howling again now and the rain was coming down with new ferocity. The rest of the squad came forward and helped the man to the ground. He looked remarkably unhurt, considering the wreckage he'd been sitting on. And while the guardsmen and the fire chief were now more or less convinced that he was of this earth, he was still a strange-looking character.

"You look like you're a long way from home," the fire chief told him, passing him a thermos of water.

"I am," the pilot said, drinking greedily from the flask until it was dry. "Very far."

"So then," the fire chief asked, taking the empty canteen back, "what's your name?"

The pilot looked up at him and then studied the rest of the men. Overhead the storm continued to roar, the rain coming on in sheets.

Still the man managed a slight, but toothy smile.

"My name, believe it or not," he replied, "is Prince Buddara Shingbang-shadzup-burin."

The guardsmen and the fire chief all laughed.

"What the hell is that in English, pal?" Sergeant Boutwell asked him.

The pilot smiled again.

"Well," he said, "my friends call me Budda-Budda . . ."

Midnight finally closed in on Cape Cod a few hours later—but again, it was still hard to tell day from night.

The storm was reaching new intensity. It had moved on-shore, and now its winds were blowing up to 140 miles an hour. The rain was coming down so fast it could not be measured. The thunder and lightning were simply incredible.

The strange thing was, it almost seemed like the storm was swirling right above the Nauset Heights section of Cape Cod. Here the wind blew hardest and the rain fell as it were a solid sheet of water. The tides were running so high, some of the waves were crashing above the Nauset cliffs, very high above the beach. It was as if the elements had decided to converge above the tiny strip of elevated land not even a mile long. It was almost as if the tempest had decided to settle here.

Somehow, the tiny farmhouse close to the edge of the cliffs was surviving the fierce battering, though many of its roof shingles had blown off and its chimney was gone. It looked dark, cold, soaked through, and, at first glance, long-ago abandoned. Just at the stroke of midnight, a tremendous crack of lightning lit up the sky above the house. The sonic shock wave from a simulataneous crash of thunder shook the farmhouse down to its foundation. The rain was now a waterfall. The wind sounded like a chorus of thousands, crying in anguish all at once. Off in the distance, an animal was screaming in shrill horror.

Another bolt of lightning, another crack of thunder. The wind rose to an inconceivable gale.

And, at that moment, up the road came Chloe.

Dominique greeted her at the door.

They had a brief, hushed conversation in which the name Hawk Hunter was repeated many times. From the sounds of it, it seemed like the two women had known each other for years. The truth was, this was the first time they'd ever met.

Dominique led Chloe inside, where it might have appeared warm and safe and dry. But the living room was not such a homey place at the moment. There was too much weirdness, too much anxiety, the air thick with the aura of too many lost souls. Frost was still on the couch, nearly catatonic with his realization that he'd actually seen the ghost of Mike Fitzgerald. The four girls, still terrified, still mute, sitting at the table, looking as lost as ever. Kurjan, the one who was probably the sanest one of them all, was keeping watch near the largest window, staring out at the storm, a massive handgun in his lap.

And upstairs, on the bed, still in his wet flight suit, still wearing his soggy boots and cracked goggles, was Yaz, still unconscious.

Chloe stood briefly in front of the fireplace and warmed her hands. Then she turned and asked an odd question.

"Is Hunter still in space?"

Dominique looked at Frost, who looked over at Kurjan, who in turn looked back at Dominique.

"Yes, we believe so," Dominique told her.

A slight smile spread across Chloe's face.

"I really don't know why I'm here," she began to explain. "I've come so far and have gone through many, many things. But I do know that something deep inside me led me here. Something I just can't explain."

"Join the club . . ." Kurjan moaned from the window.

Dominique took Chloe by the hand and led her into the kitchen, where a pot of tea brewing. The people in the living room went back to what they were doing. Kurjan especially, checking the clip in his hand cannon for the thousandth time, ready for anything.

He might have dozed off, though, because the next time he saw Dominique and Chloe, they were going up the stairs to the second floor, candles and matches in hand. Kurjan heard them walk across the ceiling, stopping briefly in front of the door leading to the master bedroom, and then proceeding down the short hallway to one of the smaller bedrooms. The squeak in the door told Kurjan they'd gone into the southeast bedroom, the tiniest of them all, but the only one to have a large picture window–sized skylight.

Kurjan maintained his vigil for another half hour, enduring every crash of thunder and every bolt of lightning, and wondering if the storm was ever going to stop. Maybe in this spooky new world, storms rise up and stay forever, he thought. Like the great red-spot hurricane on Jupiter, maybe the storms on earth would now rage for thousands of years.

Sometime around 2 A.M., Kurjan went upstairs to check on Yaz. His friend was still alive, but still deep in a strange kind of coma. Oddly, Kurjan had seen Yaz like this before. During the campaign in the South Pacific against the Asian Mercenary Cult the year before, Yaz had been exposed to a holographic hypnotic device that had knocked him out for the duration of the war. When he finally woke up, he was healthy, fairly normal, but still drunk with the psychic images that had played in his head while he was unconscious. One of these visions actually guided a search party that had been looking for Hawk Hunter after he'd crash-landed on a deserted Pacific island shortly after the end of the campaign. Yaz told the search party exactly where to look and the Wingman was eventually rescued. It was still one of the strangest things Kurjan had ever witnessed.

But the fact that Yaz had gone through this before didn't lessen Kurjan's concern very much. Yaz just didn't look good—and everyone was afraid to touch him, even to remove his wet clothes. And just how he came to be inside the upstairs closet . . . well, Kurjan decided he would let the weather calm down a bit before he looked any deeper into that one.

He came out of Yaz's room to find Dominique and Chloe just emerging from smaller bedroom next door. To Kurjan's great surprise, both women were naked and covered with a glistening powder, possibly some herb dust that Dominique was known to use on occasion.

They looked at Kurjan, who stared back, more embarrassed than they.

"Major, we were just coming to get you," Dominique said.

Kurjan just stared back at them. "Coming to get me?" he stuttered.

"Yes," Dominique said, holding out her hand to him. "Please, come with us."

Now the guy they called Lazarus found he had a little trouble breathing. *Come with us?* What the hell did that mean?

Dominique smiled slightly; her beautiful body jiggled as result. She knew why he seemed paralyzed.

"Please, Major?" she said, walking three steps and taking him by the hand herself. "We have to show you something."

Kurjan finally did follow them, numbly, as they went back inside the small bedroom and closed the door. It was now very dark inside, only a single sputtering candle was giving off the barest of light. Outside the storm was raging more ferocious than ever. Oddly, Kurjan fingered his weapon. As if massive bullets could some how affect the course of this tempest.

The women closed in on him and nudged him under the skylight. Then, pressing their naked bodies against his, they pointed, straight up.

Kurjan followed their fingers and was soon looking right out the skylight.

What he saw was . . . the clear night sky.

"This is impossible," he gasped, all thoughts of the two naked women leaving his mind for the moment. "The storm. I can hear it. *Feel it.* How can this be?"

"Look closely," Dominique whispered in his ear.

Kurjan did, and sure enough, once his eyes had completely adjusted to the dark, he saw that they were actually looking up at a huge, spiraling hole which had formed in the middle of the raging stormclouds. It looked like an enormous open drain around which clouds were swirling madly.

Kurjan just couldn't believe it. The eye of the hurricane was right over the farmhouse! At that moment, they were literally in the middle of the storm.

"This all has to do with something bigger than capturing Viktor or stopping the attacks down in Florida,"
Kurjan suddenly gasped again. "This is really something else . . ."

"It all means something," Dominique said. "These
are signs, someone wants us to do something . . ."

"Yeah," Kurjan breathed never taking his eyes off
the hole in the sky above him. "That's the scary part."

"Maybe I know what it's all about," Chloe said suddenly.

Kurjan and Dominique looked over to her.

"Before I left my mountain," she began, "one of the
priests told me something. I really didn't understand
it at first. But maybe now I do."

"Christ, what was it?" Kurjan asked her.

"He said all these weird things would start happening," she continued slowly, biting her lip. "People
would start disappearing, strange voices would ring in
the sky. Wars would break out. Nature would go on a
rampage. And then . . . well, then, the world would
come to an end."

"You mean, a nuclear war?" Kurjan breathed.

"No," Chloe replied, tears forming in her eyes.
"Something worse. Something I saw in a dream. It was
this thing. In outer space. It looked like a giant snowball. It was heading right for earth and moving incredibly fast. And I saw this huge hand behind it, almost as
if it were pushing it . . ."

Suddenly Chloe collapsed to her knees. All of the
scariest parts of her dream came flooding back to her.

"When I told this priest about my dream, he said it
was actually a prophecy of some kind," she went on,
sobbing. "He said it had been written hundreds of
years before. And now it must be coming true, because
the night I dreamt it, it got very calm up on the mountain. Almost like this . . ."

She pointed up at the hole in the clouds above the farmhouse.

Kurjan and Dominique just looked at each other, shocked by Chloe's tale.

"There are many things written about the Final Days, in many religious books belonging to many religions around the world," Dominique said. "They all claim that truly bizarre, unnatural events will occur before the world finally comes to an end."

Kurjan looked up through the skylight at the nightmarish scene above.

"Well," he gulped. "That thing up there fits the bill, I would say."

A dreadful silence descended upon them. Chloe suddenly stopped crying.

"This priest said one more thing to me," she began again. "One more word before he . . . well, before he died. It was something that seemed like it might be the key to finding out exactly what's happening."

"Well, what was it?" Kurjan asked her anxiously. "What word did he say?"

Chloe bit her lip for a moment. "He said, 'Hubble,' " she finally replied. "Is that a man's name?"

"A man and a telescope," Kurjan told her. "In fact, it's probably the most well-known telescope in history. Or it *was.*"

"But where is it?" Chloe wanted to now, now getting excited again. "Is it on top of a mountain near here?"

Kurjan almost laughed, an impossible act under the circumstances—or so he thought.

"It's not on a mountain and it ain't anywhere near here," he told Chloe. "It's up in space. It's the most powerful telescope ever built, and it can see to the ends of the universe. But it's up in orbit. That's why it works so well; it doesn't have to see through the earth's atmosphere."

"Oh, my God," Chloe suddenly cried, her hands going to her face. *"That* must be it, then! *That's* why I came here. So I could tell you about this Hubble thing and you can tell Hunter."

Again Kurjan and Dominique just stared at each other.

"God, we have to tell Hunter to get to this telescope somehow," Chloe was saying excitedly. "He has to try to find something with it."

"Find what?" Kurjan asked her. "A giant snowball?"

Chloe just shook her head. "It sounds crazy, doesn't it?"

"Everything sounds crazy these days," Kurjan said, returning his gaze to the absolutely mind-boggling meteorological event happening about a mile over their heads.

"Then we have to do it," Chloe said, her breasts bouncing slightly with renewed enthusiasm. "We have to get in touch with Hunter, we have to tell him to use this telescope to find this thing. I think he'll know what to do from there."

Kurjan looked over at Dominique, who just stared sadly back at him. She suddenly retrieved her gown and draped it over her.

Chloe detected the immediate coolness in the room.

"You can get in touch with Hunter, right? He's our only chance . . ."

Kurjan and Dominique just shook their heads. Then Kurjan slumped to the floor.

"Getting a message up to Hunter in the Zon space shuttle?" he sighed. "Now that is going to be a problem."

Twenty-four

Off UA Florida

It was the crew of the ancient C-119 Flying Boxcar who saw them first.

The cargo plane-turned-radar-picket craft was flying its usual coastal patrol down from the Kennedy Space Center to the tip of Florida and back again. It had taken off at its usual time—0400 hours—and had reached Key Largo around 7 A.M., as usual. The crew quickly took on some more fuel and began the return trip to the KSC around 0720 hours.

It was on the trip back that things started happening. Just as the airplane was passing off the coast of what used to be Vero Beach, its surface-warning radar sets began lighting up like Christmas trees. A large disruption was evident about 22 miles northeast of their present position. The scatter on the radar sets was so extensive, the C-119 crew thought at first the instruments were broken. They'd never seen anything like this before. It looked like a big blob was speeding toward the waters off the Kennedy Space Center. Indeed, this huge indication was moving so fast, it appeared as it would make landfall at the KSC—and keep right on going.

What could be that big and moving that fast?

The C-119 crew didn't even want to speculate. They

knew the area from which they were picking up this enormous radar blot was the same over which the six Sabre jets and then the huge Seamaster flying boat had disappeared just two days before. The last thing the C-119 guys wanted to do was start guessing about what the hell might be out there.

They immediately made a scramble call to KSC staff command instead. This call put the entire KSC back on high alert. It couldn't have come at a worse time. The surviving personnel were still in shock after the murderous attack the day before. Large parts of the base were still smoldering, and many of the UA facilities from the battle had yet to be identified. As it was, the base defenders had been burying their comrades all night long.

Still, as soon as the warning sirens began howling, the defenders wearily reported to their battle stations. There were just 423 able bodies left now, many of them actually technicians and support people thrust into the role of combat soldier. A huge trench line had been dug along the beaches bordering the KSC—the threat of an enemy amphibious landing was now greater than ever. The remaining Patriot missile batteries had been aligned in a no-man's land between the beaches and the space center. The shuttle runway was, of course, unusable; the pair of F-14s, the single F/A-18, the Thunderchiefs, and the Delta Dart all had to fly up to the UAAF base at Myrtle Beach in UA South Carolina following the battle, this was the nearest working airstrip large enough to accommodate the unlikely aircraft. But the distance and the time in between left the KSC woefully unprotected in the area of aerial defense. In fact, the only flyable aircraft at the KSC at the moment were the pair of battered Sea Stallions used by the JAWS infiltration team, the two Hueys, and the CH-

54 Skycrane. Any credible air cover was at least 285 miles away.

In other words, if some kind of an attack was coming, the defenders at KSC would have to bear the brunt of it with little more than rifles and a few SAMs for at least an hour and maybe much longer.

About 15 minutes after first spotting the huge radar indication, the crew of the C-119 was finally able to get a long-range TV visual on the enormous surface disruption. Their initial, if unspoken, fears proved true. The huge radar blob was being caused by 12 Cult battleships steaming west at full speed and sailing extremely close together, an old Cult tactic.

And, no surprise, they were heading right for the KSC.

It was the USS *Marconi* that sighted the battleships next.

The diminutive spy ship was positioned about 22 miles off the coast of the KSC, still looking for any signs of the missing Sabre jets or the Seamaster.

Because it had most of its sensitive visual and listening devices powered down, the *Marconi* wasn't aware the Cult battleships were in its vicinity until its communication officer picked up the original scramble alert message sent by the C-119 to the KSC.

The spy ship went to battle stations immediately. Its armament, three mounted Harpoon missile launchers and several M60 cannons, while formidable, were no match for the 16-inch guns of the Cult battleships. But the spy ship did have one great advantage: its speed. Crammed inside its engine room was not the usual set of smoky diesel engines that combined might muster up a 22-knot battle speed on a good day. Rather, the *Marconi* had a pair of GE-404 aircraft derivative gas turbines serving as its power plant. Though it hardly looked it, the *Marconi* could travel along the surface at close to 55 knots, an incredibly high rate of speed that could be well used either for attacking or leaving an area of danger.

This morning, it would be used for both.

The *Marconi*'s crew got a return message from KSC about 10 minutes after the high alert was called at the battered space base. The twelve battleships were coming, that much everyone knew. But what was their intent, exactly? Were they part of another combined attack? Or were they coming in alone? Even more important, were their holds filled with more specialty troops, meaning another attempt at an armed landing was in the offing? Or were the sinister Cult commanders planning something else?

The coded message sent from KSC command to the *Marconi* told the crew of the spy ship that it was up to them to find out.

The fleet of swift-moving battleships was still 16 miles off the coast of Central Florida when the *Marconi* first made its presence known.

The tiny spy ship emerged from a self-induced fog bank just north of the battleships, and fired two Harpoon missiles at the lead Cult vessel, the sleek new *Subshoppi*. The pair of missiles slammed into the side of the battleship, causing some damage but not enough to put the vessel in any real danger. However, it did slow it down, and as the lead vessel in the swift-moving pack, served to slow down the entire squadron of battleships as well.

This had been the *Marconi*'s intent all along. With the battleships' speed now cut in half, the swift little

spy trawler opened up its two jet engines and made a
course directly for the middle of the enemy flotilla.

The problem with a battleship was that because it
was the biggest thing on the sea, it was also the hardest
to maneuver. Turning one quickly was nearly impossible; even slowing one down was equivalent to slowing
down a supertanker, a long, complicated thing to do.
The crew of the *Marconi* knew this, which was why they
were now on the seemingly insane beeline toward the
center of the 12-ship enemy formation. They had speed
and surprise on their side. It would be enough to last
them a minute or so.

The *Marconi* made direct contact with the battleships
about 45 seconds later, speeding by the two trailing
ships, the *Fuchu* and the *Gooshu*. The elite SSSQ crewmen managed to strafe the decks of both battleships
with their M60 cannons as they raced by, taking out
several antennas and a radar set.

The *Marconi* came upon the trio of rear-flanking
ships next, the *Ishima*, the *Lareedai*, and the fiercesome
Taishima. More cannon fire, another Harpoon
launched, two more antennas, and a radar dish destroyed. The *Marconi* was up to 50 knots now, traveling
between the two rather elderly middle-flank ships, navigating a space not 30 feet wide. This put them right
on the tail of the two largest ships in the squadron, the
massive *Yumitta* and its sister vessel, the *Binashi*. Two
more Harpoons were launched, both clipping the rear
steering gears of the big ships, damaging them moder-
ately. The *Marconi* was now passing out of the formation, firing its cannons at the portside pocket battleship
Linomee and sending its last Harpoon at the bridge of
the flagship, the impressively arrayed *Sudai*.

The air was filled with five-inch shellfire from the
battleships by now—but it was too little too late. The
Marconi was already speeding away to the south, its

helmsman turning the ship this way and that, not allowing the sighters on any of the Cult ships to get a good register on it. Laying out another cloud of steam cover, they disappeared over the horizon just two minutes later.

In all, their attack had lasted less than five minutes, and the damage they'd inflicted, while bravely executed, was not enough to force the battleships to turn around or call off their impending attack. But that had not been the purpose of the *Marconi*'s brazen escapade.

Rather, the ship had just performed its usual mission: to spy. By getting in close to the battleships, they were able to see exactly how the vessels were riding in the water, how they turned, and how many people appeared on deck once they'd begun shooting.

Their conclusion: the battleships were definitely on their way to the KSC. However, they were riding relatively high in the water, suggesting their holds were probably not filled with specialty soldiers, waiting to try another landing. Instead, the ships were probably heading toward the battered UA base with the intention of simply bombarding it with their huge guns.

In the crazy state of affairs surrounding the beleaguered space center these days, that was actually *good* news.

The first barrage of 16-inch shells hit the KSC at exactly 0800 hours.

Six of them came down in all, their one-ton warheads slamming into the already useless shuttle runway, leaving a nearly perfect row of 6 craters, 45 feet wide and 25 feet deep.

Another barrage arrived at 0801, exactly one minute after the first. They, too, came down on the perforated five-mile airstrip, leaving six gigantic holes and sending tons of dust and debris into the air. No sooner was this cleared by the morning winds than another half dozen shells came down, almost in the same place.

It went on for an hour. Barrages of 16-inch shells streaking over the beaches, over the VAB, over most of the indispensible space center support buildings and landing on the long, battered, and completely deserted airstrip. At the end of just a few minutes, the runway looked like a moonscape. At the end of an hour, it resembled a small piece of the Grand Canyon.

For the hour of total bombardment, it was a matter of all the defenders keeping their heads down and their ears plugged. Just the volume at which the shells screeched over was enough to puncture an eardrum or cause an ear to bleed. The sonic waves resulting from the shells' impact could do even worse damage. *Stay low and cover up* was the order for all UA personnel manning the trenches and defensive systems positions. *This might get worse . . .*

But that was the strange thing: the huge shells were not hitting any areas where UA troopers were gathered. They were not hitting the beach, or the string of Patriots sites, or any of the command buildings within the space complex itself. The battleships' barrage, while frightfully impressive, proved to be actually harmless. A study in pinpoint shooting from more than two dozen miles away, the hour-long barrage amounted to little more than lobbing one 1-ton shell after another, hitting the same target over and over again, a target that had been destroyed long ago.

This kind of action smacked of two things—and both were very evident to General Dave Jones and his staff, still holed up inside the the command bunker below the VAB, still somehow managing the defense of the undermanned, underequipped UAAF outpost.

Between the incredible vibrations caused by the shells

landing about three miles away and the subsequent storm of dust and plaster which rained down on them after every hit, Jones and his men were trying their best to monitor the situation via closed-circuit TV, and speculating on exactly what the Cult ships were up to.

"It's a bag job, it has to be," said Colonel Catfish Johnson, commanding officer of the 1st Airborne Division. "Those ships were paid to destroy the airstrip, and that's what they're doing. Apparently they weren't paid to do anything else—so they're not."

It was a theory that few around the table could argue with. The battleships could have reduced the entire complex to rubble a long time ago and didn't. The Beagles could have bombed all of the critical launch support buildings during the battle the day before, but they didn't. The Sparvee fast-attack boats could have leveled the VAB with their Styx missiles, but *they* didn't.

It all led to the validation of what the UAAF command staff had suspected all along: the combined Nazi-Cult attack force didn't want to destroy the KSC as much as they wanted to capture it. And the only reason they would do that was to use it to launch their own payloads into outer space. With the intelligence collected during the JAWS raid down in Cuba, there really was no doubt as to what the UA's enemies wanted to launch into orbit: the hodge-podge collection of nuclear warheads waiting inside the stockyard at the mysterious, fog-enshrouded Double-Trouble base.

"If they're able to get all those warheads in orbit," Johnson continued, coming back to the discussion that had been on going inside the command bunker for nearly 72 hours, "they will quite literally be able to control the entire planet. Wherever someone didn't do their bidding, they could simply find a means of sending one, two, or more of those warheads back down, and if they survived reentry, they would wipe said place off the map.

"It's crude and it's not pretty, but it would be an effective way of gaining total power. And we'd be hard pressed to stop them. Especially when one of these things could just come falling out of the sky on top of us at any moment."

That, more or less, put it all in a nutshell. The enemy had the weapons, they had the means to put those weapons in space. All they needed was a launch facility to close the deal. The KSC was really the only working spaceport left on earth.

So now the UAAF command staff faced a very unusual situation. They were up against an enemy many times more powerful and many times more ruthless, yet one that had found itself limited by what it could do in the field of battle. Apparently there were no specialty troops left after the battle the day before, and no sizable mercenary army in the area who would want to take on a landing at KSC. To get such a landing force—whether to move a substantial force of Cult troops halfway around the world or pay an exorbitant fee to hire someone more local—would take time.

This left the unseemly alliance with the only option of lobbing their huge shells onto noncritical areas of the KSC until some other strategy could be divined. It was a situation that could persist for a long, long time.

If the eardrums of every one in the UA defense forces could last that long.

Twenty-five

Skyfire, Cape Cod

It was now morning, but it was darker than ever.

The swirl of the hurricane high above the farmhouse had not moved, and if anything, the storm had gained in strength again.

Out on the ledge of the highest peak of Nauset Heights, Dominique was standing, braving the wind and the rain, looking out onto the raging, violent sea.

There were no dramatics going on. No theatrics. No arms raised. No chanting.

She was simply standing there, the wind blowing her hair, the rain glistening off her face. She stared off into the distance.

She'd been like this for hours.

Inside the farmhouse, Kurjan had changed his position and was now watching out the back window, keeping Dominique in view at all times. Frost was at the back door, peeking out the crack. The four girls were gathered at the living room window. They were watching Dominique, too.

As for Chloe, she was snuggled up beside Kurjan, her chin pressed up against the windowsill, watching and waiting, like everyone else.

It didn't take them long to realize that getting a message out of the Cape any time soon would be impossible. The separate journeys of both Chloe and Kurjan confirmed that. The surreal weather, the conditions of the roadways, and even the conditions of the normal communications themselves—radios, faxes, short-wave—were intolerable.

So after much hushed discussion, Dominique, Chloe, and Kurjan had decided to try it this way. Maybe they could contact Hunter through unconventional means. Maybe they could contact him psychically.

This was how desperate things had become.

Though Kurjan knew it was an outlandish idea, he also knew that strange things did happen in the world—and more so these past few days. He himself had been on the receiving end of some rather incredible experiences; he was, after all, the guy who supposedly had nine lives. Or more accurately, the one with the ability to rise from the dead over and over again.

Still, that didn't mean he believed in all this psychic stuff. But under the circumstances, he was willing to give anything a try.

There was never any discussion about who should be the transmitter of this message to outer space. Of anyone in the world, Dominique was closest to Hawk Hunter. They knew each other intimately—how else could they have stayed together while spending so much time apart?

Many times, over the years, Dominique had felt that she'd communicated telepathically with Hunter. But now, this would be a test of that very nebulous connection, one that no one inside the farmhouse really believed would work.

Kurjan's eyes, though tired and bleary, nevertheless stayed on Dominique the whole time. Whatever the hell was going to happen, he wanted to see it, for himself, up close and personal. The others did, too.

But it was not to be—and the storm would be to blame.

It had grown very dark, even though Kurjan estimated that it was approaching mid-morning. Though there was really no way to tell for sure, the sky was so black with storm clouds, it still seemed as if night had been hovering over the small farmhouse for the past four days.

Suddenly there was a crash of thunder and severe lightning; it was so loud and so violent, the entire house once again shook to its foundations. The glare from the lightning blinded Kurjan; it actually knocked him from his perch. An instant later, the window he'd been sitting at exploded in a cloud of glass and wood. Kurjan grabbed Chloe and hung on. Frost did likewise, throwing his emaciated body across the four young girls and shielding them from any harm.

The wind was suddenly blowing through the tiny living room at gale force. Pictures began disappearing from the walls; the candles all went out. The sweep of rain alone was enough to douse the blaze in the fireplace. In a matter of seconds, it was as wet and cold and windswept inside the house as it was outside.

Three more tremendous cracks of thunder followed, along with many explosions of lightning, some yellow, some white, some tinged with blue. By the time Kurjan was able to regain himself and get back to the window to cover it up, he and everyone else inside was soaked.

Somehow, though, he got the window covered and blocked off most of the storm—only three panes of the sixteen had been blown out. Now wiping the glass frantically with his sleeve, he sought to regain sight of Dominique. But when he was finally able to actually see out to the ledge about 40 feet from the house, she was no longer there.

Kurjan was out the door in a second, Frost and Chloe

close behind. They battled the fierce wind and rain and somehow made their way through the blowing hay to the ledge.

They found Dominique lying on the wet grass, her hair hardly mussed, her hands resting on her midsection. She looked like she was asleep. Her face was radiant—glowing, even. At first Kurjan thought she might have been struck by lightning, and this had created the aura around her. Maybe she was only knocked out.

Kurjan reached down and put his fingers to her lips and felt no breath. He pressed his fingers to her wrist and felt no pulse. He laid his hand on her heart and felt no beat.

Chloe broke out in tears; somewhere above, the skies rumbled once more.

The glow around Dominique's face faded away.

She was dead.

Twenty-six

In Orbit

It was called the Fifth Law of Repellent Charges.

It had to do with how many electrons in a certain charge were positive and how many were negative. If there were more positive electrons than negative ones and the massive positive charge somehow came in contact with a lesser negative one, the positive charge would cancel out the negative charge, short-circuit it, no matter if it was in a tiny light bulb, a bolt of lightning, or two great spacecraft chasing each other in orbit.

There was a problem, though. Sometimes it was hard to determine whether something was carrying a negative charge or a positive one. This had to do with the difference between alternating currents and direct currents, plus volts, amps, watts, and a hundred other things. Even after studying all that, there really was no sure way to determine the true nature of a charge without putting it in contact with something you believed was the opposite charge.

Hawk Hunter was 99.9 percent sure that the Zon carried what would be considered an overwhelmingly positive charge. Though the electrical wiring throughout the spacecraft could only be kindly described as "ambitious," he was certain that the electrical supply was running on a true direct current, and this was a clue that it was a true positive charge.

He was less sure that the massive swastika-shaped space station carried a negative charge. What kind of power were they running over there? From the looks of the thing, they could be burning coal—it looked that old. But that was the clue: its age.

They'd been circling the space station for several hours now, studying it, confident that none of the Me363 Komets would ever make it back to their home base, confident that no more were coming out after them. They'd detected no defensive weapons attached to the space station. No form of AA guns or SAMs, no signs of weaponry at all. The only spoke displaying any kind of belligerence was the arm holding the collection of space mines. The terminals at the ends of the other three twisted crosses appeared to contain observation windows and, in the case of the one under most scrutiny by Hunter and Company now, what looked like a docking port.

They had reached the end of their quest. There was no doubt that Viktor was holed up inside this orbital monstrosity, no doubt that he had no means of escape, at least nothing the Zon couldn't catch up with and destroy.

They had him trapped then. All they would have to do was get aboard the space station and take him into custody. Simple as that.

There was one unknown, however. How many soldiers, minions and flunkies did Viktor have inside the space station to oppose their entry? Was it 20? Or 120? Or 1020?

The space station looked like it could hold all that and more. But this was a question of numbers more than perception. Certainly the space station was huge—"The Flying Reichstag," JT had nicknamed it.

But did it really hold many, many people? Most likely not, Ben had reported. To support a large number of people, the space station would have to be taking on supplies, such as food, fuel, and water, every day, day after day, for as long as it wanted to operate. The spacelift capability for such a supply effort would have to be enormous, and well out of range of any entity on earth, the UA included. Obviously, there was no such effort going on.

A large population inside the space station would also require an enormous amount of power. Electric power. Yet the station had no solar panel arrays—indeed, it looked like it was built long before the solar array was even invented—and, from all appearances, no alternative electricity-producing source, such as a nuclear reactor, either. The only way the space station could be powered was by batteries, and batteries wear out. Therefore, conservation is the key to their longevity—and a couple thousand people probably wouldn't be conscientious enough to turn off all the lights all the time.

Finally, a large population would have to dispense its waste products on a constant, never-ending dispersal rate, and there was absolutely no indication of this from the space station. The only sign of waste disposal were small, vaporish jets seen emanating from the underside of the station's hub, on a more or less regular basis. Ever the number cruncher, Ben counted the times the vapor jets had appeared during the hours-long fly-around and then broke this number down to an average per thirty minutes. His determination: that this was urine waste being vented directly into space, just as the Zon's zero-G toilet would do. Number of people taking a leak within a 30-minute period on the space station: 6. Factoring the nervousness of the situation and the fact that weightlessness made some peo-

ple go more often, Ben determined there were less
than 20 people currently on-board the station.

"Unless," he added, "a couple thousand people are
going around pissing in the corners."

Hunter chose to take Ben's figure of 20 or so because
he doubted the fastidious Nazis would be taking squirts
anywhere but in the proper Nazi receptacles.

So what they were facing was maybe a three- to four-
man disadvantage should they storm the space station.
Certainly this was better than 500-to-1, but still, the Zon
crew had to come up with some kind of advantage,
something to even the odds a little more in their favor.

That was where the Fifth Law of Repellent Charges
came in.

Hunter was bargaining on the fact that if the Zon
charge was positive and the space station negative, then
if the Zon made contact with it in any way, their charge
would short-circuit the station's charge. All electrical
power, or the main systems, anyway, on the space station would be knocked out. Then the Americans could
bust in under cover of darkness, sowing confusion and
panic. They would be armed with the tasers. They
would have surprise on their side.

Of course, in combat nothing ever goes right, and
the things you want to count on going in usually don't
happen or don't matter if they do.

Still, they were here, on the threshold of their dream.
They had to take that final step.

So that became the plan. Fly the Zon as close as possible to the space station, specifically, to the area
around the docking port, send out a couple space walkers, and have them determine the compatibility of the
Zon's docking ring—presently poking out of the
shaved-down, locked-tight cargo bay doors—with that
of the space station. Hunter was taking two-to-one odds
that it would be a match.

After all, Viktor's ultimate plan *had* to involve docking the Zon to this mysterious space station at some point.

Or did it?

The raiding party had been determined shortly after they'd begun closing in on the space station.

The more people they could get over into the station, the better their chances would be. There were eight bodies to pick from—the six original astronauts and the two young girls. At least one person would have to remain at the controls of the Zon during the attack, and another would have to be ready to man the pressurization chamber for both the raiding party's egress and return.

It took some creative thinking, but finally, by a committee vote, they determined that Elvis would be the best choice to remain with the Zon. He knew how to fly it, and he knew something about how to fix it, should anything go wrong during the transfer. Elvis was not particularly happy about this appointment—he, more than Hunter, wanted to get his fingers wrapped around Viktor's throat. But he knew it was a decision that made sense.

But who would remain behind to run the air lock? The mission into the space station would require every able-bodied man, and running the air lock was really just a matter of pushing the right buttons at the right times. They decided the young girl known as Six would remain on the Zon, too, and be the pressurization queen. The young girl named Eight would suit up, be given a taser, and join the raiding party. Eight was very happy about this appointment: she, too, had a huge debt to settle with the villain king Viktor.

Both spacecraft were moving into a dark period. The

earth's shadow would overwhelm this area of space very soon, and this was perfect for Hunter and his crew. The darkness would last about 35 minutes. If they could get the raiding party ready and over into the space station in that time, they would have the further advantage of attacking in the nighttime, however brief it might be.

The first step was to get the Zon close to the space station docking port, and Elvis was already well on the way to doing this. Taking over the main controls from Hunter, he had moved the Zon to within 50 feet of the port, perfectly matching the space station's rate of speed and settling in alongside it in a classic example of sympathetic movement. Throughout this entire maneuver, everyone else on board was looking out of the various portholes, keeping large sections of the space station under surveillance, ready to call out with any indication that the enemy spacecraft was going to defend itself, or that they had detected the Zon's movement. But no one saw anything. The space station just continued spinning silently, either unaware of the Zon's presence, or more likely, unable to do anything about it.

There were equal amounts of confusion and excitement in the crew compartment now. Six people were climbing into EVA spacesuits in an area built to handle four at the most. The fact that everyone was trying to do the same thing in the same space under zero-G made for a proliferation of arms, legs, and feet, with much tugging at sleeves, squirming to fit into boots, and heads trying to screw into helmets.

Surprisingly, everyone was outfitted and ready to leave the Zon inside of 10 minutes.

Geraci went out first. Armed with his taser and a huge battery-powered light, he went through depressurization and was soon floating up and out of the tiny one-person air lock. Cook went next; together they would look for and study the docking ring mechanism and see what the compatibility factor would be.

JT and Ben would follow them out. They were carrying an extra taser each, plus extra battery packs for everyone. They would be bodyguards for Geraci and Cook while they looked for the docking ring. If Geraci and Cook were successful, and were able to find a way to mate the two spaceships quickly, Ben and JT would be the first ones through the door to the space station.

Eight was the next one to go out. She would be employed as a lookout, and as she'd informed the astronauts that she'd taken several space walks before while on the Mir, she didn't require any training in the fine art of EVA. Still, she promised to stay hooked to her tether at all times.

Hunter would be the last one to go. He'd be providing the ultimate back-up, helping Cook and Geraci with their search and evaluation while at the same time helping JT, Ben, and Eight look for any enemy activity. Should they gain the station as they were hoping, Hunter would be the third man through the door.

Eight was about halfway through the depressurization process when they received the first bit of encouraging news from the outside. Cook and Geraci had located the docking ring and were fairly certain it was a match with the Zon's. What's more, there was a grounding device attached to the ring which prevented, to a certain degree, the problem of two space craft hooking up with disparate charges. The first thing Cook and Geraci did was to disconnect this device from the docking ring and allow it to float away. But this action just emphasized the need to speed things up. If there were people planing on opposing them inside the station, they certainly knew an attack was coming now. From now on, every second would count.

Eight finally went out the door, and now it was Hunter's turn. Six helped him recheck his equipment, including his oxygen supply and his taser. Then, sweetly, she floated up on her tiptoes and planted a kiss right in the middle of his helmet visor.

"Good luck!" she yelled into his ear.

Hunter smiled and stepped int the tiny air lock.

It never failed to amaze him that the Russians would make such an important piece of equipment so small, so cramped, so uncomfortable. Certainly space was a design element on any extraterrestrial craft; there was no wasted space on the old NASA shuttles, and there was none on the Zon. The difference was that the NASA shuttle designers had planned small from the get-go; the Russians just stuck everything anywhere it fit, and whatever didn't fit, they left behind.

So the small air lock was a victim of poor design, just like everything else on the Zon. Why, then, was it so dark? In a time and place where a potential space-walker had to check many elements of their survival suits, and make sure that everything was working okay in the lock itself, the Russians had chosen not to include any illumination, not even an attachment for a 10-watt bulb. The interior of the lock was mostly shaped metal, and all the cut-outs that had made it through the forming process were used up with controls for the lock's operation.

A spacewalker had to cram himself into this tiny cas-ketlike chamber and wait in the dark as the air was sucked out and his own air supply came on. It could be an unnerving experience.

But Hunter's mind was on other things as he stepped into the chamber for the minute of depressurization. Six closed the hatch behind him and successfully bolted the double lock. Then she began the depres-surization process. Meanwhile, Hunter was already projecting what they had to do once he got back out into space. They would have to double-check the docking ring, make sure there were no defense they would have to contend with, make sure there was some means of an electrical hook-up, and a few hundred other things, all while trying to beat the clock.

His mind was more preoccupied than usual as the air was sucked out of the tiny chamber, taking all remaining traces of light with it.

That's why Hunter was extremely surprised, to say the least, when he felt someone tap him on the shoulder.

He would never forget that feeling. That nudge on his right shoulder, just below his regulator hose and just above the small pocket in which he kept his extra taser battery pack.

Instinct took over as he began to spin around—who could possibly be tapping on him in this airless, dark place that was hardly built to fit one, never mind two?

When he turned, he got his answer—and from that moment on, he knew his life would never, ever be the same again.

It was Dominique.

She looked glowing, radiant—and quite transparent. She was standing right behind him, her hair flowing as if in a stiff wind, her face crinkled up in a smile. Hunter nearly went into shock. Instantly, he believed he was suffering from post-atmospheric narcolepsy, a lack of oxygen to the brain due to an equipment malfunction during the depressurization process; it was known to cause vivid hallucinations.

But he knew this could not be the case. He was still breathing, though very hard and uneasily now. Dominique was simply there with him—though he could almost see right through her.

"What . . . is this?" he was finally able to mumble.

The smile never left her face.

"This is goodbye, Hawk," she told him, plainly.

"Goodbye . . ." he stammered—it seemed like such a strange thing for a hallucination to say. "What does that mean?"

"I mean, this is the end," she said. "I'm in another place now. On another plane. I was just able to come back and talk to you one last time."

Hunter just stared at her. *Another place? Another plane? What the hell was this?*

"Are you trying to tell me . . . that you're a ghost?" he heard himself asking.

Dominique's smile widened a bit. It was the usual reaction when he got something right—finally.

"I'm a spirit," she gently corrected him. "I'm my *own* spirit, in fact. That's what it's all about. Or at least, that's all I can tell you. Your spirit and your soul are one and the same and when you pass over; your spirit remains. It's close to what a butterfly does, before . . ."

But now Hunter held up his hand. He felt like a thousand volts of electricity were running through him.

"Are you trying to tell me that you . . . that you're *dead?*"

Dominique's smile faded a bit. Then she nodded once.

"It's true, Hawk," she whispered.

Hunter went numb, the first stage of denial. What was happening? How could Dominique be dead? He would have known, somehow.

He decided to argue that point.

"You couldn't possibly be . . . deceased," he said carefully. "I would know. I know the extent of my extrasensory abilities. Believe me, I know it when the wind changes by a fraction of a degree in any direction. I know when a bad guy's airplane is going to spin out even before he does. I will feel the exact moment the sunrise cracks the horizon . . .

"If the woman I loved died, believe me, I'd *know* it."

Dominique's smile returned slightly, but it was still a sad one.

"You *will* know it," she told him. "Soon. Very soon."

Hunter began to say something else, but couldn't. He just stared at her and she at him. Time was standing still.

"Until that happens," she finally said, "you must know something. You must find out something. If you don't, then every man, woman, and child on earth will be affected."

Again Hunter tried to say something, but couldn't.

"You have to find the Hubble telescope, get it working, and point it to the segment of space your instincts guide you to."

Now Hunter almost laughed out loud. This was getting absurd. The ghost of his lifelong love was appearing to him—and telling him to find a space telescope that had probably been abandoned many years before.

"I just don't believe this—or you, or anything connected to it," he was finally able to mumble. "I just don't believe it . . ."

Dominique smiled a little brighter, even as her image was beginning to fade.

"You will believe, Hawk," she said. "Very soon."

Hunter didn't want her to go. What if this really *was* happening? What if this really *was* the last time he would ever see her? He was not prepared for this. She couldn't leave him now.

But leaving she was. Her image was now nearly dissipated. Almost pathetically, he reached out to grab her, as if he could physically make her stay inside this airless box with him.

But it didn't work. He wound up clutching nothing but empty space.

Her last words to him were, "Goodbye, Hawk. I love you very much . . ."

When Hunter emerged from the Zon air lock, he was already spinning out of control.

Never properly hooked to his tether, he began cartwheeling off into space, his arms and legs not moving, the faceplate in his helmet fogged with condensation. The girl called Eight saw him first. She was hanging on to her own tether just outside the air lock when Hunter went careening by. She tried to grab hold of him—it was obvious to her that something was wrong—but his boot proved to be just beyond her grasp. She began screaming into her radio mike to alert the others. Hunter was drifting away! In seconds, the four space walkers were swimming toward the Wingman.

It was Geraci and JT who reached him first. They were certain that he'd experienced a malfunction in his breathing apparatus and that he was suffocating, if not already unconscious. But when they yanked him back toward the Zon air lock, Hunter suddenly came alive again. He began waving them off and giving them the double thumbs-up sign, as if to say he was all right.

JT was having none of that, however; he knew something had just happened to his friend. Someone like Hunter just didn't go drifting off into space. He went helmet-to-helmet with him and stared in through the foggy faceplate. He thought he saw Hunter's face wet with tears.

"Jeezus, Hawk, what's the matter?"

But again Hunter just waved him away.

"I got . . . I got a ventilator filter stuffed up," he

replied. "Lots of water inside here. It's okay, though. I unplugged it . . . or something."

JT stared at his friend for a long moment as they floated along, weightless in space. A clogged ventilator filter would cause a lot of condensation to build up quickly inside someone's helmet—and make it appear as if they'd been crying. And JT would have fully bought Hunter's story, if not for the look in Hunter's eyes. JT had known Hunter for years; he'd never seen him look quite like this before.

"You sure you're okay, buddy?" JT asked him again.

Hunter gave him a couple of friendly taps on his helmet.

"Just had a bad dream," was his enigmatic reply.

They finally hooked up Hunter's tether and then drifted back over to the Zon cargo bay doors, which were now about 10 feet away from the space station's docking ring. The Zon would be the male functionary in this mating. Its docking mechanism was about six feet long and slightly conical in shape. The space station's receptor was slightly oval, with a collar of gold-covered-padding encrusted with a couple dozen stainless steel springs. Close inspection of the space station's orifice seemed to show that this particular docking ring had not been used very much, or at least, not recently.

"We can definitely do the deed," Geraci told them all over their helmet intercom, pointing to the space station's docking mechanism. "This looks like it works on a passive universal system. In other words, it will take any kind of docker we can put into it."

"Let's do it, then," Ben urged.

Geraci and Cook drifted back to the Zon and retrieved the pair of thick cables that had been floating just to the rear of the air lock. These were auxiliary wires used to power an ICP, an "independent components package" that might be carried inside the cargo bay itself. For their purposes, though, the cables would act as the conduit through which the Zon would attempt to shock the space station.

To do this didn't require any extra power to be sent through the wires, or a powering-down of any of the Zon's systems. If the Zon had an overwhelmingly positive charge, it would be inherent in the spacecraft itself. It would be running through it whether all its systems were at full load or not. It could almost be equated to the spaceship's "personality." Crude, problematic, yet workmanlike, and imbued with just a little more positivity than negativity.

The gamble was whether the space station was just the opposite.

Cook volunteered to make the connection between the Zon and the space station. He took the pair of heavy cables in hand and drifted over to the area of the docking ring where he and Geraci had just removed the grounding damper. The two cables had clamps on their ends that looked exactly like the alligator clamps found on a pair of automobile starter cables. All Cook had to do was attach these clamps, one at a time, to the bottom of the space station's docking ring. Then, if the Fifth Law of Repellent Forces was indeed on their side, the Zon would shock the big swastika into a massive short-circuit.

If the space station's overall charge was more overwhelming than the Zon's, then it would be the Americans who would be on the receiving end of the short-circuit. And that would be a disaster.

Cook finally positioned himself just a foot off the docking ring. Before he attached the first jumper cable, however, he did an odd thing. He took his taser, unraveled one of the lead wires, and tapped it onto the side of the docking ring. A tiny, almost imperceptible

spark was the result. He looked back at the others, now
crowded around the Zon's air lock hatch, and gave
them a shrug. His little experiment had proved that
there were opposing charges at work here—now the
only question was, whose would be the most powerful.

Cook stayed still for a long moment and then
hooked up the first cable to a large bolt which had
formerly served to hold the ground dampener on.
Nothing happened, nor was anything expected to. The
charge would become effective only when a circuit was
made, meaning when the second wire was attached.
Cook waited another few seconds, and then, like a man
attempting to hook up a cable to a bawky car battery,
he turned his face and body away and attached the
second cable.

There was a huge spark of electricity—it was blue
and green and yellow all at the same time. Cook was
sent reeling of into space, his tether line quickly
stretching beyond its limit. Everyone's helmet radios
died with a crack of static. Then the Zon began to shudder; frightening-looking sparks could be seen flowing
from its nose and tail. One of the malfunctioning steering jets suddenly came alive and began spurting
streams of gas. This started the entire spacecraft to wob-
bling; inside, Elvis was now fighting with the controls.
JT and Geraci immediately pushed themselves off to
go and retrieve Cook. He was floating and spinning
and looked as if *he'd* been knocked out. For one devastating moment, it appeared that the plan had back-
fired, that the Zon had the weaker charge and was now
short-circuiting itself to death.

But appearances could be deceiving.

It was Eight who saw it first. She was actually closest
to the space station and had the clearest view of the
double row of portholes which ran the length of the
crooked arm all the way up to the hub. One by one,

she could see the lights behind the portholes begin to blink off.

She tapped Ben twice and he in turn tapped Geraci, and now all three of them were watching as all the lights in the massive space station began blinking out, going faster and faster around the four arms. That's when everyone's helmet radios came back on and the Zon stopped shaking. Only then did everyone realize that their gamble had paid off. Their charge was more positive that the Nazi spacecraft.

The proof was in the seeing: within 20 seconds, the huge, well-lit space station had suddenly gone very cold.

It was a triumphant moment for the Americans. One of the boldest plans ever in UA history had just worked.

Yet through it all, one of the space walkers had hung back, a mere spectator in the bold gambit.

It was Hawk Hunter, uncharacteristically out of the action. He was floating in space, hooked to a loose tether, watching as the others performed all the heroics.

It was safe to say his mind was somewhere else.

Ten minutes later, they had all reentered the Zon and were now inside the darkened cargo bay, looking up from the Zon's side of the docking mechanism.

Elvis had connected the spacecraft to the Nazi station with a letter-perfect maneuver and with no loss or drain of power.

Now Geraci and Cook were working on the common hatchway which would lead them into the space station itself. For safety reasons, everyone was still in their EVA suits, and everyone had their taser guns up and ready.

It took them five minutes to get the hatchway to open. Once they'd unlocked it, a rush of air pushed the door back in their faces—it swung open so quickly, everyone thought a horde of Nazi space goons was about to come pouring through. But it was just the reaction to two different air pressurization systems quickly leveling off. No one was behind the hatchway leading into the space station; the beams of JT's powerful trouble light confirmed that. The passageway beyond was absolutely dark and empty.

Hunter was taking all this in, even as his mind continued spinning off in a million different directions. The whole space walk in which the Nazi spacecraft had been zapped seemed like a dream to him now, even though it had just happened not 15 minutes ago. Emblazoned on his eyes was not the sight of the enemy space station going dark, but Dominique's face, smiling sadly as it faded from view, her last words still echoing in his ears.

Did it really happen? Had he really spoken with Dominique's ghost? These questions were pounding inside him now like a heart that was about to burst from overuse. Why was this happening? He should be at his peak, about to fulfill his long-anticipated quest of finally capturing the world's most dangerous villain; but his mind was everywhere but on the matter at hand.

He took a series of long, deep breaths from his oxygen hose. Maybe he *had* suffered from a brief period of post-atmospheric narcolepsy. Maybe he *had* just imagined the whole thing. Maybe Dominique was alive and well and waiting for him back at Skyfire, as always. Or maybe she'd found out somehow about his relationship with Chloe—and this was just a guilty conscience playing tricks on him.

Whatever the case, he had to put it all on hold—at least, until they finished their work inside the space station. And maybe for a long time after that as well.

Geraci finally secured the hatchway into the space

station, and now the route lay open to them. As previously planned, JT and Ben went in first, tasers high, trouble lights flashing. Hunter, his weapon up, his mind clearing, was floating right on their heels.

They were drifting vertically into the space station's terminal module, heading up to the right-angled twist, which in turn would lead into the main hub. The space station looked on the inside just like it did out: heavy steel planks, lots of nuts and bolts and welds and rivets. They just couldn't get over the feeling that they were actually skin divers moving through the wreck of a World War II German battleship. Nothing they could see looked any older than 1945.

They floated up about 40 feet, Hunter, JT, and Ben in the vanguard, Cook, Geraci, and Eight bringing up the rear. There were no side doors or hatchways inside the passageway; instead, the walls were adorned with items of Nazi regalia: Iron Crosses, swords, medals, sashes, all of them encased in separate glass displays, almost as if they were part of a museum or a hall of fame of some kind.

"I've got dibs on the souvenirs," JT whispered into his helmet mike.

They continued on, passing a series of brightly colored murals, very Germanic-looking paintings applied directly to the passageway wall. Many depicted various Nazi bigwigs as conquering, benevolent heroes, entering "liberated" towns with the local population lined up and cheering them on. One showed Hitler himself as a white knight on a horse, in a shining suit of armor, complete with lance and shield and carrying a huge Nazi flag. It was the most ridiculous of the lot.

Unlike the Mir, the space station passageway was large and there was no restriction of movement. JT, Ben, and Hunter fit quite comfortably at three across. The claustrophobic feelings of the much smaller Rus sian-built space station were nowhere in evidence here. This place had been built for comfort, for movement, and obviously for many, many people to use.

They finally reached the left-hand turn in the arm; the next passageway would lead them to the hub. A hatchway was located here, and it was bolted tight. Geraci quickly solved the lock and within a minute was spinning the old-fashioned dogwheel and unclamping the hatch.

JT and Hunter took one side of the doorway, Ben and Cook the other. They had their weapons up and ready—there was no telling what they would find on the other side, even though up to now they'd heard no noise, nor had they encountered evidence of human activity anywhere.

They gave Geraci the okay sign and the combat engineer gave the door a mighty yank. JT flooded the other side with his powerful lantern. It illuminated the helmeted faces of two black-spacesuit-clad men.

They were holding rifles—down-on-the-ground, unsophisticated Mauser rifles, circa 1945. A brief stand-off ensued—no one dared make a move. Hunter studied the pair of rifles. He knew they probably fired a 7.62-mm caliber bullet and that the projectile was of the high-speed, long-range variety. In this moment an odd question came to mind: what happens when someone shoots a gun in outer space?

He got his answer a second later.

The guy on the left fired first. The explosion from his gun muzzle seemed tremendous. But the instant he pulled the trigger, the old every-action-has-an-opposite-reaction came into play. The Mauser's recoil was so powerful and violent, the shooter was sent reeling all the way up to the top of this second dark passageway, slamming himself against a bulkhead, knocking himself out, and most likely causing himself a fractured skull.

The bullet went in the exact opposite direction, rocketing over everyone's head at tremendous speed and pinging off the hatchway down at the other end of the module. But it didn't stop there. It ricocheted off the floor, up to the ceiling, back down to the floor, and up to the ceiling again. It went on ricocheting like this for ten very dangerous seconds, until it finally lodged itself into one of the regalia cases and came to a halt. If it hadn't done this, and if Sir Isaac Newton was right, it could have kept bouncing off the walls of the module forever.

The physics class ended when JT lunged forward and zapped the second shooter with his stun gun. They'd just seen the first rifle shot in space; now they were watching the first taser-induced conniption. The second JT's weapon made contact, the goon began spazzing crazily, bouncing off the walls like a cartoon character, repeatedly smashing his face mask into the heavy-steeled girders. He finally broke his neck and screamed as all the air was sucked out of his lungs.

But because they were still inside their helmets, there was no way they could hear the sound he made when he died.

It took the small party of Americans another 10 minutes to grope their way up to the next hatchway, and another five to peel off the body of the man who'd so foolishly fired the Mauser.

This door was locked, too, and once again Geraci did the honors of opening it.

To everyone's mild surprise, there were two more space-suited fellows waiting on the other side. They, too, were holding Mausers. But somehow they'd been privy to the fate shared by the first pair of spacemen who'd attempted to stop the raiding party. These two had their hands raised in surrender even before the hatchway was fully open. Almost comically, their guns were floating in place right above their heads.

Behind them was another door which led through an emergency air lock, and then into the hub of the station. It was not surprising that the hub could operate on its own pressurization system; the airlock was doubled as the inner fortress's front door. What *was* surprising was that only four goons had come out to try to stop them, and two of them had given up without a fight.

JT yanked one of the spacemen through the first hatch, giving him just a taste of a taser shot, enough to knock him out. Terrified, his companion held his hands even higher in surrender. Hunter studied this man through his helmet faceplate. Like the pair of thugs they'd iced back at the Mir, he looked underfed, unwashed, unshaven, and generally unhealthy.

JT had his taser up in the man's face now. Terrified, the man leaped to the ceiling, he was trying to raise his hands so high. Ben pulled him back down and spun him around. Hunter grabbed him by the shoulder pad and pointed at the air lock. No words needed to be spoken. The man quickly began pushing buttons and pulling levers. Soon the air lock door opened with a whoosh.

They were now just one step away from getting inside the hub.

Meanwhile, there was a great deal of panic on the other side of the air lock door.

There were now only 16 soldiers left to defend the inner hub, the remains of what had been a very small skeleton crew all along. None of these men had any weapons of any consequence with which to repel the invaders. They'd seen the brief encounters their comrades had engaged in with the Americans; they now knew that weapons such as rifles and pistols were useless, and even dangerous to use in zero-G. All they had left were their bare hands and a total of five knives between them.

They'd decided the best thing to do was imitate their comrades and simply give up.

The air lock door opened a few moments later and all six Americans came flooding into the large inner chamber, tasers held high. The 16 goons, all of them depleted, unwashed, skinny, and barely dressed, were floating several felt off the floor, lined up in a perfect row, their hands held high over their heads.

"This is too easy!" JT yelled, as he and Ben began hauling the surrending minions back down to the floor.

Meanwhile, Hunter and the others were marveling at the design of the immense inner chamber. It didn't look like a battleship in here, nor did it look like a space station. It looked like the inside of a palace. Paintings, chandeliers, velvet wall coverings, ornate chairs, and tables bolted to the walls—it looked very mysterious in the glare of their trouble lights. And, like everything else on the station, very, very old.

Hunter opened the front of this helmet and took his first deep breath of the space station air. It tasted stale and sweet.

"Anyone speak English?" he shouted at the prisoners.

No one answered—at first.

Hunter pulled down one of the goons and gave him a zap of the taser on his shoulder. The man spun away in obvious pain.

"Anyone know English now?" Hunter yelled.

Suddenly eight hands went up—fully half the prisoners spoke it.

Hunter reached up and pulled the nearest one down to him.

"Where's your boss?" he growled at the man, his taser snapping and crackling just a few inches from the goon's exposed neck.

"In . . . in the main sleeping chamber," the man mumbled, pointing to a hatch right over their heads.

"How many goons up there with him?"

The guy just began shaking his head.

"None," he said. "No goons. The only goons are down here."

"Is *anyone* up there with him?" Ben wanted to know.

The blabbermouth just shook his head again, causing him to float away a little.

"Just four officers," he replied, as Hunter yanked him back down once more. "None of them are armed . . ."

"Too easy," JT kept saying, tying the hands of one of the prisoners and then letting him float away to bounce off the walls of the very showy dark chamber.

Cook was right up beside Hunter. He seconded JT's feelings.

"It does seem like the end of the road should be a lot harder than this, Hawk," he said.

Hunter would have been inclined to agree—if they were still back on earth. But the logical view was this: Viktor had nowhere else to go. Sure, the space station looked big and old and seemed like a waste just to house 20 skinny underarmed goons. But that was a mystery for a different time. Hunter's greatest concern at the moment was that they'd get into this inner chamber and find Viktor and his officers dead—of self-inflicted wounds.

To his mind, they had to move quickly.

While Ben and Eight stayed behind with the prisoners, Hunter, JT, Cook, and Geraci floated up to the hatchway indicated by the prisoner. Geraci began fiddling with the bolt, assuming the hatch was locked from the inside. To his surprise, he discovered it was already open.

"Too easy . . ." JT whispered again, bringing his taser up to bear. "Way too easy."

Hunter nodded to Geraci, who kicked in the door with a mighty boot, which predictably sent him reeling in the opposite direction. He was caught by Cook as Hunter and JT went flying through the door.

This place was as ornately appointed as the main chamber. At first it appeared Hunter's worst fears had come true. There were two Nazi officers floating just on the other side of the hatchway, legions of blood bubbles running out of two huge neck wounds.

Two more officers were floating above a grand imperial steel-poster bed bolted to the floor at the far end of the chamber. Despite their shoulder loads of Nazi insignia, they both seemed a little too timid to take the same way out as their colleagues.

But where was Viktor, the big kahuna himself?

Hunter shot over to the two remaining officers. He mimicked his action earlier and painfully zapped one with his taser. This immediately unlocked the lips of the second man.

"Where is he?" was all Hunter had to say.

Trembling mightily, the man pointed to the space under the huge bed.

"Hiding," he said in accented English. "Under there."

Cook and Geraci had flown into the room by now, and with JT's help, they yanked a tall, skinny, almost lifeless body out from under the huge bed. This person was dressed in a very effeminate-looking nightgown, which had recently been soiled. His hair was greasy, his goatee untrimmed and full of foreign particles. He looked pitiful.

The three men yanked him up to Hunter's position and pulled his arms behind him.

Hunter had to take a long, hard look to realize that this was the man they'd come all this way to capture. The man who called himself Viktor.

It felt like an atomic blast went off inside Hunter's head. Why bother hauling Viktor's sorry ass back down to earth? Why not just get it over with, here and now? As it was, Hunter could just barely hold himself back from grabbing the terrorist by the throat and choking him until he was dead right then and there. Or better yet, applying his taser to the man's scrawny neck and squeezing out the full 80,000 volts until he was literally cooked on the inside. *Why not do it?* Why not put an end to the most feared human scourge since Hitler?

Why not just kill him now and do the whole universe a big favor?

But just as Hunter was grimly considering this, another bolt of lightning hit him, this one from out of the blue. His eyes went wild. His mouth fell open. His hands began to shake so much, he let go of the taser and it floated away.

You'll know, Hawk . . . He heard Dominique's words suddenly flood into his head, almost as if she were beside hin again, whispering in his ear. *You'll known soon* . . .

In that moment, which seemed to last an eternity, Hunter *did* know. Dominique was dead. Her spirit had visited him in the air lock. She had told him what he had to do, and it had nothing to do with capturing Viktor.

Suddenly Hunter turned to JT. His face was as white as a sheet.

"We have to go," he said quickly to his friend. "Right now . . ."

JT looked back at him and almost laughed. *"Go?"* he exclaimed. "Go *where?*"

Hunter did not reply. He had already turned himself around and was flying back out the bedroom door, back into the main chamber, heading toward the air lock.

"Come with me!" he called over his shoulder to the others, in the harshest voice anyone had ever heard him use. "Now! That's an order." They complied.

JT, Cook, and Geraci all left the bedroom on Hunter's heels. Picking up Ben and Eight along the way, they exited the main chamber, leaving behind the prisoners, Viktor, and his two very surprised underlings.

Twenty-seven

Several hours later

It looked like a big gray trash can.

This was not unusual—a lot of things looked like weightless trash cans up in space. The high-tech corrugated design was definitely the one of choice when it came to building satellites for orbit. The cylindrical lines helped in construction, launching, powering, and orbital stability.

Still, this one was particularly trash-canny. It was tumbling along on path in mid-orbital range, looking for all the world like it was about to lose its cover and begin spewing space trash everywhere.

But this satellite was different in a few ways, too. First, it was big. Much bigger than the typical KH-12 spy bird or TIRUS weather/sat. Second, it had a pair of unusual wings—actually, solar-array panels—that appeared longer and wider than most. They were flapping like bird's wings. This movement was due to the tumbling, but still, it made it appear that the wings were responsible for pushing the satellite forward.

It looked like a tumbling trash can with wings, not exactly a fitting epitaph for what was once the most famous space instrument in the world.

It was the Hubble. The huge telescope, first launched in the early 1990s and immediately discovered to have a debilitating flaw, was given a corrective lens a couple of years later. It went on to represent mankind's biggest eye in the sky. It saw things that no earth-based telescope could ever see. The first black hole. The first pulsar. The first planets outside the solar system.

But somewhere along the way, either shortly before the Big War or sometime soon after it, the Hubble was abandoned, or more likely, simply forgotten. Someone somewhere must have shut its main power supply down—the solar panels were not fully extended—and when it began tumbling, no one was around to put it back in an upright position. It had probably been going head over heels like this for years.

Watching it now from the flight deck of the Zon, Hunter felt a chill go through him. This had been a common occurrence in the last few hours. He was a psychic animal, a slave to ESP. His whole life, not just in the cockpit of his fighter, but on the ground and in his relationships with people, all of it was based, at least in some part, on his intuitive powers. It was the way he always had the edge on everybody else.

Certainly there were a lot of compulsive instincts that went along with this clairvoyance. But never, ever, had he had the compulsive override to come here to this part of space and find this thing, the Hubble space telescope.

The retreat from the Nazi Space Station had been a bizarre affair. Hunter and the others just left. They backed their way out and the Space Nazis let them go. Returning to the Zon, Hunter was sure that Viktor would send at least some of his minions out to chase them, or at least try for some kind of retaliation—but none came. The Zon backed away and Hunter began plotting its new course almost immediately. Meanwhile, once the connection was broken, the space station became powered up again—lights could be seen popping on in its windows. It also began spinning faster, a maneuver which allowed it to climb slightly in its orbit and quickly drift away from the Zon. It was out of sight within five minutes.

Everyone aboard the Zon—JT, Ben, Elvis, Cook, Geraci, and the two girls—was wondering just what the hell was going on. From their perspective, just when it seemed they'd accomplished their mission and at last had Viktor dead to rights, Hunter had suddenly called the whole thing off. He'd led their retreat without so much as a word of explanation, simply because he wasn't exactly sure himself why he'd suddenly felt the urge to go.

Yet after a six-hour dash through space, he had found what his psyche had told him to look for. The Hubble, ingloriously tumbling through the sky, had been his goal all along.

But now that they'd found it, what next?

"I assume you want to get it straight and working," Geraci asked Hunter quietly, as they brought the Zon up to pace and slightly below the rolling space instrument. Finding the Hubble had been no problem. The on-board space radar helped, but Hunter's inner self had laid out a more accurate, quicker approach.

"How much of an effort do you think it will take?" he asked Geraci.

The CE officer just shrugged.

"I know it was tumbling when NASA first came up to fix it," he said. "So stopping it shouldn't be that big a deal. Just an EVA, probably two or three people, we put a bearhug on it and slow it down. Like the Soyuz.

"But getting it to work? Well, that means getting the main juice turned on and doing some kind of diagnostic check. But getting it powered up is a long way from making it operational. I mean, I know there's no manual eyepiece over there. Everything that baby collected was transmitted back to Earth. How can we possibly capture those images?"

It did seem like an enormous problem. The Hubble used to see all these great things via remote control from the ground. Any pictures it took were sent via radio and TV waves back to a NASA receiving station. It was the equipment there that had the ability to develop the Hubble's images. How the hell would they be able to do all that up here?

"It will be easy," Ben surprised them all by saying.

Everyone on the flight deck turned in his direction, even the girls.

"Easy?" JT snarled at him. "When's the last time you did anything that was easy?"

Ben just shrugged. He couldn't remember.

"What I mean is, it won't be the hassle that you think," he began to explain. "The Hubble is not just a telescope and camera, it's also a sending station. A small TV station, if you will. That's how the images got back to earth."

"Yeah, well, if you'd been listening, you'd know we've already talked about that," JT told him snidely.

"Okay, I know," Ben replied. "But you see, when they built this thing, they must have had some kind of attachment which would allow them to check the TV relay *before* they launched. A way to connect into the transmitter to see if the lens was working even before it came up into space."

"Are you saying that there's a TV input plug on that thing?" Geraci asked, legitimately curious. "Like something we could just run a coaxial and a monitor into and get results?"

"I'll bet a hundred in gold there is," Ben replied. "We just have to find it, run a wire to one of our TV monitors, and *voilà!*"

JT was already digging into his pockets.

"Hundred in gold? You're on, pineapple boy," he said.

But Hunter wasn't paying attention to the beginnings of the wager. He was studying the tumbling Hubble through the powerful biscopes instead.

Just as Ben predicted, there *was* a diagnostic panel right on the bottom of the thing—or was it the top?—which appeared to contain a simple hook-up of the type Ben had described. Of course, the satellite was tumbling at such a rate, Hunter could only catch quick glimpses of it as it went by.

To make certain it was a TV input jack, they would have to see it up close.

To this end, he undid his seatbelt and began floating toward the hatch.

"Okay," he asked, somewhat wearily. "Who wants to stretch their legs this time?"

It took Hunter, Geraci, and JT more than an hour to stop the huge Hubble telescope from tumbling.

This was not like the Soyuz, which had responded to Geraci's acrobatic antics almost on demand. The Hubble fought them all the way, not only refusing to become stable at first, but also increasing its speed as they wrestled with it, high above the bright blue earth.

Finally, after much huffing and puffing, and nearly one complete orbit of the earth, the Hubble just suddenly stopped spinning. It was very strange; almost as if the space telescope itself had decided this was the time and place to behave.

JT was ready with the small TV monitor Ben had dug out of the navigation control panel. It boasted a modest 12-inch screen and a lot of floating wires that didn't seem to go anywhere or connect to anything. But a quick check of its battery pack and a test of its screen proved the crappy little thing did work.

Geraci located the Hubble's TV input plug right where Ben had said it would be. After a minor struggle trying to get coaxial cable to screw in, the small TV was finally hooked into the enormous trash barrel of a satellite.

The most amazing thing of all, at least to Hunter's mind, was that the Hubble still had some power left in it. It took several punches of the diagnostic panel, but incredibly, a reserve battery or something kicked in, and Hunter was soon staring at an image of the M404 Galaxy, which the Hubble's lens had just started picking up randomly.

JT floated over to him, took a peek at the TV screen, and then tapped Hunter twice on the helmet.

"What now, pardner?" he called over the radio.

It was a good question, one to which Hunter really had no reply.

"You and the G-man go back inside," he told JT unexpectedly. "I think I've got to do this alone."

JT just stared back at him, helmet-to-helmet. They'd been friends for a very long time.

"I'm sure whatever is bothering you will get better, Hawk," he said, with uncharacteristic volume control. "And whenever you're ready, we'll go back and snatch that A-hole Viktor again. Don't worry. He still can't go anywhere. And it'll be more fun the second time around. I guarantee it."

With that, JT gave Geraci the high sign and they both floated back to the Zon, waiting about 100 feet away.

Now Hunter was alone in outer space.

He could not count the number of times he'd dreamed of this moment when he was a kid. He would spend endless hours in his bed, looking out his window to the stars above and knowing somehow, in some way, he'd walk among them someday. Now here he was, just another heavenly body, doing exactly what his childhood dreams had said he'd do.

What he hadn't counted on back then—what he couldn't have conceived of—was that a weight the size of the universe would be resting on his heart when he finally did take that walk among the stars. Here, in what should have been his most supremely content moment, he was actually the saddest and most miserable he'd ever been in his life.

Dominique was dead—he knew that now. Somehow she had passed on. And she had loved him to the end, had stayed true even while he'd been waffling, dallying with an infatuation named Chloe. This was the hand that gripped the vise that was now tightening around his heart. How would he ever forget that? How would he ever reconcile the fact that Dominique died still in love with him, while he wasn't so sure about being in love with her?

Suddenly, he missed his father and mother very much. He'd been alone, without close family, since his teens. JT and Ben were his best friends; the UAAF inner circle constituted his extended family. But he'd been alone—*really* alone—for many years. Until Dominique.

Now she was gone, too.

Hunter stared out at the blanket of stars swirling above his head. A billion galaxies, each one filled with an average of a billion stars. That was a lot of hydrogen burning up there. He turned and sadly looked back at the earth. Blue was the main color with some green and brown and white of clouds here and there. They were just passing over Central America; the rim of West Africa was almost in view. The Atlantic looked particularly clear and blue, but there was a gathering of clouds up around the northeast part of the eastern seaboard. The angle wasn't quite right and Hunter couldn't see

very much, but the clouds seemed to be turning in a
very angry fashion.

For some reason, this brought him back to the matter at hand.

Some of Dominique's last words to him said that he
should point the Hubble toward a part of the sky that
his instincts led him to. Oddly enough, now that the
satellite wasn't tumbling, shifting it this way and that
wasn't so much of a big deal.

But where to point it exactly? And what would he
see when he did?

He closed his eyes and let his psyche take over. Millions
of thought fragments went through his head. He found
himself seeing bits and pieces of the images leading up
to the Zon launch, and then back to the battle of Lolita
Island, and then back further to when he first met Chloe,
to when he saw the Zon first go up with Viktor inside,
to the battle of Khe Sanh, the war in the Pacific against
the Cult, the invasion of the Fourth Reich, all the way
back through his many battles with the Twisted Cross,
the Family, the Mid-Aks, the Russians.

And then he went even further back, to the pre–Big
War days when he was trained to pilot the NASA shuttle, to his flying with the Thunderbirds, to his earning
his pilot's wings after graduating from MIT, the youngest person ever to do so.

Suddenly he was back at his home in Boston. He was
a kid again and he was lying in his bed, looking up at
the stars, picking out his favorite formations, and de-
ciding that he liked the Big Dipper the best.

That's when he felt another tap on his shoulder. He
spun around, fully expecting to see Dominique, hovering in space with him—but she was not there. Instead,
he looked straight ahead, and sure enough, taking up
almost his entire field of vision, were the stars that
made up the Big Dipper.

That's how he knew which way he should point the Hubble.

It took Hunter more than an hour to do it.

Jostling the big ash can was beginning to sap his strength, and as his colleagues watched anxiously from the Zon, they knew his air supply would be running low soon, too.

He stayed with it, finally lining up what he was seeing on his TV screen with the center of the field which made up the lower part of the Big Dipper.

That's when he saw it.

It was so big and moving so fast, Hunter was certain at first that there was something wrong with the mickey-mouse viewing system they'd set up. It looked like a tremendously huge star literally falling out of the heavens. He figured out a way to make the Hubble's lens zoom in closer and tighter, and that's when he saw this thing in all its frightening girth and color.

It looked like a gigantic snowball—or more accurately, an iceball. He could see the sparkling effect of the sun's rays glistening off its sides, just like the refracted light of a melting icicle. Yet the thing was almost entirely engulfed in flames. It was carrying a tail that looked like it extended for thousands—no, hundreds of thousands—of miles.

It was a comet, a huge, burning chunk of space dust and ice that was being sucked in by the sun's gravity at such a speed even the long-range viewfinder of the Hubble couldn't keep up with it. With shaking hands and a supercomputer-like brain that was nevertheless getting a little weary of all these revelations, Hunter used the perceived distance of the stars in the background as a measuring device and did a quick calculation on the comet's size. He was astounded to find that

it was nearly 300 miles across, or roughly one-fifth the
size of earth's moon. He did an even quicker estima-
tion on the comet's speed and found it was traveling
at more than 200 miles *a second*. This meant it could
cover 12,000 miles in a minute, 720,000 miles an hour,
or more than 17 million miles in just one day.

Hunter began a slow, but jittery calculation on the
comet's path. It took all his brainpower to figure the
angles, the rotations, the increasing effect of gravity as
opposed to the decreasing size of the comet as it
neared the sun's warmth. He reached one conclusion
after five minutes of crude calculus; he added this to
a second conclusion reached a few minutes later. More
triangulations, more bustling around with sines and co-
sines and tangents. He was thinking so hard now that
he didn't even hear the warning buzzer for his oxygen
supply system go off.

Even as the front of his mask began fogging up again
due to inadequate air circulation, he kept on calculating, reaching sums, adding them to quotients and mul-
tiplying them by subquotients. It took nearly 25
minutes, floating in space, doing in all this in his head,
and way past what would be considered a safe point
for remaining out on an EVA with such a quickly di-
minishing oxygen supply.

But finally, Hunter reached an indisputable conclusion. There was no need to double-check it. The voices
of the dead wouldn't have been whispering to him if
this was going to be some kind of fantastic near-miss.

No, the numbers didn't lie.

The enormous burning comet was heading right for
the earth.

Twenty-eight

General Dave Jones was asleep at his desk when the radiophone next to his ear started beeping.

He was hardly being derelict in his duties; he hadn't slept in 72 hours. He hadn't eaten in that time, either, or washed much more than he could by standing at his sink. He hadn't even shaved.

He would still be in the same clothes, too, if a bundle of fresh laundry hadn't shown up miraculously at his office door every morning. He had the feeling that some kind soul in the chow hall was washing it in the sink and pressing it with a rolling pin. The uniforms came cleaned and pressed, but they smelled mightily of flour and Ajax soap.

Jones was working too long and too hard, and he had fallen asleep at his desk. It was actually fairly comfortable—his head was resting on his codebook where he had brushed away the dust and residue from the day's shelling. The VAB might be the largest one-room freestanding structure in the world, but it was still made of concrete, and that stuff got pretty powdery after so many hours of vibration.

The Cult's fiercesome barrage had been going on for nearly two full days. The battleships were still cruising about 24 miles offshore and their shells were still landing everywhere around the KSC, except in the heart of the base. Sticking to the game plan, the Cult gunners were dropping their enormous 16-inch warheads on the battered runway, on parts of the deserted beach, and in the swamps to the north and west of them—all with frightening accuracy. But they still weren't hitting anything. Or at least, nothing important.

But a nonstop barrage of one-ton shells coming in at a rate of nine a minute will shake things up a bit, and before Jones had fallen asleep, he'd been reading a report from the NJ104 engineers on the extent of damage to the KSC buildings resulting from the vibration of these horrific explosions. Some structures on the outlying areas were about ready to come toppling down if the shelling continued. The only working launch platform—the famous Pad 39-A—was experiencing some "structural mistreatment," as were the VAB and thirteen other key buildings. The Cult and their Nazi cohorts might be set on capturing the KSC relatively intact, but with each passing hour, whether they realized it or not, they were slowly turning the space center into a bunch of wobbly, undermined buildings and launch platforms.

At this rate, the report had concluded, by the end of the week, a medium-sized firecracker might bring down a crucial structure. Jones knew that short of destroying it all themselves, this continuous, yet harmless bombing might actually be the best scenario for the UAAF, because either way, the KSC would not be operational if and when their combined enemies managed to conquer it. The UAAF command staff had vowed that.

It was no surprise, then, that Jones was dreaming about standing in a field with a bag of cement powder tied to his back and a heavy rain pouring down. The more it rained, the heavier the cement bag got. Eventually, it would get so wet and heavy it would harden and crush him to death. Like getting hit with a rock, except in slow motion—this was how Jones's dream state was predicting his eventual demise.

So the gentle buzzing of the radiophone sounded like a klaxon echoing across this wet, powdery field. Jones opened his eyes after the fourth series of beeps. He was up and stretching by the fifth series and answering it by the sixth.

"General?" he heard the familiar yet faraway voice begin. "It's Major Hunter. Did I disturb you, sir?"

Jones thought he was still asleep.

"Hawk?" he asked. "Really . . . ?"

Jones hadn't spoken one word to Hunter since the Zon had lifted off about 100 years ago.

"Really, sir. Please excuse me for . . ."

"Jeezus, Hawk, where the hell are you? It sounds like you're at a pay phone . . ."

"You're not that far off, sir," was the reply. "And I'll have to make this quick, because . . ."

"Christ, man," Jones interrupted. "Are you still up in orbit?"

"Yes, sir. Definitely, sir. I realize I'm using a unconventional means of communication. But the circumstances really dictated it. And I'm afraid I must be brief."

"You're calling me on my desk phone, for Chrissakes." Jones just couldn't get over it. "How is that possible?"

"Well, I'm forced to use some rather primitive communications here, sir. I'll be happy to explain it all to you later. If . . . if I can, that is. I think the best thing we can do now is have me explain why I'm calling you like this and let me relay a very important piece of information to you. Is that okay, sir?"

Jones sat back down at his desk, cleared it of debris,

and retrieved a pencil and notepad. He knew this was serious and he wanted to get it all down.

"Go," he told Hunter.

There was a long pause.

"General, I have some very grave news to report," Hunter began—and, for the first time ever, Jones thought he heard a tremor in his voice. "We were able to recover and rejuvenate the Hubble space telescope earlier today. We got it working with some unorthodox wiring, and . . ."

"Did you say the Hubble?" Jones had to ask. "That big one-eyed mirror?"

"Yes, sir," was Hunter's reply. "That's the one. We were able to turn it toward a certain section of the sky, to a coordinate that was, well, *provided* to me. And . . . and, well, sir, we detected a large object—a comet— that is heading straight for the earth, sir. It is more than 300 miles across. We estimate it weighs at least a billion and a half tons. If it hits, well . . . I don't think I have to tell you what will happen . . ."

Jones had dropped his pencil. His jaw was hanging open, but also curling up slightly. This had to be a joke. Hunter, calling him on the office telephone to tell him the world was about to end?

"I know it sounds crazy, sir," Hunter went on. "I know it sounds like a bad movie, or some tent preacher's prediction or something—but it *is* true, sir. I've seen this thing myself—and you'll be able to see it soon, too. It is enormous. I've done the calculations. It will intercept Earth's orbit in exactly a hundred twenty hours—five days from now.

"Now, I would say that at least one-third will burn up on the way in, but that will still leave an object weighing a billion tons on impact. If it hits land, the debris and dust will be equal to a million hydrogen bombs. If it hits the ocean, the hot gases alone will

vaporize more water than is presently in the Atlantic
and the Indian Oceans combined.

"The poles will melt. The tides will run up to fifty
feet in places like Kansas City and Omaha. It will be
catastrophic. Disastrous to the nth degree.

"It will be the end of the world. At least, as we know
it . . ."

Jones was still listening. Still sitting rigid, with his jaw
open. He couldn't talk. Couldn't ask a question or even
form any kind of opinion. He knew this was Hawk
Hunter speaking and knew what he was saying was the
truth, and therefore he knew that the end of the world,
Doomsday, was at hand.

For a brief moment, it suddenly dawned on him that
all of the crazy stuff that had been happening all
around the world suddenly made a strange kind of
sense to him.

Whom the Gods choose to destroy, they first make crazy. Was
that how that old saying went?

Well, damn now if it wasn't true. The earth was going
to be destroyed—and it had gone crazy first.

"Is there . . ." Jones finally managed to gulp, ". . . is
there any chance at all . . . that it might miss? Or that
the sun's gravity might . . ."

Now it was Hunter's turn to interrupt.

"The sun's gravity is making this thing come at us even
faster," he told Jones soberly. "We figured it's been going
at a rate of about two hundred miles a second for a long
time. No one saw it because it was just too far out. But
now that it's getting close, we jigged out its velocity at
three hundred miles a second. When it hits us, it will be
up to *four* hundred miles . . . a second. There's just no
way the numbers can be wrong."

Jones was now thinking about his family. His wife,
out in California. His two grown kids, living up in Bos-

ton with their families. His six grandchildren. How
would they go? Quickly? Or painfully?

"So, it is . . . the end, then?" Jones stammered.

There was a very long silence at the other end of the
phone. Jones had gone numb by now; he wasn't even
sure if his ears were even working. Or his voice.

"It is the end . . . right, Hawk?"

Another short silence.

"Maybe . . ." he finally heard Hunter say.

"Maybe?" Jones breathed.

"I mean that we have a one-in-a-billion shot at doing
something about this," he heard Hunter reply. His voice
was suddenly as chilling as the news he'd just delivered.

"Well then, spill it, man!" Jones ordered him. "If
there's a chance for us to do something, then hell,
we're better off going down fighting than ending with
a whimper!"

"My feelings exactly, General," Hunter replied.

There was another short silence, followed by a brief
burst of static.

"So, sir," Hunter came back on. "This is what we
have to do . . ."

Fifteen minutes later, Hunter was hanging up the
very ornate, highly stylized telephone.

Like everything else in the huge, circular room
around him, the phone looked like it had been manu-
factured some time back in the thirties, by hands who'd
spent most of their idle time raised in a one-arm salute.

It looked so old, he was amazed it worked at all.

"Well? Did he buy the idea?"

Hunter looked up at the man standing right over his
shoulder. He was tall, thin, ugly, and had bad breath
and bad skin, but his black uniform was nearly cleaned
and pressed, as were his gloves, his socks, and his cap.

"Fuck you," Hunter told him, floating up from the Bavarian antique desk and depositing himself on the long velvet salon couch. "I'm not talking to you—or any of the other flunkies. If I talk, I'm talking to the Man himself."

The officer in the black uniform smiled. His teeth were crooked, too.

" 'The Man,' as you so rightly call him, will not speak to anyone directly," he sneered, floating over to a spot right in front of Hunter's nose. "Least of all, you. Therefore, you have to report your conversation to me and then I will transmit it to the *Fuhrer* . . ."

Hunter burst out laughing. His voice echoed around the cavernous compartment and came right back to him again. He just couldn't get over how big the Heavenly Space Station was inside.

"The Fuhrer!" he spit derisively. "Jessuzz, you guys kill me. That asshole can't come up with a better name for himself than the *Fuhrer?*"

The man in the black uniform looked authentically puzzled.

"He is our leader," he reasoned out loud. "Why shouldn't we call him the *Fuhrer?*"

Hunter resisted the urge to deliver a boot to the man's crotch. But how far could he kick him if he did, Sir Isaac? At least across the huge compartment. Maybe if he aimed it correctly, he might be able to kick the man right out of the room.

But that just wouldn't do right now.

Right now, no less than saving civilization was at stake. He could go around kicking Viktor's flunkies in the balls all he wanted after this was over.

So he just grabbed the man by the lapels instead and yanked him to within one inch of his nose.

"Listen, *Schultz,*" he sneered. "You tell your A-hole

fearless leader to come down here, *schnell!* That's the only way he'll get what I just got . . ."

Hunter was suddenly aware of another presence in the room. An evil one, fucking up the last of the positive waves. He looked up at the set of mahogany doors right above his head and saw the grinning, sinister, Luciferian face of Viktor staring down at him.

In his hand he was holding what looked to be the world's oldest tape recorder. In reality, it was the world's oldest telephone tapping device. There was a gaggle of grinning, smelly goons surrounding him; these were the same people Hunter and Company had captured just the day before.

"I *already* have what you got, Fly Boy," Viktor hissed with obvious satisfaction, indicating the wires and the headphones and a long piece of thin paper that appeared to be a transcript of some kind. "So we don't even have to fuck around with that point. Let's progress to step two . . . shall we?"

Hunter shoved the officer he'd been holding away from him, lodging the man high up on the room's curved ceiling.

"Step two?" he asked Viktor in a mocking tone. "Now, exactly what would that be?"

Viktor looked momentarily surprised, but then he started laughing. Softly at first, but building in volume with each guffaw, until it was booming around the entire space station—theatrical, mocking, and not in a small measure feminine.

"You're asking me?" Viktor roared. "I think you should be *telling* me, that's more like it, isn't it?"

Viktor's minions were all laughing now, too. Including the guy Hunter had just deposited up on the ceiling.

"After all," Viktor continued with a well-rehearsed sneer, *"you're* the one who came to *me,* Mister Wingman. *"You're* the one who wanted to make a deal . . ."

Part 4

Twenty-nine

Off the Coast of UA Florida

It was close to midnight when the Cult battleship known as the *Sudai* retired from the KSC firing line and began steaming further out to sea.

The *Sudai* was now the flagship for the Cult battle fleet; ever since the loss of the *Miajappe,* all orders for the battleship flotilla had come from its command center. Its officers and crew had been elevated to the status of *mushimushi,* or "most holy," meaning they were just one step away from being divine in the eyes of the Cult members. It was a high honor, though one that carried with it the disturbing fact that the bodies of the last people to have it bestowed upon them—the crew of the *Miajappe*—were now providing a feast for the sea creatures of KSC Bay.

No matter, because of the *mushimushi,* the *Sudai* was close to being a deity, and as such, many of the people on-board believed they were invulnerable, even immortal, and completely protected from any sort of outside harm.

The battleship had just reached its new station about 55 miles off the coast from the KSC. The crew, enraptured by the elevation to divine status, were hardly on the highest alert. Few of the small AAA gunposts were manned and none of the big 16-inch turrets was occupied. The officers' housing section was alight with candles and incense sticks, and weird atonal music filled the passageways. Bowls of saki were being passed among the officers; soon many of these men began disrobing. Below decks, a more intense if informal celebration was going on. The sailors were drinking "iki-juice," a combination of *sake*, beer, tea—and hydraulic fluid. This potion could attain alcohol levels as high as 190 proof. Its ingestion frequently produced hallucinations and in some cases total blindness. Regardless, gallons of it were flowing within the crews' quarters.

Still, there were some people on duty this night—some very special guests were holed up inside the ship's stateroom and a high security presence had to be maintained. However, none of the radar warning sets were being attended to up on the bridge or in the ship's combat control center, nor was anyone watching the air defense radars.

This is why none of the antiaircraft weapons onboard were fired when the sleek F/A-18 came out of the night and deposited the UAAF's one and only laser-guided smart bomb onto the rear section of the *Sudai*. Penetrating a predetermined weak spot in the hull, the bomb traveled down through the enormous steering gearbox and exploded with a dull thud, destroying two of the battleship's four propellers and heavily damaging the third.

Had this happened in a combat situation, the entire crew would have been called to battle stations and firefighting teams would have been dispatched to the scene of the explosion. But the noise onboard the *Sudai* was so loud at the moment, and the celebrating on all decks so boisterous, few people even heard the smart-bomb go off, and those who did chose to ignore it. After all, this ship was now protected by the gods.

Nothing untoward could happen to it or its crew. Nothing . . .

Which is why no one saw or heard the pair of Sea Stallion helicopters approaching the ship, either. Their engines refitted with noise dampeners, their holds bursting at the seams with heavily armed 1st Airborne troops, the first chopper was able to set down on the aft loading pad just behind the *Sudai*'s third gun turret and disgorge nearly all of its 44 troopers before anyone on-board the battleship really knew what was happening.

Only after the second chopper set down was there any return fire. It came from the security troops guarding the stateroom directly under the bridge; they alone had been alerted by the sound of the bomb going off below the rear steering systems. When they rushed to the rear of the ship, they were astonished to see dozens of dark-uniformed soldiers running free on the aft deck.

A sharp, violent gunfight ensued, but the ship's security troops were quickly overwhelmed. Two squads of UA troops climbed up to the massive rear turret and dropped a satchel full of plastic explosives into the crew compartment. The charges went off, their sounds somewhat muffled, but producing enough damage to foul the guns and prevent any immediate discharges.

Now the main body of UA troops, swelled to 80 men, began a headlong charge up to the bridge of the ship. Acting in concert with this advancement, the F/A-18 returned and laid down a murderous barrage of cannonfire across the main bridge wind screen, killing most of those on duty and destroying what was left the ship's steering control and all of its communication equipment.

It took just four minutes of hard fighting for the UA troopers to reach the bridge and another two minutes of brutal hand-to-hand combat to capture it. At a cost of six dead and three times as man wounded, the 1st Airborne troops were in control of the *Sudai*'s most important location not ten minutes after landing on the ship.

Incredibly, the majority of the crew had no idea what was happening. The *Sudai* was enormous, and many of the sailors could not hear beyond the next bulkhead, never mind up on the bridge.

This made it even easier for the UA troops to flood down through the decks, surprising and shooting dozens of Cult officers as they still celebrated in their quarters, and entombing many nonofficers by sealing entranceways leading in and out of the vast sailors' housing.

Less than 20 minutes into it, the leader of this bold and unusual operation—Catfish Johnson himself—was able to send a coded, scrambled message back to KSC command in the VAB bunker: "Objective secured. Minimal casualties. Beginning phase two now."

To the people gathered in its luxuriously appointed state room, the first sign that anything was wrong aboard the *Sudai* came when the main cabin door suddenly vaporized in a puff of magnesium-laced smoke.

The twelve men sitting around the long, slender table had been eating octopus and drinking *sake* when the door suddenly disappeared. Up until then it had been a pleasant if not perfect evening. After firing more than 100 shells at the KSC, the *Sudai* had retired to its command station and was about to transmit a load of communications data back to Cult headquarters in Tokyo. Much of that same information was to be uplinked to Fourth Reich headquarters in Berlin as well. This daily procedure had actually been raised to the level of ceremony—just as the bestowing of flagship

status had been on the *Sudai*—because of the VIPs who
were now gathered inside the stateroom.

Five of them were the top commanders of the Cult
flotilla, the battleship captains who had also just recently been elevated in the wake of the *Miajappe*'s sinking and the demise of the Far-Away Boys. A sixth man
was Admiral Migi Kutigutti, the highest ranking officer
in the entire Cult Navy.

But it was the half dozen people sitting across the
table from these officers who made this meeting so
unusual, and in a perverse sort of way, somewhat historic. They were all impeccably dressed in gray uniforms with white shirts and black ties. They were all
wearing knee-high black leather jack boots with hob-
nails.

Each one of these men was wearing a bright red arm-
band high on his right sleeve. Emblazoned on each
band was a gold swastika, the mark of the highest officers in the Fourth Reich.

To say the alliance between the Cult and the Fourth
Reich was a troubled marriage of convenience was a
vast understatement. Many times throughout this six-
month bonding, both sides had come very close to firing on each other, as opposed to working against their
common American enemy and gaining what both recognized to be the most important prize in the world
at the moment, the Kennedy Space Center.

Simply put, the Fourth Reich and the Cult operated
on two entirely different levels. The Cult obviously took
the blunt, uncivilized route toward attaining its goals;
the Fourth Reich strove to take the more sophisticated
approach. Yet they were both bound by their common
infatuation with the world's most dangerous man, Viktor II. And it was he who'd ordered their union forged,
he who'd ordered it to do his bidding.

The six Fourth Reich officers were even higher on

the command scale than the half-dozen Cult members.
Two of the six Germans were field marshals, one was
an *Oberfuhrer,* and the remaining three were admirals
in the Fourth Reich's powerful naval aviation corps.
Sitting inside the *Sudai* stateroom, then, were twelve of
the most powerful officers in the Cult/Fourth Reich
alliance.

And now they were staring down the barrels of several dozen UA guns and peering into the eyes of several
dozen extremely determined-looking UA soldiers.

Twenty minutes later, the majority of the officers captured inside the *Sudai*'s stateroom were being marched
out onto the deck of the ship and herded to the rear.

Two of the captives—one of the Cult captains and
one of the Nazi admirals—had chosen suicide over ac-
companying the raiding UA troops. The Nazi had swal-
lowed a poison tablet; the Cult officer had impaled
himself with a knife. It made little difference to Catfish
Johnson and his men. To their minds, ten captured
officers would be that much easier to spirit away than
an even dozen.

It was now 0100 hours, and the amazing raiding operation was still on schedule. But time was becoming
precious. The main fleet of battleships, though still battering the empty areas of the KSC with its huge guns,
was only 20 miles away. It would be just a matter of
time before one of the other captains tried to get in
touch with the *Sudai* and upon receiving no reply, become suspicious.

For one or more of the Cult battle wagons to show
up now would be disastrous, and no one knew that
better than Catfish Johnson. He had no doubt that the
Cult would sink one of its own, and even kill a top layer
of officers, if it knew that the hated Americans had

taken over the ship. More officers and another battle wagon they could get anytime. Killing a large number of Americans, when permitted to do so, was the Cult's number-one priority.

So that was why Johnson and the rest of his men were waiting, rather anxiously, for a single red beacon to appear on the horizon.

That important crimson light was attached to the nose of the largest UA aircraft currently operating out of the Kennedy Space Center: the CH-54 Sky Crane.

The Sky Crane was about as far removed from a combat airframe as one could come. It was actually a cargo craft, a large, spidery-looking affair with a disjointed cockpit, a huge power plant, a large rotor set, and four long grossly extended legs. The Sky Crane could pick up and carry an external load roughly the size of a railroad boxcar. It could lift such a load over a range of about 100 miles. It could do so swiftly and under the right conditions relatively quietly.

The KSC's Sky Crane was making a lot of noise at the moment, though. It was flying very close to the surface of the Atlantic, too close for a machine of its size and girth. Escorting it were the pair of overworked Huey helicopters, their holds filled with troops from the Football City Special Forces. All three aircraft were flying at top speed, no more than 50 feet above the wavetops, heading toward the recently captured battleship *Sudai*.

The Sky Crane was carrying a steel box about 20 feet long, 12 feet high, and roughly 12 feet wide. There were air holes punctured into the top and sides of this steel box and within, several empty gasoline cans that could serve for toilets in a pinch. There were two portholes on the container, one at each end. These were covered with heavy bars and reenforced with barbed wire.

The container was a makeshift portable prison cell. Its intended inmates were waiting on the deck of the *Sudai*.

Catfish Johnson finally did see his long-awaited red light around 0110 hours.

It broke the southern horizon as a faint patch of pink at first, growing steadier and brighter until finally it formed itself into a discernible little red ball.

Johnson immediately alerted his troops and now, finally, the third and last phase of the daring operation could begin.

As several squads of UA troops roamed the ship destroying its two forward turrets and all its main navigation systems, the 10 prisoners, stripped of their arms, their ties, and their boots, were put under the overlap of the ship's still-smoldering number 3 rear turret. They were handcuffed, blindfolded, gagged, and injected with a small amount of sodium Pentothal. The well-known truth serum wasn't being given to the enemy officers as a way of information inducement; rather, it was being administered to take advantage of its other talent as a sleeping drug.

Within a minute, all ten officers were out cold.

By this time, the Sky Crane was circling the captured battleship, its pair of Hueys in tow. Using an incredibly deft touch, the Sky Crane's pilot brought the huge chopper to a hover above the rear of the ship. Then, slowly, on cables installed on lift motors hanging underneath the chopper's four long legs, the container was lowered to the aft deck of the *Sudai*. Working quickly now, the prisoners were loaded on-board the container end-to-end, each one laid out on a blanket.

Once the human cargo was on-board, the Sky Crane was given the okay to lift the container. It did, but with much squeaking and groaning. Finally, though, the steel box was tucked underneath the Sky Crane's very slender fuselage and locked into place.

Without a moment's hesitation, the pilot turned 180 degrees and began slowly to move away. Covering his rear were the pair of Hueys, still bulging with Football City Special Forces troops. Somewhere overhead, the captured F/A-18 was providing cover, looking out for any high-flying aerial threats that might disrupt the delicate operation below.

So far, none had been spotted.

Once the Skycrane and Hueys left, the two Sea Stallions appeared once again. Slowly, carefully, they came in, one at a time, and picked up their load of Airborne troopers, both living and dead. Johnson himself was the last one off the big battleship. As his Sea Stallion was moving away, he nodded to one of his officers to push a button on a radio-activated control device. There was a series of muffled explosions below decks on the *Sudai*. Two more powerful explosions followed, then two more.

Within sixty seconds, eight separate fires had broken out on the battleship, the results of incendiary bombs left behind by the 1st Airborne sapper squads. Now many of the sailors, previously held behind the locked doors in their housings below, were making their way to the decks above. It was a testament to the UA's grudging humanitarianism that several of the explosions were placed in such a way that when detonated, they would free the sailors caught below decks.

These sailors arrived up top to find their ship quickly becoming engulfed in flames. There were life rafts and life preservers available for anyone who wanted to use them—at least it could not be said the UA didn't give them all a fighting chance.

But even as the Sea Stallions moved away, the *Sudai* was nearly totally engulfed in flames and beginning to list to port.

By the time the Sea Stallions were 20 miles away, the *Sudai* was just a faint glow way out on the horizon.

The small group of helicopters made its way around the line of Cult battleships still firing on the Kennedy Space Center, gained landfall about two miles south of the VAB, avoided the handful of fire zones where the Cult shells were falling onto the base—and kept on going.

They flew over the Banana River, and over the abandoned cities of Titusville, Warm Springs, and Doreena. Finally, after 25 minutes of flight, they saw a very unusual skyline on their horizon: a huge artificial silver ball, thick forests of ugly skyscrapers, a bevy of artifical islands sitting in artifical lakes, and artifical vegetation covering artificial mountains. They were looking at a place just outside Orlando, once known as Disney World, the sprawling pre-Big War amusement park. Now it was empty and long abandoned.

It was odd that this artificial place would be the destination of the five UA helicopters and the captive cargo Sky Crane was carrying. Truth was, in the ultraflat terrain of UA Florida, this place was the highest location for many miles around.

It was called the Super Space Mountain, a ride constructed in the amusement park shortly before the Big War erupted. It was more than 500 feet high, and as its name implied, it was built to look like a mountain that might be found on some other planet besides earth.

It was a slight mushroom shape, with a restaurant, game rooms, and observation deck sitting above the ride itself, a roller coaster whose rails pointed nearly straight down in places.

The observation deck was the goal of the five helicopters. The Hueys reached it first and circled a few times, their gunners looking out for anything or anyone who might intefere with a landing. The pair of Sea Stallion set down, the two huge choppers just fitting onto the south edge of the observation deck, their rotors almost touching. The load of 1st Airborne troops were disgorged once again; their area of defense was much different this time than ont the battleship *Sudai*. Now they found themselves looking out on vast stretches of swampy Florida real estate—it seemed to go on for so long, they imagined they could see the Keys by looking south, and the Gulf by looking west.

The Sky Crane came in next. Its pilot gently lowered the steel container until it landed with a bump about 20 feet away from the resting place of the Sea Stallions. The observation deck was only about 400 square feet in area, so the container took up whatever room the Sea Stallions hadn't.

Once the container was unlashed from its constraints, the Sky Crane backed off, turned back to the east, and departed along with the pair of Hueys. They would now fly to a hidden cache of fuel about 20 miles away, gas up, and return.

The 1st Airborne troopers carefully opened the door to the steel container and were greeted with 10 very groggy enemy officers. The Cult prisoners were still laid out on the floor of their flying cell, groaning as the Sodium Pentothal began to wear off. The Fourth Reich officers were already on their feet, though, and loudly protesting as soon as the UA troopers opened the door. One soldier slapped a Nazi admiral who was too shrill.

Another slugged the *Oberfuhrer* who'd begun a loud protest of the admiral's *unmenschlich Behandlung*—"inhuman treatment." The raising of a dozen UA weapons finally shut up the German officers. One by one they were led outside.

New fear gripped the Nazis as they realized for the first time where they were. It was dark and windy and very high and they were all sure this was to be the site of their execution. But the UA soldiers took them to the edge of the observation deck, retightened their manacles, and sat them down. Then they went in and brought out the groggy Cult officers and did the same thing.

The prisoners sat like this for thirty minutes. It was close to 2 A.M. and the sky above them was clear and ablaze with stars. Off in the distance another rumbling of helicopter engines could be heard. The Hueys were returning. They circled the Super Magic Mountain once and then came in for a landing.

The Football City troopers piled out of the first chopper, but this time someone else was with them.

He was a short, wiry man with a baggy black UAAF uniform, a baseball cap, and a pair of bifocal glasses. Every UA soldier on top of the artificial mountain snapped to attention at first sight of him. It was General Dave Jones, the Commander-in-Chief of the United American Armed Forces.

He dismissed all the attention with a quick salute and then walked quickly over to where the prisoners were being held. Jones scanned the 10 angry, yet expectant faces in front of him, selecting one of the Nazi admirals, the man who to him seemed to be the most mature looking of the bunch.

"You are—?" Jones asked him plainly.

The slightly graying, slightly balding Fourth Reich

officer got to his feet, wearily clicked his heels, and
saluted.

"I am Admiral Karl Doenitz, the Fourth," he brayed
in strong, accented English. "I am commanding officer
for all surface and underwater fleets of the . . ."

Jones interrupted him with an impatient wave of his
hand.

"I could not care less what you command," Jones
told him. "Or who you are related to. All I want to
know is if you are an educated man . . ."

Doenitz seemed stunned.

"Educated?" he repeated. "Of course I am! I have
a degree from the University of Cologne, from the
State Institute of Technology, from the War College
at . . ."

Again Jones interrupted him with a wave.

"Did you ever take astronomy, Admiral?" he asked
Doenitz. "Or astrophysics? Or cosmology?"

The German officer hesitated again.

"I am familiar with these things," he said finally.
"Not as much as other areas, but certainly . . ."

But Jones was not listening to him any more. He
nodded to the pair of Football City Special Forces
troopers next to him and they picked up the German
officer by the arms and led him over to where the second Huey had set down.

The troopers on this aircraft had been busy putting
some kind of long, tubular instrument onto a slender
metal tripod. In the darkness and shadows it looked
like a weapon, but on closer inspection, it was revealed
to be a large telescope.

Jones waited silently as the troopers finished setting
up the powerful Meade 1660 75X telescope. His own
personal possession, it had an automatic viewfinder,
motorized controls, and a small microprocessor unit
attached to aid in gaining preprogrammed targets.

Doenitz waited silently, too, the pair of huge troopers flanking him on both sides. What the hell was this? he couldn't help but wonder. Exactly how insane were these United Americans?

Finally, the troopers backed away from the telescope and turned back to Jones.

"It's all yours, General," one reported.

Jones stepped forward.

"Thanks, guys," he said to the soldiers. "Why don't you see what's cooking on the other side?"

The troopers took the hint and quickly cleared out, leaving Jones and Doenitz alone.

Jones put his eye to the telescope's lens and began punching numbers into the microprocessor. The telescope began turning slowly on its pan, the small motors nudging it along with a slight buzzing sound. When it stopped, Jones sighted the eyepiece again.

Doenitz heard him gasp.

"Damn," Jones then whispered. "It gets bigger every time."

By now Doenitz was was bursting with curiosity.

"General, I demand to know what this is all about!" he huffed.

Jones looked up at him and gave a grim smile. Hunter had been right about one thing: the Germans would have to see it for themselves.

"What this is about, Admiral," Jones finally said, "is the end of the world."

Twenty minutes later, all of the captured officers had taken a turn looking through the telescope. All of the UA troopers atop Super Magic Mountain had, too. Each man was shocked by what he saw, even the near brain-dead Cult officers.

What they had seen was a tremendously bright light

coming right out of the lower part of the Big Dipper. Even the dullish Cult members knew this was not an ordinary star or planet they were looking at. It was a comet. One that was moving so fast, it was actually growing larger as they were looking at it, filling up the telescope lens right before their eyes.

The Germans were especially shaken. They knew what this meant, and they believed Jones when he told them that all calculations indicated that the comet was heading right for the earth. They also knew that if such a large object, moving so incredibly fast, actually hit the earth, it *would* be the end of the world, no question about it.

The shock of this knowledge was so great, it took almost ten minutes of silence before the Germans regained their arrogant bearings.

Doenitz sought Jones out in the small crowd gathered atop the fake mountain.

"So, General," he began. "You have shown us this thing. And you claim it will hit the earth in, what . . . five days?"

"Four and a half . . ." Jones replied.

"Whatever," Doenitz sniffed. "So, let's say this is true. What do you expect from us? We are close to overwhelming you. Our forces are much stronger than yours, and we have more on the way. Do you really think this changes anything?"

Jones just stared back at him, astonished but not surprised that the Nazi officer seemed to be advocating continuing their little war, even in the last few days of civilization.

Doenitz waited for a reply, and when he didn't get one, he gulped uncomfortably and straightened up a bit.

"What is it that you want from us?" he asked Jones

directly. "Do you actually expect us to surrender to you?"

Jones just shook his head sadly and wiped his tired eyes. This was the moment he'd been dreading.

"No, not surrender," he said finally. "Just the opposite, in fact."

Thirty

The helicopters came in first.

They were Mi-6 Hooks, enormous flying machines capable of carrying up to 11,000 pounds in cargo, people, or weapons. Four of them began circling the Kennedy Space Center shortly before sunrise, the sound of their rotors cutting through the unusual calm that had befallen the battered American base.

Many of the weary UA defenders climbed out of their trenches at the first sight of them. Shielding their eyes against the brightening sky, they tried to get a closer look at the copters as they began descending one by one toward the center of the space complex. Helicopters like these had never been seen around the KSC before. They were too big and too noisy, and these were painted in a very strange way.

It was only when the Hooks got closer to the ground that it became obvious they were not carrying the blue and white colors of the UAAF; they were covered in a dull silver and gray low-level camouflage pattern instead. In defiance of this bland color scheme, bright red swastikas had been plastered all over their fuselages, tail sections, and noses, and anywhere else they could fit. There were a number of splashy Iron Crosses painted onto the copters as well.

The Hooks belonged to the Fourth Reich's 81st Combat Lift Squadron. They landed, one right after another, in the parking lot next to the battered VAB. Though the parking lot was surrounded by heavily armed UA troops, by strict order, not a shot was fired to prevent the copters from doing so.

A small group of United American officers was waiting at the landing site. They were not a welcoming committee. They were simply on hand to tell the Nazis where they could park their gigantic helicopters.

A dozen high-level Nazi officers climbed out of the first Hook and greeted the UA officers with a round of bootclicking and curt bowing. They were from the command staff for the 5th Bavarian Engineering Korps and, they said, they were glad to be here. The UA officers did not introduce themselves or attempt any formal greeting in reply. They gave the German officers a set of preapproved photocopied maps, showing them where the Hooks could be unloaded, and then left.

It was 0545 hours.

The "peaceful" Nazi occupation of the Kennedy Space Center had begun.

It was 0600 hours when the second wave of Nazi helicopters arrived.

Unlike the first group, which had been carrying advance supplies such as radio sets, fuel oil, tents, and K-rations, these Hooks were carrying troops, specifically, the elite Himmler Company from the 1st Berlin Special Ops Brigade.

Twenty-four Hooks set down in all, each one disgorging about 50 Nazi troopers. Inside of 30 minutes, more than 1,200 German shock troops were lined up along the main road connecting the VAB and the KSC's launch pads. Each one was carrying a machine gun, extra ammo clips, a half dozen hand grenades, and a personal rocket launcher. Each one was also wearing sunglasses.

The sight of so many Nazi soldiers was disconcerting, to say the least, for the UA soldiers assigned to watch the landing areas. After all, there were only about 500 UA soldiers left. Many were wounded, and all were low on ammo, food, and sleep. If the Nazis suddenly re- neged on this unusual agreement—or if it was an elabo- rate deception all along—then a battle between the German storm troopers and the UA defenders would be extremely violent, extremely bloody, and over pretty quickly.

This was the price the Americans had to pay if they wanted to save the world.

At 0630 hours, another fleet of Hook helicopters ar- rived. They were carrying the main force of the 5th Bavarian Engineering Korps. They landed astride the pummeled shuttle runway, some of their gigantic cop- ters carrying large pieces of construction equipment as well as full loads of combat engineers.

But by 0645 hours, more than 500 of these combat engineers had been landed, along with a squadron of bulldozers, front-end loaders, and other pieces of earth-moving equipment. At exactly 0655 hours the CEs declared themselves ready for duty. At exactly 0700 hours, and with permission from the UAAF high com- mand, the Nazis CEs went to work.

Quickly collecting vast amounts of debris thrown up from the 48 hours of bombardment of the shuttle run- way, the Germans mixed the rubble with gasoline, tar, and thick lubricating oil, and using sheer manpower, pushed, pulled, and shoveled the mixture into dozens of crater holes over a two-mile stretch of the airstrip. The Nazis had previously boasted that their concoction would harden quickly enough to allow heavy aircraft

382   Mack Maloney

to land on the section of recovered runway within an hour. The unbelievers scoffed. But sure enough, at exactly 0835 hours, a handful of Antonov An-22 transport airplanes appeared overhead. One by one the huge cargo planes came down and landed safely. The miracle patch job had worked.

After the first group of Antonovs had been unloaded and sent on their way, more German airplanes began showing up. Coming in at a rate of one every four minutes, they landed more cargo, hand tools, fuel, and heavy equipment. Many were carrying troops as well. By 0815 hours, a second section of runway had been repaired and was ready for use. By 0820, ten more troop-carrying Antonovs had arrived.

By 0845 hours, there were five times as many German soldiers on the ground at the KSC as there were UA troops.

The first of the Nazi XHL cargo planes arrived at the Kennedy Space Center just after 0930 hours.

The Fourth Reich had somehow secured four of the most unusual XHL ("extremely heavy lift") airplanes ever built. They were 377-PGs, also known as "Super Guppies." The four-engine cargo planes had an upper fuselage that was so extended, so puffed up, they looked more like huge flying blowfish than guppies. Originally designed to carry oversized components for the NASA space program, each plane's airframe was so bulbous, it seemed like it would be impossible for the aircraft to get off the ground, never mind fly.

But fly they did, and now a quartet of these strange-looking beasts was circling the KSC, waiting for clearance to land.

Watching the scene from the top of the still-smoldering VAB building, even General Dave Jones was impressed. And considering what the Super Guppies were carrying in their enormous cargo bays, he knew the sooner they came down, the better.

So he grudgingly keyed his hand-held radio set and spoke three words to the KSC main control tower: "Bring them in."

Immediately he could hear the engine pitch on all four airplanes change. A minute later, the first Super Guppy was touching down on the newly repaired shuttle runway.

"Magnificent airplanes, no?" the man standing beside Jones asked.

"Sufficient airplanes," Jones snapped back. "And most likely obtained as a result of killing some innocent people."

Admiral Doenitz laughed.

"General Jones, you are being far too dramatic," he declared. "Don't you think in light of the dire situation that it is wise to lay aside our differences?"

Jones stared back at him through the midmorning sunlight. Doenitz had been his shadow ever since the Nazis began arriving at KSC. It was just another part of the agreement he'd hammered out with the German commanders atop the Super Magic Mountain earlier this morning. Jones knew that the only way he could really keep an eye on the Nazi CO was to have him always within arm's reach. And Doenitz knew it was the only way he could keep tabs on Jones, too. So they'd been joined at the hip for the entire morning, and would be for most of this unsettling operation. Doenitz, though, was proving to be an enormous pain in the ass.

"I could never lay aside my differences with a Nazi," Jones replied plainly, and for the fourth time of the morning. "You people are the most repugnant A-holes on earth. Throughout history, you've brought more suffering and more pain and misery to more innocent people than any other entity I can think of."

Doenitz looked genuinely confused. He sucked in a load of smoke from his long Parisian cigarette and let it out with a spit into the high wind.

"But what is your point, General?" he asked.

Jones's angry reply was cut off by the roar of the first Super Guppy reversing its engines upon touchdown. The bizarre airplane quickly taxied off the main strip, allowing the second of its kind to set down. Behind that came the third and fourth. With frightening efficiency, the airplanes were directed to an unloading area where four separate armies of handlers waited.

The first group of handlers scrambled aboard the first cargo plane even before it had stopped rolling. Soon doors were opening, fork trucks were screeching, and loading ramps were being lowered. The first huge package slid out of the first plane so quickly that Jones was once again silently impressed. The bubblelike cargo planes didn't even have to shut down their engines. Once their cargo was unloaded, it was back to the runway and a roaring take-off inside of 120 seconds.

It was all happening in an unbelievably short amount of time. Jones had put his stopwatch on the fourth plane's unloading. Sure enough, the big package was taken off and the Super Guppy was back in the air in less than two minutes.

Throughout it all, Jones could hear Doenitz chuckling in the background. The German officer knew exactly what Jones was doing and what he was thinking.

"Your timepiece is probably slow," the Nazi said through a perpetual haze of cigarette smoke. "Unless, of course, it is of German manufacture . . ."

* * *

Just like the big Antonov cargo planes before them, the Super Guppies just kept on coming.

There were twelve of them in all. They would arrive in groups of four and would be attacked by the horde of the off-loaders as soon as they touched down. Once their cargo was disgorged, they went back out on the runway for take-off. The only thing it could be compared to was an auto race like the Indy 500, where a pit crew could gas up a race car and change all four tires in seconds. The Germans managed to make even that kind of operation look slow.

The Guppies were making the round-trip to the Double-Trouble base in the wilds of Cuba in record time, too, cutting down what should have been at least an hour-and-a-half flight and turnaround to a round trip lasting no more than 45 minutes.

This meant that shortly before noontime, all of the nuclear warheads that had originally been stored down inside the weapons stockyard in Cuba were now lined up in neat little rows, just off the partially reconstructed runway at the KSC.

The first Cult battleship was spotted off the coast at 1300 hours.

Unlike their Nazi allies, the Cult were not slaves to keeping a schedule. This battleship, the rather infamous *Ishima,* had been the first gunship pulled out of the firing line once the Cult command had ordered their battleships to stop bombarding the Florida coast around 2 A.M. that morning.

Under new orders, the *Ishima* had made for Cuba at top speed, arriving in the northern port city of Talmero around 6 A.M. Here it took on a piece of cargo that was too heavy even for the Supper Guppies to handle. Just as the *Ishima* began securing this load, two more

Cult battleships appeared off Talmero. Then two more, and two more. A total of seven Cult battleships had been pulled off the line and sent to this Cuban port. At the moment, their mighty engines and tremendous draft were needed for something other than supporting nine enormous guns.

The special cargo were the components for the three Energia rockets that had also been kept at the secret Double-Trouble base. Only the battleships had enough deck space—barely enough—to take on all stages of the rockets and transport them up to Kennedy quickly. Loading them was no problem, as it turned out. It was getting them up to the KSC where the Cult nearly dropped the ball.

The *Ishima* was late in arriving back at the KSC because its captain had miscalculated the tides getting in and out of Talmero. He was two hours behind schedule, just as the six other ships would be. But this time was more than made up during the unloading of the Energia pieces off the battleships, once again due to Nazi efficiency.

In anticipation of the battleships' arrival, the Fourth Reich engineers had laid a pontoon bridge out into KSC Bay, building an unloading platform at its terminus. As soon as the *Ishima* reached this floating dock, Nazi engineers swarmed aboard her, and taking over the battleship's cargo crane, unloaded the first three stages of the first Energia rocket.

These components were quickly put on a rolling cart the size of two railroad cars and using a track laid down previously by the engineers, they were pulled by hundreds of Nazi troops up to the beach, through the dunes, and over to the area around launch pad 39-A, deep inside the space complex.

Once the *Ishima* was unloaded, it sailed away to be replaced by the second battleship, and then the third, and so on. This gigantic unloading and transporting operation proceeded throughout the afternoon and into the night until, by 2200 hours, all of the pieces for all three Energia rockets were close by the 39-A launch pad and already in some process of reassembly.

The only involvement of the UAAF in any of this was the employment of the Ch-54 Sky Crane, which helped out by taking some of the more delicate Energia components off the battleships and depositing them up near 39-A. This was the only assistance General Jones would allow in the unloading operation, though UA equipment and manpower would have sped things up even more.

But Jones was already weighed down with the burden of dealing with the Nazis and the Cult in the first place.

He would rather risk being late for the end of the world than to have the mortal sin of collaboration on the souls of all his men as well.

It was near dawn the next morning—three days before the end—when the Cult battleships anchored in KSC Bay began disgorging cargo of a different kind.

Each ship was now being served by its own floating gangplank, courtesy of the Nazi allies. The huge vessels had been silently riding the tides since the unloading of the Energia rockets, their lights extinguished, their crews silent and out of sight.

But now—symbolically, with the rising sun—the Cult sailors began appearing on deck. They were dressed in combat fatigues with sidearms but no larger weapons. There were seven ships in the harbor in all; combined, this put the number of Cult seamen on hand at close to 7,000.

On word from each individual ship commander, the sailors began filing down their walkways. Several ships' bells began ringing and klaxons began blaring in tra-

ditional Cult fashion as this small army trooped across
the pontoon bridge and up into the KSC.

If the sight the day before of the Nazi troops landing
at the KSC had rankled those in the remaining UAAF
forces, then the appearance of the Cult members coming ashore was enough to get their blood really boiling.
All of the KSC defenders knew what was happening,
knew about the comet and why the Fourth Reich and
the Cult were here. But actually seeing the loutish Cult
members land unopposed was almost too much to take.
Many of these UA soldiers had fought against the ruthless Cult in the last Pacific War and against their allies
in the recent Southeast Asia conflict. By their actions
alone, they considered them to be subhuman, thor-
oughly brainwashed, and not worthy of the ground
they walked on.

As it turned out, this was an opinion shared by the
Fourth Reich Nazis as well.

It took two hours for the crews of the seven battleships to disembark and walk to the agreed-upon staging
area out near the rebuilt shuttle runway.

Jones was still in his perch atop the VAB building,
watching over the KSC like a king trying very hard to
prevent his domain from being further infected by the
heathens. For once, Doenitz was not at his side. The
Nazi commander was down on the field, where the Cult
crews were gathering. He'd told Jones his staff had
planned a short ceremony to welcome and show soli-
darity with the Cult crews and that he would have to
preside over it. He invited Jones to participate as well.
Jones replied that his desire was to be far away from
this event as possible; he vowed to stay on top of the
VAB until the ceremony was over.

Now, staring out through his powerful binoculars at

the area abutting the runway, Jones could see the long, ragged line of Cult sailors standing at what approximated attention in their ruffled, undisciplined ranks, their brows beginning to sweat in the hot Florida sun.

A small platform had been constructed in front of them, and sure enough, Doenitz and the rest of his officer corps had taken their places on it, as had the five remaining top officers for the Cult. Lined up also as part of the ceremony were the crisp heavily armed troops of the 2nd Dresden Combat Brigade, which had landed the night before. At approximately 6,700 men, they nearly equaled the number of Cult sailors who had come ashore.

A public address system had been set up, and even in the high winds atop the VAB, Jones could hear Doenitz's distinctive Prussian voice droning on and on in front of the restless Cult troops. While the speech was going on, a team of Nazi construction troops had continued working on a trench directly behind the Cult assembly point; the sound of their heavy machinery nearly drowned out what Doenitz was saying.

Still Jones watched the whole thing through his spyglasses, taking special note of how long Doenitz's officers spoke, as opposed to the Cult COs, who'd barely croaked out a few words before the Germans had whisked them away from the microphone. This went on for about a half hour. Finally, Doenitz took to the podium again.

Jones considered putting away his spyglasses at this point. The last thing he wanted to do was hear Doenitz speak again. But then he noticed something very unusual happening down on the parade ground. Doenitz had just spoken a few distinct words in German into the microphone. But unlike his speech, these were more direct, almost as if he were giving orders. Jones could see looks of confusion and bafflement come across the Cult officers on the stage and the sailors lined up before them. The soldiers of the 2nd Dresden Brigade took one step forward.

Then they all fired their weapons . . .

There were screams and a kind of mass grunting—Jones could hear it all the way on top of the VAB. There was also a huge cloud of white smoke and the *pop-pop-pop* of many automatic weapons firing at once. But it was over very quickly. When the smoke cleared and Jones was finally able to refocus his binoculars, he was astonished to see piles of Cult soldiers lying shot at the feet of the Nazi troops. Those who weren't dead were now being dispatched by Nazi troops walking among the massive sprawl of bodies. The Nazi construction troops now came forward, the same ones who'd been digging the trench behind the Cult troops as they'd listened to Doenitz drone on and on. Using the backhoes and bulldozers, they began pushing the bodies of the Cult sailors into the huge trench and covering them over, even though some of the victims were wounded and still alive.

Jones stood frozen while he watched the surreal scene, not quite believing it. With typical Nazi efficiency, all of the bodies were buried and the ground atop their mass grave covered and smoothed over in about ten minutes' time. Then the Dresden Brigade packed up its gear and returned to the Pad 39-A area, where they'd been helping the Fourth Reich combat engineers restage the Energia rockets. The Nazi construction crew also returned to work, going about the business of fixing up the odd holes still left in the five-mile runway as if they'd done nothing more than take a short coffee break.

As for Doenitz, he jumped into one of the Fourth Reich's trio of swift Lynx command and control helicopters and was soon setting down atop the VAB build-

ing. He approached Jones with an arrogant smirk, the
ever-present cigarette holder dangling from his lips.

Hardened combat veteran though he was, Jones was
actually sickened by what he'd just witnessed.

Once again, Doenitz was able to read his thoughts.
He just shrugged and shook his head.

"There will now be more breathing room for both
of us," he explained to Jones coldly. "And it will smell
a whole lot better around here, too."

Another full day passed.

For the most part, Jones maintained his vigil atop
the VAB, Doenitz rarely leaving his side.

Though Jones remained reticent, the Fourth Reich
officer persisted in many attempts to engage him in
conversation about a wide variety of subjects, from music, art, history to various military campaigns, to the
comet that was speeding towards Earth.

As the sun began to set and the stars came out on
this particular night, the unnamed comet was now visible to the naked eye. It was now much larger than the
brightest star in the Big Dipper, brighter than everything else in the sky at the moment, save for the three-
quarters waning moon. Very soon, it would be brighter
than this as well.

But Jones refused to talk with Doenitz on matters
other than the mission at hand, which was constructing
the Energia rockets and getting them launchworthy as
quickly as possible.

Still, the UAAF commander was amazed at how fast
Doenitz's troops were doing just that. The Nazi CO
received updates on the work out on Pad 39-A every
half hour, and he never hesitated a moment to relay
the news of their progress to Jones. By 2200 hours, the
first two stages on the first rocket had already been

powered up; the third would be on-line soon. The loading of the first batch of nuclear weapons for lift into orbit was progressing swiftly as well. A total of 14 warheads would go up on the first launch attempt. If these made it, another 18 would go on the second Energia rocket, and then the remaining warheads would launch on the third. If everything went right, there would be 44 nuclear bombs of all shapes and sizes in orbit in less than 18 hours.

After that, the whole matter would be out of the hands of all those at the Kennedy Space Center and in the hands of those who were orbiting high above it.

It was close to midnight when Doenitz received a report stating that the first Energia rocket was ready to go, all stages were in place and powered up, the load of 14 nuclear warheads tucked snugly inside its payload bay.

When the Nazi officer snidely passed the news on to Jones, the UAAF commander came very close to accusing him of lying.

How could it be? Jones pressed himself, staring at the ghostly glow coming from Pad 39-A, about five miles away. How could a huge Energia rocket, the most powerful in the world, be moved, reconstructed, powered, loaded, fueled, and ready for launch into orbit in less than 36 hours—and actually 10 hours *ahead* of schedule?

It just didn't seem possible.

As always, Doenitz read his mind.

"The answer is simple, General," the Nazi told him, his face dark, his lips dispersing streams of cigarette smoke as he talked. "You see, we've been planning to do just this for a very long time. Capture this base, construct the rockets, load the nuclear devices, and launch. My men have been going over this very procedure every day, every week, every month for nearly a year. Believe me, after all that time, they know how to do it, when to do it, and how quickly it can be done. So you see, the actual completion of the mission is the only challenge left for them. They've chosen to do it both quickly and efficiently. For their spirit. For their beliefs. For their Fatherland. It's hard to beat that kind of enthusiasm, is it not?"

Jones was loath to give Doenitz any reply, but finally his Irish got the best of him.

"Werner Von Braun and his Nazis put NASA into space the first time," he replied icily. "You're just doing it again under different circumstances. I mean, let's face it, you guys are the follow-up crew. The *Wiederholenz*. And surely you, above anyone else, would agree that while history always seems to repeat itself, it usually forgets the guy who comes in second place."

Doenitz's reply was a long, angry stream of cigarette smoke that came fairly close to touching Jones's nose.

"Fair enough, I suppose," he said, in his most sinister voice. "But believe me, General, there are some things that history *won't* repeat . . ."

It was exactly 0600 hours that morning when the bottom stage of the first Energia rocket ignited.

It sent a huge billow of flame across the bottom of Pad 39-A and out onto the wetlands and marshes beyond.

The rocket remained frozen for five long seconds. Then, slowly, gradually, it began to rise. It cleared the tower easily enough and, as these kinds of ballistic missiles usually do, began to pick up speed at an incredible rate the further it climbed into the sky.

Jones watched the thick missile rise into the air, the enormous swastika adorning its sides making him cringe. His eyes actually got moist with anger and hopelessness as the rocket began to disappear from view. Doomsday was coming, he thought, and we're relying on the Nazis to give humanity one last shot. After all his years of fighting, and sending men to die for Liberty and what was right, what kind of an end was this?

But it was another question that had been really haunting him, one that was even more disturbing: what will the Nazis want if this impossibly bold plan actually works?

The very notion felt like a kick in Jones's stomach every time it occurred to him. As he watched the Energia finally fade into the morning sky, he could see the Nazi ground crews already moving the second Energia stages to the launching pad, this even before all the smoke from the first had cleared away.

As always, the efficiency and coordination was rather frightening.

Maybe it would have been wiser, Jones thought, to just let the comet hit the earth and be done with it.

The second Energia went up at 1300 hours, seven hours to the minute after the first, and according to Doenitz, a full 90 minutes ahead of schedule.

The third and final rocket went up at 1800 hours, 6 P.M., just as the sun was beginning to set in the west, maybe for the last time.

Jones had watched all three launches from the VAB, Doenitz at his side, never missing a chance to pester him about the fabulous job all his good little Germans were doing. For the most part, Jones continued to ignore him, while also secretly marveling that what was happening before his eyes was real and not some kind of bad dream.

Night fell again and the great comet came out and stayed out. It was brighter than the moon this time, and tomorrow it would be brighter even than the sun. The only time Doenitz ever shut up was when he was staring up at the huge chunk of space ice that seemed so unflinchingly on course toward the earth.

They stood like this, watching it in silence, for a long, long time. The base below was quiet, too. There really was nothing left for anyone to do but wait. All of Doenitz's troops had undoubtably gone to sleep. All of Jones's very anxious UA soldiers were undoubtably awake, eyes lifted in rather pathetic hope, like Jones. And even a little like Doenitz.

The night grew clear, and with each passing hour, the comet got bigger and brighter. Around midnight, Doenitz began speaking again. This time, his voice was less stern, almost human.

"You know, General," he began, "we had a number of very mysterious occurrences happen to us during this long ordeal. Missing men. Missing ships. Strange radio messages. Especially recently. We thought it was you. Your counterintelligence people, trying to spook us, as you say. It wasn't you, was it? Reading biblical passages out over the airwaves?"

Jones nearly laughed out loud. "Are you kidding? We thought it was you guys . . ."

They looked at each other. Their eyes went wide with realization. Both men started to say something—but couldn't.

"We lost men, too," Jones finally said, breaking the silence. "A flight of Sabre jets. A big Seamaster. About fifty miles due east of here. Were your people involved in shooting them down?"

Doenitz shook his head no.

"We lost three troopships dropping off the Norse Army, who attacked you first," the Nazi officer suddenly revealed. "They simply disappeared as well. Into a fog. About fifty miles off this coast, too."

"We certainly didn't sink them," Jones told him. "We didn't know anything about the Norsemen until they hit us."

Doenitz waved his hand in a very imperial manner.

"They were simply fodder," he said plainly. "Expendable louts. Just like our little yellow friends beneath the ground over there, we're all better off without them."

Suddenly angered again, Jones bit his tongue. He wanted so much to launch into a lecture on the basic regard for human life, even in the case of Norsemen and Cult members, but he held himself back. What was the point? Why try to educate a Nazi while up in the sky, hanging like a huge, glowing electric lightbulb, a rock of ice more than 300 miles across was heading right toward them at 72,000 miles an hour? Jones's only regret was that he would never see his wife again, or his family or any of his friends. He couldn't believe a sophisticated animal like Doenitz could share such feelings—and he was right.

"We had a number of missing airplanes as well," Doenitz said, breaking the long silence again. It was clear his mind was firmly rooted on military matters, not those of love, hopelessness, and loss. "They just seemed to disappear, too. We sent them on an attack against you ten days ago. Off Key West. They weren't shot down. They simply vanished, on their way back to base. They were two F-14s and a single F/A-18. Do you know what happened to them?"

Once again, Jones began to say something, but held his tongue for a moment.

"Lost off Key West, did you say?" he finally replied, with a shake of his head and the beginnings of a sly smile. "Nope. Can't say I know where they are."

Thirty-one

In Orbit, Twelve Hours Later

The string of space mines was more than 10 miles long.

It stretched from the docking ring atop the cargo bay doors of the Zon shuttle to the end of the one of the twisted arms of the Heavenly Space Station, now more than 50,000 feet away.

Strung out along this astral clothesline, several groups of space walkers could be seen moving about; they were the Nazi space-mine technicians, men originally housed inside the space station. For the past two days they'd been spending just as much time aboard the Zon spacecraft as they had inside their orbiting home.

The ten-mile-long necklace of bombs was the grandest, most ambitious project ever undertaken by the Nazi space techs. Before this, their stint in space had merely involved taking the various pieces of space junk retrieved by the Me-363 Komets and adapting them into small-yield, chemical-explosive remotely controlled space mines. Eventually these techs believed they would be working on nuclear warheads that would be boosted into orbit by the Fourth Reich for refitting onto reentry rockets with which Viktor could then bombard the Earth below at will.

Now the space techs were working with nuclear weapons—each of the bombs along the 10-mile string had some kind of nuclear device attached to it, but this string of orbital megatonnage was not intended for use by Viktor to rain thermonuclear explosions down onto the earth.

Rather, it was being built to save the planet.

At the very least, the Americans inside the Zon could boast that it was their design being constructed 10 miles out in front of them, although the Nazi space techs were doing all the work. Once the string of bombs—44 in all, they'd all arrived safely from the three Energia launches—were properly fused and set, the string would then be broken into three separate lengths. These would then be attached to the rear of the Zon by a series of cables. If everything went according to plan, this trio of bomb lines would be flown out to a position in very high orbit, where a EVA would unhook them and connect each length into a ring, each one with a descending diameter.

The trio of concentric rings—one would be five miles around, the second three miles around, and the third two miles around—would then be placed in space, about 20 miles from each other. They would be arranged in such a way as to intercept the comet just as it was being drawn into the thick of the earth's gravitation field. It was hoped the 44 nuclear blasts, going off mere microseconds from each other, would be enough if not to destroy the comet, then at least to alter its course and push it away from the earth.

There were three problems with this scenario, however.

First, the trio of nuclear rings had to be placed exactly in the right position at exactly the right moment; second, all bombs would have to detonate at the same time for the full impact of the 442,000 megatons to be effective; and third, whatever spacecraft placed the bombs in position would undoubtably be vaporized, either by colliding with the comet or by getting caught up in the string of nuclear explosions.

The only spacecraft available to make this suicide mission was, of course, the Zon.

And there was only two people who could actually pilot the spacecraft that high and perform the crucial EVAs needed to place the nuclear rings in proper position.

One of them was Elvis.

The other was Hawk Hunter.

There had been a huge argument among the Zon crew as to who should or shouldn't go. The near universal feeling was that the two girls should be left in the dubious care of the remaining Nazis aboard the space station, and the rest of the original Zon members—Ben, JT, Cook, and Geraci—should join Hunter and Elvis on their last mission. There were some merits to this case: after all, the alternative was for the odd men out to retire to the space station with the girls, knowing full well that if the desperate plan didn't work, then the best they could hope for would be that the mysterious space station would be incinerated along with the earth when the comet hit. If that wasn't the case, then they'd be doomed to a slow death orbiting high above the devastated planet, with absolutely no hope of rescue or resupply.

Even if the plan *did* work, they would still have to wait months, maybe even years, for any hope of a rocket being blasted off from the earth to orbit in order to take them back home. And all this time they would be under the yoke of the Nazis still inside the space station. What kind of life would that be?

But Hunter had vetoed the plan that they all go on the suicide mission together because he didn't want to be personally responsible for killing four of his best friends. Knowing he was going to die with Elvis was hard enough. One soul on his conscience was already a load—four more would be unbearable, in this life or the next.

The most amazing thing about the past two days was that Hunter had come to a kind of truce with himself. It was not some acknowledgment of a tremendous inner peace that would give him the strength to go on this, his final mission. It was more an understanding that this was what he'd meant to do all along. All his skill, all his knowledge, all his adventures, and all his battles had been in preparation for this moment, this one-in-an-epoch chance of saving the entire planet. After all, he'd been trying to do it piecemeal for the past six years or more. He recognized the beauty in trying to do it all in one fell swoop.

There was also another kind of peace running through him as he sat on the Zon flight deck and watched the Nazi space techs string the line of space nukes together. In plain and simple terms, he had nothing to live for after this. Dominique was gone, just as his family and many of his friends had gone before, and now he felt it was his time to go, too. He made no pretenses that there was a warm, fuzzy feeling attached to such a tragic conclusion—the part of the soul where this idea had come from was a cold and dark place. But it was also a logical place—or at least, in Hunter's present frame of mind, it seemed to be.

It had been a very strange 48 hours since he'd radioed Jones with his plan to let the Nazis come into the KSC and let them try to launch the nuclear warheads into orbit. The UAAF would have to step aside and let the goosesteppers do their thing.

That was exactly the same attitude shared aboard the Zon as the nuclear payloads arrived and the space station techs began stringing them together. *Let the assholes do all the work,* was how JT had put it over and over again.

The people on the Zon had better things to do—like say goodbye to each other.

They had devised a kind of reverse clock to count down the hours to the comet hitting the earth.

The string of space nukes was finally completed and pre-fused, and this clock stood at minus 6 hours and 32 minutes.

This gave the Zon crew absolutely no time for leeway—which was okay with Hunter. They had to collect the three bomb strings and be on their way. As it was, he was worried whether the Zon still had enough fuel in it to get them up to the place in high orbit where the triplet of bomb rings had to go. One thing was in their favor, though: they didn't have to worry about conserving fuel for the return trip. There would *be* no return trip this time.

For this mission, the ticket was strictly one-way.

At minus 5 hours and 55 minutes, they got a report from the Nazi space-tech CO that the three strings had been separated as needed and if the Zon came over to the space station docking point, they would be able to fit it with the tow lines.

Hunter quickly drove the Zon the five miles over to the space station, positioning it next to the docking arm as requested, all the while being careful not to waste any fuel. The battery of space techs began hooking up the three strings to the three tow lines, a task they estimated would take twenty minutes at most.

But now came the hardest part of all.

It was time for those not going on the Zon's final mission to transfer over to the space station.

Hunter was entrenched in the flight commander's seat and Elvis, stoic as ever, was strapped into shotgun when the word went out that it was time for the others to go. Cook and Geraci were the first to come up to say goodbye.

They both shook hands with Elvis and then floated over to Hunter. There was really no sense in avoiding the issue. This would be the last time they'd ever see each other again.

"Wouldn't have changed a thing, Hawk," Geraci told him after a zero-G bearhug. "Not a blessed thing . . ."

"Thanks, G-man," Hunter replied. "Tell all the guys in the 104 I said thanks . . . for everything."

Cook came next. They'd known each other for a very long time.

"I'd do anything to trade places with you, Hawk," the JAWS commander told him. "Be glad to do it, too."

"Are you kidding, Cookie?" Hunter replied, trying like hell to be upbeat, but failing miserably. "You think the JAWS team would ever forgive me for that?"

Cook nodded sadly, shook his hand again, and was gone.

That's when Hunter looked up and saw Ben. His heart caught in his throat. It was going to get progressively harder.

They shook hands vigorously.

"See you, Hawk," Ben said, trying to make it as quick and painless as possible.

"You got it, pal," Hunter was just barely able to croak out. He looked away for a moment, just to clear his eyes, and when he turned back, Ben was gone.

At that moment, one of the Nazi space techs appeared just off the Zon's portside window. He gave Hunter and Elvis a stern thumbs-up. They took it to mean the three strings of nukes were attached to the tow lines.

"We can get going any time now," Elvis told Hunter.

Hunter began pushing buttons and clearing computer screens in anticipation of the huge main engine burn they would have to accomplish if they had any hope of getting up to higher orbit.

As he was doing this, Hunter was aware of someone else looking over his shoulder. It was JT.

"So, how long do you figure *this* little adventure is going to take?" he asked Hunter, in his usual nonchalant way.

Hunter was momentarily stumped. Exactly *how* should he reply to that?

"About a lifetime, I suppose," he finally answered.

But JT was shaking his head.

"C'mon, Hawk," he said. "This is JT you're talking to. You know how this book will turn out just as well as I do. You guys will go up there, blast the big snowball to smithereens, somehow have just enough gas left to get back down here, rescue us, capture that asshole Viktor again, and bring him back to *terra firma*—just like we planned to do. I mean, this is all just a mild diversion. You know, to make the plot more interesting . . ."

Hunter just stared up at his friend in disbelief.

"Your powers of denial are rather strong," he told JT with a grim smile.

"What denial?" JT insisted. "I've been with you through the whole kit and kaboodle. Don't you think I know how it's going to end? Sure, it will get hairy. And sure, it will come right down to the last second. And you'll have one last nuke that won't go off like it's supposed to, and you'll have to do a quicky EVA to get it back in line. But you know, and I know, and everyone knows you'll pull something out of your hat and save the day and come back in one piece, and then, we'll all live happily ever after . . ."

Hunter was laughing at him now—so was Elvis, a rare treat. They just couldn't help it. JT was actually being funny.

"So, just remember one thing," JT concluded. "While you're up there icing the biggest hero-move in history, we'll be sitting aboard the floating *Reichstag,* doing God knows what. So get it over with in a hurry, will you? Save the planet and then scoot back and save us, okay?"

Hunter just continued staring up at his old friend; his face looked like he was completely serious.

"Okay, buddy," Hunter finally told him with a hand-shake. "We'll try to make it as quick as we can."

JT smiled and then mock-saluted them both. Then he was gone, too.

Now an eerie silence descended on the flight deck. The lights were dimmed as the main power systems began coming on-line. Elvis had a long conversation with the Nazi space-tech CO. They'd done everything they were supposed to, was the gist of this guy's message. Now it really was up to Hunter and Elvis.

The clock was at minus four hours and forty minutes now. Hunter leaned forward and then looked out the window back at the rear of the Zon. He could see the three strings of space bombs floating in three straight lines right beyond the tail section. Beyond that, the glare of the unnamed comet was rising like the sun over the edge of the earth.

It was so bright, it hurt his unprotected eyes. They said it would soon be brighter than the sun, he thought, and they were right.

He looked over at Elvis who had just completed the last diagnostic check. Everything that still worked on-board the Zon was up to near-peak efficiency. Hunter suddenly felt a pang of grudging admiration from the all-thumbs spacecraft. There was certainly a lot to complain about in its design and construction. But it had stayed together for them this long, and there was some kind of beauty in that, he supposed.

Elvis finally completed his check and gave Hunter a solemn thumbs-up. The others had already transferred over to the space station, and now it was time to break the docking connection, turn the Zon around, and begin the last main engine burn. But just as they were about to do this, they saw the airlock activation indicator light up on their control screen.

Someone was coming back aboard the Zon.

"Who the fuck is this?" Elvis blurted out.

They heard the commotion below as the airlock sprung open and first one, then two, then a third person got out. Then the first person floated over to the hatch leading up to the flight deck.

"If this is JT to finally kiss goodbye I'm going to slug him," Elvis said. Like Hunter, he was understandably anxious to get the show on the road.

But then they saw the figure rising up through the hatch from below and both of them felt their breaths catch in their throat.

It wasn't JT or Ben or any other part of the Zon crew coming for the one last goodbye.

It was Viktor.

He was rising out of the hatchway like a vampire rising from a coffin—except that he was going straight up.

"You've got to be shitting me," Elvis cried out.

Viktor smiled as his pointed head touched the top of the compartment and he hung there like some kind of strange animal. He was dressed in all black, of course, his outfit complete in all its Luciferian regalia, from the foppish satin slippers to the long silk cape.

Both pilots were infuriated to see him.

"If you're here for a pep talk, it's a little too late," Elvis told him sternly.

Viktor waved his protestations away. "Be still, you hill-billy," he said. "I've come to chat with the man who will soon be the earth's greatest hero—posthumously, of course."

Hunter chose to ignore him. In light of the circumstances, all the hate he'd had inside for this man had dissolved into indifference. When compared to what lay ahead of them, Viktor was rather insignificant now.

"You're using up our air being in here!" Elvis shouted at him. "You're smelling up the place, too!"

Once again, Viktor just waved his words away.

"I've not come to speak with you . . ." he sneered at Elvis. "So just shut up."

He drew closer to them. His shadow cast a dark silhouette across the control panel.

"Nothing to say on this momentous occasion, Mister Wingman?" he taunted Hunter. Elvis was right—Viktor did smell. It was a perfume-thick scent that tried to mask the undeniable stink of the body odor of someone who'd ingested a lot of drugs. Viktor's eyes were as red as the warning lights on their control panel.

"You know, I do have a question for you," Hunter told him suddenly.

"You mean, like a last request?" Viktor mocked him. "Go right ahead . . ."

Hunter pointed out at the huge swastika-shaped station hanging in space before them.

"Where the hell did you get *that*?" he asked directly.

Viktor looked out at the space station, and then to Hunter's complete surprise, just shrugged his shoulders.

"You know something," the superterrorist said, in a voice that sounded so sincere it was frightening. "I have no idea where the hell it came from . . ."

Hunter turned around and looked him straight in his very red eyes.

"I really don't," Viktor continued. "It was up here when we got here . . ."

Hunter stared at him and found his jaw dropping.

"Jesus Christ," he swore. "You're telling the truth, aren't you?"

Viktor just nodded. He seemed genuinely mystified by it, too.

"We needed a place to go, and suddenly there it was," he said. "One moment it was just empty space. Then we went around in the Mir and the next orbit, it had appeared. Empty, powered up, ready for us to use. Even the design was just right, if a little too Forties for my taste . . ."

"You have no taste!" Elvis screamed at him.

Again Viktor infuriated the pilot by ignoring him.

"But that was certainly a good question, Mister Wingman," he continued, talking to Hunter. "A good parting mystery, no? I'm sure you would have been able to drag out a whole new series of your adventures just finding out where the hell it came from. Too bad you won't have the chance."

"Like hell he won't!" Elvis suddenly screamed.

The red-faced pilot was out of his seat and hovering next to Viktor. His face was crimson with rage. Suddenly the superterrorist looked terrified himself. He tried to get away and call out for the two guards who had come aboard with him and stayed below. But Elvis yanked on his floating cape, pulled him back, and cuffed him hard across the mouth.

Hunter just stared at Elvis, who looked like he was about to pop a vessel, he was so angry.

"I'm sick of this fucking guy," Elvis screamed, as he continued to pummel Viktor in the kind of violent slow-motion of zero-G. "Sick of every thing he's done to me. To you. To everyone."

He was wrapping Viktor's cape around his neck now. The terrorist was so aghast at what was happening, he couldn't even cry out.

Elvis looked up at Hunter. He was crying, he was so furious.

"And you know what I say, Hawk?" he whispered angrily. "I say if we ain't coming back, then we take this asshole with us."

Hunter looked up at Elvis, then down at the terrified, struggling Viktor, and then back up at Elvis.

"You know what?" Hunter then replied. "I say we do, too . . ."

What the others aboard the space station saw next would be a matter of some dispute.

JT and Ben were in the observation deck of one of the station's twisted arms, brought there by the Nazi space techs, who, while now doubling as guards for the practically empty space station, were still unsure exactly what they should be doing.

They were aware that Viktor had gone over to the Zon for one last taunting session against Hunter, and that he had brought his two remaining officers with him for protection and support.

But now, the Zon was pulling away from the space station after having quickly broken the docking connection. Those two officers were floating motionless in space behind it—without any space suits on.

In fact, it appeared the two men hadn't exited by way of the air lock. Rather, they had come out of the bottom of the Zon, through a hatch that was used for emergencies during launch and touchdown, but never in space.

But however they'd been expelled, the two men were now clearly dead.

As for the Zon, it had slowly moved away from the space station, had turned, and was now pointing right at the comet, which was lighting up the dark sky with a tremendous unholy glow.

What JT and Ben saw was an explosion of flame coming from the rear of the Zon—obviously the main engines had lit properly. The spacecraft started to gather more speed by the second. It was an astonishing sight for them—they'd never seen the Zon from this angle before, never believed it could really move that fast. But it did.

Very quickly, it became a blur of motion. It went straight up toward the oncoming comet, trailing the three strings of nuked-up space mines far behind it.

JT and Ben watched it open-jawed for as long as they could, which was about a minute or two, but not much more.

Then, very quickly, it left their field of vision, disappearing into the glow of the enormous approaching comet.

Thirty-two

Nauset Heights, Cape Cod

Donn Kurjan was the last one left.

He was sitting on the edge of the highest cliff on Nauset Heights, looking out on the gradually calming seas.

The storm had finally ended 24 hours before. The rain had stopped first. Then the lightning and the thunder. And finally the wind.

The seas were still high, but at least they were no longer breaking up on the cliffs. The sun had come out, though it seemed dull, compared to the huge glare lighting up the eastern sky now. This was the comet, Kurjan knew now. The one Chloe had dreamed about, the one that Hunter was trying to either destroy or divert.

The one that had taken Dominique's life.

They'd buried her at sea, as she would have wanted it, the day before. Frost, Chloe and the girls were there on the beach when Kurjan got Frost's old seaplane working again. He managed to sail it about a mile off-shore. Weighted down with the books she'd loved and other momentos, Kurjan had dropped Dominique's lifeless body over the side and watched as it slowly slipped beneath the waves. Then he stayed over the spot where she'd finally disappeared and cried for at least an hour. Then he made his way back to shore.

The UAAF helicopter arrived from Boston about two hours later, the result of a message Kurjan had finally managed to get out over the ancient radio in Frost's seaplane. On-board were two people attached to the NJ104 engineering battalion. The joy Kurjan saw in their faces when they first laid eyes on their four missing girls was almost enough to erase the pain of Dominque's sudden death.

Almost . . . but not enough.

The hows and whys of what had happened here at Skyfire would have to be answered later—if there was to be a later. Right now, all that was certain was that the enormous comet, so bright it was almost impossible to look at, would collide with the earth in less than two hours—if Hunter somehow failed in his final mission.

Kurjan had decided to stay here, at Skyfire, to await the end, if that's what was coming.

He felt it was the right thing to do—a kind of tribute to Hunter and to Dominique. This is where they had lived for just a brief period of time, yet those days were their happiest. Kurjan was sure of this, because when he was here before, those had been some of his happiest days, too.

So he felt it was only fitting that he guard this place, this last outpost of Hawk Hunter's life, and be here for whatever was about to happen. He would serve to the end, just as Hunter and Elvis and the others had done. He would be the last UAAF soldier, guarding the last place the hero for their age had called home.

It was here that he sat down, shortly after the helicopter had left, bearing Frost and Chloe and the four girls and the newly awakened Yaz. It was not long after

412   Mack Maloney

Dominque's death that Yaz had suddenly come to life.
Walking down the stairs, still in his soaking wet flight
suit, like a ghost from decades-old airplane crash, he
began to speak about the dreams he'd had, about the
explanations of missing people, missing ships, missing
airplanes, and how they would all turn up, somehow,
somewhere, if the world didn't come to an end.

It was a question of metaphysics, he'd try to tell Kurjan, but at the time, the guy nicknamed Lazarus just
wasn't listening. Other things were consuming his
thoughts. He'd promised Yaz he'd spend a week hearing the story of what had happened inside his head
after he'd suddenly appeared in the old ramshackle
farmhouse, but not now. There were just too many
other things to do.

He'd lifted Yaz onto the helicopter, and bidden fare-
well to him and Frost and the four young girls, and the
absolutely beautiful Chloe. His arms were still warm
where he had held her in those terrible hours of the
storm's mighty rage, and in those unbearable moments
after Dominique had died. When Kurjan touched his
hands to his face, it reminded him of her—and the
warm kiss she had given him before the helicopter took
them all away.

If there was another life after this one, he hoped he
would meet up with Chloe again.

He had fully intended to await the fate of the planet
alone, but just when he figured that the comet was only
about an hour away from hitting the earth, he saw a
man trudging up the road leading to Skyfire.

He was dark-skinned and Asian in feature, wearing
a pilot's suit, with his helmet and oxygen mask still
clinging to his side.

Kurjan met him at the ledge and the man introduced

himself with the unlikely name of Budda-Budda. He was the man, he said, who had flown Chloe to this place, and since their plane had crashed two days ago, he'd been searching for her.

"You're too late," Kurjan had told him, even as the glare from the comet began to envelope everything in an all-encompassing hellish red glow.

Budda-Budda took the news very hard at first. But then, strangely, he looked up at the monstrous glare in the eastern sky and smiled.

"I knew her for a while," he said. "That was enough for me."

With that, he took up a station on the rock a few feet from Kurjan's own. They sat there in silence, the two strangers who had only the knowledge of Chloe and her beauty in common, to await the end together.

The explosion, when it came, looked like a thousand suns had suddenly been blown apart.

The glare alone was blinding. Many people around the world who now knew of the comet's deadly approach were rendered sightless, the explosion had been that bright.

The shock waves that hit the earth mere seconds later were enough to trigger massive earthquakes and tidal waves and set all of the planet's major volcanoes erupting. The seas seem to catch fire. They became tremendous and wild, and their waves were like waves from a nightmare. Animals hid, flowers closed up, electricity stopped running, streams and rivers reversed themselves. Birds all over the world fell from the sky.

Then the clouds came. All over the planet, from pole to pole, the angry black cumulus blotted out everything, including the glare from the great explosion. Then it seemed as if these clouds themselves had caught on fire, because the skies looked as if they were totally in flames. Everywhere, a deep, massive rumbling could be heard. Some said it was the combination of all the people of the world crying, now that the end had apparently come. Others said it was really God laughing. At last, the punchline for the great cosmic joke had been delivered.

But slowly, almost imperceptibly at first, the clouds ceased to burn. And at an even slower pace, they began to clear. On that part of the globe where it should have been daytime, the sky reemerged blue and clear.

Slowly the sun came out again.

No one really knew what had happened.

The huge explosion in the sky had come—and then it had gone away. The comet's glare no longer fouled the skies, and all of the strange, unnatural things that had preceded its approach to earth finally stopped happening.

So the bold plan conceived by Hawk Hunter must have worked to some degree. The earth was still here, in one piece, and Doomsday had been postponed, at least, for the time being.

But had the comet been destroyed? Or simply diverted?

The answer to this question came for those on the American continent when night finally arrived. For as the sun went down and the stars came out, they saw in the sky not one moon, but two.

This new satellite, smaller, fainter than Luna, was hanging about 50 degrees above the moon, almost like a little brother, slightly red, slightly glowing. From this astounding event, the scientists and the physicists, and then the holy men, and then the regular citizens of earth finally divined the truth.

Hunter's plan had indeed worked. The massive comet had not been destroyed, but was diverted by the 44 nuclear blasts. What remained of it had taken up a wobbly orbit around the planet. It was closer but smaller than the old moon. Just enough to lend an additional beauty to the night sky, but not enough to upset the delicate balance of the tides.

And this, the people of earth would learn, was the lasting result of the brave mission to save the planet. To look up into the night sky now, they would forever remember how the new moon had come to be there.

As for the men who had brought all this about, the truth was not so certain. For many nights and weeks on end, the people of earth searched the skies, hoping, praying, speculating that somehow, somewhere, the Zon would suddenly appear, a long, fiery tail behind it, looking for a suitable place to land. Many people claimed they saw it streaking overhead, its battered wings wagging in greeting, twisting this way and that, as if it was looking for a safe place to land.

But the new and growing myths aside, the truth of the matter was that in the many weeks following the saving of the earth, no sign was ever seen of the Zon, or of the person who had been behind its controls on its last mission, Major Hawk Hunter, the one they called the Wingman.